LOST
GENERATION

ERALIDES CABRERA

Book Vine Press
2516 Highland Dr.
Palatine, IL 60067

To immigrants all over the world.

Blessed are the meek,
For they shall inherit the earth.

Matthew 5:5

CHAPTER ONE

THE CARIBBEAN WINTER WAS REALLY showing its teeth that year. Frank stood by a ditch near the road, trembling inside his corduroy jacket. He felt a biting breeze beat harshly against his face. Shivering, he looked for the bus on the road. Nothing. He paced over the sandy ground and leaned against the wooden gate leading into the farm. The house was a good 300 yards from here, but Frank could hear the ranting of the animals in the early morning. He walked back to the edge of the road and faced the twisting highway up ahead.

Rows of leafless *piñon* trees connected by barbed wire marked the boundaries of the peasants' lands on the sides of the road. This was the season of the *piñon* tree and in a few more days, they would bloom with clusters of tiny violet flowers. The local peasants used them as fence posts because of their astonishing ability to change from skimpy twigs into full-blown pillars that would sometimes reach the thickness of a man's torso. They extended along the highway and seemed to stretch forever into the horizon. Now, in the heart of winter, the grass and foliage had changed from Kelly green to a soft dredged olive with touches of opaque brown. The broad plain was rich in carob and the ubiquitous palm trees growing sparingly throughout the flat terrain. They rose high and erect against the sky, defying the threat of cyclones and tropical thunderstorms that had battered this land for centuries.

Amid this scenery, eight-year-old Francisco Ochoa braced himself for another day of rural school, this one different in that today was the day before Christmas Eve. Frank heard the labored sound of an engine coming from the east. He instinctively turned to look and saw the square frame of a jeep approaching fast, a white star painted on the drab background of its hood. He quickly turned away, hoping that his nervousness had not been noticed. The sound of the engine kept getting louder and showed no sings that the vehicle would stop. Frank felt relieved. He waited until the noise reached a crescendo and was directly across from him. He then glanced at the vehicle without turning his head. Although he could see only the two helmeted heads of the driver and front passenger, Frank was sure there were others crowded in the back, bodies bulging as they leaned over. The jeep kept moving ahead then disappeared as it went around a curve, its engine echoing feebly in the air.

They were *casquitos*, Frank thought. He walked back to the gate and pressed his body against the splintered surface of the boards, hoping for any audible sign of the bus. No more than five minutes had passed when suddenly he heard the loud discharge of what could only be a shotgun. The sound was first steady then seemed to break and echo rapidly all around. Immediately after that, Frank heard another discharge. This one was a solid thud, as if it had struck a target. Then came the goading crackle of machine-gun fire. Frank didn't know what to do. He thought for a second about crawling inside the culvert underneath the entrance. He dropped his leather bookcase on the ground and quickly stumbled into the ditch. He squatted in front of the circular opening and moved the high grass that surrounded it when he heard a horse galloping on the dirt road coming from the house. He lifted his head to look and, recognizing the rider, he hurriedly climbed out of the ditch. He had barely reached the gate when the rider's arm reached over the top board to lift him. In one clean sweep, he pulled him off the ground and brought him over into the back of the saddle. The man held Frank in place while the horse turned and headed back towards the house, gaining speed. The rider jerked the reins and bent his body over the animal's mane to spur him on. The horse stopped abruptly near the entrance to the house and Frank jumped off running towards the porch and into his mother's arms.

The woman folded her arms around him. She was pretty and of short stature, with a fine shape reminiscent of a figurine. Her skin was very white, and she had long, straight black hair tied into a pony tail with a rubber band. She had a small round face with dark brown eyes, a button nose, rosy cheeks, and thin lips. Frank buried his head in her bosom. He wasn't scared anymore. Back there, when he had heard the shots, a terrible fear had overcome him, but he had reacted quickly, as if knowing exactly what to do. He was very proud of himself.

"I'm fine, Mom," Frank said. "It was nothing."

He turned back to look at his father.

"What do you think happened, Dad? Were they shooting somebody?"

"No," his father said. "They were probably shooting in the air to scare some animal."

"What about school, Mom?" Frank asked. "I don't want to miss school. We're having tests this week. And my books! I forgot my books!"

"I'll fetch your books later, Frank."

"But Dad, if I miss school, they'll fail me."

"No, they won't Frank," his mother said. "I'll talk to your teacher. She'll give you a make up. Besides, there might not even be school today."

"I don't want a make up, Mom, I want to go."

"Come on, Frank," she said. "You'll take the exam tomorrow."

"What do you think happened, Aldo?" she questioned her husband.

"I'm not sure. I find it strange that the Army could be in this area."

The woman took Frank inside and Aldo followed them. He took a good look at the highway before closing the front door.

From here he could see farther into it than anyone on the road. He followed the road until the gray stretch of asphalt became blurred among the bounding trees and shrubbery. *No sign of life*, he thought. What could it have been?

"I don't like it, Aldo," the woman said inside. "Those shots sounded awfully close. Frank could have been hit. Anyone could have been hit. Was it the Army?"

"I think I saw an Army jeep, Amanda," Aldo replied. "It might have been in jest. It's almost Christmas, remember? Soldiers are bound to get loud with the spirit of the season. They probably just saw a good target on the road and shot at it."

"Yeah, near the houses of dozens of people."

She gave him a contemptuous look, as if he were to blame.

"Peasants from Rios," Aldo remarked ironically. "I don't know. Why don't you just wait and see? I'm sure if something serious had really happened, we'll find out about it. Are the girls still sleeping?"

"Yes."

They walked through a tiled room with four rocking chairs and a table and went into the dining room, a small room with a square wooden table and several chairs built from carved logs and cow skin. Aldo pulled one out and sat down. Amanda went into the kitchen, which was merely an extension of the dining room, divided only by a doorless frame and a small gate.

"Whether they're peasants or doctors, the Army has no right to practice target shooting in front of peoples' houses."

"Ah, you're on the opposite side of Batista today, Amanda. Talk to him about rights," Aldo said.

He heard Frank sobbing inside one of the bedrooms.

"That's not the only thing I would like to talk to him about," Amanda replied.

She walked towards the table and placed a plate with two fried eggs in front of him.

"Do you have milk with coffee?"

"It's coming."

She went to the kitchen and took an enameled cup. She took a ladle hanging from the edge of the stove and gently pushed it over the surface of the steaming milk, causing the froth to glide over to the sides. Then she filled the cup and added a teacup of espresso coffee and two spoonfuls of sugar. She stirred the mixture, grabbed the handle with a wet rag and gave it to Aldo. She took an aluminum can from a mantel on the wall and snapped the lid open with her fingertips, taking out some country crackers.

"Maybe there are insurgents here," Amanda commented.

"I doubt it," Aldo said. "Rios is too populated for them. Besides, we would have seen more than one jeep if that was the case. Don't worry, Amanda."

"Don't worry, don't worry. That's all you ever say."

She had been standing at the head of the table. She brusquely turned away from him and went back into the kitchen.

"How do you know there was only one jeep with soldiers?"

"I saw it," Aldo said calmly.

"Then it was them who did the shooting?" Amanda asked.

"Probably. That kind of rapid shooting had to come from soldiers' weapons."

Amanda gazed at his back from the kitchen and shook her head in dismay. She leaned on the cast-iron sink facing the wall. She had left the evening dishes and silverware soaking in soapy water and now rubbed them with a wet sponge. She dipped some in the other section of the sink to rinse them then began drying them with a white cloth. Sometimes Aldo's passiveness was too much for her. It was the peasant in him that could never be hidden, she thought. Like a curse. At such times, she felt she might as well have married a black man. Why hadn't she seen it? How could she have been so shortsighted? She, a city girl born and raised in the best of neighborhoods, married to a peasant. If she had only listened to her father, she would not be here washing dishes right now.

Aldo drank his milk and coffee and stared serenely ahead. The heat of the mug handle burned his fingers. He loved the sweet blend of café au lait. He left the empty cup on the table and got up.

"I've got to go," he said.

He went into the living room and brushed aside one of the bedrooms' curtains. There were two bedrooms in the house, facing each other off the living room. There were two other small beds in the room parallel to each other in front of Frank's. Aldo bent over and kissed the boy. Frank jerked his head back at the feel of his father's unshaved face.

"I'll bring your books back now, Frank."

"Will I be able to go to school tomorrow?" the boy asked.

"I'm sure, Frank," Aldo replied. "Listen," he added, "stay around the yard this morning. Don't go too far."

Frank nodded and Aldo left the room. He went across the living room into the other bedroom. And he stood by the marital bed, staring at the two round little heads sunk into their pillow. They were his most precious possessions. He could not sleep without them. The girls would begin the night in their own beds but later Aldo would carry them, one in each arm, and lay them on his bed next to Amanda. It was a tight fit and he had to lay on the edge of the mattress with the box strip biting into his back as he slept.

The girls were truly adorable. With long light brown hair, the identical four-year old twins Teresa and Clara, were like characters from an animated cartoon. Nothing could make Aldo feel so overwhelmed as seeing them. When they were born he had quickly learned to tell them apart and then had shown the secret to Amanda. The twins had very white skin, sprinkled with clouds of freckles around their shoulders. But he had discovered a tiny black mole on the left shoulder blade of one of the twins which the other one didn't have. They had named her Clara. Because of this, both girls had already experienced great inconvenience. Visiting relatives would always pull down the girls' top garments to check the back of their shoulders. It was by now a practice against which the girls had stopped rebelling. Aldo bent over and kissed them. He quietly left the room and went through an open door into a small room adjacent to the dining room. It was completely bare, except for a medicine cabinet on the wall and was used as the bathroom. Here each of them bathed in a washbowl. Aldo opened a side door that gave access to the yard and he went outside.

The yard wrapped around the house. It had scattered patches of Texan grass around it, and was surrounded by a fence made of chicken wire at the bottom and barbed wire on top. The thatched-roof house, built with thin wooden planks, stood in the middle. It was painted a soft green and had long, white colonial windows with vertical iron bars. A water well faced the bathroom door. It was operated by a manual pump. A few feet behind it was a big elm tree, and under it rested a leashed German shepherd. The animal wagged its tail after seeing Aldo. Several chickens moved aimlessly about the yard, poking at tiny pebbles with their beaks that only they could see. It was Amanda's job to tend to them.

Aldo went towards the rear of the yard. He went inside a narrow latrine built of boards and zinc roof tiles to relieve himself. He heard a voice call him so he opened the gate out of the yard. The cabin he entered had no walls except in one side where two compartments had been built with palm tree barks. One served as storage for tools and the other was Alfredo's, the man who had just called him. Only the tool compartment had a door. Alfredo's room was walled only by pieces of sack material sewn together into one large canvass.

Alfredo was Aldo's hired hand. He seemed shaken. Since hearing the shots, he had been sitting on a chunk of chopped wood. Aldo had not seen him at first. Alfredo raised himself at the sight of his boss. He was short, dark complected, and slim. He had high cheek bones, small black eyes, and a pointed nose. He had a thick mustache, as black as his eyes, that grew into two long tufts, in a daring but futile attempt at an imperial flair. No one, including Alfredo, knew exactly how old he was, but he appeared to be in his mid-fifties. He wore a maroon flannel shirt and thick brown trousers, a wide-brimmed straw hat and dusty short boots. From his waist hung a machete encased in a long leather sheath with a waxed butt that was strapped to his hip by a thick brown leather belt.

"They came from over there!" Alfredo said.

He pointed with a crooked index in the direction of the road.

"I know," Aldo said.

"Let's get the cattle rounded. It's already late."

The herd had gathered idly by the gate of a cattle chute. The calves snuggled against the loins of their mothers. They had been together since dawn after the men had finished milking the cows and their feeding was done for the day. It was a daily competition between man and calf, in which both sides seemed to always win out of necessity. The men would have their turn first, extracting the precious liquid with their quick, choppy tugs. Then the calves would suckle the last reserves.

The animals were creatures of habit and waited patiently. The cows were used to leaving their calves in the morning to spend the day pasturing, coming back to the same spot at sunset. The bull, a very important member of the herd, stood indifferently by. His work day was merely beginning. He bore the responsibility of insuring that the herd reproduced.

Alfredo limped towards the gate, his leather sheath dangling from his hip. His left foot seemed to drag more noticeably as he gained speed. Aldo watched him work his way through the herd and disappear among them. He walked around the boundary of the yard fence and opened a gate separating the cattle chute from the front of the property.

Aldo was tall for a Cuban, just over six feet. His face was long and austere and his hazel eyes sometimes looked green. His nose, somewhat crooked at the bridge, was thin and gave him an interestingly-disarranged profile. He wore no mustache and his lips were thin. His jaw was unremarkable. His light brown hair was short under a broad-brimmed straw hat. He wore a dark blue flannel shirt tucked into grey slacks and a wide leather belt fastened by a square silver buckle. His trousers were neatly tucked inside long cattleman's boots with chrome spurs.

Aldo untied his horse's reins and mounted the chestnut-colored mare. She had been a gift from a horse breeder from the Oriente province. Aldo had traveled to the area with his friend, Pablo, to deliver cattle to a local businessman. While there, the men had become acquainted with Antonio Carroso, a fat-belly old man known for breeding the best studs and mares in the region. The cattle deal worked well for Pablo and Aldo. As they approached the portico of the mansion in Carroso's jeep, Aldo saw from a distance the beautiful mare, trotting gracefully along its sorrel mother. He asked Carroso later if he would sell him the mare. Carroso would not hear of it. He summoned an aide and ordered that the young mare be separated from the mother and herded into one of Aldo's cattle trucks.

Aldo's roots were in the deep impoverished country of Rios, where the meager peasants toiled their minute lots for some food. That world was a thousand miles away from Carroso's Eden farm of high prized horses and fine cattle. Aldo worked hard on the mare. It had been a tough job training her. This was no task for a peasant. Peasants were used to donkeys and mules and this elegant mare, trotting the plains, was somewhat incompatible to their needs and a luxury for which they had no use.

With Alfredo's help and the advice of some of his newly-acquired acquaintances in the cattle trade, Aldo was able to turn the young mustang into a disciplined and reliable cattleman's horse. After endless hours of patient work, Alfredo had set the bridle paths and snatched the first pair of blinders on the mare's head. She had to wear a muzzle for a long time because of her efforts to bite at her tormentors, and when she finally got to wear a bridle, a snaffle had to be attached to the bit. She developed a red gash where the nose band of the muzzle had been which had by now turned into a dark scar running across the face. Aldo was happy with the way the mare had turned out. She had not only proved to be an excellent herd horse but also provided him with a distinguished tool of the trade to the delight of other cattlemen. She was more than just a horse. She was a symbol of status, a sign of success and one that Aldo needed to survive in the world of cattle trading.

Aldo led the mare out of the shabby path towards the main road. He preferred to trot the animal on grass where the ground was softer and would not strain its hooves. He kept his eyes fixed on the road and saw no movement or other sign of life. He reached the gate and flipped the ring over the left leaf, pushing the door ajar. He dismounted and picked up Frank's leather bookcase off the ground.

As he went back to the house, Aldo thought about Amanda's remarks. He was disturbed by the latest events taking place around the country. It was no longer an isolated occurrence of insurgents ambushing an occasional Army truck or a mad attempt at Batista's life in the National Capitol. This was an organized war movement that seemed to be rapidly gaining momentum. Aldo was concerned about the long-term effects of the rebellion. What would it bring? What effect would it have on his life and that of others like him? He was not for Batista or the rebels, or anybody else for that matter. The rebels could come and take over tomorrow for all he cared. In his mind Batista was only a dirty politician, one that, like many before him, had plundered this small country of what little resources it had. But there was the insecurity and apprehension that accompany any change, the fear of the unknown and the knowledge that they could be in a worse predicament after the change.

Aldo thought himself a lucky man. He had graduated from secondary school but then discontinued his studies because of his infatuation with boxing. He had started out early and smartly in life. At twenty-eight he owned his farm and had earned the admiration of many of his peers. He had married Amanda at nineteen, shortly after he left prize fighting. Then he had moved back to Rios into a peasant's hut, a *bohio*, and saved enough money to buy three heifers which he later sold at a profit.

He had swung similar deals until he could lease the land where he now lived with his family. It was six hectares of land, about fourteen acres, which he had rented from Orlando Aparientos, a wealthy local landowner. He began a small milking herd so he could have a steady income. At the beginning, he cultivated and toiled the soil like any other peasant, building the home his family now lived in, an improvement over his old *bohio*. But he knew there was little opportunity to get ahead by cultivating the land. He was good with cattle, and Aparientos had kept him on as a hired hand. The ailing landlord had taken a liking to Aldo and agreed to sell him the six hectares for two thousand *pesos*. Aldo used his every penny for the purchase. He borrowed money from his aunt. He even sold some milk cows. But he achieved independence. He continued milking his tiny herd and selling and buying whatever cattle he could find. Eventually he stopped cultivating the land and his herd grew. He and Pablo now owned seventy-five heads of cattle and were about to buy more. The two friends hoped to do well when they sold the herd. Then maybe Aldo would not have to milk any more cows and could be a full-time cattle tradesman. But what about this revolution? How would it affect the future?

With these thoughts, Aldo arrived at the house. No one was on the porch waiting for him. He carried the bookcase into the living room and placed it on the table. He looked at the dining table and saw Teresa and Clara, each toying with a cracker. They were small, and their chins hardly reached the table. Aldo approached them and hugged them.

"Did you see anything on the road?" Amanda asked from the kitchen.

She had mopped the floor and splashed the residue water out into the yard with a bucket. She lay the bucket underneath the sink.

"Not a thing," Aldo replied.

"Well, so what do you think?" Amanda inquired.

Her tone of voice was less tense. She appeared to have overcome her earlier discomfort.

"I think it's like I told you before. Just horseplay."

Aldo did not want to alarm Amanda. Deep inside, though, he suspected that something was amiss. It was true that it was unlikely that any rebellion would emerge in this area. The people here were too involved in their work to care, too poor, and too ignorant to even want a change. Also, the region was not suitable for any kind of subversive activity. There was no place for anyone to hide in these prairies. But the fact remained that a jeep full of soldiers had gone by, and they apparently had fired their weapons at something or someone. It was unlikely that at a time when the present government faced serious political opposition and insurrection, it would send a segment of their special forces, badly needed in other troublesome areas, on a joy ride to the peaceful poverty-stricken, Rios. Aldo thought about all this and did not know what to make of any of it. He suspected that these soldiers had come here for a purpose. Perhaps Amanda was not over reacting entirely. Still, he did not think it prudent to inquire just yet. He was well aware of the reputation of the feared special forces known as *casquitos*. They were known for their brutality and their ability to silence troublemakers. Whether the shooting had been a reprisal against someone here or merely a warning, surely anyone becoming too inquisitive about it might run a chance of being suspected of subversion. That would be fatal. There would be no hearing, no tribunal, no witnesses; only the execution of an inevitable sentence. Specially at a time like now.

"Where is Frank?" Aldo said. He was ready to leave.

"He's still in his room."

Aldo looked at the twins, then quickly walked outside. At the sight of their father leaving, the children began to cry. Amanda stood by the kitchen window. The morning chill had not gone away. Christmas was here, she thought. Christmas 1958. She saw her husband walk in the direction of the cattle house. It was a large open structure, the size of a barn, built with round studs, a cathedral-shaped ceiling covered with zinc tiles, and concrete floor. The sides were enclosed by four rows of braces that connected the studs, giving the building the appearance of a corral. Here the men would milk the cows during the night. Amanda watched Aldo slip inside between two braces and then walk behind Alfredo who was busily shoveling cow manure into a wheelbarrow. Then, Aldo suddenly seized him by the arms and shook him. Alfredo became startled and dropped the shovel while Aldo laughed heartily. *He is such a kid*, Amanda thought. His unconcerned attitude in the face of crisis disconcerted her. It was his nature. He came from a world where the only thing that mattered was that food was served on the table. She despised it. She hated this world of oxen and mules, of barefoot, dirty children, and ugly shanty shacks.

Amanda had been born and raised in the city of Camaguey, about fifteen miles east of Rios. Her education had been abruptly interrupted by her marriage to Aldo. When she was barely fifteen she had met him in the outskirts of the town's recreation and sports center. She was smitten by the tall boy's impressive physique and pleasant manner. But most of all she was driven to him by his reputation. Aldo was then seventeen, an accomplished amateur boxer almost at the peak of his career and competing in the national golden gloves. After their first meeting, Aldo asked to see her again. She replied as was expected of a girl of her status at the time. He would have to court her at home.

When the handsome young man came to her house, she immediately became the envy of her two sisters, Ana and Aleida, sixteen and thirteen respectively. They could not believe that their sister would have outdone them this way. Bewildered, they looked at Aldo's wistful face when he was introduced to them in their father's elegant reception room. He was tall and handsome, with light-brown hair and sun-browned skin. As he stood before them smiling, with his broad shoulders and muscular biceps, he reminded them of a gladiator about to go into battle.

They all walked through the loggia and entered the garden alcove on the far end of the house. Then they sat on wicker chairs, observed by water-spitting gargoyles hanging from the roof that aimed at round earthen jugs on the ground. A maid brought them sandwiches made with pasted guava shells, cream cheese, salty crackers, and also cups of espresso coffee. Aldo's fluent speech and nice manners stole Amanda's sisters' hearts. From then on, they secretly became his most supporting accomplices. They instantly appraised the young man's qualities and saw in him what Amanda never could. This was no ordinary youth. He was only seventeen and had little or no family distinction to fall back on, yet he already seemed as accomplished as any full grown man. He worked in a kiosk until late and lived with an aunt while attending school in the mornings. The two sisters unanimously agreed that there was no one in their social circle of friends that could compare with him.

The conversation went well for all except Amanda's father. Gillermo Diaz was an accountant born in Andalucia, Spain. He had come to the island with his parents as a small boy. He received a degree in accounting at the University of Havana. Then he went back to the provincial capital and became a successful business man like his father. He had worked hard to establish his family as one of the most socially prominent in the community. He was a member of the League of Lyons and his family attended frequent gatherings within the exclusive confines of his private country club. He inquired about Aldo's family background. Aldo explained that his parents had been small farmers who lived in Rios and that he was in town only due to school and his boxing career. Gillermo understood immediately. Orlando Aparientos, the landlord of Rios, was one of his clients, he said.

Guillermo was disappointed. Like his two young daughters, he had perceived this young man's strength and had seen something extraordinary in the boy, something reckless yet terribly calculating, something that would get him places. But he had to act. He could not afford to ruin his hard-earned reputation. And act he did. Guillermo got up abruptly from his chair and went to his study where he remained during the rest of the visit. When Aldo left the house, escorted by the three girls and Francisca, Amanda's mother, he summoned Amanda to his presence. He stood behind his roll-top desk and assumed a military stance.

"I don't want to see that boy in this house ever again," he said. "I also don't want you to see him or talk to him again."

Amanda looked at him incredulously. She had already become so infatuated with Aldo that she could not conceive of anyone rejecting him. How could anyone not accept this hunk of a man? What reason on earth could anyone possibly have not to like him? Yet here was her father, the very person whom she thought would be most impressed by the young man's austerity, forbidding her to see him.

"Why?" asked Amanda. "What did he do wrong?"

"He is not a man for you," her father replied with a slight Spaniard accent. His many years in the island had done away with all but a trace of his native accent. "This boy has no future of any kind. He does not have a suitable education. He cannot provide for you in any respectable manner. Next to him you are like a jewel mixed with a piece of crayon. Don't you see what I tell you?"

Amanda was speechless. A knot formed in her throat. She covered her face with her hands and she screamed at the top of her lungs. Then she fled from her father's presence and secluded herself in her bedroom. The other women in the house thought that a real tragedy had happened. They had been sitting in the living room, conversing in whispers when they heard Amanda's scream of anguish. The three of them ran towards Gillermo's study, only to find Guillermo leaning back comfortably on his barrister's chair. Amanda had vanished.

"What happened to Amanda?" Aleida asked.

"You girls leave the room for now." Guillermo directed. "I need to talk to your mother alone for a moment."

"Where is Amanda?" Ana asked. "What happened?"

"Go to Amanda's room and stay with her," Francisca said to both girls. Upon entering her husband's study, she knew immediately what had happened. She gazed at his wrinkled face with the square black-rimmed glasses, and waited patiently for an explanation, one that she knew only too well.

"I have prohibited Amanda from seeing this boy Aldo again," Guillermo said. "I think that it is very plain, and I am sure you will agree, that he is not a good choice for our daughter. He is a peasant." Guillermo shrugged his shoulders and stretched his lips in a gesture of disdain. Although he had tried to speak as assuredly as possible, his wife's insensible look made him feel uneasy.

"Plus," Guillermo added, "Amanda is too young."

He waited for his wife to speak. He became restless and shifted his bulky body on the chair.

"I have to agree with the last part," Francisca said. "We will see what the future brings."

She was a short woman with a stout body. She had long, black, silky hair streaked with gray. She was strangely attractive with a small, round face and wide eyebrows. She had eyes the color of olives, a tiny nose, and very thin pink lips. She turned, leaving her husband in the room alone, and went to see Amanda.

The days passed without turmoil. At first Amanda seemed withdrawn and melancholic, but then her usual frisky ways returned. Her father noticed this change and became convinced that his daughter had successfully overcome her silly passion. He spoke with self-confidence about it to his wife. She merely nodded. Ever since the incident with Aldo, communications between the middle-aged couple had broken down. Although Guillermo had made valiant attempts to reestablish them, his efforts had received only superficial acknowledgment. A yes or a no, or a simple facial gesture. He had also tried to resume sexual activity in the marital bed, but his advances had been rebuffed. "Go see your concubine," his wife had jeered.

Francisca's parents had emigrated to Cuba from Santa Cruz de Tenerife, a port city in the Canary Islands. They had met in this provincial town, married, and then moved to the country. Francisca was the only surviving child of that union. Her mother and two brothers had died from nineteenth-century plagues, during the war of independence. It was only then that her father had decided to move her to the city where she went to school. Then, out of tenacity and perseverance, she had become a primary school teacher, a profession that she still practiced despite her husband's wealth. No one could tell her that two plus two made four, she thought. She had been through it all. And no one knew her family better than she did. When she entered her husband's study and saw his face, her heart had sunk, foreseeing the mutiny that was about to come. She knew that Amanda was like her father. She had inherited his thirst for prominence, his pomposity, and his bigotry. But she also had some of her own pernicious qualities. She was as stubborn as Francisca had once been. Aleida and Ana, on the other hand, had their mother's wise intuition, her foresight and her endurance.

Francisca tried to put herself in Amanda's place. What would she have done at Amanda's age if she had been smitten with a handsome Aldo and her father had banned her from seeing the boy? Would she have complied? Would she have crumbled at her father's feet and begged him for acceptance? No way, she thought. She would have fought and challenged her father head on until she triumphed. But, like her father, Amanda was also a politician and an actress. She had tried to make everyone believe that her feelings for Aldo were over so that her freedom would not be curtailed and she could keep seeing him. Inside, her passion burned and grew by the hour with ferocious intensity. She and Aldo were now in love and nothing and no one could stop it.

Francisca wondered about the young Aldo. She agreed with her husband that he was not a good match for Amanda, but for a different reason. Aldo was, in her eyes a fighter, not only of other men but of life. At his young age he already had started on a warpath. And she was sure he would conquer whatever he was after. What did it matter that he came from a peasant family? He rose well above any other youngster in their class. Amanda, with more educational opportunities than he, could not speak as intelligently as this young man. Francisca was, after all, a school teacher, and she recognized wits when she saw them. But despite all his cleverness, Aldo had missed his target. Of her three girls he had picked the one most incompatible, the one that could not ever make him happy. Amanda could never blend into the strife-filled life that awaited Aldo. She was meant for a life in Castile, as the Spaniards said. She needed someone from her own world, Guillermo's world, someone that would fill her with prestige. But Ana and Aleida were different. They were warriors like their mother. They were waiting for that one triggering boost that would tip them into conquest. And Aldo was it, she thought. He was the type of man they needed. She thought about Ana because she was her oldest. She and Aldo would make a dynamic couple. May be it was not too late.

Francisca noticed that the three girls had been arriving together from school lately. She suspected that this was because Ana and Aleida were helping their sister in her clandestine relation with Aldo. They were probably acting as guides for the couple, surveying the area when Amanda and Aldo met to prevent sudden unwelcome encounters with family friends and acting as messengers between the two. More than once, she had seen Aleida enter the house and hastily disappear into Amanda's room where whispers were exchanged. One evening, as the family sat in the living room, Francisca called Ana aside. They moved to a sofa in a corner of the room. Francisca sat down and looked at her husband asleep on a chair in front of the radio, his head resting heavily against the back.

"Well," Francisca said, "now that things are back to normal again, I thought that we could talk about Aldo a little bit."

"Aldo?" the girl said in surprise.

"Yes. I think he is quite an impressive young man."

"You do?" Ana was puzzled.

All this time, she had wondered about her mother's opinion on Aldo's courtship of Amanda. She had thought that perhaps she was not as opposed to it as her father. But why, after so many days, was she bringing up the subject? She trembled thinking that perhaps her mother had found out that Aldo was still seeing Amanda. It was not easy to fool her.

"Yes," murmured Francisca, "I think he's very handsome. What do you think?"

Ana felt herself blush. Suddenly, she felt betrayed. She had not expected this bold assault on her deeply-hidden feelings. She had been ambushed, she thought. That afternoon when she had first seen Aldo, she had been touched by a powerful emotion. But she had quickly recovered. She understood immediately that the gorgeous young man was off limits. He was Amanda's. Nevertheless, she had felt a tremendous envy for her sister. And she had wondered how it all happened and why it had happened to Amanda and not to her. Later, as she listened to Aldo, she found herself wishing she were Amanda. And ever since that fateful afternoon she had not had a peaceful moment. But why was her mother now taunting her this way? Could it be that she had noticed her feelings?

"Yes, he's handsome." Ana mumbled without thinking. She was trying hard to sound casual.

Francisca gazed at her daughter for a moment. Ana was a graceful, beautiful child. She was taller than her sisters and her face was long and better formed. She had jet-black hair combed back and woven into a long braid, thin arched eyebrows, and olive-colored eyes, like her mother's. Her eyelashes were thick and long. Her lips were thin and formed a tiny bubble of flesh at each end. She was small breasted and her legs were long and shapely. Although Francisca deeply loved her three daughters, she had special feelings for Ana. Ana had been her first child, her first maternal experience. She despaired at the thought of Ana marrying and leaving her someday. She did not want to ever lose her. And now, as she looked at Ana and noticed her despair, she realized for the first time the suffering her daughter had been going through. She felt guilty about it and for not noticing it before. She also regretted the thoughtless punishment she had just inflicted on her daughter, probing into forbidden territory and unmercifully poking at her wounds. She reached for Ana and embraced her. She felt her breath on her shoulders and heard her sobs. She gently patted her, just as she used to do when she was a newborn baby and she rocked her to sleep.

"My little girl," Francisca said, "my pretty little girl."

Francisca's own tears rolled down her face. She could no longer contain herself. What a fool she had been. All this time she had centered her attention on Amanda, thinking of ways to make her happy, but she had totally disregarded Ana. She had failed to see her pain. Not once had Ana tried to sabotage Amanda's sizzling relationship with Aldo. On the contrary, Ana had acted as Amanda's strongest ally. She had probably carried messages between the two, arranged surreptitious meetings and who knew what else. All this she had done because she was thinking about her sister's happiness and ignoring her own. Inside, she must have known that by helping her sister she was destroying any ray of hope of ever winning the boy she loved. *What a beautiful daughter I have,* Francisca thought.

She wondered what to do. But what could she do? How could she interfere with the capricious flow of events that had entangled her family in this crazy web? The first thing she must do, she decided, was to find out the true state of things. She had to know whether Amanda and Aldo were really involved. She hugged Ana tightly and waited until her sobs subsided. Then, while still holding her, she spoke.

"Ana, I know this is difficult for you, but you must tell me the truth so I can help. What do you think Amanda feels for Aldo?"

There was a long pause. Ana did not move. She had stopped crying, but now her tears began flowing again.

"Amanda loves Aldo very much. And he loves her," she said gently and without hesitation, leaning her head against her mother's neck. Francisca felt her cold tears streaking down her back. The two women stayed in this position for a long time. There was nothing Francisca could say at this moment. She felt as if she had been trapped in a cage, watching the lions devour her daughter outside. What in the world could she do?

After a long while, Francisca felt Ana's warm lips on her cheek. Ana kissed her, got up from the sofa and without saying a word or looking at her mother, she went to her bedroom. Francisca watched her disappear in the darkness of the loggia. She felt rage building up inside her. She wanted to strike at something or at someone. But who could she blame for this disaster? She hated having to decide on a course of action. Maybe something would happen to change this situation, something that would spare everybody the pain.

The miracle that Francisca hoped for never came, and perhaps she had known it all along. She raised her hopes in the next few days, thinking that either Amanda or Ana would perhaps forget Aldo. She tried to rationalize both situations, to see which one would have a better result but then she gave up. She no longer cared. All she wanted now was their happiness. Then one afternoon, as she prepared to leave her classroom for the day, she saw the wimpled heads of two nuns, one tall, one short, walking towards her. Francisca recognized them immediately. They were from the exclusive Saint Teresa School her three daughters attended. She knew these nuns and had met with them occasionally to discuss her daughters' academic performance.

"Good afternoon, Francisca," they both said politely.

"Good afternoon, sisters," Francisca responded. "How can I be of service to you?"

"Well," said the tall nun soberly, "we wish to speak to you for a moment about your daughter, Amanda."

Francisca felt a cold chill running down her spine. She knew immediately that this involved Aldo.

"We have been very concerned about Amanda for the past few weeks," the tall sister added. "We were hoping that we wouldn't have to bother you but we don't want to let it go too far."

"Amanda's academic performance has deteriorated," the short sister interjected. "She is constantly late for class and sometimes she leaves early. We have tried to control her but we no longer can. Then yesterday she disappeared. We looked for her and found her in an alleyway, kissing a boy."

"We thought you should know," the tall sister added. "We really cannot allow this behavior to go on in our school."

"Yes," said Francisca impassively, "I understand."

And she really understood, she thought. They were trying to tell her that if she could not set Amanda straight, her daughter would be expelled from their school. They, too, were worried about their own reputation.

"Tell me something, sisters," Francisca said. "What does this boy look like?"

"We have noticed him walking around the school many times," the short nun said. "He is tall, with light hair and a stocky build. Do you know who he is?"

"No," replied Francisca, "I do not know who he is. But I will talk to Amanda immediately, sisters."

Francisca watched the two nuns cross the school yard, a square cemented section in the middle of the building surrounded by hallways and classrooms. As the nuns reached the exit, they turned simultaneously. Now was only the beginning of her troubles, she thought.

When Francisca arrived home that afternoon, she went into Amanda's room. She did this everyday while the girls were at their afternoon school session. Today, as she turned the knob of the heavy wooden door and glimpsed inside, she immediately noticed a change. The dresser would have looked normal to her husband and even to the maid but not to Francisca's vigilant eyes. Some perfume flasks were missing and a large powder case was gone. Francisca knew Amanda could not live without those things. She opened the drawers in the highboy and found two of them empty.

Francisca was now shaking. She leaned her elbow on the edge of the bed and crouched on the floor. She looked under the bed and saw two strapped, black leather suitcases. She pulled one out, un-strapped it, and turned the top flap open. Inside were Amanda's night clothes, her shoes, and some make-up articles neatly packed. She did not have to look anymore. She now knew that she must act. She closed the suitcase and slid it back under the bed. She stepped outside her daughter's bedroom and, shaken, she sat on the living room sofa.

It was a difficult evening for Francisca. When the girls arrived, she hid all signs of affliction and carried on with all the evening house chores. She helped the maid get the table ready for supper. Then she fetched her daughters and asked them to come to dinner. All three had bathed and changed from their school uniforms into more casual attire. They sat at the table. Guillermo's place remained empty. Not one word was spoken. Everyone seemed to sense the tension tonight. After supper, Francisca sat on the sofa and looked out the window. She was waiting for her husband. The girls turned on the radio and sat on their rocking chairs. Francisca knew then that Amanda's sisters also knew her secret.

The girls had already retired when Guillermo came home. As he opened the front door, Francisca smelled the odor of brandy on his breadth. *Whoring around again*, she thought.

Guillermo walked in, briefcase in hand, and greeted his wife. Francisca returned his greeting and waited for him to go to his study. Guillermo had barely sat down in his chair when he saw his wife enter the room. She was still wearing her work clothes, a white cotton blouse and black pleated skirt. Her countenance was somber. She sat silently on one of the two brown leather chairs facing him.

"The time has come to allow that boy Aldo back in this house," Francisca said dryly.

"What!" Guillermo exclaimed. "What are you saying woman? Have you gone mad?"

"I said that the time has come to allow Aldo back in this house," Francisca repeated.

Her voice was calm, yet Guillermo could see that this serenity hid a giant volcano about to erupt.

"You realize the meaning of what you are saying? Don't you know that letting our daughter be snared by that boy could be her ruin? And what about our reputation? What do we tell our friends?"

"Crap, *mierda*!" Francisca exclaimed.

She slapped the smooth surface of the desk with her open hand. She stood up and leaned towards her husband's face, unleashing all the frustration and anger towards Guillermo that had built up inside her during the past few weeks. And she knew it was wrong but someone had to pay. Guillermo was apprehensive as he saw lightning and thunder in her eyes. His wife was an islander, *una isleña*. These Canary Islands natives were dangerous people. The Spaniards had never trusted them. Even here in Cuba, thousands of miles away, they retained their reputation for obstinacy. One had to move out of their way and let them pass, as people said. He waited for her outburst to pass.

"Your reputation is the only thing that worries you, Guillermo," Francisca thundered. "That is your only real concern. Well, I tell you, there is more than that at stake. There's my daughter's happiness, and that is of real concern to me."

"Of course I am concerned about Amanda's happiness," he answered. "That is why I did what I did. And if you are concerned as you say, then you must agree that she should not ever see that boy again."

"I am afraid that it's not up to you, or even me," Francisca replied. "Amanda has a say in this, and she has decided. She has not stopped seeing the boy because of you and she won't."

"But she's barely fifteen," Guillermo protested.

"What I am saying to you is that regardless of her age, neither you nor I can keep Amanda away from that boy. She can win one way or the other. She already has. It's too late. I want this boy to visit her here instead of in the streets. Otherwise, we will lose her forever."

For the first time Guillermo looked his wife in the eye. He knew he could not win. He was henpecked, he thought.

"I warn that you will be responsible for the results," he cautioned, "and you will regret them."

"Don't warn me about anything, Guillermo," Francisca shouted. Bearing a stern look, Francisca turned around and left. She closed the study door and walked through the loggia, passing two doors and stopping in front of the third. No light was seen at the bottom of the door. She rapped on the door and heard the shuffling of sheets inside. Then she saw the light reflecting on the tile floor. Amanda opened the door wearing a long white night gown. Only the tip of her toes were visible. Her black hair was mussed and bundled into a net. Her face looked quite beautiful in the darkness. Her black eyes showed her surprise.

"I have to come in for a minute," Francisca said softly.

She closed the door and motioned for Amanda to sit on the bed. Amanda pushed the mosquito net aside and sat down at the edge. She stared at her mother with alarm.

"I want you to talk to this boy Aldo and tell him that he can come visit you in this house from now on," Francisca said. "Visiting hours will be from 7:00 to 9:30 in the evening, four days a week. I want you to stop seeing him in the streets, you understand? You keep going to school until you marry him, if you marry him. Now we will find out what kind of stuff this boy is really made of."

Amanda could hardly believe what she was hearing. She had thought all along that her mother was opposed to her relationship with Aldo. She had been sure that Francisca supported her father's position, although she had never expressed it. She thought she was merely letting her father handle the matter and that Francisca, too, saw no future in her marrying Aldo. But more surprising was the fact that her mother knew Amanda was seeing him. She felt embarrassed and outsmarted by the grave-looking lady with the penetrating olive eyes.

"Does my father know?" Amanda managed to ask, still bewildered. "Does he approve?"

"He knows and he will not interfere. Just do as I say."

Suddenly, Amanda felt her mother's warm lips on her cheek and two arms that enfolded her head. She was too dazzled to respond. She merely sat there perplexed. Francisca walked to the door and turned towards Amanda.

"Amanda, now it will not be necessary for you to elope. Unpack your things right now," Francisca said. "I'll send someone to tell Aldo. Sleep tight." Before Amanda could look up, she was gone.

In the days that followed, the proper arrangements were quickly made. What had seemed like an inconceivable feat to the three sisters a few days before soon became real. Francisca immediately ordered two mahogany rocking chairs with upholstered cane bottoms and backs and had them placed parallel to each other near one of the living-room's arched windows. The long sofa behind them was dragged back against the wall. The maid was instructed to change supper from the usual time of 7:00 P.M. to 6:00 P.M. to avoid interference with Aldo's visits, and coffee was to be served every night at 8:00 P.M. Francisca asked for Aleida's assistance in chaperoning the couple and allowed Ana to be out during visiting hours if she so wished, to spare her pain. She could never explain to her daughter the reasons for her decision but she hoped that time would heal the wounds in her eldest daughter's heart. For now, she only wanted to prevent any conflict between Ana and Amanda, preferring to see it focused on her.

Amanda and Aldo's relationship bloomed. In the enchanting Caribbean nights, the two of them sat by the window talking in whispers while Francisca and Aleida listened to the radio and Guillermo secluded himself in his study. Here, for the first time, Aldo started calling Amanda "figurine," and she came to adore him with a boundless passion. He escorted her to parties and a year later, they were married at the Mercedes church. At their insistence, there was no large reception, only a small gathering of close relatives at the family home. Amanda and Aldo moved to the country. One year later, when their first child was born and Amanda's mother had died, Aldo persuaded Amanda to name the boy after her mother, the brave and noble lady who had made it all possible.

CHAPTER TWO

THE DAILY CHORES MADE TODAY'S cold morning go by quickly.
Alfredo, with his usual energy, moved swiftly about, performing
all the mundane daily tasks. Milk pitchers and buckets had to be
washed and water pumped into troughs for the cattle. Aldo would
ride into the rear section of the farm and check the pasture to see
if weeding was needed. Today, however, he chose to stay in the
house. He did not want to lose sight of the road, still thinking about
possible explanations for this morning's events. He did not like what
had happened and felt uneasy about not having seen the Army jeep
return after the shooting. He was sure that the vehicle had stopped
where the soldiers had fired their weapons. If they had come to
do a job and finished it, then why had they not turned back? He
thought it unlikely for them to keep going in the same direction.
Vertientes, a small sugar-mill town, was at the end of that road but
there was hardly anything happening there this time of year since
it was off sugar season. The town was empty now, with only a few
locals staying behind. All the important people had left and would
not return until the sugar mill started up again in the early months
of the coming year. Logic dictated that the soldiers would have to go

back to Camaguey, the provincial capital, which was at the other end and from which the soldiers had come.

Aldo spent most of the morning rearranging the chicken coop behind the outhouse. Chickens were in high demand during the holidays. He would let Amanda have the first pick on those she wanted for their own family and for gifts for close relatives.

Aldo took his time. At 11:30, he saw Alfredo enter the open cabin and waived for him to come into the yard.

"Let's go inside," Aldo said, "it's time for lunch."

He knew that Alfredo's internal clock read noon. Alfredo never used a watch, yet he always quit work exactly at the same time each day. They walked together toward the house.

"I have heard nothing since this morning," Alfredo commented. "Have you?"

"No, I haven't," Aldo replied. "Listen, Alfredo. Don't say anything about this in front of Amanda and Frank. I don't want to alarm them."

The two men scraped their shoes on the coarse-grained cemented square at the rear of the house to shake the dust off their feet. Aldo tapped the door, and Frank opened it. He was a thin kid, tall for his age, with reddish-brown hair and a freckled face. His eyes were the color of olives.

"Where were you all day, Dad?"

"I was right here in the yard. What have you been doing?"

"Nothing, I was bored."

"I'm going to need your help in this afternoon, Frank, so you won't be bored."

"What are we doing?"

"We are catching some chickens."

"We're going to chase chickens?"

"Yes."

Aldo went to the living room where Teresa and Clara were playing on a blanket. He picked them up in each arm and carried them to the dining room. He sat them on two chairs in front of the table. The table held a soup dish and three pieces of silverware. The twins had their own baby spoons and forks. Aldo took his hat off and hung it on a long nail. Alfredo hung his by Aldo's. Aldo sat at the head of the table with Alfredo two spaces from him, leaving the chair closest to Aldo empty for Amanda. Frank sat at the other end and Teresa and Clara to Aldo's left. Amanda brought in a hot steaming pot of stewed red beans from the kitchen and rested it on a hot-plate.

"Did you notice anything else on the road?" she asked.

"No," Aldo said. "Nothing."

"Well, I've been listening to the news on the radio and it all sounds normal."

Aldo picked up the ladle and filled his soup plate with the clay-colored broth.

"I am sure the newscasters would never admit that the government is now in trouble," Aldo added. "That would be silly. Right now the news is the last source of information to listen to."

"Well," Alfredo said, "I bet you if Batista sends troops into action all these guerilla war games will be over in one day."

"They better not wait too long if they want to win," Aldo said.

"What do you mean?" Amanda asked.

She walked behind Frank and filled his plate. Although she would never admit it, she couldn't help but respect her husband's analytical mind and looked to him for guidance.

"I mean that the situation has gotten critical for the government. The rebels have gained a lot, may be not militarily, but support wise. The general population wants them to win."

"The general population doesn't know what it wants." Amanda turned to Alfredo. "You don't want them to win, do you?"

"I like Batista," Alfredo said humbly.

Aldo looked at Amanda. During her nine years of marriage to Aldo, she knew it was alright to challenge him. Aldo was not an irrational man, an exception to the crude egotistical macho man of Cuban society. He would let her have her way. She could air her frustrations and anxieties freely but there was always one boundary she could not cross. When she became offensive or sarcastic, she knew she would reach an impenetrable wall.

"If you are having a bad day," Aldo commented, "maybe you should stay in your room, Amanda. We can probably manage just fine without you around here."

Alfredo quietly dipped into his plate. Teresa and Clara broke the silence and, becoming impatient at the sight of their empty plates, they began crying. Frank reached out and pinched one of their cheeks. Amanda went back to the kitchen to fetch some bean-puree. She was still afraid to feed them whole beans.

After the men ate their stew, Amanda brought in a pot of white rice along with jerked beef and a tray of green fried bananas. She also brought high glasses for everyone and a pitcher of fresh water. She kept feeding the girls but never sat down to eat.

"I will probably need you around the house by mid-afternoon, Alfredo," Aldo said.

"Are we catching any pigs?"

"No, not yet. But I need to see Pablo about that so I'd like you to stay put just in case we decide to do it today."

It wasn't a real lie. Hogs were another source of income for Aldo and Pablo. Since Aldo already cared for the dairy cattle, the two friends had agreed that Pablo would keep most of the hogs, with Aldo keeping only a few. The two would split the profits at time of sale. A hog was a high-priced item during the holidays.

Amanda brought Alfredo a cup of espresso. Alfredo drank, picked up his hat, and went outside.

"I'll be back for you in a little while, Frank," Aldo said.

He followed Alfredo who crossed the yard and went inside the rear cabin. He entered his room, a small space with a dirt floor that had been tamped hard and smooth. His few possessions were kept inside a chest. The only light in the room was an oil lamp on a shelf, next to Alfredo's oak guitar. A hammock from pieces of sack material and tied into the corner studs served as his bed. Alfredo laid down, trying to nap. He was still unnerved about the morning shooting. He had never before heard automatic weapon fire. The first two shots had made him jump but they were not an unfamiliar blast. Hunters looking for wild guinea fowl in the nearby valleys would sometimes fire their guns. But the machine-gun stutter was definitely different. Now, Alfredo closed his eyes and tried to sleep and forget about this morning. He thought about Aldo. He felt safe thinking about him. And then he fell asleep.

Although Alfredo was his hired hand, Aldo respected the man deeply. He thought of him as a talented person, someone endowed with great natural talent but who, because of his environment, had lacked the opportunity to develop them. It was a tragedy that a man who played the guitar and sang self-composed verses could not read and write. Alfredo could sing a *decima,* a ten-line stanza with a complicated rhyme scheme, that could describe you in detail. He could compose verses about any event. He had a photographic memory and could recite details in verse about his family history and childhood that he had composed many years ago. He had never gone to school and like most peasants, he had never traveled farther than twenty miles from the prairie.

Aldo untied his horse and trotted through the cattle path near the house. He reached the end and dismounted. The gate was built with thin studs and barbed wire and lead to the section occupied by the calves.

Aldo had split this section in two, and alternated each for pasturing the herd. He
opened the gate and moved his horse to a well shaft. He tapped the mare on the crest, allowing her to drink and then rode back to the house.

Aldo looked down the highway as he neared the house but saw nothing. He tied the mare and went inside the yard to call Frank.

"Ready?"

He unbuckled his spurs and threw them on the ground.

"How many chickens are we catching?" Frank asked.

"Probably fifteen or twenty for now."

They passed the water pump inside an open cabin similar to Alfredo's but even more squalid. Its floor was covered with chicken waste and surrounded by a wire fence. One of its sides was walled with palm tree barks. The latticed ceiling, where the chickens slept, was reachable by a ladder. Aldo opened the gate to the storage compartment and took out some ears of corn. He grabbed a basin and placed it on the ground. As he threshed the corncobs, the chattering sound of the grain hitting the basin made the chickens rush towards them. In seconds, they surrounded Aldo and Frank.

"Get out of here, birds," Frank yelled, "not yet." "Frank, keep away from the hens and roosters."

Frank circled around them. The birds ignored him, hustling one another to get at the corn.

"Come on, Frank, "Aldo called, "they won't be hungry forever."

Frank seized one by the legs. The others dispersed for a second at the sound of wings flapping, then rushed back. Frank grabbed another one then he ran towards the coop and threw them inside. Father and son worked until they filled the coop. Frank counted twenty-one chickens.

Then they went inside to drink the chilled water from the jug. Even in the hot summer the fat clay jugs would act as thermos and had become a cultural symbol for the region. They varied in sizes and were popular for their ability to hold the water's coolness. The peasants also used them for storing salted meat. It was said that the early Conquistadores had hid treasures in earthen jugs, *botijas*, as they were called, and later buried them in hidden spots throughout the country. The site of an abandoned well or of a *ceiba* tree was always cause for speculation. It was not uncommon for people to dig around such sites in the hope of finding a *botija*.

Aldo met Alfredo standing by his curtained door, sharpening his machete with a flat file. He always sharpened the instrument even if he did not plan to use it and was proud of its razor like sharpness. He was slumped forward, the butt of the machete nipped against his stomach and the tip poked into the wall, as he worked up and down in short strokes over the blade.

"How did the chicken hunt go?"

"We don't have many left."

Aldo unclipped his key ring and turned one of the keys in the lock. The door creaked as it was released from the chain. Aldo pushed it and stepped inside the pitch-dark, dusty room full of tools and artifacts. From an old disc harrow in a corner, he heard a shrill cry. He scuttled back and caught a glimpse of a long wiggly tail racing by his feet and out of the room.

"There's a rat for you."

Alfredo had positioned himself near the door, his right arm above his head, ready to strike. As the rat ran by him, he swung his machete. Aldo heard the dull chop of the blade and turned around to see the creature cut in half, its blood oozing on the floor.

"This rat was making a nest in there," Alfredo said. "We got to her just in time."

He took a piece of sack cloth, picked up the two hairy pieces with the tip of his machete, and put them in the sack. He sprinkled some dust on the bloody spot. Then he wiped the blood from the blade and sheathed his machete. He tied the cloth into a bundle and threw it in cow manure.

"That was great timing, Alfredo."

Aldo searched through a box of tools and picked up a short pointed spike. Then he took a coiled nylon rope hanging on the wall and went outside. He sat on Alfredo's chunk of wood and worked on the rope. When he was finished, he coiled it and tied it to the saddle.

It was around 4:00 P.M. when Aldo noticed three vultures circling the sky near the spot where the shots had been fired this morning. There was no doubt as to why they were there. They must have spotted a target down below. The fact that there were only three meant that it was fresh carrion, not yet discovered by others. They would pounce on any carcass and strip it of its skin. Then they would maul the rotting flesh and entrails and greedily devour the torn pieces, avoiding each other as they ate. The grim sighting did not escape the eye of another observer farther away. As Aldo moved ahead, Alfredo ran behind him.

"Aldo!" he called. "There are vultures out there."

"I know," Aldo said.

"But that's where we heard the shots this morning," Alfredo added. "There must be something dead out there."

"Yes."

Aldo studied the road, looking for signs. It was strange how quiet Rios had been since this morning.

"I think that those soldiers shot somebody on the road this morning," Alfredo said. "The people here won't move the body because they are afraid."

"Afraid of what?"

Aldo was thinking. The soldiers had not fired for nothing. Alfredo was right. They were probably scared.

"Afraid to get involved. Don't you think we ought to try to find out?"

"You want to go and see?"

Aldo was being unnecessarily cruel, and he knew it. He was baiting the poor man.

"Me?"

"I'm teasing you, Alfredo. Calm down."

Aldo rode his horse to the front of the property passing his children who were playing in the yard. He trotted on the low grass and headed for the road. He noticed the black birds ahead, circling in the air. By nightfall the birds would have finished pillaging their prey. He didn't want to be seen probing around. If people in Rios were afraid to remove carrion dropped at their doorstep, then they might tell the Army who had done it when questioned. It was best not to get involved. But the thought of leaving a human body to be plundered by vultures repulsed him. He headed back toward the house.

He tied up the mare and looked into the distance. There were more birds circling the air now. Time was running out. The sun had set and it would soon be dark. The short winter days were nearly over by 6:00 P.M. Aldo saw something move on the road and waited. It was a human figure walking away from the spot where the vultures were circling. Aldo walked towards the fence and leaned his arms on the top wire. The man was walking towards Aldo's front door. He turned towards the gate and came through. Aldo thought he recognized him. It was Tomas, a local peasant who lived in one of the shacks in Rios and who had shared many meals at Aldo's house. Tomas was a loner and cultivated Arapientos's land. He wore the usual attire, brown cotton trousers and a wheat-colored flannel shirt. He also wore short brown leather boots and a wide-brimmed straw hat.

"Good evening," Tomas said.

He was short and dark. His lank black hair jutted out from beneath the rim of his hat in shiny, greasy tufts.

"Good evening, Tomas," Aldo replied.

"I must talk to you about something."

"Yes?"

"I don't know if you know," Tomas began, "but Patricio is dead."

Aldo was genuinely surprised. Patricio was another local farmer who lived in one of the shacks in Rios. He and his wife had two small children. Aldo knew immediately how Patricio had died.

"Yes," Tomas continued, "Well, you, of all people, knew Patricio. He was causing problems for the Government. They had to do something."

Aldo was on guard. "Did the Government have anything to do with Patricio's death?"

"He was problematic."

"I don't know that he was. Did they kill him?"

"Well, yes."

So there it was. Army men had come here this morning to shoot the poor soul. A whole regiment had been sent to execute a peasant who would not kill a fly. Aldo remembered that day at the country grocery store when Patricio had had too much rum and shot his mouth off in front of the others.

"Look at Aldo," he had said, "he had to go to town to look for a wife. He could not marry a peasant girl, oh no, they are not good enough for him."

"Mind your business," Aldo said.

"What business?" Patricio yelled. "What fucking business? Everyone knows who your wife is. She doesn't belong here. She's a fucking city girl."

Aldo stood, about three feet from Patricio who was poking him with his left index. Aldo leaned back and jabbed him in the mouth. No one saw it coming. Patricio dropped like timber, his bottle crashing on the floor, spilling its urine-colored fluid everywhere. The other men held him by the shoulders. He was bleeding from his upper lip in a thin red streak that ran down to the chin and stained his shirt. The men dragged him onto a chair. No one said anything. The storekeeper came out with a baize and a bucket and picked up the broken glass. Patricio just sat there with his arms hanging. Then two men helped him to his horse.

A few months later Aldo, had passed him on the road. Aldo greeted him but Patricio turned his face away. Aldo figured this was the man's way of dealing with the incident. He would not fight him back or face him, but he also would not speak to him again. So be it. Aldo did not hate him or held any grudges against him. A man had to have his pride.

Now Aldo looked into Tomas's eyes and pondered over his announcement. He knew Tomas was a Batista sympathizer. He was trying to cover for the men in khakis, but there was something else here too. How did Tomas know so much? Why was he the only one that dared speak about what had happened? "How do you know that the Army did it?"

Tomas's eyes shifted to the ground and he stuttered. "Well, they had to execute him this morning," he said. "He had been helping the rebels. The government can't let these things happen. They have to take a stand. Otherwise the country would soon be run by bandits. They have to get tough."

Poor Patricio. He had probably gone on another of his drinking sprees. May be he took a crack at Tomas. Tomas, the ignorant son of a bitch. What rebels was he talking about? There were no rebels around here. Besides, of all people in this area, Patricio would have been the one least likely to get involved. Like most peasants, his life had been controlled and shaped by his work and the need for survival. His only other interest had been drinking. Sometimes late at night, his screams could be heard all over Rios. As he drank from a bottle, sitting outside alone, he would sing *décimas*. When he was pleasant, some of the other peasants at the site would join him with maracas and guitars to sing along but most of the time, Patricio's mood was too foul for him to be good company.

There were times when he would be impudent such as when he had badmouthed Aldo. It was during those moments that the other peasants avoided him. But when he was sober, everyone talked to him. They knew about his habit and had learned to live with it.

"But how do you know?"

Tomas lifted his head. He could not quite look into Aldo's eyes, so he gazed down again.

"Well…"

"How do you know it was the Army?"

"I heard the shots."

"I heard them too."

He and Tomas both knew. May be Aldo wasn't supposed to know all of it. Aldo became aware of his precarious position. He had opened himself by needling Tomas too hard. If Tomas decided that his secret was not safe with Aldo, he too could end up like Patricio. Right now Tomas had the upper hand. Aldo would have to pretend. He would have to make believe that he didn't know who had tipped the Army.

"Well, I happened to see an Army jeep speed out of the area right after the shooting." Tomas had regained his composure but his voice was fuzzy.

"So what do you want from me?" Aldo said.

"Well, his body is out there on the road, and I want you to help me bury it."

The creep must be feeling remorse. Inability to cope with his ugly deed. Fear that Patricio might get up as he bent to pick his body and slit his throat. He needed Aldo.

"Patricio's body is out on the road?"

"It is lying at the bottom of the ditch by the entrance to the site."

Tomas was now speaking with assurance. He felt relaxed after hearing Aldo ask the question and felt a sense of power by providing Aldo with genuine facts that Aldo didn't know.

"There are vultures out there."

"I put a palm tree leaf over him. They can't get to him for now."

Aldo was silent for a moment. He tried again to rationalize Tomas's possible motives for seeking his help. He probably felt safe with Aldo. For now, he thought it might be best to have Tomas trust him. But was it worthy? Was it worth securing his own personal safety in exchange for his honor? If he agreed to help Tomas, Aldo sensed he would become an accomplice in his treason. But then there was Patricio and the business of a poor peasant murdered and left like a dead dog on the highway. His riddled corpse would soon be despoiled by vultures. The man needed a decent burial at least. What was done was done. He would need Tomas if only as protection for the burial.

"All right," Aldo said. "Let's have some supper. When it gets dark we'll go and bury him. Don't mention anything about this inside."

"Why?"

Suddenly Aldo felt overpowered by anger.

"You want to come in my house, you keep your mouth shut, understand?" Aldo ordered.

They both walked inside through the living room. Tomas sat down at the dining room table. Aldo pulled a chair from under the table and sat next to Alfredo.

"Good evening, Alfredo," Tomas said.

"Good evening. How is everything at the site?"

Everyone was trying to avoid the subject, but it was hard not to mention it.

"Nothing is new," Tomas said.

"You didn't hear the shots this morning?" Amanda inquired from the kitchen.

She was stirring a steaming liquid cooking in a nickel casserole.

"Yes, I did."

"Do you know who was shooting, and why?"

"No, I don't. It could have been anybody. It's almost Christmas, you know."

"Yes."

Amanda did not pursue it. She felt depressed and wanted to be alone with Aldo. She felt badly about this afternoon. Suddenly, this morning's incident had lost its significance. All she wanted now was to be with her husband.

"Are there many shindigs at the site this year?" Alfredo asked.

Alfredo could tell Tomas had been warned. He respected his boss's decision not to discuss it with the family. He, too, itched to know what had happened this morning. It looked like Tomas had the answer, but he had to wait until he saw Aldo alone.

"I don't know," Tomas said curtly. "I don't know much about what goes on at the site anymore."

"There's only time for the Arapientos, right?" Alfredo smirked.

"No, that's not true either."

"Are the brothers getting along any better now?" Aldo inquired.

Ever since the old Arapientos had died, there had been nothing but discord among his sons. The harvests had been poor and the cattle was not as productive. The old man was survived by two boys who knew nothing about running a farm. Many of the cultivated land was now marabou weeds. What remained was only a small portion of land where the cane crops seemed to grow smaller and thinner every year.

"Things are better than last year. They hired two more men to look after the harvest."

"Since when do you need to look after sugar cane to grow?" Alfredo interjected.

"They seem to think so."

Amanda brought in several plates and silverware. She called for Frank and the girls to come.

"Frank, set the table," she said. "Would you please turn the oil lamps on, Alfredo? It's getting dark."

Alfredo left his seat and went to the kitchen. From a mantel in a corner he grabbed four kerosene lamps and took them out. The sky had now darkened with the first shadows of the approaching night. Alfredo set the lamps on the floor. From underneath the mantel, he took a vat full of kerosene shaped like a coffee pot and brought it outside. He filled the lamps with kerosene, cleaned the glasses and lit the wicks. He brought the lamps inside.

Amanda carried a pot full of steaming soup to the dining room. She placed it on a straw hot plate. Alfredo and Aldo dragged their chairs to the table. At Amanda's insistence, Tomas came around and sat near Aldo. Frank brought Clara and Teresa in and tried to sit them down on their chairs.

Aldo dipped the ladle in the pot and poured scoopfuls of noodle soup in his plate. They all had some and also helped themselves to white rice, fried rubble beef, and fried ripe plantains. Amanda was not eating. She kept busy feeding the girls. After they finished, the men pulled their chairs back and leaned them on the wall.

"I have to unsaddle the mare," Aldo said.

He went outside. It was pitch dark but above the frail clouds was the splendor of moonlight. He opened the gate and untied the horse's reins. He brought the mare to the cabin in back of the house. He untied both cinches, reached into one of the rafters, and pulled the looped end of the rope. He tied the pommel of the saddle with it. He suddenly remembered something and reached inside one of the saddlebags taking his revolver out of it. The silver-plated handle shone in the darkness. The gun was wrapped inside a brown leather holster.

Aldo clutched the handle and pulled the gun out. He checked the safety, then opened his shirt and slipped the holster on. One could hardly see the small bulk. He pulled on the rope until the saddle reached the ceiling. Then he tied the end of the rope to a rafter. He saw Alfredo wriggle into the open cabin.

"What happened, Aldo?"

"They killed Patricio."

"Patricio?"

"Yes. Those shots that we heard this morning. I still don't know why."

Alfredo stood there, open mouthed. He had suspected a tragedy.

"There's no reason to be afraid. I will need your help though. I'm going out there to bury him so I'll be gone for a couple of hours. I want you to keep an eye on the house while I'm gone," Aldo said.

"Shall I stay inside?"

If it had been daylight Aldo could have seen his paleness.

"No, stay in your room as normal. Just keep your ears open. Now unleash the dog, please, and get back inside the house until I leave with Tomas."

Aldo lifted the sweaty packsaddle from the mare and laid it on one of the trestles by the tool room. Alfredo scurried away to unleash the dog. Aldo unbridled the mare and patted her head. The animal moved out of the cabin making swishing sounds.

Aldo unlocked the chain in the tool room door. He pushed the door open. The tools were so neatly arranged that he knew exactly where to find everything, even in the darkness. He took a pick and shovel and carried them outside.

"Down, boy, down," he whispered to the dog that had rushed to greet him.

Aldo leaned the tools against the house and tapped the door lightly.

"I am going to change, Tomas. Then we can go."

Aldo went to the master bedroom. He saw Amanda lying on his side of the bed. He stooped and unfastened his spurs. As he stood, Amanda embraced him. He shielded the gun to keep it from view.

"Oh, Aldo, I'm sorry," she whispered. "I love you so much."

"I love you too, Figurine."

"I feel so bad," she said. "It's all because of politics."

"Yes, politics." Aldo stroked her hair. "I have to go with Tomas for a while, Amanda. I won't be long."

"Why?" she asked. "Why do you have to go with him?"

"I want to look at the hogs he has for Christmas. Pablo and I may be able to use them."

"Why not go in the morning?"

"He's not there in the morning. I won't be long."

Aldo hung the spurs on a peg on the wall. Then he reached for a black leather jacket and put it on. Amanda clung to him.

"Please, don't be long Aldo. I need you with me."

"I won't, Figurine. Watch the kids."

Aldo kissed her on the forehead. Then he walked to the curtains and peered through them. The girls were playing in the living room while Frank listened to the radio. He went out through the bathroom and stood by the kitchen door.

"I'll meet you outside," he whispered to Tomas.

Aldo picked up his tools and loaded them on his right shoulder then he went

quietly around the house and exited the yard through the front gate. He walked a few steps and waited for Tomas. The dark man walked slowly, overshadowed by the lights behind him. Aldo started to leave before Tomas reached him.

"Aren't you cold?" Aldo said.

"I'm never cold," Tomas replied. "Why did you bring those? I have some at home."

"I don't mind carrying them."

Aldo kept talking as he walked ahead of Tomas who was rushing to catch up to Aldo's long strides.

"It's a pretty dark night," Tomas commented.

"There is some moonlight," Aldo said. "We won't need a light."

"That's good. That way, nobody will see us."

"Sooner or later they'll have to know."

"It's better that they don't find out just yet."

If the bloody fool thought that those peasants did not know by now that there was something dead on the road, he was crazy. There was a hamlet of about twenty-five shacks, or *bohios*, not far from the road. The peasant families that lived in them were not as ignorant as Tomas and Amanda made them to be. They were scouts of these plains, able to forecast the weather with more accuracy than modern laboratories. Surely, they had heard the shots this morning and seen the vultures flying by the road. And by now everyone would miss Patricio's hollers. Most of them probably had connected the pieces.

"His family must know that he is missing," Aldo said.

"Patricio was such a drunkard that not even his family would know whether he's dead or out on a spree."

Aldo became silent. He did not want to answer such an insolent remark. Tomas's lack of sensitivity was abominable.

They went through the front entrance and turned left, walking on the dirt strip next to the road. Tomas was behind Aldo who could see the weak flare of lights deep inside the meadow to the right of the highway. They were the first few shacks of Rios visible from the road. Each tenant built his own home on his parcel of land. Some, like Tomas, were more fortunate and had a permanent job as hired hands for the Aparientos family. Those had a steady income and did not need to cultivate their parcel to survive. Some would sublease part or all of their own land to others. The Arapientos also owned the land in front of the site next to Aldo's property. It was there that the luxurious Arapientos family ranch was located and where the old man had lived most of his life. It was now occupied by his incompetent sons.

As they neared the entrance, Aldo crossed the road, with Tomas behind him. Aldo turned left and headed for the gate. It was built with *piñon* tree logs and four lines of barbed wire. As he approached, Aldo heard a rustle and saw a heap of small figures fluttering. The dirty creatures could not wait. He flapped his left arm in the air as he got closer, and they retreated a bit. The vultures had found a source of food and were reluctant to abandon it. Aldo unloaded the tools from his shoulders. He startled some of the vultures and they flew away. Aldo picked up some stones from the ground and threw them at the remaining birds. They flapped their wings and they too flew away.

Aldo stepped into the ditch. At the bottom was a *yagua* leaf covering something. It had been poked in several places by the vultures. Aldo anchored his feet on the walls of the ditch, one on each side, being careful not to step on the *yagua*. He slowly removed it and put it aside. Under his feet he saw Patricio's battered corpse, lying face up. His eyes started blankly and his mouth was partially open, the wide gap of his broken front teeth conspicuous in the moonlight. Aldo felt shaken. Once he had pulled his brother's crushed body from under a truck, and he had help carry his father's corpse from a lagoon back to the house. But those were accidents, and the dead looked relatively peaceful compared to this. This man had died in agony. He had been beaten and cut unmercifully. His clothes were as mangled as if they had been put through a shredding machine. There were numerous wounds all over his body and face. He had been hacked and jabbed with a bayonet, and the left side of his head was gone. His forehead was charred around the hairline, scraped by ammunition. There was a red gash on his left cheek, and his chest was riddled with bullets. *What reason could someone have to kill another this way?* Aldo thought. Men who killed like that were worse than beasts in the jungle that killed only out of hunger. These men had taken their time to inflict the maximum amount of pain. It was obvious from these wounds that Patricio had suffered the death of Christ.

"When did you put this *yagua* here?" Aldo asked without turning to face Tomas.

"This morning,"

Tomas was standing by the entrance to the site. He did not dare look down into the ditch.

That's probably why he did it, Aldo thought. Tomas wasn't concerned about the vultures picking at Patricio's body, but he must have figured he had to cover the body to prevent neighbors from seeing it. Then when it got dark, he could fetch someone to help him bury it, someone he could trust to keep his secret. Aldo felt rage and had an urge to use his gun on Tomas but he couldn't. He hadn't really seen him do anything and had no proof that the man was involved in Patricio's death. Only his own mental reasoning found Tomas guilty. He must wait. That was the difference between he and the butchers who had executed Patricio without any evidence, relying solely on someone else's unsupported accusation.

Aldo wondered for a moment if he himself might not now be suspected of being the stool pigeon responsible for the murder. After all, he and Patricio had not been in good terms, although he had no reason to hate the man. He decided to get to work. He had been standing there, his feet spread apart on the ditch, staring at the body for a few moments. He could feel Tomas impatient gaze on him. He didn't care. He wanted to give Patricio a decent burial. He bent forward and brushed aside a swarm of flies on the dead man's head. The body was beginning to swell. He climbed out of the ditch and looked around.

"I'm going to get another leaf," Aldo said. "I'll be right back."

"I can go," Tomas said.

"No. Just keep an eye on those vultures."

Aldo didn't want him touching anything. He didn't want his help. He felt Patricio did not deserve to be disgraced this way by having Tomas prepare his funeral. He would do it alone.

Aldo entered the site and looked at the palm trees nearby. When their combs of leaves dried up, they usually sagged down, then shed along with the broad flat stem attached to their base. The leaf called *yagua* was coveted by the peasants because of its versatility. The shell was hard but also flexible and easily bent like a thick piece of cloth, fluffy inside and coarse outside. It was used to sheath the walls of the peasants' shacks, as a tray for roasted pork, and for many other purposes. Tonight, Aldo was going to use one for a coffin.

He couldn't see well in the dark so he went toward a grove of mangos nearby. It got darker as he went under the branches. He looked carefully around. The bottom area was usually grassless. The hogs had worked it into a puddle where they bathed and laid in the mud for hours. The tree stump was brownish, with a currycomb-like surface, and exposed roots. Aldo walked under the tree until he saw a leaf on the ground. It was pretty dry. He kept walking and found another leaf. The leaves were a little stiff from the dry mud, but the shell was intact. They were broad enough to cover Patricio's body. He carried one of them back to the road.

Tomas was pacing back and forth at the entrance. Aldo passed by him without saying a word. He walked along the edge of the road and positioned the *yagua* in the bottom of the ditch. He placed the shell in front of the dead man's head and wished he had brought a machete to cut the comb of dried leaves off. He needed rope.

"Do you have a knife, Tomas?"

"Yes."

Tomas unbuttoned his shirt.

"No, not now," Aldo said, "I'm going to need it later to trim the shell."

Aldo stepped into the ditch, spreading his legs apart. The *yagua* was so broad that both sides overlapped. Aldo spread them apart. Patricio was a big man. Aldo might have to use the other *yagua* to cover him. Then he moved back along the sides of the ditch. He fixed one foot over each end of the *yagua*, stooping and passing his hands between his legs to haul the body. He didn't want to touch the head so he carefully grabbed the shoulders and pulled forward. The body was very heavy. The chilly weather had helped prevent its quick decomposition but too many hours had passed, and it had now begun to swell. Aldo dragged it over the *yagua* with much effort. The head and shoulders went through his open legs, the corpse's eyes staring at him. Aldo brushed the flies away. Then he placed himself in front of the body again. He kept pulling it forward this way until the head reached the base of the comb. The wings of the shell came around the shoulders, leaving the rest of the body exposed. He would have to use a cover. He looked back and saw that the feet protruded.

"It's the best I can do for you, old pal," he murmured.

"What?" Tomas asked.

"Nothing."

Aldo gazed at the spot where the body had been. The grass there was bloody. He saw bits of flesh and bone on the grass stems. He would have to pick up as much as he could, the rest he would cover. He didn't want Patricio's family seeing the mess. He moved quickly. He picked all the debris he could from the ditch with the shovel, emptying it on top of the body. He dug a hole in the ditch at the other side of the entrance and took dust to cover the bloody spots. Aldo took the *yagua* that Tomas had used and placed it over Patricio. Then he tore the leaves out of the comb with his knife and fashioned four strings. He slipped each string around the *yagua* leaves and tied them. Only the feet were exposed. He pushed the body onto the dirt strip along the road, then climbed out of the ditch, dragging the *yagua* forward and using the comb as a handle.

"I'll take the tools," Tomas said.

"No, it's all right, I'll carry them."

"But why?" Tomas protested. "I can help."

"Relax, Tomas," Aldo said irritably, "I know what I'm doing."

Aldo hoisted the pick and shovel onto his left shoulder and dragged the *yagua* coffin onto the site, heading in the direction of the mango trees. He stopped a few feet from them and surveyed the area. He didn't want to bury the body under the trees. There were too many animals wandering around during the day so he decided to dig the grave out here on the grass. He would have to dig a deep hole and for the first time, he realized how much work it would be to do it alone.

"You are going to bury him here?"

"Yes."

"Why not go under the trees or by the coconut grove?"

"The animals come under the trees. They might smell the body. I can bury him out here and then cover the spot with grass."

"The ground is hard out here. It's going to be a lot of work."

"I'm doing the digging."

Aldo took his leather jacket off and hung it on one of the trees. The exertion had made him warm. He was now ready to dig. He grabbed the pick and began to break up the ground. First he turned over all the stumps of grass in a large circular area around him. Then he measured a strip inside with his feet. He made it long so he wouldn't have to dig down vertically. He saved the stumps on the side. Tomas was right, the ground was hard, and it took Aldo a long time to break through the first footing. Underneath it was softer, so he used the shovel. He dug down to chest height, piling all the dirt outside. Tomas stood near the edge silently, watching him work. Then Aldo pulled himself out of the trench.

"All right, give me that knife now."

Tomas unbuttoned his shirt and handed Aldo a broad concave knife. Aldo pulled the coffin to the edge of the grave, then cut the comb off at the bottom. He handed the knife back to Tomas. Then he lowered himself into the hole and pulled the body inside. For a moment he bore all its weight on top of him. Then he gradually let it rest on the bottom while he stepped aside. He placed his hands on the edge of the hole and pulled himself up. He looked inside one last time. Seeing Patricio's exposed feet, he took his jacket and covered them. Then he shoveled all the dirt in. After the grave was filled, Aldo took the time to replant the grass stumps. He dug out others nearby and moved them, making sure that the whole grave area was covered. Then he picked his tools and turned to leave.

"I'm finished," he said.

He slung the tools on his shoulders and walked toward the gate.

"Are you going to tell his wife?" Tomas said.

"No."

"Don't you think maybe you should?"

Aldo again felt anger. He dropped the tools and grabbed Tomas's shirt collar. "Listen," he bellowed, "you have a lot of explaining to do."

Aldo lifted Tomas off the ground and kept jouncing him up and down as he spoke. Tomas was now gasping for air and could hardly hear him.

"Aldo…no, please," he managed to say.

Aldo released him, and Tomas fell on his back. Then Aldo turned, gathered his tools and walked away without looking back.

CHAPTER THREE

It was well after midnight when Aldo returned home. From the road, he saw the dim lights of the cattle house. Alfredo had begun the milking without him. The milkman usually arrived early and Alfredo dozed off before starting but tonight he had missed his nap and had to make up for Aldo's absence. Aldo stood silently on the road and waited for Champ's barking to subside. The dog came rushing towards him, jumping around him.

"Down, Champ," Aldo whispered, "down."

Aldo went to the tool room and put his tools away. He had moved stealthily in the darkness to prevent the milkman from seeing him. His involvement in the incident had been purely humanistic, but a curious observer might interpret it otherwise. He wondered what Alfredo might have told the milkman to explain his absence. It was cold, and Aldo missed his leather coat, so he went in the house. He reached underneath his shirt and unbelted the gun. Then he wrapped the belt around it and hid it above one of the eaves. He walked across the yard and entered the house through the bathroom.

Amanda slept quietly. She had endured in this scruffy environment for which she felt she was never meant. Aldo was the only one who really knew the cause of her torments. He knew it wasn't politics. Amanda couldn't have cared less about that. It was this inner struggle about this place that was constantly assaulting her heart. It brought out the worst in her and was slowly consuming her and him. Even at this moment, he knew the flame still burned secretly inside her and would soon flare up again.

Aldo searched inside the mahogany chest for a woolen shirt. He saw Amanda's body shift on the bed. She was a light sleeper. He could never move at night unnoticed. He saw her tip her head forward.

"Go back to sleep, Figurine," he said. He bent forward and kissed her in the forehead.

"Is everything all right?" she asked in a sleepy voice.

"Yes, go back to sleep."

"Please, Aldo, stay with me."

"I'll be back later, Figurine."

"Where are you going?"

"I have to milk the cattle. It's already late. I'll be back shortly." He bent forward and kissed her once more.

"What time is it?"

"I don't know. After midnight."

The cattle house served as the dairy for the farm. The men worked around the cows, filling buckets with milk and emptying them inside the milk pitchers. They worked solely by the light of the two oil lamps placed high at each end of the structure. The lamps had no glass enclosures, and their flames looked like flickering crimson red tongues that reflected ripples of light over the animals' bodies.

Aldo entered the cattle house and went to where the dairy tools were kept. They were fastened to the stakes with ropes coated with dried cow manure. A small cinder block house was used to store cheese and jerked beef. One gate at the other end led to a corral where the cows were kept away from their calves until milking time. The other gate led to a small pen holding the calves.

"Well, it's about time," the milkman said.

He had stood up when he heard Aldo. He bought milk wholesale and sold it to private homes in town. Aldo had been his supplier for years. The milkman often acted as the boss and would carry this pretension to extremes.

"Thanks for the help," Aldo said.

It was customary to address the milkman by his trade name of *lechero*, milkman, rather than his own name. Aldo waited for him to speak first since he did not know what Alfredo had told him about his absence.

"How was the cattle run?" the milkman asked.

He was a big man, maybe an inch taller than Aldo. Aldo's vision had not yet gotten used to the dim light of in the cattle house and he could not see the man's face.

"As good as ever," he replied.

Aldo ran the end of a rope through the back of a small bench, pulling the ends and tying them to his waist with the bench on his buttocks. Then he took two ropes, one long and short one, and chose a cow to milk.

"I did not see you come in," the milkman commented. "Where did you leave your horse?"

"I unsaddled her right in front of you," Aldo said. "What are you, blind? It's a good thing I'm not a thief. You and Alfredo would let me walk away with the whole house." Aldo entered the pen at the end of the cattle house which was accessible by a narrow gate built from stakes like the walls. Aldo knew each calf and to which cow it belonged. He drifted among the impatient little animals until he recognized one. He swooped a sorrel calf, mottled with blotches of white. The calf was light, and Aldo wrapped him in his right arm and reopened the gate.

"Aldo, this might not be the best time to be wandering around in the night," the milkman shouted. "Have you heard the news?"

"No."

Aldo took the long rope and tied one end of it around the calf's midsection. Then he pressed him against his mother and tied the other end around her. She acknowledged her calf by turning her head back and licking his face. Aldo moved around the cow.

"The rebels are taking positions all around the city," the milkman asserted. He moved away from his cow and came closer to

Aldo, his voice high with excitement. "If they are rounding up the city, you know they got to be around here, too."

"Be careful on the road," Aldo said.

Aldo grabbed a pail and placed it underneath the cow's udder then sat on the bench that was tied around his waist.

"Believe me, Aldo," the milkman went on, "if I didn't have to I wouldn't be here smelling the shit of these cows. I'd be home sleeping with my woman. But a man like you, with what you have, you don't need to take these risks anymore."

"Not really."

"Come on. I wish I had half of your money."

The milkman was now into one of his favorite themes and would go on for the rest of the night. Aldo felt happy about it as the milkman had obviously failed to see the flaw in Aldo's alibi. Alfredo's ploy had worked beautifully. But now it would take forever to get him to stop talking. It was the price he had to pay for keeping the affair secret.

Aldo reached under his cow with his left hand and whirled the short rope around the animal's hind legs. Then he crossed the ends of the rope between the legs and tied them with a single knot to prevent the cow from kicking.

"Do me one last favor, *lechero*," Aldo said. "Finish milking that one cow. You can even help me count my money then."

"I have no choice but to milk cows," the milkman replied. "It's my destiny. But you, you're going places."

He went back to his cow, still muttering. Aldo grabbed an udder in each hand, held them firmly, and tugged each one at a time, aiming down at the bucket between his knees. A thin string of white liquid shrilly spattered into the bottom of the bucket and a cloud of bubbles began to from inside.

"If the rebels take over, you'll have it made," the milkman said. "The country will be ripe for opportunity."

"Yes?"

"That's right. That's what we need, opportunity. Everybody will be trading, selling, or buying something. If you have a couple of dimes saved, there's your chance to get on the bandwagon and make them grow."

"Yes."

"Aldo, do you really think that we have a market now? People are scared to make a move. Not even the very rich are doing business anymore. We have…"

"Shhhhh, keep it down," Aldo said.

The milkman got up and left his cow again. His deep voice was carried through the cattle house like thunder. "If he only knew what had gone on here today," Aldo thought

The milkman turned back and again sat behind his cow. He mumbled a few words and went on milking. If there was anything he hated was to admit that he had been indiscreet. But here was Aldo warning him about his imprudence and he was right. In these times of violence and confusion, any patrols could be wandering the prairie searching for rebels in the darkness, and they could easily overhear their voices. This was a time when a big mouth could mean big trouble. He trembled at the thought of having to travel through the desolate roads in his milk wagon at night. But that was his livelihood. What else could he do?

Aldo felt the cow's udders deflate and he switched to the other two. He squeezed them hard and fast, one at a time, in perfect harmony, aiming the steady flow into the bucket. Aldo was warm now. He would have liked to know more about what the milkman had heard in town but was afraid to ask. He thought about Patricio at the bottom of the hole he had dug.

Aldo got up and carried the full bucket towards the gate. Standing by the stakes were two long milk pitchers. Aldo lifted the bucket and poured the milk into one of the pitchers. Then he went back inside the cattle house and untied the cow's legs. He walked around her and released the calf on the other side. The two animals huddled together, the cow licking the calf all over, he pressing forward to reach the udder. Aldo petted her and led her and the calf outside through the main gate. He closed the gate behind them and went back to pick another cow. He saw Alfredo and tapped him on the shoulder.

"Good work, old buddy," Aldo said.

Aldo opened the gate and let another cow inside. "We are doing good, actually ahead of schedule," he said.

The milkman had finished his cow and released her.

"Watch they don't trample the pitchers outside," Aldo warned.

"I'm going out there," the milkman retorted.

He untied the rope holding the bench around his waist. He hung it from a stake by the supply house and then went outside.

He had been a milkman since he was eight years old when he began making rounds with his father who had been a milkman in the city and knew no other life. They had been hard times, and he was happy that he had survived them. He had been one of eight children, five of whom had died from smallpox. He and his two younger sisters had been the only survivors. He had had to quit school and start milking when his older brother had died. The old man needed help and could not afford to pay for it, so he had been the answer. He had learned how to lift heavy milk pitchers and to drive the wagon. He also learned how to add water to the milk pitchers and double their volume. His father always said that was the only way for a milkman to make a profit. He called it "the water pennies." Everything else went for overhead. The practice would soon allow him to own a wagon, and if he used his brain, he might eventually have his own route. The trouble was, he had been doing it all his life and had nothing but a miserable milk buggy and one farm supplier to buy his milk from. He was tired of the sleepless nights, the non-paying customers, and the smell of cow shit. Meanwhile, he thought, his supplier was getting richer.

"I hope we get a cyclone this year that destroys every fucking thing in sight," he murmured.

He knew Aldo couldn't hear him. He envied and respected Aldo. Here was a lucky man. Fifteen years younger than him, and Aldo had already been able to achieve three times as much as he.

"Damn," he repeated to himself, "if I could only get myself started with some cattle."

He looked inside the two milk pitchers, noticing that one was more than half-way full. He pulled a small notebook and pencil from his pocket and scribbled some figures on it. "I've got three-fourths of one in here already," he yelled to Aldo. "I'm going to start mixing."

He went to his wagon parked a few feet away and carried a milk pitcher back with him. He pulled the round top off it and lifted the pitcher from the bottom, pouring water inside the one that was nearly full. He always carried the extra pitcher of water in the wagon, preferring to do the mixing at the farm. It was too dangerous in town or on the road. Getting caught would mean paying a heavy fine to Sanitation, if one did not have the money to bribe them. His only concern was making sure that he jotted down the actual quantity of pure milk he was taking, or a little less if possible, so he would not end up paying for his own water. He was not worried since, although Aldo probably did not approve, he knew he would never tell.

Time passed quickly. Alfredo and Aldo moved from one cow to the next. Alfredo would usually sing *décimas*, his high-pitched voice echoing inside the cattle house. Aldo welcomed the tunes as a diversion from the harsh task. It also set the pace for him. The milkman would grimace at the tunes, displeased at the interference with his speech. He also considered himself a city man and pretended to be intolerant of the peasants' ways. He discarded *décimas* as a backward form of music and did not consider himself a part of it. But after the milking was done and he started back to town, he would often hum some of Alfredo's catchy tunes.

Aldo and Alfredo finished the milking. Although the milkman had substituted for Aldo at the beginning, he was far too slow to make up for Aldo's absence. Aldo and Alfredo had to put on their best form, milking cows while the milkman let cattle in and out and emptied the men's buckets into his pitchers. He filled two-and-a-half pitchers of pure milk, which became three with the help of water. He loaded them into the back of his wagon with the fourth empty one where he had carried the water. He ran a rope across the open back of the buggy, tying one end on each side. Then he swung the tailgate closed, tying its top board to the sides. The buggy was a light, two-wheel carriage built for one horse and a seat for the driver. The wheels were two automobile tires which made the carriage faster on the paved roads. Its maneuverability was limited by the rugged terrain, especially during the rainy season. The milkman, however, had no desire to venture upon any unknown territories and had no need for hard wheels. He liked Aldo's farm because of its proximity to the highway and the city. The idea of going into any of the remote areas looking for better buys to expand his business did not appeal to him. He made enough to live and besides, he liked Aldo.

He went to the front of the carriage and picked a lasso wrapped around the lamp enclosure. Because the milkman traveled great distances at night, the buggy was equipped with oil lamps, a clear one for the front and one dyed red for the rear. He slipped his right arm through the lasso's loop and looked for his horse.

He found it standing near the well at the end of the cattle chute. He pulled him gently from the rope and walked him back to the cattle house.

"Go to sleep, Alfredo," the milkman heard Aldo say as he got close.

"Yes, yes, go to sleep Alfredo," mimicked the milkman. "The night is still young and your boss doesn't need you anymore, so take advantage of it. The hell with tomorrow."

Alfredo headed for the tool house. Aldo watched his figure in the shadows as he opened the gate to the yard and entered the outhouse.

"I wonder when that old bastard is going to wash up," the milkman bolted.

"Now," Aldo replied.

"Shit," the milkman said, "that fuck never washes. I don't know how you can live with him. I'm not even sure he should be milking these cows. It's unsanitary."

"He washes," Aldo said. "Besides, what do you care?"

Aldo glanced at the big man guiding his horse backwards into the arms of the buggy. Then he turned and saw Alfredo's darkened figure exit the outhouse and walk towards the well to wash. Aldo thought it was pretty incredible that Alfredo could withstand such cold water in the middle of winter.

The milkman reached into the front section of the carriage and gathered the harness. He moved to the head of the animal and put the bridle and blinders on.

"Well," he remarked, "you know what I always said about people like that. Stink if you like, friend, but stink to yourself. Don't stink the whole world, for Christ's sake."

Aldo looked up at the sky for a moment. It was a beautiful winter night. Some of the stars were bright against the black sky. The moon had disappeared behind the clouds. He felt the chilly breeze now that he had stopped working.

"I'd rather get through delivering early," the milkman said. "With all this commotion, I don't want to spend anymore time on the road than I have to." He threw the leather straps over the ribs of the horse and let the stirrups hang loose.

"That's good thinking," Aldo replied. He walked around the buggy and grabbed the arm on the other side. "Just say when you're ready."

"Now," the milkman called. Each man lifted one arm and drove the end of it through the stirrup. The buggy tottered unsteadily. Aldo held the arm on his side while the milkman connected the chains from the frame of the carriage to an iron ring and then to the horse's breast strap.

"You're not scaring me, Aldo," the milkman said. "I've seen all this before."

"All right," Aldo said, "but look, just be careful out in town, okay?"

The milkman did not respond. "Can you open the gate for me?" he asked.

"Sure."

Aldo walked towards the gate at the end of the cattle chute. The milkman lit the two oil lamps in the front and rear with a match. He mounted his wagon and grabbed the reins.

"Let's go, Shooter!"

Aldo was waiting by the opened gate. The carriage went by slowly, and Aldo said good night. The milkman acknowledged him and prodded the horse. Aldo closed the gate behind him, watching the glare of the pitchers in the back of the buggy until it disappeared in the darkness. Then he went toward the tool house. Alfredo was there waiting for him.

"What happened, Aldo?"

"I had to bury Patricio," Aldo said.

"Where did you find him?"

"He was lying at the bottom of a ditch by the road. Tomas found him there. You know, where we saw the vultures today."

"Was he killed?" Alfredo asked.

"Yes, he was shot many times."

"Who do you think did it, Aldo?"

"Now, Alfredo, you know the answer to that."

But did he? Aldo looked at Alfredo's eyes shinning in the dark and wondered if the old wizard knew who had passed sentence. Everyone who had heard the shots would know but few would know about the actual murderer.

"What do you think will happen now, Aldo?" Alfredo's voice sounded choked.

"I don't think anything is going to happen now. Who knows, may be they'll patrol the area more often. Just keep quiet, Alfredo, and don't talk to anyone. I think that may have been Patricio's mistake."

"Why? What did he do?"

"I'm not sure at this point, but you know how loud he was. He may have said too much to the wrong person."

"Let his mortal remains rest in peace."

"Yes. Keep your ears open now and let me know what you hear."

Alfredo stood there silently. He knew the poor devil would worry, and he tried to calm him.

"Come on, Alfredo, go to sleep. There's nothing else for us to do. We'll talk more in the morning."

Aldo patted him on the shoulder and turned to go inside. Alfredo saw him disappear in the yard and went toward his own quarters. He brushed the sack curtains aside and entered. The room was pitch black. He hung his hat on a nail and felt for the leather sheath of his machete. He grabbed it and laid it in the hammock under his blanket. He sat down and untied his shoes. He laid back and covered himself with the blanket. He was afraid. He thought about Patricio, about the time when he had heard that Patricio had reviled Amanda's name at the store in front of Aldo. And Aldo had now buried his body when nobody else would dare touch it. He admired Aldo, he admired him very much.

Aldo went into the house through the bathroom door. He felt dirty and wanted to wash up, but he was very tired and it was cold. He hung his hat on a peg, took his woolen shirts off, and hung them on the bed's headboard. Then he sat on the edge of the mattress, hoping not to wake Amanda, and pulled his cowboy boots off. He remembered the twins and Frank in the other room and got up gently from the bed.

"Aldo?"

Aldo saw Amanda's head tilt up.

"Yes, Figurine."

"Please don't bring the kids here. Just come to bed with me."

"I'm just going to check on them. I'll be right back." Aldo knew this was a lie. He could never stand sleeping away from them. He crossed the darkened living room and went past the curtains into the kids' bedroom. A dim light shone from an oil lamp on top of a high chest. Amanda always left this light on for the children. Aldo stood by Frank's bed for a second. The boy slept soundly, a solid blue blanket covering his body up to his neck. Aldo went to the two single beds across from Frank's. The girls were both sleeping on their stomachs, their backs covered with pink blankets. Aldo reached into one of the beds, with his left hand and folded his arm around one, then the other. He carried them to his own bed and put them next to Amanda.

"Aldo, no…"

"Shhhh, you are going to wake them up. They won't bother you."

Amanda sat on the bed and embraced him. She needed to be with him tonight. All afternoon she had yearned to talk to him and tell him how much she loved him, but she couldn't. She had to wait for the results of her tongue lashing at the table to abate. It would only be then that she would have the courage to beg him to bring her back, to the world they had forged with their dreams in those early and beautiful days when they had first met. It was also then that she felt most sexually attracted to him. It was as if her younger self was reincarnated into her older one. And she could again feel the burning passion that could only be quenched by the man she loved.

She pulled him towards her side of the bed with short tugs that made Aldo giggle. He let himself be carried. Then he spread himself on the bed and let her undress him. She clung to him while he grasped her body as if it were a toy. She felt her whole body tremble in ecstasy and tried to visualize for a second if there was a limit to her lust, as she used to do in the beginning. She saw huge voids, flawless rivers, and raging seas, but never the end. Then she was breathless, totally overcome by her emotions, with Aldo's warm body next to her. Aldo opened his eyes to the crowing of a rooster. He glanced at the clock on the night table and saw that it was after 7:00 A.M. Amanda was already up. He was lying on the edge of the bed with the twins next to him. He must have gotten up during the night and moved to his side of the bed. It was his way of protecting the girls while preserving his narrow edge. He remembered Frank and jumped up. He put on his trousers and two woolen shirts and went quickly to the kitchen. Frank was at the table having breakfast.

"Wait, Frank, I want to take you to the gate to wait for the bus."

"Why, Dad? I can manage."

"No, I don't want you to go alone."

"Good morning, Aldo," Amanda called from the kitchen.

"Good morning, Figurine."

Aldo went back to the bedroom and put on his black cowboy boots and his hat and went outside. Alfredo was busy tending to the dairy cattle. He had rounded most of them up near the cattle chute and was separating the calves from the cows, leading them into the section. Aldo saw his horse tied to a post inside the tool house, all saddled up.

He always marveled at Alfredo's reliability. He could depend on him down to the smallest detail.

Aldo turned back towards the house. He fetched toothbrush and toothpaste from the bathroom and carried them to the well. He pumped the handle down and up a few times until a stream of sparkling water oozed out of the mouth of the pump. He plunged his right hand into the flow and made a scoop. He splashed water on his face then filled his hand again and gargled. He brushed his teeth and then made ready for his horse.

Aldo and Frank traveled together on the mare. At the main gate, Frank dismounted and stepped through the gate, with his leather bookcase in hand and walked near the road. Aldo saw two men walking out of Rios to the road. Flanking them were the mango trees near which he had buried Patricio last night. He saw the men turn and come toward him and Frank.

"Someone's coming, Dad," Frank said.

"I see them."

As they came closer, Aldo recognized them. They were locals who lived in the hamlet. Aldo guessed they were here because of Patricio. He leaned over the mare's neck and waited.

"Good morning," the two men said.

They were both short with swarthy skin and wore wide brimmed straw hats. One wore a beechnut-colored corduroy jacket and the other wore a woolen shirt. They both wore oak-colored trousers and short brow work boots.

"Good morning," Aldo replied. "Working today?"

"Later," one of the men said. He was slim in comparison to the other and his name was Rodolfo.

"There is no rush," the other said. "Work will not do you any good anyhow."

He looked older than Rodolfo. He had a puffy face and a broad forehead, with eyes buried deep under the eyebrows. His name was Oscar.

Aldo heard the pithiness in the man's voice. These men were not here to talk about the weather. They had come to discuss the grim news. They looked at each other for a moment, then one of them turned towards the highway where the bus was now approaching. It was a red and white bus that could seat about twenty. Frank was already at the edge of the road and waived his arm.

"Good luck in school, Frank," Aldo said.

"Good luck, Frank," the men repeated.

"Thank you," Frank said.

The bus came to a full stop in front of the gate and the driver beeped the horn. Frank climbed in and sat by a window seat. The two men and Aldo waived at the bus driver as the bus started again slowly.

"You're a lucky man, Aldo," Oscar observed, "such a smart little boy."

"Well, Aldo," Rodolfo added, "the reason we're here is Patricio."

Aldo looked at him. He had been expecting it but not quite so bluntly. He had pondered his answer to the inevitable news they brought. He did not want to let on that he already knew, but he also worried about Tomas and what he might have said about last night. If he pretended ignorance when they already knew about his involvement, it could call in question his veracity and his role in the affair and could implicate him even further. He decided to tackle the issue head on.

"What about Patricio?"

"He's dead," Oscar announced.

Aldo tried to express astonishment, but he couldn't. He was no hypocrite. He stared at them silently for a second.

"Those shots yesterday morning?" he asked.

"We think so," Oscar said, "wouldn't you?"

"Maybe. Who was doing the shooting?"

"*Casquitos*," Rodolfo said.

"I heard the shots," Aldo commented.

He was trying not to appear defensive. He was afraid by trying to hide what he already knew, he might prove over sensitive to the men's comments and questions, which were probably borne out of ignorance.

"Tomas found Patricio's body in a ditch by the road and he buried him last night," Oscar said.

His voice was bleak and serious and matched his composure.

"When did he find him?" Aldo inquired.

"Last night," Rodolfo replied, "he was lying right by the main gate to the hamlet."

"Well," Oscar said, "maybe he was lying there all day."

"One of you would have seen his body, no?"

It was Aldo's turn to goad. If Oscar was trying to snub him for not having found Patricio, he would poke at his own cowardice. Patricio's body had been lying right at their doorstep all day. Did Oscar really think that Aldo believed him? Of course they had seen his body but no one had had the balls to pick him up. They would have left the vultures devour him if it meant exposing themselves to danger. Only Tomas had had the courage to bury him. Or was it really Tomas? Maybe that was the real reason Oscar had dragged the ignorant Rodolfo here. He knew that Tomas could not have done it. He was too indifferent. It had had to be someone courageous but he wanted to be sure. Aldo felt good about having cornered Oscar. He waited.

"I didn't see him," Rodolfo blurted.

Aldo gazed steadily at Oscar. He was not going to let him use Rodolfo as a scapegoat if he could help it. Oscar looked pensively at the ground his uneasiness apparent. Aldo knew then and it almost embarrassed him to press the issue because he understood the reasons for Oscar's behavior. These people had homes and families to protect, and they were scared of the *casquitos*, of the rebels, of the whole bloody mess. They only wanted to survive, to keep their *bohíos* and their diminutive parcels of land which they had worked so hard to gain.

"Oscar," Aldo said curtly, "I know that you don't want to get involved in whatever happened with Patricio. Nobody does, and I can't say that I blame you, but don't put your burden on somebody else."

"I would like to be able to do something for his wife Julia and his kids," Oscar replied.

"Does she know what happened?"

"Yes," Rodolfo said, "Tomas told her this morning."

"I was thinking that maybe we all could get together and help," Oscar added.

"I agree. What do you have in mind?"

Aldo felt a certain compassion for the man. He was sure that his intentions were good. He did want to help Patricio's family but he was afraid, knowing that the government was behind his death and that there had been a purpose for the execution. What it might not be clear, but Aldo could see that Oscar was smelling a rat and that he was looking for support. Yet Aldo could not help but ponder the ugly question. If he had not removed Patricio's body from the ditch the night before, would Oscar or the other peasants have let the vultures finish their plunder?

He felt disappointment. After all, Aldo was one of them.

"It would be a good idea to visit them today. Maybe we all could bring something. You know, it's Christmas Eve. Then we could see about other things they need. The whole neighborhood could help."

"Sure, fine. I can meet you at your house in a couple of hours, and we can go together, all right?"

"Yes. Actually, some of the women are going there this morning, and I was thinking that we should all go late in the afternoon after they've consoled Patricio's wife. It's much harder for the men-folk to do."

"Yes." Aldo watched Rodolfo's approving nods. "I have to do a couple of things today, so that's even better."

"Shall we meet, say, at 4:00?" Oscar inquired.

"Yes," Aldo said. "Your house."

"We will see you later then."

Aldo turned the mare towards the house and trotted away. Oscar and Rodolfo walked back towards the hamlet. Aldo thought about Patricio's wife and his two daughters. What would they do now? Would they be able to stay in their *bohío* or would they be kicked out by the Arapientos? Who would provide for them?

At the house Aldo sat at the table near the girls having breakfast and he wondered whether he should tell Amanda. She would soon know anyway, but he thought she should hear it from him first. He weighed the possible effects that the news would have on his wife. The glow of last night was still very much present in her. The topic of politics would surely change that. He decided to wait.

"Well, Aldo," Amanda inquired, "do we have anyone to do the milking tomorrow night?"

That would be Christmas Eve and the entire family would dine at Amanda's father's house. Old man Guillermo lived alone with his daughter, Aleida, in the big house since Amanda's mother had died. Her sister, Ana, had married. She too would come with her husband, Blanco. Aldo and Amanda had made it a custom to be with them since the first year of their marriage.

"I haven't actually talked to anyone yet, but I'll find someone today."

"Aldo," Amanda protested, "how could you forget?"

"I haven't forgotten, Amanda, I just haven't had the time. I will do it today."

"Please do it this morning."

"Can everyone come?"

"Yes, why wouldn't they?"

"Wasn't Blanco away?"

"Yes, but it's Christmas Eve, Aldo. He should be back."

Aldo thought about Blanco. He was a cattleman Aldo had met sometime ago when he had first started in the cattle business. He was older than Aldo and came from a reputable family. He and Aldo had become acquainted over snacks at a well-known saloon in town where most of the high-powered cattle traders met to discuss business. They had put a good cattle deal together and had become friends. Aldo had forgotten about him. Then one day, Amanda was talking about Ana who was seriously contemplating celibacy and becoming a nun all to Aldo's astonishment. He remembered Blanco and thought him a good candidate for Ana. Without knowing the implications of this fateful decision, Aldo mentioned it to Amanda who became excited at the idea. After Amanda spoke to her sister, Aldo approached her.

"Do you want to meet him?"

"If you think I should meet him, I will meet him Aldo." Aldo looked deep into her olive eyes that reminded him of Francisca. He was surprised at her nonchalance, and thought her too docile. What happened next made him even feel more perplexed when he saw her become tearful. For a man who had so much foresight, he was acting incredibly clumsy in failing to see Ana's true feelings.

"I will arrange it."

Things happened very quickly from there on. Blanco came to discuss business with Aldo at Guillermo's house one day. As usual, the old man kept to himself while Aldo was in the house. He had never gotten over the humiliation Aldo had caused him, although deep inside he admired him as the man he never could be. During the discussion, Aldo introduced Ana to Blanco and then took a passive role during the rest of the meeting. A few days later, Blanco visited Aldo at his own house. As soon as he saw him, Aldo knew the tall-silver-haired man had taken the bait and he felt happy about it.

"I have a business matter that I would like your father-in-law to consider," he had said to Aldo.

Aldo knew this was only a scheme to see Ana again.

"Listen," Aldo had said, "we can arrange a meeting with Guillermo and then, if you like, my wife and I, and Ana and you, can go out for the evening."

"Yes, that would be nice."

It was the only time that the relationship had needed any encouragement from Aldo. From then on, after Guillermo became acquainted with Blanco and learned of his resources, the old man did all the pushing. Not that Blanco needed any persuasion, but Ana kept tottering about his courtship. And she acted strangely when Aldo was present at the meetings. Aldo interpreted this behavior as embarrassment about his part in arranging the union. He thought it was cute and kept out of the way. The relationship bloomed and at Ana's request she and Blanco were married in the same church where Amanda and Aldo had taken their vows. The two moved into a ranch house on Blanco's parents' cattle farm. Ana was well taken care of. Aldo thought them a happy couple, and he was fond of "the silver man," as he called Blanco. He thought of him as the kind of individual born with a silver spoon in his mouth but who was not spoiled by it.

Aldo got up from the table and kissed Amanda. She kissed him back. Then he turned to the girls and bumped heads together. He kissed each in the forehead.

"I will be back early. I have to go to Pablo's house."

"Don't forget about tomorrow," Amanda said.

Pablo lived in a ranch about four miles east of Rios, off the main highway leading to the city of Camaguey. Although not as populated as Rios, this section was much more lively and pleasant. The peasants in that area were better off financially and owned more land. Their houses were closer to the highway than those of Rios, and there were fewer trees, allowing more open space. There was also a store nearby, the same store where Aldo had once knocked Patricio to the floor. Some of the peasants from Rios went there to buy their groceries.

Pablo's house was only a few feet from the road. It was a ranch-type cabin similar to Aldo's but smaller. Its walls were thin, carved wooden boards painted in blue and surrounded by a well-kept yard. The front porch was enclosed by a short picket fence. There was another porch at the rear of the house about five feet tall and screened on top which was the dining room. Part of it was sided by brick and was the kitchen. The roof, like that of most of the houses in the region, was thatched. Aldo pushed the front gate open. He eased the mare inside and closed the gate. Then he trotted through the path leading to the house. It was a short, narrow road marked by whitewash colored stones stuck in the ground. Aldo dismounted and tied the reins to a post. He walked inside the yard. A woman came out to greet him.

"Good morning, Olga," Aldo said, "is Pablo here?"

"Good morning," she replied. "Yes, he is here. He is waiting for you."

She was a stout handsome woman. Her weight made her look rather short, but she could look into Aldo's eyes almost without tilting her head. Her dark brown hair was short. Her face was plump, her cheeks round. She had big hazel eyes that seemed to flicker as she spoke. Her nose was very thin and contrasted with her other chubby features. Her lips were thick and her broad mouth showed her gums as she smiled. She started to go inside, then turned quickly to Aldo.

"Oh, Lord, come inside, Aldo. I wouldn't think of leaving you outside."

Aldo opened the gate and stepped into the porch.

"I'll wait out here," he said.

"No, come on back with me. Pablo is there eating breakfast."

"Breakfast this late?"

"Right," she said, "now, you tell him, okay?"

She took Aldo through the living room and into the back porch. Pablo stood up and shook Aldo's hand. The sound of a radio turned on high vibrated behind him.

"Well," Pablo said, "the man finally shows up, ah. I knew you'd come today though."

Pablo smiled. He was a man in his late twenties, and his manner was pleasant like his wife's. His trunk was trim, and his legs were long for his stature, making him look slimmer and taller than he really was. He had a pronounced receding hairline and jet-black hair that grew in tufts on the back of his neck. His eyes were very black and his thin and carefully-trimmed mustache shadowed straight, thin lips. He wore wide black slacks, pointed black cowboy boots, and a blue woolen shirt. The two men shook hands.

"Sit down," Pablo said.

Aldo pulled one of the chairs from the table and sat down. On the table there were crackers and a glass half filled with coffee and milk. Pablo resumed his seat.

"Bring some breakfast for Aldo, Olga," he said. There was no door separating the tiny kitchen from the dining room, only a partition, leaving enough space on one side to walk through.

"I am not having any breakfast," Aldo said, "I already ate."

"I won't offer you coffee because I know you don't drink it," Olga said.

She walked toward the table and stood before Aldo, hands on her waist.

"I made some hard cheese yesterday, though. I want you to try it."

"Now you are putting me on the spot," Aldo protested.

"Come on, man," Pablo said, "you're not training, are you?"

"Just one skinny slice," Aldo said.

"Olga, bring the whole thing over, would you? And turn the radio down, please."

"Yes, sir," she mocked him.

She moved swiftly about the room and lowered the volume on the radio. Then she disappeared into the kitchen.

"Well," Aldo began, "are we ready for those hogs?"

"There are about twelve orders."

"Let's do it this morning, then."

"How are things down by you?"

Aldo looked steadily at Pablo. They had been friends for many years. They were only one year apart in age, Pablo being the oldest, and they easily communicated in silence. Pablo returned Aldo's gaze then turned towards the kitchen.

"I can come up with three," Aldo replied.

"Leave all the Chinese ones, Aldo. I am going to use the ones I've got over here, and we'll mix them up with your American ones."

Olga came back and placed a small plate in front of Aldo. Then she brought a large salad plate holding a square molded cheese and a butcher's knife and laid both items on the table. She cut a slice of cheese for Aldo.

"Let me know if it's salty," she said. "Sometimes I overdo it."

"Not the ones that we sell, though," Pablo corrected.

"Good," she answered, "you'll have to buy one from me then, Pablo."

"It's great," Aldo said.

"Now I'll have a piece," Pablo added.

They all laughed heartily. Pablo finished his milk and coffee. Then the two went outside to the back of the house.

"Thanks for the cheese," Aldo said.

"Oh, for nothing, *de nada*," Olga replied from the kitchen, "I'll wrap a piece for Amanda before you leave."

They went toward an open cabin in the rear, passing a short distance from an outhouse. Pablo opened a gate built with studs and screen leading into the cabin. There was a pinto dog tied to one of the cabin's posts. The animal barked and waggled its tail at the sight of the two men.

"Anything the matter?" Pablo asked.

"They killed Patricio yesterday."

"What?"

"It seems like the Army did it. I saw a jeep of *casquitos* pass by the house early yesterday morning. I heard machine gun fire coming from the entrance to Rios. Then last night, Tomas came to my house and told me he had found Patricio's body inside a ditch by the road."

Pablo listened attentively and looked at the dirt floor of the cabin.

"I can't believe they would leave him out there," Aldo said incredulously. "And why would they kill him?"

"The worst part is that I had to bury him."

"You buried him? Are you crazy?"

"Everyone knows who did it, Pablo. It was done right out in the open. The thing is, nobody would pick up his body so I had to bury him. That's why Tomas came for me."

"And you went with him, of all people."

"He wouldn't have done it if I hadn't gone with him. Nobody would have. The vultures would have eaten the body."

"Still, Aldo," Pablo said, "that was a crazy thing to do. How could you get involved in anything like that, the way things are?"

"You didn't see that jeep pass by here yesterday?"

"No. I'll ask Olga."

"I wouldn't yet, Pablo. Wait until it's common knowledge."

The two men exchanged glances. Pablo didn't doubt his friend. Nothing needed to be said to anyone, not even to their wives. Pablo tried to absorb the news he had just heard, then quickly prepared to move on with their plans. Like Aldo, he was a man of action.

"I have collected a few hogs already but I left all the big ones for today."

Pablo went to unleash the dog, a low-bodied hunting animal. Aldo reached up and grabbed a lasso.

"You should have left them all."

"Olga helped me a little bit. We've been doing it on and off in the evenings."

They walked to a corral, with the dog following. It was a big pen built with a fence of heavy studs and boarded with palm tree barks. The top was covered with chicken wire. There were at least ten hogs inside. Some rested on the muddy ground below the shade provided by boards placed above a corner of the fence. The others roamed around the dry sections of the corral.

"You and Olga didn't do too badly," Aldo observed.

"Now let's get the big ham," Pablo said.

The two men went into the back woods. Not far behind the cabin, the grass grew high enough to cover the men's calves, and was interspersed with bare ground. Aldo and Pablo reached a group of guava trees where the grass receded. The trees grew everywhere from this point on, forming a sea of branches that extended deep into the rest of the land. Pablo brushed the branches aside and crouched, moving inside. Aldo was behind him. Hardly any sunlight seeped through the branches that helped keep the soil moist, a heaven for the hogs to wander in and feast upon the pulpy ripe guavas that fell on the ground. Aldo and Pablo straightened up and looked around.

"There's a couple right by you," Aldo said.

"I see them."

They moved slowly, brushing aside the branches hanging down in front of them. The dog bounded by their side. A few feet ahead, two chubby pigs sniffed the ground around the trunk of a guava tree. Pablo waived his right hand. The dog moved quickly ahead of the men, and at the sound of Pablo's voice, he darted toward the hogs. One of them disappeared into the shrubs. The other whirled and tried to run away but was held by the dog that had jumped on its left side and was biting its ear. It was a tight grip, and the hog tried to shake it desperately. Then Aldo came behind them and tipped the lasso over their heads.

"Let go, Fury," Pablo commanded.

Instantly, the dog let go. The hog dashed forward straight into the open loop of Aldo's lasso. It ran a few feet then reeled and fell on its side when it reached the end of the rope. The impact yanked Aldo off his feet as he pulled. Pablo motioned the dog to goad the hog. The hound had positioned himself in the rear and quickly bit one of the hog's hind legs. The hog jerked himself free and ran forward, with Aldo following closely behind, in the direction of the corral. As they emerged into the clearing, Pablo rushed to open the corral gate. Aldo walked towards the hog, rolling rope until he was so close to it he could touch its neck. Then with a sharp pull he dragged the hog toward the open gate. The animal quivered and slumped to resist. When his head reached past the gate, Aldo quickly loosened the noose on his neck and pushed him in. The hog charged into the corral.

"It would be nice if we could get a whole bunch of them together," Pablo said.

"We'd probably end up losing them," Aldo replied, "and then they'd be wild and hard to catch."

Pablo looked at his friend. He had always been impressed by Aldo's quick thinking. The pride of a peasant mind. And behind this powerhouse stood the most prevalent of virtues, caution. Pablo, too, was a cautious man and thought of himself as such. That was why now, no matter how much he went over Aldo's version of the previous night, he could not believe it. What had overpowered Aldo's reason last night to do what he had done?

They went back to the guava trees. Aldo had rolled the lasso on his left hand and held the noose on his right.

"Who's going to tell Patricio's family?" Pablo inquired.

"I made Tomas tell them," Aldo replied.

"How?"

"I just told him to."

"What makes you think he will tell them?"

"Oscar told me he has."

"Fine. And what exactly has he told them?"

Aldo knew that behind the questions lay a real concern. He appreciated it.

"The truth."

"That some soldiers must have shot Patricio outside, and he buried the body," Pablo guessed.

"Right."

"It does not make you uneasy to put your fate in the hands of a man like that?"

"The alternative would be to tell them myself, which would really do me in."

"No," Pablo answered, "the real alternative was not to get involved."

"I know that," Aldo said, "but I had to."

With that they entered the guava grove, Aldo, lasso in hand, scouting the trunks and the thin foliage, Pablo alongside him, leading the dog. They worked until late afternoon, tying and dragging the un-wielding hogs into the corral.

"We'll have to get some out of here today," Aldo said. "It is too crowded."

"I've got five people coming this afternoon." Pablo said. "Then tomorrow you and I can take some to the market in town."

"Early in the morning."

Aldo coiled the rope and hung it. Then he and Pablo walked through the open cabin, out into the yard and inside the kitchen where Olga waited. "We are here, Olga," Pablo said.

"Do you know that it's past one?"

She spoke from the kitchen where she had been sitting listening to the small radio.

"Really?" Pablo exclaimed.

"You are going to have to excuse me, Aldo," Pablo said.

He started to pull off his boots.

"Go ahead."

"There's water if you want to wash your hands."

Aldo went to a corner of the room. He slipped his hands into a washbowl and rinsed, then wiped them dry with a white cotton cloth hanging from the stool. Olga came into the room carrying a plate full of rice and a bowl of fried sweet potatoes.

"I thought you two had forgotten about lunch."

"We wanted to finish," Pablo said. "What have you heard on the news?"

"Nothing much," she replied. "It's Christmas Eve."

"Except that this year it's really not," Pablo retorted.

He put on his slippers and went to wash his hands.

"Pablo, no one can overthrow Batista. You're doing the right thing by going through the holidays as usual because nothing will change," Olga said.

She glanced at Aldo for approval. She had now brought a black pot of jerked beef in a sauce to the table.

"Not the way things are, Olga," Pablo replied.

His voice had taken on a note of gravity.

"Why, do you know something I don't know?"

"No," Pablo replied, "but I see the confusion, the weakness in the system. Never before have I seen it this bad."

Olga went into the kitchen, returned with three plates and silverware, and sat between Aldo and Pablo.

"Let me serve you, Aldo," she said. "You are too shy. What do you think, Aldo," she asked while filling his plate.

"I think the system is too feeble to survive this last shove," Aldo responded.

"I agree with you that the government is rotten and that there's turbulence, but there's been turbulence before."

"You can sense the changes in the air."

"Aldo, you and Pablo must have seen prophesy outside. What is it with you two?"

"It's our masculine sixth sense," Pablo said.

"Men do not have one," she countered. "Women do."

They were interrupted by the dog barking.

"Someone's coming," Pablo said.

He got up from the table and moved quickly towards the front door. There was a car at the gate, a light-green 1956 Chevrolet. A man exited the vehicle from the passenger side and opened the gate. Pablo stepped out and motioned Fury to be quiet. He had recognized them. A short man wearing a broad-brimmed hat got out. He was dark skinned and wore a leather jacket, jeans, and black cowboy boots.

"Happy holidays," he said, offering his hand to Pablo.

"Happy holidays to you, too, Don Fernando," Pablo replied.

He shook the man's hand. The passenger in the car had closed the gate and walked up to the porch. He was short but slimmer than Don Fernando, wore gray slacks, a blue sweater, and black boots. He too wore a hat.

"Come in and have a seat," Pablo said. "Can I get you a drink?"

"Well," Don Fernando said, "if it was another time may be I'd pass, but this being the season to be jolly, I'll take some brandy."

"Sure," Pablo said, "how about you Senor Sanchez?"

"I wouldn't pass even in the non-season," the slim man said laughing. Then they all laughed. Pablo motioned them to cane upholstered rocking chairs.

"Felipe II all right?"

"Fine," they replied.

Pablo turned to the kitchen and called Olga into the room to meet the men.

"I already know Aldo," Don Fernando jarred jauntily, "and so does Sanchez, right?"

He pointed to Sanchez as he shook Aldo's hand.

"Bring four shots of Felipe, Olga" Pablo said.

"Well, do you boys have anything good for us during these holidays?" Don Fernando asked.

"You have plenty to choose from, Don Fernando. We've barely finished rounding the hogs this minute."

"Good!" Don Fernando said, "I want lean, clean meat."

"I take it that with the pugilist along, it shouldn't have been much trouble," Sanchez added humorously. "How many did you knock out, Aldo?"

Olga came into the room with a tray, four shot glasses, and a bottle of brandy. She placed the tray on the center of the table. She filled the four glasses and passed one to each man.

"*Salud*," Don Fernando said.

He guzzled his drink down in one gulp. Sanchez took two gulps to put his away.

"I'll have one more," Don Fernando said.

Aldo reached for Don Fernando's glass and filled it with the dark liquid. An odor of malt filled the room.

"May the new year bring us lots of prosperity and lots of money," Don Fernando said.

His voice had become boisterous. It was obvious he had been at it since early today.

"*Salud, señora,*" he yelled into the next room to Olga. Then he gulped his drink down.

"I think the new year will bring more than just money," Sanchez added. "It will bring changes, may be a new government."

"Ahhhh!" Don Fernando exclaimed, "Batista is the man. Leave these shabby little loudmouths alone, *hombre*. What the hell are they going to do? We don't need any new governments."

He threw his hands up in the air in disgust. Then he abruptly stood up and led the other men outside. He had talked enough and now wanted to see the hogs. That was his only purpose here. Pablo took him to the back of the house through the yard. Aldo and Sanchez followed them. They stood by the fence of the corral. Don Fernando leaned on the chicken wire and studied the lot carefully.

"You've got a nice lot here, son," he murmured, "indeed a nice lot."

Aldo went inside the cabin and climbed a short ladder to a roof attic. He brought down a steelyard scale. It was made of a horizontal flat arm with numbers, suspended by a hook on top and low-friction support on the zero end. It had a counterbalance that slid back and forth on the beam and another hook on the bottom attached to the support. Aldo grabbed the lasso and tied it around a beam, leaving some slack. Then he hung the upper hook of the scale on the rope. He took a short rope with a noose at the end. Don Fernando had already made his pick and he had fingered one of the animals to Pablo.

"I'll get him, Pablo," Aldo said.

He handed Pablo the rope and then opened the gate, squeezing himself inside. It was so crowded that he could hardly move among the hogs.

"Be careful, now," Pablo warned as he handed Aldo the rope. "It's the red one, down there," Pablo said, pointing at a husky reddish hog in the middle of the lot.

Aldo slowly worked his way toward it. At his every step, the animals would jiggle, trying to move aside, only to find themselves stopped by a wall of their own. When he got behind the red hog, Aldo quickly locked his left arm around his midsection. Then he tied the noose around his nose and pulled it tight to keep him from screaming. He put his right knee against the hug's ribs while turning the body flat on the ground. He turned the rope around the nose to make it into a knot, then pulled the head down low and tied the four legs together with the rest of the rope. He grabbed two of the legs and lifted the animal in the air. Pablo met him at the fence and grabbed the other two legs. They carried the hog inside the cabin where they hung his legs from the bottom hook of the scale. Pablo slid the counterbalance until the arm stood in a horizontal position.

"Ninety-five pounds," Pablo called.

"I am going to take two," Don Fernando announced.

He moved back towards the corral, and after studying the lot once more, he picked another. Aldo staid inside, anticipating Don

Fernando's announcement. Pablo threw Aldo another strip of rope, and he artfully performed his act again.

"Ninety-one," Pablo called as the second animal hung from the scale.

"Good!" Don Fernando exclaimed. "Let's put them in the trunk of my jeep."

Aldo and Pablo carried the two animals to the front of the house. Sanchez opened the trunk and Aldo placed them inside, side by side, shutting the door. Pablo went to the house for more brandy. Don Fernando had another shot, then he took out a stash of bills from his right pocket.

"You've got one hundred and eighty-six pounds of pure meat in there, Don Fernando," Pablo said.

"I know what I got son," he replied. "I also got guts and bones to get rid of."

"Twenty-five cents a pound makes forty-six pesos and fifty cents, forget the cents, all right?"

"Have a good holiday," Pablo said.

"Have a good one, boys."

Don Fernando eased his bulk inside the car while Sanchez walked to the road and opened the gate. The car sped out of the driveway, making Aldo's mare scamper away. Don Fernando stopped at the gate and waited for Sanchez to close it. Sanchez had barely gotten into the passenger side when the vehicle made a quick right turn and dashed out into the road toward town.

"Impressed with the cursory way we do business, Olga?" Pablo asked. Olga had joined the men outside.

"I think he is smug," she blurted.

"May be," Pablo said, "but he pays."

"He has got as much self-esteem as he does money," Aldo said.

"Well," Pablo said, "let's finish eating."

"No, I'm done," Aldo replied. "I must get going."

He grabbed the reins of the mare and mounted.

"Wait Aldo," Olga said, "I have some wrapped up cheese for Amanda."

"Oh, that's fine."

"How about another drink, *hombre*?" Pablo asked.

"No, I need to get home and try to find somebody to cover for me tomorrow night."

"Are you going into town?"

"To Amanda's father's house as usual. You want to join us?"

"I have the same plans as always, too. Olga's parents' house. There will be time on New Year's Eve."

Olga reappeared carrying a tray wrapped up in white linen. She handed it to Aldo, and he put it inside one of the pouches of his saddle.

"Thanks for the cheese. I will be here at 8:00 A.M. sharp."

"Take care."

Aldo and the mare trotted out of the driveway and headed in the direction of Rios. They rode on the dirt path between the road and the ditch. Two cars passed him, headed in the direction of the city. Aldo glanced at the faces of the front seat passengers. They looked somber, as if presaging the future. Aldo thought it odd to see only two vehicles this time of year. During past holiday seasons the highway would be a beehive of trucks, cars, and wagons, traveling in both directions in search of pork meat which was a delicacy at Christmas and New Year, or simply looking for a place to drink and party. The hissing sound of the breeze radiated serenity. For a second, one could almost dream there was no war.

Aldo kicked gently the mare in the ribs to start her on an easy gallop. He liked the feel of the breeze on his face. As he entered his farm, he saw Amanda and the kids sitting on the porch. "This is from Olga," he told Amanda.

He ruffled Frank's hair and opened his arms wide to the twins who rushed over to him.

"Something terrible has happened," Amanda said.

"What?" Aldo asked.

Had people discovered the illicit burial? No, Tomas must have spread the news.

"They killed Patricio." Amanda replied.

"Patricio?" Aldo feigned surprise.

"Yes, right out there, on the road. The shots yesterday, remember?"

"How did you find out?"

"Two of the women were here this morning. They asked me to console Julia, his wife. I was waiting for you."

"What else did they say?" Aldo was genuinely interested now.

"Just that Patricio was dead. I am scared, Aldo," she said, "I'm afraid for the children and for all of us."

"Don't panic, Amanda."

"Frank, you heard what happened, right?" Aldo said, turning to Frank.

Frank knew exactly what had happened. He had been closer to the crime scene than anyone else in this house. He had heard the women talking to his mother, and he had been afraid. For the very first time, he had been exposed to the whisper of death. He now knew it was real but he wasn't afraid anymore. Like yesterday, his father had come to his rescue when he needed him.

"You can't repeat what you heard here today, Frank, not even in school."

"I know," he said. "I won't tell anyone."

"And you know it could be dangerous, right?"

"Yes."

Aldo stroked the boy's head.

"Let's go get two chickens from the coop for Patricio's family."

Aldo left the twins with Amanda and strolled with Frank around the house toward the chicken coop. Frank was more inquisitive alone with his father and felt he could let his true feelings show. Aldo did not have to spoon feed him answers. Although elusive by nature, Frank was a smart boy who understood the essentials. They tied two chickens by the legs and brought them inside. Aldo went back outside to unsaddle the mare and let her run free in the chute.

"I am going to go to Patricio's house with Amanda and the children to offer my condolences. Everybody knows already," Aldo said to Alfredo.

"I saw the women come," Alfredo said. "Two of them."

"I know. It's all right. Watch the house while I'm gone. Then once we come back you can go if you like."

"How's everything at Pablo's?" Alfredo inquired.

"Same as usual. I'll be back later," Aldo repeated. "Now, don't worry. Everything will be fine."

Alfredo walked silently to the cattle house. He sat on a stake board from where he could see the road and watched Aldo and his family walk down the lonely dirt path out into the highway and turn left. He saw their figures disappear behind the *piñon* trees as they approached the hamlet. He remained there for a long time, as if trying to hear the yelps of mourning in Patricio's house.

CHAPTER FOUR

THE RIOS HAMLET CONSISTED OF a number of huts huddled near the road. Its houses were built on small parcels of land. This structure had its roots in early feudalism and was normally known throughout the country as *sitiería*. It was an urbanized form of living in a nation poorly equipped to handle the transition from farmer to urbanite for those who sought it. People living in a *sitiería* had, for the most part, come to accept its limitations. They were in a limbo of sorts, having neither broken off their masters' chains to own land of their own nor achieved enough autonomy to move out of country life. They were, in short, bound by their environment and tied by their destiny, which had been somehow decided by their ancestors long ago. Their life was monotonous and their future predictable.

* * *

Aldo and Pablo were from this *sitiería*. Aldo's parents had migrated from the Canary Islands as children during the early part of the century and had settled with their respective families deep within the countryside. When the young couple married, they could not aspire to anything beyond Rios and they were actually lucky to find a spot within the confines of the Arapientos' *sitiería*. It was Aldo's father, with his self-determination and physical strength who had made it all possible. A mulish, curt young man, he had come to Arapientos asking for work. Aparientos saw no harm in hiring the tall, muscular islander. He became a lowly hired hand at first, but he had so impressed Arapientos with his stamina and hard work that when he had asked for living space in Rios, Aparientos had promptly agreed.

Then Aldo's father got a parcel of land at the rear end of the sitiería. He quickly built his *bohío* and settled in with his new bride. Years later this house would become Patricio's.

Aldo and his older brother, Emilio, had grown up together. The only surviving children in a succession of miscarriages and infant deaths that had aged their mother Cecilia and thwarted their father. Then the worst came. Aldo was a freckled ten-year-old when his father failed to show up from work one night. His brother, an already-husky young man who toiled the Arapientos' fields alongside his father, had not seen him at the farm that day. That was a terrible night for Cecilia. While the boys slept, she sat by the front door, keeping their bedroom door ajar. She stared in silence at the moving shadows of the palm trees swaying against the dim moonlight, occasionally hearing the restless tapping of a woodpecker on the bark of a tree. Dusk came, and her husband had still not shown. She brought her chair inside, blew the flame of the oil lamp out, and stood sobbing softly in the kitchen. She was a short woman of raw beauty with small, intense black eyes and white freckled skin. Despite her young age, her once-auburn hair was now a tufted sea of gray, which made her appear much older. She possessed immense courage and had resolutely withstood the desolation and misery of these prairies. But now, in the wave of disaster, she cringed. She knew something tragic had happened. In seventeen years of marriage, her husband had never spent one night away from her.

Aldo's brother was the first one to awake. He entered the kitchen and found his mother by the stove preparing breakfast. He would have almost overlooked his father's absence but when he noticed the large nickel casserole still covered, he realized his father had never come home. He immediately went to look for him. Cecilia woke Aldo and told him to go help his brother. Aldo, in turn, ran to find his friend Pablo. The two boys learned from a neighbor that Aldo's father had been seen cutting cane in the lagoon section the day before. He never kept much company, and it had been such a humid and hot April day that everyone had quit early.

Aldo and Pablo headed for the cane fields. Barefooted they crossed the first furrowed fields and then cut through a clearing in the dense sugar cane sections to reach the lagoon. The cutters assigned to these fields had opened up space for a path. The proximity of the fresh water made the high temperatures a little more bearable. The cutters would freshen up and then slowly work their way back through the field at the end of each day.

The boys took a good look around but saw nothing. They searched for any trace of life from the day before, a water jug, a kettle, a machete, but saw nothing. Then they began circling the lagoon. Suddenly, Aldo saw something in the water that made his heart jump. Near the opposite shore, an object was sailing across the water, pushed by the early morning breeze. Aldo ran like a madman, with Pablo trailing behind and asking what he had seen. He recognized his father's straw hat floating on the surface like an abandoned ship and immediately understood its ominous message. The cutters were beginning to arrive at the scene when Aldo's brother rushed past them in a frenzy. He was yelling to Aldo and Pablo to stop. Aldo had dived into the lake followed by Pablo. Both boys were excellent swimmers, having spent long afternoons in the deep ponds and lakes of the prairie. Aldo reached for the hat and turned back to shore. His brother grabbed it from him and began crying. Then he undressed. Aldo and Pablo discussed which side they would search first, but Aldo's brother shouted for them to be quiet. He would do the searching. Some of the men came over and offered to help. Those who could swim dove in and helped search the bottom. In a little over an hour, they covered the whole section where the hat had been found but found no body. Some went as far as the middle of the lake without any luck.

Aldo and Pablo stared at the divers. They watched them submerge and come up for air time after time. Aldo looked at the tall sugar cane stems bent by the wind which was blowing towards the other end of the lagoon. But then it occurred to him that the hat could have come from the other end and could have been sitting at this end all night, perhaps trapped among the high grass growing sparsely at the shores of the lagoon. His father was no swimmer and he must have been near the shore line, perhaps bathing to alleviate the heat. He could have trampled or fallen asleep in the water.

Aldo drifted slowly away from the divers, some of whom had now come out of the water. He motioned Pablo to follow him. They both reached the other side and separated. They decided they would swim from the opposite sides of the lagoon, each one working his way through the bottom in a straight line until they met, then farther toward the center and back to the sides. Their technique seemed more apt to produce results than the disorganized search of the older men.

The lagoon was deep and very steep at the shore line. Two or three steps into it and one would sink up to the neck. Although the surface appeared clean and clear, its bottom was murky and full of algae. The boys submerged slowly to prevent being heard by the men at the other end. They each came within arm's length of the bottom, then drifted towards each as agreed. As they met, they would emerge for air, swim back towards the bottom, and away into the shore line. During one of these sweeps, Aldo saw a blue bulk ahead, nearly touching the dark floor. He felt his heart pound at the thought of finding his father drowned. He thought it impossible for him to glance at the face, and his arms ceased stroking for a moment. He padded his feet and moved cautiously ahead. The body slouched with its back facing Aldo, and the feet dangled loosely amidst the brown weeds.

Aldo recognized the blue cotton shirt and pants. It was the outfit most cane cutters wore in the fields. He thought about tugging the body to shore by pulling the loose ends of the shirt, but his anxiety had worn him out, and he needed to come up for air. As he pulled himself up to the surface, he saw Pablo swim quickly towards him. A look of excitement was on the other boy's face.

The two boys reached the surface. They both had been jolted by the encounter and now needed time to release their emotions. Aldo, even though he had not seen the dead man's face, knew immediately who he had found. Pablo had looked into Aldo's father's eyes and had been shocked. It was an experience neither would ever forget, one that would ironically help seal their friendship in years to come and serve as a basis for their long- lasting partnership.

Pablo yelled at the men at the other end that they had found the body. Aldo, always the more placid of the two, motioned his friend to submerge. They both swam to the bottom and looked around. They lost their bearings momentarily, but ahead of them was Aldo's father's head, its dilated pupils staring blankly at the bottom.

Aldo grabbed one end of the shirt. He began pulling steadily while swimming forward. Pablo got behind him and pushed. With much effort, the boys carried their load to the shore. Aldo saw the sunlight at the surface and heard the shouts of the men. He was on his last gasp of air and felt dizzy. He lifted his head out of the water and took deep breaths. Pablo was behind him, floating on the surface face up and catching his breath. Both boys were worn out. But more was needed. Aldo felt he must be first to bring his father up, and he hadn't let go. Ignoring his brother's wild screams, he shot out of the water in one last pull until he could stand on firm ground. He steadied himself and pulled on the shirt. He turned to see his father's face sag lifelessly out of the water.

Since that day Aldo could not recall a pleasant time between he and his brother, Emilio. Even then, as their father's corpse lay on the wet grass, his brother assumed an over zealous and tyrant role over him. He shoved Aldo to the side, ordering him to go home. Aldo refused. A struggle ensued. The brawny Emilio smacked Aldo across the face, sending him awkwardly to the ground. Emilio had inherited his father's stubbornness and anger, and he was releasing all his frustration over his father's death on Aldo. Perhaps it was the realization of his new fatherly role over his younger brother, or bitterness at having seen him rescue the body, which Emilio had been unable to do. Aldo never quite understood it then, but he had his father's tenacity and was determined to stay around at this critical moment. He quickly stood up and launched himself at his brother. His head smashed against Emilio's flat stomach, sending him staggering. But the yet-undeveloped Aldo was no match for Emilio who grabbed the boy in a nelson hold, and, with a blow to the ribs, laid him flat on the ground. At that point, the men wrestled with the grappling Emilio who kicked and punched at them like a wild animal. It took four men to appease him. It was a scene that was to repeat itself time and time again in years to come.

That night had been a terrible one for Aldo. The pain from the corporal punishment inflicted by Emilio was nothing compared to the agony he felt over the death of his father. He could not recall many tender moments with him. His father had been rude, unable to express his feelings and insensitive to Aldo's inquisitiveness. Aldo could not remember as much as a smooch from the bristly, tall islander, but he had loved him. In years to come he found himself reminiscing about those brief moments when his father had sat quietly with his family. He felt a deep sense of loss and insecurity, as if a layer of protection between him and the world had been surreptitiously removed.

That night his father lay motionless in a wooden coffin that had been hastily built by the neighbors that afternoon from rough-hewn planks nailed together at the edges. They had placed the coffin on a skeleton skid so it wouldn't touch the floor and had dragged it near the living room's window. Cecilia sat quietly near her husband's body, her hands clasped around a red handkerchief on her lap and her gaze fixed steadily on the floor. She was never the same after that.

* * *

Aldo found himself reminiscing about these memories as he entered Patricio's house tonight. This was the house where he had been born and where he had lived in as a boy. The house was crowded, with many neighbors seated solemnly around the room. Aldo now saw the bright moonlight through the open window and heard the visitors' small talk as the door opened. They were speaking in whispers. "There was a tragedy here many years ago," they were saying. They stopped speaking as they saw Aldo and his family enter the room.

Aldo looked at the sullen woman on the rocking chair with mussed hair and swollen eyes and again thought about his mother at his father's wake years ago. Now there was no coffin. The dead had already been buried. He extended his right hand to Julia, Patricio's wife, and gently tapped her wrist. She acknowledged the gesture with a slight movement of her head.

"I'll put these in the coop," Aldo said, raising the chickens he had brought her.

Amanda, who had remained standing near the door with the children, waited for Aldo to leave the room, then she waded through the group of women sitting and standing around Patricio's wife. She embraced Julia and quietly offered her condolences. Julia sobbed on Amanda's shoulder. Amanda felt the warmth of her face and kept her arms around her until Julia could slowly let go off her.

"If there's anything we can do for you, please don't hesitate to ask," Amanda said.

She wondered what would become of this woman and her two little girls. Who would provide for them now that their breadwinner was gone? Would the Arapientos allow her to stay in their home? It seemed inconceivable since the right to hold land was based primarily on the vassal's ability to either work the lord's property or pay rent. It was obvious that the widow could do neither. Most likely, she would have to abandon her house. Amanda thought that at least she'd be rid of the hideous prairie. She could migrate to the city, be human again. And Patricio had not been much of a husband anyway.

The thoughts passed through Amanda's mind like a bolt of lightning. She felt guilty. It was amazing how fast her of view could change, the result of her own unhappiness. "It is this wretched place," she thought. Her life, the political unrest around them, Patricio's death. And where was Aldo that he could not see this? Their kids should not have to grow up in this environment. Frank was fast approaching his teen years. If they didn't get him out of here, he too, would end up like these people. Something had to be done.

Amanda's thoughts came to an end when she heard her husband's soft voice outside talking to the men. They spoke in whispers, as if afraid any noise they made could disturb those grieving inside. It was odd, but it seemed to come to them naturally, as if they were somehow aware of the present state of affairs and did not wish to upset the prevailing peace surrounding them. The day was now coming to an end, and the flickering lights of the first stars shone on the distant blue-gray sky. A cool chill came into the room, and one of the women closed the window. Another lit an oil lamp.

Outside, Aldo let the chickens loose inside the coop, then came around the house to talk with the men that scattered by the front door, next to an oak tree. They were all locals who lived in the *sitiería* and worked the Aparientos's land.

"I remember when we brought him here from the cane fields," one of the men said.

"There is a spell on this house," another one added, "this has happened four times, and it will keep happening for as long as people live here."

They stopped as they saw Aldo approach them. One of the men was short with a face wrinkled by his years and a strange paleness. He had small black eyes and wore a hackneyed straw hat, brown flannel shirt, tawny slacks, and short leather shoes. He was known in the village as a *santero*, or voodoo man. Aldo stood next to him. He had known the old man since he was born and considered him an astute charlatan who managed to make a living from his wicked and strange arts.

"We are nothing, Aldo," the *santero* said, "only dust."

Aldo nodded. He felt the gaze of the other men upon him.

"It's a terrible thing when it happens this way," someone else said. "His family didn't get to bid him farewell."

"Under the circumstances," another man said, "it's better that they did not see him."

Aldo met the speaker's candid gaze. It was Oscar. He seemed more at ease now than this morning. He seemed resigned to the present estate of affairs, perhaps satisfied now that Aldo had shown up.

"When it's time to go," the *santero* said, "we go without saying goodbye."

"It didn't have to end like this," Oscar said.

"That's right," someone else said.

"But it did," the *santero* responded, "and that was his destiny."

"Well, now we must see about the living," Aldo said. "What's going to happen with his family now?"

The men all raised their eyes to him. That was after why Oscar wanted him here. And he had come.

"No one knows. It's in the hands of the Arapientos brothers," the old man said.

"Arapientos will not let her stay here unless she can give something in return."

"And what can we do to change that?" Oscar inquired.

"I think," Aldo responded, "that we can talk to the Arapientos."

"Do you really think we could persuade them to do that?" Oscar shot back.

"We may buy some time for Julia and the kids," Aldo said.

"I honestly don't think she will be able to stay, Aldo," the old man said, "that's reality, let's face it."

"It's like Aldo said," another man argued, "she doesn't have to be kicked out the next day. It's not fair."

"All right," the old man said. "Who's going to place the bell on the cat's collar? Who's going to talk to the Arapientos brothers?"

All eyes went to Aldo. They knew the young man's powers of persuasion. He had, after all, achieved the impossible with Arapientos when he had bought some of his land and became independent.

"I will," said Aldo, "but we all need to do something for Julia and the kids in the meantime. She has no money and no food."

"She will not lack anything," Oscar said, "not with all of us men here."

"Clearly," the old man added, "and with help from the saints, anything is possible. We all have to have faith."

The others looked at him approvingly. Despite his many lies, they respected him.

"Fine, then," Aldo agreed, "I will see the Arapientos tomorrow, and I'll get back to you afterwards, old man."

"That's good," he replied.

Here was a man of action, the old man thought. Someone who wanted to do something right this minute.

"Then we can all talk to Julia. Where will you be in the morning old man?"

"On a day like tomorrow, where else would I be but with my *viejita* and my saints?" the old man said, his yellowish teeth showing in his crooked smile.

"I'll be at the old man's house," Oscar said.

Aldo turned towards the house. The breeze had picked up as darkness closed in. It gushed through the dense foliage of the oak tree top tottering its branches and casting shadows on the men's faces.

Aldo tapped lightly on the door. The old plain heavy sheet of wood had been replaced by rustic planks skimpily joined with nailed studs. Aldo thought that there was no art in the structure. His old home had been simply neglected. Patricio had not had the time for anything but drinking and making a fool of himself to the neighbors. The bark on the walls had begun decaying, and the roof thatch looked flimsy and worn.

The door creaked as it opened. Aldo met Amanda's sullen stare. She moved aside, and he went in. Things weren't much better inside. The dirt floor appeared unkempt. The walls dividing the two bedrooms had started to cave in at the bottom, an ominous sign that the house was doomed. Aldo could not see the whole kitchen from where he stood but he could see the reddish mason wall behind the stove. He remembered when he lived here as a boy the many tender moments sitting in the kitchen with his mother, staring thoughtfully at the bricks while she moved busily around. She was the best memory he had of this house. Cecilia, his Cecilia. After his brother Emilio was killed, she was so shocked that she had to be institutionalized and was never the same. Now she was a quiet and lonesome lady with copious hair, living with her sister in town, who mumbled her words and wore black all the time.

Another family moved quickly in this house after Cecilia and Aldo left. But their stay was cut short. Like Aldo's family, their life was soon filled with trauma when their breadwinner was run over by a tractor in the Aparientos' farm. The widow and her children disappeared into the deep country. Then Patricio and his family moved in. Already, tragedy had struck again. No wonder the peasants thought this house was cursed.

One woman walked hastily in the room and handed Julia a cup of steaming linden tea. This was the natural tranquilizer for the peasants. It grew abundantly in every yard, along with many other medicinal herbs that normally served their purpose.

Another woman came from the kitchen with a tray of coffee cups and passed it around. She came by Aldo who declined politely, then she turned to Amanda.

"Could I have a cup of tea," Amanda asked softly.

"Ah, yes," said the woman while she waded past the others.

She was short, with a lean face and very black eyes. Her white hair was hidden under a gray handkerchief that looked much like a bandanna, and she wore a black cotton dress.

"We have to start heading back," Aldo whispered to Amanda. Everyone spoke very softly. Only Julia's periodic sobs could be heard over their voices. She held a white handkerchief to her cheek and she kept her arm folded over her stomach as if in pain. The other woman stood in front of her holding the cup of tea.

"You have to drink some, Julia," the woman said, "it will do you good."

Julia raised her tearful eyes then she began wailing loudly. Aldo turned and grabbed the twins who had been sitting with Frank and other children. He held them in his arms and motioned Frank and the other children to come outside. He closed the door behind them and walked towards the group of men. Someone asked if everything was all right inside.

"Yes, she'll be fine."

"The twins are looking more beautiful each day, Aldo," Oscar said.

"Thank you."

"Oscar," Aldo called, "I have a favor to ask of you."

"Sure, Aldo, anything." Oscar looked complacent. All the animosity and distrust seemed to have vanished from his face.

"I need someone to cover for me with the dairy cattle tomorrow night. I plan to go into town. Can you do it? I know it's asking a lot on a day like tomorrow."

"No, no. It's fine, Aldo. I'm not going anywhere."

"Alfredo will be there, but he'll need help maybe for two hours."

"That's fine," Oscar said. "At midnight then?"

"Yes, and I will pay you the next morning."

"No. I'll not accept it."

The front door opened and Amanda came out.

"Well," Aldo said, "I will see you and the old man tomorrow as agreed. Good night."

"Good night," the men said.

"Good night," Amanda replied.

The two of them and the children walked down the narrow path out of the hamlet. Patricio's house was behind the rear of the village. Behind it was the open prairie covered with high pasture and pervasive carob trees that looked like gigantic shadows in the night. Far into the horizon, the silhouettes of palm trees swayed against the night sky.

They moved down on the dirt path, first passing Patricio's house then going right, away from the highway. Amanda carried one of the girls and Frank followed behind. They walked in silence, seeing the dim beacons of light that escaped through the cracks in the windows of the houses along the way. They came to the dirt road and turned towards the highway. They were now passing the front end of the Rios. A few yards to their left was Patricio's grave, something that only two people in this world knew about. As they reached the highway and turned in the direction of their house, Amanda spoke.

"Aldo, have you heard where he buried him?"

"No."

"I can't believe his wife doesn't know. That would be the first thing I would ask."

"Do you know whether she did?"

"No one mentioned it. I just presumed she doesn't know."

"Maybe she does."

"Maybe," Amanda said, "but it sure is strange that no one mentioned it."

They arrived at the gate and opened it. Aldo waited for Amanda and Frank to pass and then pushed the leaf back again. As he engaged the bolt, he looked over at the other end of the highway opposite from the village. Something had caught his attention. In the distance, he saw headlights and he knew immediately that they weren't cars. Then he saw two more behind them, and then two more. He knew then they were trucks and did not need to speculate which kind. He turned calmly and began walking. Amanda and Frank had started towards the house and were a few feet ahead. Aldo could hear the rumbling of the engines.

"Amanda," he yelled, "walk away from the road, quickly!"

"Why?" she asked in surprise.

She turned and faced him as she stopped. Frank, who was ahead of her, was also facing Aldo. But neither of them could see his face in the darkness.

"Never mind," he said, "come, quick."

He rushed towards them and hastily grabbed Amanda's arm, leading her off the road and into the grass. He then motioned for Frank to follow.

"Come on, Frank, walk towards the fence, fast."

"What's happening, Aldo?" Amanda asked.

She could not understand what her husband was doing. He still had her by the arm, moving away from the dirt road in the direction of their neighbor's fence, opposite the Aparientos' land. Aldo had intuitively chosen this course.

"There are trucks coming this way, Amanda," he said. "I think they are military, so we better keep clear of them."

"Oh, God!"

"It may be nothing, but I don't want them to see us in the middle of road at this time of night. Come on, hurry."

They were now walking very rapidly, each pressing the sleeping body of a girl against their shoulder. Frank was running alongside of them. They could see the trucks on the highway to their left now, their beds rigged in a canvas and approaching at a moderated rate of speed. Aldo judged that despite the moonlight, the soldiers inside could not see them. He and his family were already too far away from the road. He kept his eyes on them, listening for any warning in the engines that would show they were coming inside his property. His thought was that it was ludicrous that they would send three trucks to get one man. Could they perhaps be going to Rios?

The trucks had passed them. Aldo slowed down, pulled on Amanda's arm and stopped walking. There was no sign that they were headed for his gate.

"Where are they going?" Amanda whispered.

"I don't know."

"Could they be going to Rios?"

"Wait and see. I sure hope not."

Throughout the whole ordeal, Aldo had kept his calm. He did not want to alarm his family. He knew Amanda would easily break down. Aldo marveled at how close a call it had been. A couple of minutes earlier, he and his family would have been out on the main highway when the trucks passed. And then what would have happened? The way things were, there was no telling.

"They are not going there," Aldo said.

"Where are they going?" Amanda asked.

"They are probably going to Vertientes."

The guerrilla situation must really be gearing up. He knew the region well enough to know that very few locals would participated in any type of insurrection. They were simply not interested in changes. But if the rebels were serious about overthrowing the government, they would have to have be an offensive, and this quiet land formed a bridge to Cuba's northern provinces where most of the important cities lay. The rebels would have to cross near here if they wanted to take their fighting there. Perhaps that time had come.

Aldo and his family turned back towards the dirt road. Aldo saw the red tail lights disappear in the distance. He made a decision. Amanda and the children were not safe here anymore.

"Do you think there's going to be fighting in Vertientes, Dad?" Frank asked.

"I don't think so, Frank," Aldo replied, "There are no rebels there."

"That we know of," Amanda said.

"Amanda, if there were, we'd be the first to know."

"I'm not so sure about anything any more, Aldo. I don't think anyone is."

Frank looked at his father as if expecting an answer that never came. This was the only sensible thing Amanda had said lately. Nothing was certain anymore.

As they slowly approached the dark outline of the house, they heard the dog bark but it quickly realized that the approaching figures were those of his masters. He raced towards them, threw himself at Frank who petted him lightly and then moved away from him. Aldo saw a figure behind the gate and realized it was Alfredo. He could see his face staring at them through the spaces between the boards.

Aldo unclasped his keys from his belt clip and unlocked the front door. He moved unsteadily in the darkness of the house towards the children's room and laid Clara on her bed.

"I am going to see Alfredo," he said to Amanda. "Please turn a light on for me."

Aldo met Alfredo in the ranch house and talked to him for a few minutes. The devoted hired hand had been alert and worried all evening. Not surprisingly, he had seen the Army trucks on the highway. Aldo patiently reassured him that things weren't as bad as they seemed and that he should get some sleep. He started to have second thoughts about leaving Alfredo alone in the house the next night. He considered him more than a trusted employee and was genuinely concerned for his well being. He knew Alfredo leaned on him during time of crises.

Aldo went back to the house. He felt sticky and yearned for a bath. He grabbed one of the milk buckets outside and pumped water in it until it was half-way full. He brought it into the kitchen where Amanda had left an oil lamp burning. He took out a few pieces of charcoal from under the stove, set them in a bundle on top of one of the grills, and lit the fire. He waited a few moments until the flames died down, then placed the bucket on top of the burner.

"I would have done that for you," Amanda said from the dining room.

She wore a light blue night gown and white slippers. She had unpinned her hair and wiped her lipstick off.

"I don't mind."

He came to the dining room and sat at the table. Amanda sat across from him.

"I wonder what kind of Christmas Eve it will be," she commented.

"An unpredictable one," he replied.

"Were you able to find someone for tomorrow?"

"Yes."

"Who?"

"Oscar."

"And do you think it's a good idea to leave the house alone?"

This was a concern he didn't think she would have. Amanda's deepest wish for the holidays was always to spend them with her father and sisters. The trouble was that she also wished the same the rest of the year. He knew she desperately wanted to leave the country. But had he underestimated her? When faced now with potential danger, was she prepared to sacrifice her utmost wishes in order to defend what was hers? Was this a facet of her character that he had never known?

"I don't think there's any reason for that," he replied. "The house will be fine. Alfredo will guard it with his life."

The hissing noise of boiling water summoned Amanda. She went to the kitchen and took a rag. She wrapped it around the handle and lifted the bucket, moving slowly through the dining room, working her way around the table, and entering the bathroom. The room was dark so she opened the door behind her to let some of the light from the kitchen. There was a large water basin leaning against the wall where she and the kids had washed earlier that afternoon. She turned the basin over and poured the water in. She went to the bedroom and slipped a sweater over her gown.

"I'm going to get some water from the well," she said.

"Leave it, Amanda," Aldo said, "I'm coming."

"Too late, I'm already going."

Aldo reclined in his chair, thinking about the last events. He had already decided that it was not safe for Amanda and the children to remain in the house. The situation seemed to be getting explosive.

He still did not think that the rebels would turn the area into a fighting post, but if the Army was meeting nearby, that meant that trouble. With the holidays coming, there was no harm in sending Amanda and the children to stay in town. She would welcome the idea of spending the season near her family.

Aldo heard Amanda enter the bathroom and pour water in the basin. He got up and went inside. She prepared his bath neatly and left the washtub near the wall so he could rest his back against it. She moved a chair in front of it and set a bath towel, wash towel, and bar of soap on it. She went to the bedroom and brought his inner garments. Aldo stripped his clothes off and got in the warm water. He leaned his head back against the wall.

"Poor Patricio," Amanda commented as she came into the room. "I don't know why they had to kill him. He could not hurt a fly." She was silent for a moment. "I am going to listen to the radio for a while before going to bed," she said.

"I'll be there in a few minutes."

He laid comfortably in the tub, still thinking about this evening. He worried about safety. What if Tomas had talked? Although he was tired, he knew he would sleep lightly tonight. He wished it was already morning.

Aldo washed and rinsed himself with handfuls of water and dried with the towel. He dressed and opened the bathroom door that led to the yard and emptied the washbasin on the ground. He fell on the bed. Through the light openings of the living room curtains, he heard the soft chatter of the radio. Later, he thought he heard Amanda whisper in his ear that the Army was moving in on the rebels, but he remained motionless.

There was a slight tapping on the window around midnight. It was Alfredo. He always awoke Aldo at this hour. Aldo rose instantly, got dressed and went to the cattle house to meet the men for the night's work. The milkman had been nervously waiting. He was bringing fresh news about the revolt. The rumors in town were escalating, announcing, for the first time, the threat of an ultimatum by the rebels. There was talk of a strike, and the populace seemed to anticipate a showdown. The government, meanwhile, was not giving in, but the rebels were taking positions around the outskirts in town. On his way out of town, the milkman's carriage had been searched by an Army patrol. The situation was truly explosive, the milkman said.

Aldo and Alfredo indulged him. Aldo gestured for him to speak softly. They looked at each other. The milkman apparently hadn't learned of the more immediate news and they were glad as he was likely to repeat what he had heard and where he had heard it. Aldo whisked the milkman inside the cattle house and told him to be more discreet. Voices carried far in the night, and there was no telling who could hear him. As usual, the milkman became petulant. Aldo didn't care. It made their task easier with fewer interruptions, and it incited Alfredo to sing his *décimas*.

In the morning, Aldo woke up feeling fresh and energetic. This was going to be a busy day but an enjoyable one, he hoped. It was Christmas Eve, one of the biggest holidays in the country. The first thing he planned to do was to visit the Aparientos and then go to Pablo's house to help him deliver some of the hogs. He had a light breakfast with Amanda and then left the farm on his mare. He passed Rios without seeing anyone. A few yards down the road, he came to a wide iron gate and pushed on one of the heavy leaves, following a gravel path to the family mansion. Aldo trotted the mare to the house. He arrived at a long portico passing a garden of pink roses and white lilies. A white picket fence surrounded the house.

"Keep the horse off the fence," a servant warned who came outside to greet him.

He was short, had very black skin, and wore a shiny straw hat, a light blue outfit and black suede shoes.

"Is Juan or Jose Arapientos in?" Aldo inquired. He dismounted and led the mare by the reins to the rear of the house.

"Yes, Jose is here."

"I would like to see him."

"Well," the servant said, "he might be asleep. It's very early."

"I still would like to see him."

The servant looked despairingly at Aldo. He had pretended not to know him and tried to summarily get rid of him but the big fellow had outsmarted him. He turned and disappeared into the house.

Aldo walked to the rear of the property. A jeep was parked by the fence gate. In the back was a large cattle house. Two small cattle trailers were parked nearby. Several men were inside tending to the cattle. Aldo stood near the back porch, holding the reins of his mare as he watched the cattlemen.

"Good morning, Aldo."

A short, plump middle-aged man stood by the gate. Aldo turned to face him. He had a chubby face with large black eyes and his manner was grim.

"Good morning, Jose," Aldo replied, "happy Christmas Eve."

"The same to you and your family," the man said. "What brings you here?" He ran his left hand through his bushy gray hair. He wore a black sweater over a gray high-collar shirt and his pot belly seemed to peak at the belt line, trapped under a black leather belt and a silver buckle.

"I guess you heard about Patricio."

"Most unfortunate," the man responded.

"I was at the wake last night," Aldo said, "and I was saddened by his family's plight. I wonder if you and your brother would allow them to stay in Rios for now."

"Well," Arapientos scoffed, "Aldo, why don't you take them in?"

He looked at Aldo, yet Aldo felt the man's gaze go right through him as if he was not really noticing him.

"I just might have to do that if you and your brother don't let them stay."

"I don't run a charity house here, Aldo. My father worked very hard for what we have. If they're going to stay, then they will have to pay. It's their choice."

"How much?"

"Well," Arapientos said, "same as they always. Why would it be any different now?"

"Jose," Aldo said, "I do not want to suggest that they shouldn't have to pay you. I understand that. But a widow with kids would be no replacement for Patricio. So I thought you might consider letting them stay for less money."

"Who's going to pay? You?" Jose asked.

"Aldo," Arapientos went on, "charity is not our family's business. If it was, we wouldn't be where we are today. We need hands that produce, not burdens."

"I suppose you also need cooks and maids. His wife is a good one."

Aldo decided that it was time to go. He had made his point. Jose Arapientos studied him for a second. If someone else had dared propose it, he would have had one of his peons chase the fool out. But coming from Aldo, the proposition seemed interesting. Somehow, it gained respect. His father had always said that Aldo was different. He had potential. Aldo had always seemed to have an edge on the old man until the day he died. He had talked old Arapientos into selling him a nice piece of land adjacent to his empire, something unattainable by anyone else.

"I've got my own," Arapientos muttered.

"This one's white," Aldo said as he mounted the mare.

He felt guilty about mentioning it, but he knew it was the only hope and he knew it would appeal to the Arapientos. Old Arapientos had an appetite for black and mulatto women, yet he had remained deeply prejudiced until his death. Aldo had heard that his sons had inherited the old man's habits. Julia would be a noted exception among the colored servants. He hoped the strategy would work.

"Happy Christmas Eve, Jose," Aldo said.

"You also have one, eh? Talk to me about business next time."

Aldo turned the mare around and lead her onto the gravel path. He didn't turn to look at Arapientos. Near the French doors on the side of the brick mansion, he caught a glimpse of the servant who had received him. Next to him was a short, black, heavyset woman. As they saw him pass, they both pulled back, two souls of the Arapientos' empire.

Aldo rode to Rios. It was still early, and no one was on the dirt trail, leading to the village except for a curious face here and there peeping through a window. Aldo turned onto a narrow path, squeezed his horse between two houses with long back yards, and reached the end. He stopped in front of a small hut with an open porch and a small garden filled with sunflowers, red and pink roses, and a few Christmas flowers. An old woman came out to greet him.

"Good morning," he called, "is the old man here, *viejita*?"

Since he was a child, Aldo had always addressed the voodoo man's wife as *viejita*, meaning little old woman.

"Aldo, God bless you, my boy. It is so good of you to come here."

She rushed to greet him. He leaned to receive her embrace.

"May Saint Lazarus always guard you, my boy. No one can ever harm my prince."

She held his head tightly in her arms and then she placed her cheek near his, as if he were a little boy. Her face was boney, the skin sagging around the cheekbones. Aldo made no effort to pull back until she loosened her hold. Then he sat erect on the saddle and smiled at her.

"Where is he?"

"Inside." Her pale blue eyes were teary.

"Will he come out?"

"You are not going to come in?"

"I must go quickly. I have much to do. Is Oscar here?"

"Ay, my boy," she lamented, "not even some milk and coffee, ah?"

"No," he said, "I will send you something."

He glanced at the porch and saw the *santero*.

"Good morning, Aldo."

The old man was leaning against the door frame, his yellow teeth showing through his ever- present smile.

"It will be all right, I'm sure," Aldo said. "Jose Arapientos will give Julia some work. She won't have to leave."

"My saints do not fail me ever, Aldo," the *santero* chirped confidently. "You see, ah?"

"Tell Oscar not to forget about tonight."

"You are a bit early, but he'll be here. Wait for him."

"No. I've got no time."

Aldo turned to the old lady: "I'll send you something with Oscar, *viejita*."

She smiled and opened her arms to him. He again crouched his torso and let her hug him.

"Goodbye, *viejita*."

"The saints are looking after you, my boy," she said. "Don't worry. They can't harm you. Not he, not anybody. You are an angel, my angel."

Then she let him go. "May the virgin guide your path, my boy," she said.

Aldo again went through the narrow opening between the two houses. Then he let the mare trot out of the village. Once on the road, he went straight to Pablo's house.

She already knows, Aldo thought. The old lady knew. All those years when she had seen him grow, she had learned to love him, and she had chosen him as her trophy. The *santero* resented it but admired him too much to say anything.

A small Ford pickup was parked behind the house. Pablo had borrowed it the night before from another cattleman. The road was too busy for a wagon.

Aldo unsaddled the mare, took the bridle off, and let her run free.

"Good morning, *hombre*," Pablo said, "some milk and coffee?"

"No," I had breakfast.

"We heard about Patricio."

"I figured you would by now."

"We also heard about another one."

"Who?"

"Someone near Palmas, five or six kilometers up the road."

"How?"

"Pretty much the same as Patricio, I think. I don't know all the details."

"That's not good news."

"What do you make of it?"

"I think the government is getting desperate. They're in trouble."

"They're taking it out on these poor folks. That's insane."

"They want to scare us. They don't want anybody getting any ideas."

Like Pablo, Aldo could not be thought of as a peasant, yet he always included himself in their lot out of respect for his roots. He would never betray this prairie. Not for Amanda, not for anybody. Aldo had everything needed to mingle with the upper levels of society, yet he would never deny his heritage and his upbringing.

"Good morning, Aldo," Olga said from the kitchen door.

Her hair was parted sideways and neatly combed. She wore a white cotton flowered blouse and black skirt. She was an early riser, unlike her husband.

"Good morning, Olga."

Aldo and Pablo got to work. They gathered their lassos and in a few minutes, they filled the truck bed with about fifteen pigs. Aldo locked the rear of the truck and hopped inside the cabin with his friend.

The drive to town was short. The narrow winding road went through the heart of the beautiful prairies, green even in December. The symmetrical rows of pinon trees along the highway seemed to lead the way. There were no other housing developments near the road. The land in these parts was owned by cattlemen. It was well kept and quite scenic. The cows roamed under the trees, giving the prairie a picturesque touch.

There were two or three houses to a farm. They were usually built of wood but closer to town, some brick houses could be seen. The piñon fences also began to be replaced by wooden fences. Then the pasture gradually eroded and the big trees faded. Power posts appeared along the road.

At the end of a curve, Aldo and Pablo passed a row of one-story houses. They were small wooden homes with little space between them and skimpy gardens. The two men were flagged down by two soldiers holding carbines, one standing at each side of the road. They were *casquitos*, dressed in khakis and drab commando helmets. The truck came to a halt.

"Out of the car," the one on Pablo's side said. He was slim and dark and spoke without emotion. Pablo and Aldo exited the truck.

"Where are you heading?" inquired the soldier near Aldo.

He was short and stocky. The helmet covered most of his forehead, and he had to tip his head back to look at Aldo.

"To the slaughter house."

"For what?"

"To take our hogs."

The soldier walked to the edge of the bed and surveyed it.

"Where are the papers?" inquired the soldier near Pablo.

Pablo pointed to the inside of the cabin. The soldier tapped the door open with the tip of his gun and gazed inside.

"All right. Move out."

Pablo got behind the wheel and shifted the engine into gear. They began moving again. Instinctively, he and Aldo turned to look at the military transport truck parked behind the skinny soldier. The rear was shrouded by a drab canvas.

"Looks like it's loaded," Pablo observed.

They moved slowly ahead. Both sides of the road were now populated by modest-looking houses, with narrow windows and doors. They were unpainted and all had some sort of a garden. It looked like a Caribbean ghetto. It was the beginning of the city.

They reached an intersection. The intersecting road was a single-lane asphalt highway, fairly wife, and known as the Central Highway. It connected both ends of the island. All local roads of any importance connected to it.

Pablo turned right. The traffic in the opposite direction seemed to be increasing. That was the way to Havana, the country's capital. Pablo sped up. A high cinder block wall to their left extended for almost a mile. Inside its confines, marble angels and crosses could be seen. Undoubtedly a cemetery. At the end of the wall, Pablo turned left and entered a dirt bumpy path bordered by one side of the cemetery wall. The road ended at a wide triangular dirt space surrounded by corrals. Four quays had been erected, high enough for the cattle trucks to reverse and unload their cargos. All four were occupied this morning, and two medium sized trucks were already waiting in line.

Pablo and Aldo got out. They went through a high stable gate at one corner and met a rosy- cheeked man, wearing a white baseball cap and wrinkled dark clothes. He leaned comfortably against one of the stakes. He seemed not to notice Pablo and Aldo.

"Good morning," Pablo said, his voice barely audible over the noise of the truck engines. "We have our first load of pigs."

"Good morning," the man replied.

He straightened up and stretched while he looked at Aldo.

"How goes it?" Aldo said.

"Ahhh." He rubbed his cheeks with the palms of his hands.

"How many?" he asked.

"Sixteen," Pablo answered.

"That's so? What's the matter, you sold them all this year?"

"No, in fact, we have another load coming," Pablo said.

"Oh, really? Well, let's see what you got. I don't want you sticking me with shit."

"How much are you paying per pound this year?" Aldo inquired.

"Twenty, if they're good."

All three walked to the truck. The man examined the restless animals inside.

"Not too bad. How's the next trip going to be, better or worse?"

"Same," Pablo said.

"Yeah, sure." He smiled at Aldo. "If they're any worse I'll have to throw them over that wall."

He pointed to the cinder block wall ahead of them.

"Give them to the dead to eat. That's probably all they're good for anyway."

"They're well bred," Aldo said. "Look at them, not too fat, not too slim. Just right for roasting."

"Wait for your turn, boys," the man said, ignoring Aldo's comments. "Then we'll weigh them."

He turned away and disappeared behind the gate. Aldo and Pablo sat inside their pickup, waiting. The drivers in the cattle trucks appeared impatient. Most of them worked by contract loads. They wanted to move out fast so they could go on their next trip. The Christmas season and the political unrest only added to their anxiety.

When their turn came, Pablo backed the truck into one of the quays. The floor of the truck bed came much lower than the platform. Aldo hopped in the rear and Pablo climbed to the edge of the quay. The man they had talked to appeared by their truck.

"Be careful that one of these wild animals doesn't get loose here, ah. You really should not be unloading them from a pickup. You don't have enough to hold them back."

"I'll make sure they go down the ramp," Pablo said.

Aldo began handing the squealing animals to Pablo, one at a time. Pablo grabbed each one and pushed it so that it would run down through the chute where they would go into the weighing room and later be butchered. After they were finished, both men went to look for the attendant.

"Let's see how much they weigh," he said.

They followed him through a chute into a platform. The hogs had all been shoved inside it.

"Six-hundred and seventy-two," the man said. "Pretty slim bastards."

"You don't want fat this time of year," Aldo corrected.

"Well," the man said, "it's nineteen per pound."

"Come on," Pablo said, "these animals are pure meat"

"Take it or leave it, things are bad." He looked at Pablo and smiled. "What are you going to do, load them again? In any event, I got no time for pigs. We have too much cattle coming in."

"Today is Christmas Eve. Pigs are a delicacy today. You wouldn't take them in if it weren't so. It's twenty a pound," Aldo replied, "that's the going market rate."

"That's in the market. This is the slaughter house. You can't sell them at the market this year, I bet you."

"Someone will always buy," Aldo said. "Twenty a pound."

The man stared at Aldo. He started to say something, then stopped.

"No," he repeated, "go to the market, Aldo."

"Leave it, Aldo," Pablo interceded. "Let's move on."

The man retreated to a space improvised as an office. He came out holding some bills and change and handed them over to Pablo.

"One hundred and thirty-seven pesos and seventy-five cents," he said.

Pablo and Aldo drove out of town. They were stopped again by the same soldiers
who, upon recognizing them, let them pass without a check.

"That son of a bitch got us," Pablo shouted, "he really got us."

"There will be a next time," Aldo replied.

"We ought to try the market, the hell with him."

"How many trips do you figure we got?" Aldo asked.

He knew the market would be slow, but later in the day he figured it had to pick up a bit.

"We could probably squeeze them all in two."

"Then let's try one more time at the slaughter house. Play it by ear. Then on the last one we can try the market."

"I see your point. I just don't like to be taken for a sucker, that's all."

"I know."

They loaded the truck again and immediately headed back to town. They were stopped again at the check point by different soldiers than before. They looked bored and inattentive. But there was no doubt that this was a major shake up. Something big was coming.

"How much per pound this time?" Pablo asked the attendant. He had asked Aldo to stay behind. The two men exchanged glances.

"What was it this morning?"

"Twenty."

"No, it wasn't," the man said.

"It was twenty cents a pound this morning, you bastard." Pablo shouted. His face was red with anger and his eyes gleamed in contrast to the carefree man who had walked out of his truck a minute ago.

"What did you say?"

The man started towards the pickup. Now he turned abruptly to look at Pablo."

"You heard me."

Pablo stared at him. "*Guajiro*, you are lucky it's Christmas Eve today."

The attendant stared at Pablo then turned toward the pickup.

"Eh," Pablo called behind him, "forget Christmas Eve. I don't like being lucky. So call it. Call the price." He paused. "The pound was twenty cents this morning, and it is still twenty."

The man ignored him. He kept on walking and then paced around the bed of the pickup. Aldo was leaning on the passenger door.

"They're not too bad," he murmured.

Then he glanced at Aldo to indicate he was speaking to him.

"What are you paying for them?" Aldo asked calmly.

"Unload them," the man commanded.

He began to walk back to the corrals and away from Pablo who had had followed him to the rear of the truck.

"Only twenty a pound," Pablo screamed, "not one cent less, or I get them out of here right now."

Pablo made a motion to go after the attendant but he did not respond his move. The attendant walked a few more steps then turned to Aldo. He was standing a good ten feet away from them, but Aldo could see the smirk on his face.

"Take your chance Aldo."

"I'm talking to you, you sucker," Pablo shouted.

The man disappeared behind the cattle truck.

"Let's get to work," Aldo said.

He opened the passenger door.

"No, Aldo," Pablo replied, "who the fuck does that son of a bitch think he is?"

"It's all right. Come on."

"I'm not taking anything less than twenty."

"I know," Aldo said.

The men unloaded the hogs, then had them weighed.

"Seven hundred and twelve pounds," called a peon, his gold front teeth shining.

The man reappeared holding a few green bills and three coins. He gave them to Aldo who was standing a few inches from Pablo without looking at either of them and said nothing. The peon gazed insolently at them, hands on hips.

Aldo flipped the sheaf of bills with his long fingers as if they were cards. Seven twenties, two pesos and forty centavos.

"How do you like that?" Pablo said. "He paid the twenty cents per head."

"We'll be back one more time," Aldo said.

The attendant went back to his makeshift office shaking his head.

CHAPTER FIVE

THE NIGHT HAD STARTED OUT mild then became windy and chilly. But it fit right in with the season. This was a memorable time for all. Families would gather and dine together tonight, each house sparkling with festivity and the pleasure of this yearly reunion. The city would be flowing with the noise of cars, moving rapidly through the narrow streets. Each block would vibrate with music and the yells of happy dancers.

In the countryside, it was also a time of jubilation. The peasants' misery seemed to dissipate on this special night. Reality would no doubt return tomorrow, but tonight the peasants would play their guitars and sing their *décimas* while mingling with their neighbors. And their nostalgic songs would reflect upon the sanctity of the season, as if to remind themselves why they were here.

Aldo returned home late in the afternoon. He and Pablo had stopped in town at a local cattleman's club where Aldo had agreed to meet a mutual acquaintance. They returned the borrowed pickup and took their jeep, the vehicle the two of them shared. After dropping Pablo off, Aldo drove home alone. The children and Amanda were almost ready when he arrived. While Aldo bathed, they finished dressing. Aldo went outside to talk to Alfredo who was leaning on the fence by the open cabin, waiting.

"You will be back before twelve, won't you?" Aldo asked.

"I will be back by eleven," Alfredo answered, "and I will bring Oscar with me."

"Go back after you finish with the milking if you want."

"No," he said quickly, "not on a night like tonight."

"You should have some fun at the party," Aldo insisted, "have a drink."

"Not tonight Aldo, maybe next year."

Aldo turned, as if to leave him, then turned to him again.

"I will sleep well tonight knowing you are in charge."

"Just be very careful in town, Aldo," Alfredo said.

Driving the same route he and Pablo had used this morning, Aldo and Amanda headed for town. They went through the checkpoint, with soldiers peering cautiously at them. Then they were waived through and Aldo drove on, going south on the Central Highway. After about two miles, they were entered a busy section of town. The road became a circle that enclosed a small park with a statue in the middle. Aldo drove half-way around it and turned right. The houses dwindled gradually as they entered the suburbs, filled with beautiful block houses. They stopped in front of a large Spanish style mansion surrounded by an iron fence with round columns and a white portico. The gate was open, and Aldo and his family walked in. Aldo knocked on the elaborately carved door.

A short black woman, wearing a pin-striped blue dress and white embroidered apron, opened. Her hair had been carefully fashioned into two braids. She had a sunny smile and a pleasant look about her.

"God bless you, my child," she said to Amanda.

She kissed her on the cheek while holding her hands. Then she bent down to kiss the children, whispering softly to each of them. They all went through a large living room, Amanda first, then the twins, Frank and Aldo. They entered a recreation room, before the courtyard where everyone was sitting on comfortable white wicker chairs. A man with bushy gray hair stood up as they entered.

"Aldo," he said as if surprised to see him, "Happy Christmas Eve."

"To you also, Blanco."

Aldo thought he would have been happy just to go to Rios tonight. Something was different this year. But this could not be seriously considered. There was Amanda and the children. They had made it a ritual to visit Amanda's father on Christmas Eve and dine with her sisters and their families. It would be unforgivable not to attend. This was Amanda's night.

"Happy Christmas Eve," Ana said.

She leaned forward to kiss Aldo's cheek. She was no longer the pretty school girl that he had once known, tantalizing the imagination with her raw, developing beauty. She was now a strikingly beautiful woman. Her long silky black hair touched Aldo's shoulders.

"The same to you."

She stood briefly before him, her olive eyes searching his face. Then Aleida came to hug him. She held hands with a dark-haired man of medium height dressed in a full khaki uniform. Aldo shook hands with him. Last, came Guillermo. He wore square glasses with tinted lenses and a starched white *guayabera* over brown slacks. He silently shook Aldo's hand.

"Let me get you a drink," he said.

He motioned to the tuxedoed butler standing in a corner with a silver tray and white cloth napkin. The man handed Aldo a shot glass of Phillip II brandy.

Everyone sat down again, Aldo at the end and Amanda next to him. The twins stood next to Aldo for a few moments, then followed Frank inside where the maid had turned the television on for them.

Aldo and Amanda's arrival had temporarily interrupted the others' discussion, but as soon as they sat down Guillermo spoke and addressed Aleida's companion who sat directly across him. He still hissed somewhat when pronouncing the s's and z's.

"By the way," he said solemnly, "may I present to you my daughter's husband Aldo."

He pointed in Aldo's direction.

"This is Roberto," he said to Aldo.

Both men stood up and shook hands again.

"Roberto is a sergeant in the Army. He will be leaving us early because of his duties."

"Not a good night to be a soldier," Blanco joked.

"It is men like Roberto who make Batista strong," Guillermo said with pride.

"Unfortunately, I think we will need many more Robertos for this government to remain strong," Amanda said. "Batista's walls seem to be crumbling."

"Daughter, what in the world gives you that idea?"

"There are soldiers everywhere. The guerrillas are spreading even to Rios."

"Ah," Guillermo mumbled in disgust, "Rios." He looked sheepishly at Aldo.

"We heard shots yesterday morning and saw Army trucks on the highway last night. And on our way here, there were soldiers stopping and searching cars by *Nadales.*"

"It is a different holiday season this year," Blanco said.

"No one can overthrow Batista." Guillermo said dismissively.

"Well," Blanco said, "the situation is serious and at this point, anything can happen. Nothing is moving. Business is stagnant, and everyone is waiting."

It was obvious that Blanco was an objective man. Everyone in the room was struck by his realism, even Roberto, who was, by all measures, the one person in the group who stood to lose the most. A defeat of the status quo could mean at the very least his job, at most his life. Blanco had been prudently discreet about his prognosis of the future but at some point he felt he had to tell the truth. Aldo agreed silently and felt sympathy for Roberto.

"So what do you think? Is it war?" Amanda strained forward to get a better look of Blanco.

"You are seeing nothing more than Batista's stronghold of forces moving in to quash a bunch of ragged ruffians, something that he should have done a long time ago." Guillermo said. "Roberto can tell you," he added.

Amanda switched her gaze to him, still looking for an answer.

"Much of it is confidential at this point," Roberto explained with authority, "but I can tell you that the insurrectionists have their hands full."

He was in his mid-twenties, certainly much too young to be a sergeant. He had baby- soft skin, flat cheekbones, and very black eyes. His most striking feature was his thick, jet-black hair. He looked of Spaniard descent.

"I will drink to that," Guillermo exclaimed, raising his shot glass. He drained it in one gulp.

"I think the movement has gained much momentum at this point. It is very dangerous, and one has to prepare for what may be coming."

Blanco was again rationalizing. He kept looking at Aldo as he spoke, as if looking for support.

"From what I hear," Aldo said, looking at Roberto, "I think your peers also have their hands full, sergeant. It's like Blanco says, we are almost at a standstill at this point."

"We have to fight fire with fire."

"But is it too late?"

"No, I do not think so. I cannot comment except to say that the mobilization is justified and that it will overwhelm any resistance."

"I do not think that you are going to meet any overt resistance," Blanco interrupted. "The Army is probably going to override small rebel pockets. But the real problem now is that the movement has gained popularity, and once a flame is lit, it may not die."

"True," Aldo agreed.

"I have to say that once our forces move in, they will crush whatever popularity there is for the rebels."

Roberto knew that he had failed miserably to address his friends' worst fears.

"Of course," Guillermo said. The deep lines in his forehead seemed to almost come together as he frowned.

"What an idea," he continued, "the rebels have not yet realized the might of Batista's Army. It is easy to talk when no one is whipping you but it's a different story when your ass is on fire. They will see now."

"Yes, Ramona?" Aleida had stood up to address the maid who had appeared at the door and patiently waited for an opportunity to speak.

"Ms. Diaz," Ramona said, "the roasted pork has arrived."

"Oh, great, we should all go to the dining room, no?"

"Yes, my child. The salad is already on the table. Your butler is cutting the meat. Please come."

She went through the hallway into a dining room. It was an elegant room with a high ceiling and flowered arches. The walls were paneled with beautifully hand-crafted mahogany. There was a long rectangular table in the middle exquisitely set with a white tablecloth and red candles set in gold candelabras in the middle. There were two pitchers filled with beer. China and green cloth napkins folded like fans and held together with silver napkin holders had been placed before each chair. The silverware shone, with fork, knife and spoon lined up at the side of each.

The maid began serving them iced shrimp on salad plates. Then she transferred more salad from two silver trays on a serving cart into a large plate on the table. It was a mixture of Chinese lettuce with radish, with a vinegar-and-oil dressing sprayed slightly with sugar.

They all took their seats, Guillermo at one end of the table and the others on each side. The other end of the table remained vacant as a sign of respect for Francisca. The smell of roasted pork filled the room as the butler walked in, carrying a round silver pan filled with brown meat.

"May this Christmas Eve be filled with happiness and prosperity," Guillermo announced.

He solemnly raised his glass then drained it. Gradually, the others followed suit. They exchanged toasts by raising their glasses and tapping them.

"Where are the children?" Amanda asked.

"I have served them, child," the maid said. "I brought them into the breakfast room, and they're eating."

"I will go check on them," Aldo said.

He got up and went to the next room. It was a smaller room with a countertop connecting it to the kitchen and an open archway on the side. The children were seated at a large oak table, holding red candles and Christmas plates.

"We are eating pork, Daddy," one of the twins said.

"Eat everything. Ramona will be mad if you don't clean your plates."

"Dad," Frank said, "how is Mama doing tonight?"

"She is better, Frank."

"I don't think so, Dad. She is worried. She told us."

"I guess everybody is, Frank. People worry about changes. But it's Christmas Eve, soon it will be Kings' Day. There's no reason to worry."

The butler came into the room, followed by Ramona.

"Go with the others," Ramona said to Aldo. "You should spend time with your wife tonight. I'll take care of the children." Her tone was almost reproachful. Aldo went back to the dining room and sat down.

The maid and the butler came back to the dining room. Ramona filled a large bowl with brown roasted pork meat. The butler stood by her, patiently holding the silver pan on the flat of his palm while she picked from it with a serving fork. She filled the bowl then motioned for him to place the pan on the cart and bring the next course, a casserole filled with purple rice and beans, a typical rice course called *congrís*. The butler placed it before her. Using a ladle, she quickly filled an oval-shaped plate on the table. Then the butler handed her a tray of smoking *cassava*, made with starchy bread and warm water and resembling hard tortillas, a pre-Columbian food of the Indians of this region that had survived through the centuries of Spanish occupation.

She added a plate of fried sweet potatoes, cut into long thin slices and salted. She also served them *yuca*, a tropical vegetable cooked in water and soaked in *adobo*, a tasty sauce of garlic, larded meat, and fried green and ripe bananas in syrup.

"There is white rice and stuffed potatoes for anyone that wants them," Ramona announced. "If the gentlemen would prefer any special part of the pork, let me know, and I will cut it for you." She turned to Amanda. "I know what part you like, my child."

"Can I have some?"

Ramona turned to the cart and grabbed a knife. She speared the meat with a fork and cut the skin until a large portion of the section was exposed. The tan-colored meat seemed tender and juicy as she sliced through it, separating the lard, and the meat steamed up as she skillfully pulled the pieces away. She placed several on a plate, salted them, and brought them over to Amanda.

"Like in the old days, my child."

"Ah, it's great Ramona."

"Eat, and tell me if you want more."

Ramona went over to Guillermo, took his plate, and filled it quickly from the trays in the center of the table. No words were exchanged. She seemed to know exactly what he craved. He leaned back, making colorful remarks about the strength of the government troops as if to reassure everyone, including himself, that its massive power could not be overcome.

Ramona went to Roberto and served him and Aleida. Then she surveyed the others' plates, making sure that Blanco and Aldo had been served. She pointed to the center of the table and the cart several times, reminding them what they had missed. As the large plates became empty, she would summon the butler who would quickly move near her to fill them.

"Let's have more beer," Guillermo said.

The butler approached with a full pitcher, removing the empty one. He placed it on the table, and Ramona filled Guillermo's glass.

Then they heard the sound of firecrackers in the distance, and they remained silent for a moment.

"It's a holy Christmas Eve," Guillermo said.

"That's gunfire," Amanda said.

She looked helplessly at Aldo. They all fell silent for a moment. The distant waves of music from homes nearby reached the room. No doubt the dancing had begun. Amanda concentrated on the sound outside but could not hear anything else. Then Roberto spoke.

"Any plans for tomorrow, Don Guillermo."

"Definitely not any work plans!" Guillermo exclaimed.

His accounting practice had grown since Francisca's death, and his office remained open during holidays, as was his custom. He himself, however, never worked during one and he now let employees run it in his absence, still demanding that they work through the holiday season.

"I have Amanda and the kids all day tomorrow and many visitors, like in every year," he added. "You are welcome to come, if you are not on duty."

"I start at 4:00 A.M. tomorrow. I am on guard duty at the airport. From there, I do not know where I will go."

"I hope you can be with your family at least tomorrow night," Blanco said.

"When I leave here, I will spend some time with my parents and tomorrow night also. That is a relief."

"Well," Blanco commented, "I just hope the roads are cleared of the restrictions so that cattle can move again. Right now I am unable to bring any trucks in. Are you moving anything, Aldo?"

"Barely," Aldo answered. "Mostly hogs, right now, like most Christmas Eves."

Ana had been quietly dipping into her plate. She raised her eyes and smiled at Aldo. No one else at that table, she thought, appreciated the humility of his statement. Despite his success as a cattle trader, Aldo was still not afraid to admit that he sold hogs, like a peasant which he was at heart.

Ramona reappeared. She began collecting the plates of those who had finished. To each she would ask to make a selection from a choice of three dessert. She had rice pudding, baked custard and cream of milk. She began serving them in small plates and passing them around to each. She gave each a small silver spoon, then she asked who wanted coffee.

The old man had started telling stories when Ramona served him his espresso in a small china cup. He took a spoon and poured sugar, stirred it and drank it all at once.

"Delicious," Aleida said after she tasted it. "Do you drink much coffee?" she asked Roberto.

He whispered something in her ear.

The couple got up from the table and asked Ramona to get the living room ready. They were planning to marry and wanted some privacy during the few moments they had left together before Roberto went away.

Ramona moved quickly about, her embroidered white apron sometimes flapping as she turned. She turned on the lights in the living room. A silver chandelier came alive with the bright yellow glare of several bulbs. Then she turned on the television set and moved several pillows to a corner of the sofa. She disappeared into the kitchen for a few moments then came back with Frank and the girls. The children were still eating and Ramona asked the butler to bring portable tables for them into the living room. She placed them in two armchairs in front of the television set.

"The room is ready," she said to Aleida.

Aleida and Roberto sat down on the sofa holding hands. The children watched television and giggled while they ate. Ramona took turns attending to those in the living room and the others in the back.

"Would you like a drink," she asked Roberto.

"No, thanks, I am done for the night."

The couple went on talking, Roberto speaking to Aleida in whispers as she whispered back to him.

In the dining room the conversation turned more mundane as Blanco talked business with Aldo. Guillermo fell suddenly silent. He had had much to drink, and his breath reeked of cognac. Amanda sat next to her father, talking to him intimately.

"It's a little unnerving," Blanco said cautiously. "The trailers are not bringing any cattle for fear of roadblocks. There's talk that something imminent is about to happen."

"We listened to *Radio Rebelde* today before coming here," Ana said.

She spoke in a low tone of voice as if no one else in the room was supposed to hear. The three of them were sitting at the end of the table, Ana and Blanco next to each other, and Aldo on the other side.

"I see soldiers everywhere. There is no road that you can take right now where you will not meet some."

"So what did you hear from the station?" Aldo asked.

"They promise that the end is near," Ana said. "They say Batista will be down before the end of the year."

"They're obviously trying to build up momentum with the people," Blanco commented. "But I think that there's much more anticipation this year than last. You can see it."

"If a change comes," Ana said with concern, "how do you see it, Aldo? Do you think it will be a good thing for us?"

Blanco looked at Aldo. His wife was gullible for a woman of her education, but he could not blame her. Times were hard, and one needed all the security one could get. Aldo, too, wondered why she looked up to him for an opinion when her husband was constantly on the road and saw more of the world than any one in this room. But he said nothing about it.

"It's difficult to say right now," he said carefully. "The moment you start giving an opinion you get mixed up with your own personal desires. What you want may not be what everyone else wants. I would like to see some changes. I think we probably all do. But from the little I have seen, I am not sure yet whether the rebels can really deliver. We just don't know."

"The rebels represent the masses, the humble people," Blanco said. "But the rich also want a change. The political situation is not desirable, even for them. I think that class, too, is represented by the Rebels."

"I haven't seen enough of them to know," Aldo said.

"You will in the days come. I know."

"Shhhh." Ana hissed to her husband.

She did not want Guillermo to hear. Maybe not even Amanda, who still sat by her father, carrying conversation that seemed very personal.

"Yes. Next thing you know, Roberto will be taking me out in handcuffs for interrogation. We don't want that for Christmas."

"Shut up," she said. "It's not funny."

Blanco smiled mischievously at Aldo. His taunting of Ana could have been either jest or drama. Members of the same family sat at opposite ends of the table, sufficiently concerned about each other's political views to avoid discussing them openly among themselves.

"Tell me about the rebels," Aldo said softly.

"They are, for the most part, inexperienced young men, some with good ideas but most, very cynical of authority."

"What do they want?"

"There is no doubt that at this point their leader is Fidel Castro. He's very nationalistic. The students are still behind him, even after their movement was practically crushed last year."

"Yes. I remember."

Aldo was about to ask the obvious question of how Blanco knew so much about the rebel movement but thought better of it. Could he be one of them? It would be ironic that a member of one of the most powerful and rich families of the region could join a movement that was, for the most part, the champion of labor and the poor. Blanco could have passed for an intellectual, and this side of him on a path that could prove catastrophic. For Aldo, there was a principle but the principle had to remain clear. He was a man of action, and he considered the philosophical couching of ideas useless.

"Do you think this movement is about one man, then?" Aldo said.

"No," Blanco replied, "I think there's unity. But like in every movement and in every idea, there has to be a leader. He is that."

"So he represents the movement?"

"Yes," Blanco replied hesitantly.

"What little I know of him is that he comes from a rich family. He is a lawyer and although probably quite intelligent, he appears to be a bohemian radical, someone who probably had pampering parents and never quite grew up. Is that who this movement has picked to lead them? If so, that doesn't say much for the movement, no?"

"It's not that simple, Aldo," Blanco said defensively.

Some of the traits that Aldo had described could also apply to Blanco, and although he did not show it, this made Blanco uncomfortable. For a moment, he thought Aldo knew it, and he felt some anger but rationalized that maybe Aldo was feeling him out. Aldo, whom old man Guillermo had once rejected as the son of ignorant *guajiros*, was no fool.

"There are all sorts of reasons why a leader is chosen," Blanco went on. "To start with, you have to recognize that Fidel Castro is no coward. After he masterminded the attack on *Moncada*, Batista put him in jail for a few years. Then he was released. If that had happened to me or you, what would we do? We'd go home and call it a day. But what did Fidel do? Next thing you know, he's outside planning the revolution again, and he comes back with an invasion and wages war from the mountains. No matter how you slice it Aldo, that's guts."

Blanco knew this would play favorably on Aldo who was a man who backed his words with actions.

"Second," Blanco continued, "movements need intellectuals. They don't move just with actions. There has to be a background to the movement, a central idea to the cause. That's where the leader comes in. You can have a leader who will fight the battles, but when the smoke clears you need someone to remind you what you are fighting about."

He could see Aldo listening attentively, eyes fixed on him. He didn't know why he kept talking, but he now found it a challenge to make the point clear to his friend.

"And that's what Fidel is, right?" Aldo said. "He's the man with the torch, setting the sugar cane fields on fire then explaining to the common folk why the fields had to be burned."

"But what bothers you about it? What do you find corrupt in it?" Blanco said, sensing Aldo's displeasure.

"I have difficulty accepting a philosopher or theorist who is untested in the rigors of everyday life as a leader. I am suspicious of his motives."

"But his motives have been proven. He does not need to be a revolutionary. As you yourself have said, he comes from a rich family. Why would he need to go to the mountains to fight when his future is secure? As for his lack of experience or whatever you want to call it, show me one single president that this country has had who was first a common man. You'll find a needle in a haystack faster."

"Blanco," Ana whispered, "please be careful what you say. My father is hearing this. Let's talk about something else."

"That's probably the reason why we have had such bad governments, Blanco. We need someone who can really relate to the people. This country has never had that."

"I don't think that will do any good, Aldo. If anything, you get a poor soul in Havana, and he will steal the country blind as Batista has done so he can then retire in glory. The difference with this movement is that the population is involved. That is the difference I see."

"Then either the movement is out of touch with their leader or the leader, is out of touch with the movement, for the two don't match."

"Boy," Blanco said in frustration, "you are really cynical about this, ah?"

"Not really, Blanco," Aldo said, "you know I'm not political. I just follow my own instincts, what I see. If I'm wrong, I'm wrong."

"Well," Blanco sighed, "at least give the man a chance."

"See, the problem is that for a start, you are focusing too much on one man. I think that is dangerous. If the movement is about the people, why do we need to talk about the qualities of one man?"

"But he's the leader."

"You said he represents the movement. That's more than just being their leader."

"Enough!" Ana said, turning to Aldo. "We are spending New Years at the *Casino*, Aldo. We want you and Amanda to come."

"I would be glad to go except, that I must find someone to do my milking for the night."

"You may not have to this year," Blanco commented slyly. "Batista may have fallen and we will be in total chaos."

"Stop, Blanco," Ana said, "I've had enough."

"Does any one want more coffee?" Ramona inquired from the door. Hearing no one answer, she approached Guillermo and asked him if she could release the butler for the night. Guillermo frowned and was about to speak when Amanda interrupted him.

"Please, Papa, let him go, he's got a family too."

"Bah," he said glibly, "the night is still young. We need service, and he's being paid."

"Let him go," Amanda ordered Ramona.

Guillermo did not contradict her. He merely looked at the group at the end of the table as if seeking their company. Ramona turned away quietly. No one had mentioned her name. Unlike the butler she had no place to go.

Ana stood from the table first. Then Blanco and Aldo followed.

"Let's go to the living room," Amanda said.

They all left the dining room and passed the open arched door into the hallway of the loggia. The loggia was classic Spanish architecture. A long passageway with eight doors displayed ornamental wall light fixtures and potted ferns at the entrance of each room, giving one the impression of entering a dark, misty arena. It had been built by a Spanish army officer during the past century when Spain had control of the island. Guillermo, a Spaniard, had been careful to preserve the original Mediterranean quality. The floor was made of hunter green ceramic tiles with splashes of pink and matching flowered moldings. The walls were white.

They entered the living room and everyone sat in front of the television set around the children. Aleida and Roberto, who were sitting on the sofa, seemed oblivious to their presence and continued their lovers' chat. Then Amanda switched the channel to a local station. Everyone was interested in the news, and not even the children protested when she switched the channels. They had begun to understand that their elders were up to something big.

"I don't like him," Amanda said about the commentator on the screen.

Mr. Conti-Aguero was an older statesman who expounded on topics with criticisms that sounded like advice to a child.

"He says nothing new," Guillermo said.

"He says what he wants though," Blanco added, "nobody stops him."

Ana looked at him with imploring eyes.

"I think he favors them," Amanda said.

"Of course he does," Guillermo added, "he's scum like them. He has no class."

The liquor had now begun to affect him, and his accent was getting even more pronounced.

"Papa," Ana said, "no more drinks tonight."

"It's Chrismas, daughter."

"Leave him alone," Amanda said. "He works too hard."

"The man doesn't really take a position," Blanco said defensively. "He just comments on issues."

"Hear him now."

Amanda turned to Blanco while the commentator went on camouflaging the present calm in the country as a symptom of passive restraint due to frustration during the holiday season. "And after the calm comes the storm," the speaker warned.

"Yes," Guillermo said, "Batista's storm is going to put scum like you out of business."

Blanco stared and Aldo and shook his head. There was no point in talking to the old man. His stance was that of a defeated general who refuses to accept the truth. He bordered on ignorance, and to engage him would be foolish. One could not reason with him.

Roberto and Aleida stood up. Roberto shook hands with each of them. He would see them at New Year's, he said. Then the couple went outside by alone. They stood together at the gate for a few seconds, Aleida's back turned toward the house until Roberto drove off in his car, a 1956 Buick he had borrowed from his father.

"I feel so bad for him," Amanda said. "He doesn't get to enjoy the holidays. He's going to his parents now, I hope."

"He will see them for a while, then he's going on duty," Aleida replied.

Her eyes filled with tears. The farewell was always a sentimental act but under the present circumstances, it was especially hard. Her fiancé was not just saying goodbye for the night. He was going on military duty during a very unpredictable time when, for all purposes, the country was thought to be at war.

"And where will that be?" Amanda asked.

Her curiosity and desire to pry into anything that might inform her about the political situation knew no limits.

"Nobody knows. He doesn't know himself. He can't even say where he's going tonight."

On television Mr. Aguero spoke of the difficulty in traveling into some areas of the province due to a massive military build up. Many roads were blocked, and fighting was reported in the *Cubita* mountains the only mountainous region in this very flat province. The city of *Camaguey* was at peace tonight, celebrating the holiest of all Cuban holidays, Christmas Eve. In churches, mass had been said early and families had gone home for dinner. Many military men had come home to see their mothers, and he wished their families a peaceful supper together, as he emphasized. "And may we all stay together in the future", he added.

"Shut-up, you old fart," Guillermo said.

"Papa!" Ana reproached, "you had enough. Stop."

"Oh," Amanda said, "leave him alone. Let's put on some music and dance."

She stood up and went to the record player, a richly polished piece of furniture that had been pushed against the wall. It was the latest General Electric model. Above it, on the wall, a large section had been carved with shelves of dark brown mahogany that held a wide selection of records. Amanda searched through one of the stacks and pulled a few records. She stacked them on top of the record player and placed one record inside. She fiddled briefly with the button and arm until the music started playing, then asked Frank to turn the television set off.

The music was a classic *cha cha cha*, played and sung by the Aragon Orchestra, a famous band that had created a flow of hits with their unique erotic dance style. Their sound was a combination of violins, piano, and bass against the insistent beat of *timbales*. The lead instrument was a flute that gave the music a Latin flavor and was its most distinguishable feature. The tempo was moderately fast with occasional bursts of percussion.

Amanda took her father by the hand. They had last danced together on the previous Christmas Eve. They did not spend much time with each other through the year. During Amanda's marriage to Aldo, Guillermo had visited their house only once when the twins were born, always mindful of the misery of country life and resentful of its inhabitants. But their relationship had grown. They had much in common, and tonight she sought to make him happy.

Amanda was a fine dancer. She could carry the rhythm in perfect harmony with the beat. She had participated in many dance competitions with Aldo before they were married. Aldo had been her partner in the flesh, but incompatible in the soul. Like her, he had been an able dancer, handsome and strong willed something she had always sought in a man. But there was something deep inside her that she shared only with her father.

The old man was slow and clumsy. He danced to his own swings, unaffected by the beat. He moved in a style of *danzón*, an old form of dance that had evolved from the *danza*, a slower, waltz-like type of dance of the nineteenth century. The *danzón* had had its heyday during the first three decades of the century but had been overtaken by the rumba and the latest creation of the populace, the *cha cha cha*. Guillermo would lay his left foot flat while pulling his left hand down alongside his thigh, then moving his shoulders back and fourth, bringing his right hip and foot forward, then slowly back. Amanda followed his moves and laughed happily.

"Can Aldo and I dance?" Ana asked.

"Of course, you can," Blanco said.

Ana grabbed Aldo's arm. He got up and followed her. They stood next to Amanda and Guillermo and began a colorful interpretation of the *cha cha cha*, tapping twice with one foot forward, up two steps, skipping on the sides, then back. They took turns with Blanco and Aleida and when Guillermo sat down, Amanda joined them, dancing by herself. Eventually, Frank and the twins joined in.

At the end of a record Ramona, appeared with a tray. She offered everyone nougat made with almond and nuts, a Spanish delicacy popular during the holidays. Then she asked each what they wanted to drink. She came back shortly with several mixed drinks and some shot glasses. Aldo and Amanda finally danced together, Aldo leading, and Amanda following his steps. They looked beautiful together.

As the night wore on, the twins fell asleep on the sofa and Aldo reached to pick them up, but before he could, Ramona appeared.

"I'll put the children to bed," she said dryly. "No need."

Then she turned to Frank and asked him to come along. Blanco stood and drained his drink, motioning to Ana that it was time to go.

"I will be back tomorrow," she said to Aleida, "when Blanco comes into town."

"We have a surprise for you," Aleida said.

"So do I. Your present is under my tree."

"I want it under mine."

The two sisters hugged and kissed. Aldo and Blanco shook hands, saying they would see each other in town. Amanda spoke to Ana softly and embraced her. Guillermo shook Blanco's hand and kissed his daughter. Afterwards, Guillermo said, "Aldo, make yourself at home. I am going to bed but you and Amanda can sleep in her old room."

He turned to Amanda to kiss her but she put her hand around his waist instead and led him down the hallway. The two disappeared in the darkness. Aldo sat near the television set opposite Aleida who was still drinking from her glass.

"You're such a good dancer, Aldo," she said, "I wish you could live closer to us."

"It's difficult with the farm."

"Does Amanda like it any better?"

"Not really."

"Would you consider selling?"

"With the kids, I'm afraid we'll probably have to make some arrangements. The only school in the area goes to the sixth grade."

"That's good. Then we'll get to have you closer."

She smiled at him. Aldo thought she had turned into quite an attractive young girl. She looked a lot like Amanda, short and with very black, long hair. She had a small nose and bright black eyes.

Ramona returned. "Do you want me to make your room, Don Aldo?"

"That would be fine."

"It will be ready in five minutes."

Aldo heard her enter one of the bedrooms then came back shortly thereafter.

"Your room is ready, Don Aldo," she announced. "Follow me."

"Aleida, I hope Santa treats you right tomorrow," Aldo said. "And you too," she replied. "Don't let Ramona boss you around. Sleep where you want to."

Ramona ignored the comment. She led Aldo down the hallway into the third door on the left. This was Amanda's old room, just as she had left it years before. It was a big room, and although the bed was full size, it left plenty of space for the rest of the furniture. Ramona had lit a small lamp on the dresser.

"Leave it," he said softly, "I'll turn it off later."

She quietly left the room. He slowly undressed and put on the pajamas she had left for him on his side of the bed. He undressed, removed the cover, and pushed the pillow up as he liked it. He waited for a few moments then dozed off until Amanda woke him as she entered the room.

"I was putting my father to bed," she said. "He's so lonely."

"He seemed to have had a good time tonight."

"He pretends a lot, Aldo. Not really, he didn't. He's worried."

"Tell him not to worry."

"You really think so?"

"No need to worry. It wont solve anything."

She put on the night-gown Ramona had meticulously folded on the other side of the bed. He thought he heard her speak again, but he could not quite make out the words. Then he felt her turn on the bed, and he woke up. He opened his eyes and glared at the ceiling. The room was pitch dark. He could hear the faint rumble of a faraway car engine that gradually faded. He thought the town's silence foreboding.

He pictured his mother sitting in the kitchen, silently watching the food casseroles boil, and again he felt he had betrayed her. One more Christmas Eve he had not gone to see her. He remembered his last boxing match long ago when he had heard her scream from the audience as she saw him pushed against the ropes. He had then momentarily forgotten his opponent and had turned to look at her. This mistake would cost him the fight and later, by his own choice, his boxing career. He took a punch to the jaw that "turned all the lights out," as his trainer later said.

He remembered the smallest details of that night and would remember them forever. His opponent was a lean, tall black man with cropped hair. He had a handsome face. He was light for a heavyweight at 190 pounds but he had large biceps and moved very fast and gracefully. There was no hesitation in his movements.

Aldo was tall with muscular shoulders and longer arms than his opponent. He weighed 201 pounds which, because of his young age, meant he would eventually be a top heavyweight. His face was free of scars and his nose had never been broken, odd for a white fighter in those days. He could punch hard and what had made him exceptional was his quickness and his ability to dance fight in an unexpected style for his classification. None of the local fighters wanted to confront him. His coach no longer scheduled local fights for him and he was waiting for word from Havana about a second professional bout. What made this fight special was that this opponent came from Aldo's town. Two local boys fighting in the Havana golden gloves.

Aldo's coach was an old fellow with a glass eye who squinted when looking at people. He was strong and could handle the toughest fighters with an iron grip when he wanted their attention. "I want you to deck him," he had said to Aldo. "I don't like his fucking attitude. I never liked that kid. Just deck him fast, then we're out of here. No more rinky-dink fights. We'll never fight again in Camaguey."

It was an understatement. Aldo had made it through the golden gloves, had achieved fame at tournaments where, before his last fight, he won each bout by technical knockout. Aldo's opponents were mangled by his relentless jabs. Then the rumor started that the big islander could not punch hard enough to put anyone out, and his coach had reacted with rage. "Knock the socks out of him fast," Aldo's trainer had said during the previous fight. "No dancing this time."

But Aldo had danced his way until he saw an opening, then jabbed his opponent's face. The young man fell like timber and never made the count.

That night Aldo's mother Cecilia had come to the arena. She had missed all of her son's fights. She didn't like him being a fighter and would have done anything to keep him away from the sport. But her sister had said that it was obvious that Aldo was on his way up. He would be famous one day. So she had gone to the match, much to the consternation of Aldo's coach who did not want her there. She sat on the second row, in tears most of the time.

The first round went fast for Aldo. He danced around his opponent who tried to cut the ring on him without success. He put his hands down and circled him, and when the fighter charged him, he quickly brushed aside the punch with one arm, jabbing him with the other. It looked like an easy win to his coach who kept yelling for Aldo to put his opponent out.

By the third round Aldo's opponent had a bloody eye. His left cheek was puffy and his upper lip swollen. But he kept coming at him. He would hit fast to give the impression that he was getting the best of Aldo, but his punches never landed past Aldo's shielding arms.

Then the fourth round came. The black man charged in. He pushed and shoved and kept cutting the ring on Aldo while getting himself jabbed. When he thought he had him, he charged and punched repeatedly into Aldo's mid body, hoping to land punches in his mid section. Aldo kept blocking him and backing away, knowing that the man would only tire himself out and become an easy target.

Purposely, Aldo let himself be backed into a corner, trying to wear his opponent out. He placed both arms in front of his chest. The punches kept coming. Then Aldo's coach yelled for him to get out of the corner. It gave his opponent a boost, and he suddenly began to punch Aldo's arms, desperately trying to hit his midsection.

Then Aldo heard a scream from the audience. He recognized his mother's voice. And then he made the second biggest mistake of his life. His first would come years later. He turned his head to look in the direction of the noise and saw Cecilia standing in the gallows, arms flapping and yelling for the fight to stop. It was only an instant, but it seemed like an eternity for immediately after that, his opponent landed a punch that almost turned his head backwards. Aldo felt time stand still. His knees weakened and his eyesight became hazy. He felt calmness gradually overpower him. For a fraction of a second, he lost all control. He could have just let himself go, and it would have been all over. But he preferred to fight. Then he saw an opening. It was what he needed. His thoughts raced, and suddenly he was out again, looking straight at the fighter's eyes, and the punches kept coming at him. He raised his gloves up to block them. Their impact made the gloves bounce against his face. He felt a rush of strength coming.

Suddenly, a hand grabbed his shoulder and the same scream he had heard before ruptured the air. Only this time it was right by his ear. It was Cecilia. After seeing her son struck, she had gone berserk and rushed toward the ropes, trying to stop the fight. Aldo's coach saw her coming and tried to cut her off but could not reach her in time. Then, seeing his fighter being held, he climbed into the ring and ran towards the corner. He immediately realized his mistake. He had technically stopped the fight by entering the ring.

It was then that Aldo began to strike back, pushing his opponent away and breaking loose from his mother's grip. He immediately moved to his left to gain his balance. When the other fighter came back at him, Aldo was in position and met him with a right jab and a left uppercut that lifted the man off the ground. But it was too late. The referee turned toward Aldo's coach and crossed his hands in a sweeping motion. "Over!" he yelled, "over!"

Aldo's opponent staggered back and would have gone down if not for the ropes. There was a blankness in his eyes. But his coach was holding him fast and slapped his face several times. For a second, Aldo had the urge to turn the bout into a real street fight. But the referee was now blocking him. He went to his opponent and lifted his right arm up in victory. The crowd booed. They knew it wasn't his fight.

"Winning by technical knockout, Eugenio Santana!" More boos.

Aldo made up his mind that night that he would never fight again. He held no grudge against his mother. Boxing was only a sport, something that he was good at and loved but could live without. Cecilia was only thinking of him but by her actions that night, she had literally taken him out of the sport. Aldo felt compassion for her and understood. She was all he had left. What he didn't realize until years to come was how deeply he cared for boxing and how much he had given up that night for his mother.

"I never want to see your mother at a fight again," his coach said.

"Shut up," Aldo replied. "There will be no more fights."

"Kid, you don't know what you're saying. I never saw a fighter shake a punch like you did. Had it not been for your mother, that chump would have never touched you. You know that, don't you?"

"Shut up," Aldo said again. "It's over."

"Like hell it's over. I'll see you at the gym in Camaguey."

Aldo never went back. A few days later, he went to Rios looking for work at the Arapientos' farm and began his rise into the cattle business. Many times his coach had gone after him berating him for throwing his career away but he could not move him. When Aldo was in town, he would see the now-frail mulatto, wearing dirty slippers and pants made from flour bags. He would discreetly slip him a peso and tell him to stay away from the bottle. The old coach would gaze up at him and squint, then he would grip Aldo's forearm, and squeeze, as he used to do in the old training days.

CHAPTER SIX

IN MOST NEIGHBORHOODS, A MILKMAN delivered his product to each home at dawn. In areas where cooking gas had yet not arrived, the charcoal delivery man delivered charcoal for cooking. Later in the day, other delivery folks would come by selling vegetables, bread, and even roasted peanuts. There were specialty stores and markets where one could buy these same items, except milk. The milkmen still enjoyed a trade monopoly, although they lived a life of sleepless nights.

The Diaz house was located in an exclusive suburban area. The homes were protected by high fences for privacy. It was a status symbol to say that one lived in a suburb. Amanda and her sisters had profited from this as children and had met elite folk. Their life had been sheltered by this environment. Guillermo felt his family deserved the best in society and worked hard to get it. After all those years, he felt he had succeeded. All of his daughters had received a good education. Ana had married a man of her class and Aleida was engaged to a military man. Amanda, his favorite, was another story. He never felt that she married the right man. Guillermo could never accept Aldo as his daughter's husband.

Aldo awoke early. He was used to nights of interrupted sleep that he would supplement with afternoon naps. Not having awakened during the night had given him a rare opportunity to sleep straight through. He felt fresh by 7:00 A.M. He quietly got up, careful not to wake Amanda. He changed his garments and put on his woolen shirt, blue jeans, and black cowboy boots. He opened the door and went to the end of the hallway to one of the bathrooms reserved for the guests. He brushed his teeth and let the faucet run for a while before rinsing. There was a knock at the door.

"Don Aldo," Ramona called, "can I make you breakfast?"

"Yes, Ramona, thank you."

He heard her footsteps recede. He opened the door and went into the kitchen. He and Ramona were the only ones up.

"Can you please make me a plate of pork meat for my mother and aunt? Give them some ribs, please."

She did not answer. Her back was toward him.

"Did you sleep well, Ramona?" he asked.

"No," she answered dryly without turning.

She wore a different dress from the night before, this one of white background and pink stripes. Her hair was neatly combed as before. She came into the room and stood before him.

"And what will you have, Don Aldo?"

"Only milk and coffee and some bread. I can get it myself Ramona. No need to trouble you."

"I do what I have to do."

She turned brusquely from him. Deep inside, she admired him, as she would a black man if he had married a white woman and crossed the color line. But she could not acknowledge it. She was part of the Diaz's household and had to play the part. She could never accept him and had to make it obvious that she tended to him only because he was Amanda's husband. Aldo had observed this and his reaction was the same as anything else that related to Guillermo. He did not need Guillermo, his name, or his fortune. He had married Amanda only out of love and did not care that her father or his servants were critical of his peasant roots.

"How are you these days?" He asked as she moved to the kitchen.

"I'm all right."

"Our kids are getting big fast, eh?"

"That they are."

"Soon Frank will have to go into a school in town. You will be seeing more of him then."

"Is he going to stay here?"

"No, he'll commute."

"Too much for a young boy his age. He needs to stay in this house to be tended to properly, not going back and forth."

"Explain that to his mother."

"Don't tell me about Amanda, I have known her since she was born."

"What is bothering you, Ramona?"

Aldo thought he could not let her go on. Her sarcasm was now nearing rudeness. He was willing to forego her insults up to a point because he thought her a victim of the old man whom he knew she considered her master like the Arapientos servants. Their masters were their world to them, all they knew. Their fate was embedded in the webs of this complex society. And he hoped such archaic system would end once Batista was gone, if this ever happened.

She remained silent. Then she came into the room with a glass of warm milk, coffee, a round piece of hot bread, and a square block of sugar on the side. Aldo removed the top of a silver sugar bowl and emptied two spoonfuls of sugar from the bowl into the glass, stirring the contents. Ramona handed him a paper bag.

"There's your pork."

"You can tell Amanda that I went to see my mother. Then I will be in town on business, and I will come back this afternoon to pick her and the children up."

She did not respond. He knew she had heard him. He ate the bread without any butter and then drank the rest of the milk. He took the empty glass and saucer and placed them on the counter that separated this room from the kitchen.

"Can you tell me where the children are sleeping, or shall I knock on every door and wake everybody up?"

"They are in Number 5," she said dryly without turning.

He went through the dining room and along the hallway, four doors down. He opened the doors gently and looked inside. He saw the twins lying side by side on a large bed. Frank slept alongside them. It was a room like Amanda's with a high ceiling and wallpapered in a lively design of yellow, red and blue sailboats. The bed had a high canopy with a curved top of yellow and green fabric, like the comforter. It was flanked by a night table and lamp on each side. There was an oak dresser with a large mirror shaped like a fan, and a chair. A small lamp had been left on.

Aldo closed the door gently. He went inside his room for a moment and put on his leather jacket then walked through the living room and stepped outside. It was a cold clear day. There was no sign of dew or fog. He walked toward the gate. The jeep was parked by the sidewalk. He got in and started the engine.

He drove out of the suburbs and into the center of town by taking the Central Highway, exiting into a narrow cobblestone street that made the jeep bump clumsily. The structures on both sides were contiguous making them appear as one long barrier of concrete and bricks, their doors being their only point of demarcation.

Aldo liked driving through town in the early hours of the morning. He thought about people he knew as he passed their homes. He had spent a great deal of time in town after finishing primary school in the country. His mother had insisted in sending him to the city to continue his education. She had thought him a bright boy and, ignoring her husband's disregard for such things she had sent Aldo to live with her sister. Aldo's aunt had taken him in, and he quickly adapted to his new surroundings. But his education was doomed when he began fist fighting with his school mates and then boxing at a gym by the age of ten.

The street got wider, and the jeep turned into an asphalted street. He passed an old church, the local museum, and several theaters then a square used for public gatherings and an open market. One of the most elegant churches in town, the Mercedes, stood there with a light-blue bell tower and a diocese house. Several streets ended at the plaza, and Aldo took one of them. It was narrow, and the jeep had very little room to maneuver.

He passed an old movie theater, then the street widened, and he began to slow down. He stopped and parked the jeep behind an old Chevrolet. He took the brown bags from the back of the jeep and walked to a flimsy door with a small barred window. He knocked and heard slow footsteps approaching. As the door opened, he saw Cecilia's solemn face.

"Aldo, my boy," she said.

He walked up the step and hugged her. There were tears in her eyes. She could have been sixty or more, but her wrinkles and long gray hair with a yellow ribbon made her look seventy. She was short, with fair skin. She had a short nose, black eyes, and a thin face with flat freckled cheeks.

He gave her one of the bags. "How are you, Mama?"

"You did not come to see me yesterday."

"You know how my Christmas Eve is. But I am here today."

"Ay, yes." She tapped him affectionately on the shoulder, gazing up at him.

"Where is Aunt Dulce?"

"She is in the back, come on in."

They walked together as he hugged her shoulder. It was a small house. The floor was cement, cleverly marked to resemble tiles. A small living room connected with a short hallway with a bedroom to the left. A second bedroom adjoined a small dining room off an open kitchen and a third was in the back next to the bathroom. A curtain covered the entrance to the dining room. Aldo's aunt stood by the stove, a lean woman, taller than Cecilia and looking much younger. With hands on her waist, she greeted him.

"Well, so the Marquis finally shows."

He went up to her and kissed her on the cheek. She held him by the back of the neck and pressed his face against hers. She was flat cheeked, and her hair was gray and long, like her sister's.

"I brought you some eggs and pork."

He gave her the bags.

"We still have some of the pork you brought us this week. One thing we don't need is food. We just need love."

She went to a blue refrigerator located in a corner of the dining room. The room was crowded and the table and chairs hardly fit. Dulce looked inside the bags, placed them in one of the compartments, then began taking the eggs from the bag one by one and putting them inside the egg holder in the door. She was in her mid fifties, and it was obvious that she was in charge. Her movements were swift and energetic. Her sister, in contrast, seemed weak.

"How are the children and Amanda," Cecilia asked.

She pulled a chair from the table and sat down. Aldo sat across from her.

"They're fine, still sleeping. They will come later."

"Oh, I would like to see them so much."

"You will."

"Make sure they come," Dulce said.

Dulce folded the empty bag and closed the refrigerator door. She walked to a small pantry behind Aldo and placed a bag inside a drawer.

"I know you don't drink coffee," Dulce said, "but how about some nice fresh milk with coffee. I know you like that."

Aldo smiled at her. She knew him better than his mother. She had raised him during his teenage years, knew his weaknesses and strengths, and those secrets that Cecilia had never learned.

"You are such a twit, Aunt Dulce."

Cecilia smiled at him. Her hard life on the prairie of Rios had gotten the best of her. Her son Emilo's death had been the straw that had broken the camel's back. She had lost her sanity after his death and had to be committed to a sanitarium for the mentally ill. She had needed her sister to take care of her after she left the institution and never went back to Rios. Dulce would have never allowed it.

"And what would you like to eat today, Mama. Tell me and I will bring it."

"Oh, it's not important Aldo. I just want you to be here. Stay with us."

"I will stay until noon. Then I have to meet Pablo at the Centro. I will bring Amanda and the kids in the afternoon."

"How are they? Frank and the girls growing?" Dulce asked.

"Yes, they are fine. Sleeping."

"And what about Pablo?"

"He is good. He is in town today."

"Why don't you bring him for lunch?"

"I don't know if we can be here for lunch. We are in business today."

"May the Lord guide you," Cecilia said.

"He'll do well in whatever it is, Cecilia," Dulce assured her.

She handed him a glass of milk and coffee. She poured just the exact amount of sugar, the way he liked it. She brought him some country crackers. It was Aldo's second glass of milk and coffee this morning.

"I hope."

"No, don't hope," Dulce corrected him, "just do what you think is best, and it will be fine."

"Things are not that good, Aunt Dulce. There's too much insecurity in business right now with the rebels around. Commerce is slow"

"And what do you think will happen, Aldo," Cecilia asked.

"I don't know, Mama."

"What are you doing, selling or buying?"

"We are looking to buy. We think we can gain an advantage now because of the low trading. It could be our chance but if things get any worse, then we may get stuck with the lot for a long time. That could be disastrous."

"How can you go wrong?" Dulce said. "If the rebels take over, commerce will move again. It will skyrocket. The people are expecting it. Don't doubt that for a moment, Aldo, and don't be afraid."

"You really think the rebels have it, eh?"

"I think Batista can't hold out. He let this thing get too far. Now his time is up."

"You are one of the few who thinks it will happen, Dulce. I think most people expect he will carry on, especially now with all the maneuvers they are doing. They do have the military on their side."

"Can Batista fall, Aldo? Do you think so?" Cecilia asked naively.

"It's possible, Mama. It's very possible."

"Batista won't fall," she affirmed, suddenly serious. "Nobody can take him. And I hope he's there for a hundred years."

Dulce gave Aldo a meaningful look.

"What has he done that makes you root for him?"

"And what would these rebels do?"

Aldo looked at her. For someone whose sanity had deserted her, he thought she was asking just the right questions, the same everyone should be asking themselves. What would these rebels do? Were they really going to do what they say or is this just euphoria among the people who want a change, any change?

"We shall see," Dulce said.

She and Aldo exchanged glances. Her sister's condition had taught her not to rely on her logic. At the least expected moment, she would lose all reason and repeat anything she might have heard wherever she might be. Dulce was a strong woman, like Cecilia had once been, and she had achieved what nobody else could. She had lived with the insane woman without straight jackets, cages, and ropes. She could handle Cecilia. But her life was full of bounds and she never overstepped them. One could never trust Cecilia.

"I don't know what they will do, Mama. We will find out, as Dulce said."

"I don't want to find out," she intimated. "Let Batista stay."

"You sound a bit like Alfredo, Mama. He likes Batista."

At the mention of Alfredo's name she looked past Aldo as if trying to remember. It was a name from Rios, someone she had known well. Aldo knew he had made a mistake by mentioning Alfredo. It was taboo in this house to mention anything that related to the prairie. Dulce had learned the hard way the dangers involved in having her sister remember the past. She could easily go into a tantrum. The mention of the slightest reference to Rios, the place where she spent her youth, would sometimes trigger it. It was an impossible task to avoid references, and only Dulce could. Aldo hoped it would pass.

"It's not important, Mama," he said casually, "forget it."

"Did you drive here, Aldo," Dulce asked, looking at Cecilia.

"Yes. I have the jeep."

"You need it all the time, Aldo. If I had the money, I would buy you one. Sell my two calves and use the money to buy yourself a jeep."

She was referring to cattle that Aldo had given her, as he did with members of his family.

"No, we can't do that. Pablo and I share the jeep and we do just fine. If I do well on this deal, a house for the family is next on my agenda. Then I can come see you everyday."

Dulce was still looking at Cecilia. She studied her face as her sister continued to stare into space.

"And here I thought we would have a pleasant Christmas Day," Dulce said.

"Pardon me, Aunt Dulce, really," Aldo said.

"Not your fault my boy, not at all."

The church bell tolled, calling for the eight o'clock mass. It was an old church located in the next block behind the house. Its steeple could be seen from the kitchen window, protruding above the low-tiled roofs. For a moment, Aldo was surprised to hear it so near. Then he remembered when, years ago, he would wake up to its sound.

"Oh, I have a headache," Cecilia said softly.

She rubbed her temple wit her fingers.

"Let me get you a *mejoral*," Dulce announced.

Dulce reached quickly into the pantry and retrieved a transparent cellophane wrapping containing a white thick tablet inside, a sedative equivalent to aspiring. She handed it and a glass of water to Cecilia. "Here, take this," she told her sister.

"No," Cecilia interposed, "just leave me, Dulce. Leave me, please." Suddenly she started to sob and covered her face with both hands.

"Cecilia," Dulce said, raising her voice, "listen to me now. You have to take this, come, your son is here. It's Christmas Day. Don't let yourself get sick now. Come on."

Cecilia did not hear her. She was groaning. She had rested her face on the table, tears dripping from her face. She was shaking.

"Cecilia!" Dulce patted her neck, trying to make her come back. "Cecilia, please, no. Come on, no."

Aldo, who had sat silently, stood and went around the table. He too began to caress her. Cecilia's groans turned hoarse and seemed to vibrate from deep inside her throat.

"Come on, Aldo, let's put her to bed," Dulce commanded.

Aldo took her by her armpits and pulled her from the chair. She put her head back and screamed at the top of her lungs. Dulce dragged the chair back to give Aldo more room to handle her. He put an arm underneath her thighs and lifted her. Dulce pulled aside a curtain behind him so he could enter the room. It was dark, with a double bed dressed in pink and a chifforobe with a large mirror in the middle. Aldo laid his mother down gently. She did not resist him but moved away from him. Dulce went back to the kitchen to fetch another pill. She gave Aldo the glass to hold, then wrapped her arm around Cecilia's head and held her jaw with her hand. She forced a green tablet into her mouth. Cecilia tried to spit it out, but Dulce held her mouth. She took the glass from Aldo and forced her to drink. Cecilia spurted water into the glass and in the struggle, she swallowed the pill.

"You have to take another one," Dulce said.

She gave her the *mejoral* tablet. Cecilia's screams waned and she now sobbed inconsolably. Aldo and Dulce stood by the bed looking at her. It was a sad spectacle, one they had seen too often. As her sobbing diminished, Aldo and Dulce moved away. They both knew that the effect of the medicine was quick and would make her doze. She would sleep for a while, then be groggy for the rest of the day, but it was better than her present condition. They could do nothing else. They went back to the dining room and sat down, listening to her sobs in silence. There was a knock at the front door.

"Oh, that's probably Leticia from next door. Let me see."

Dulce walked to the door. A woman in her mid-forties, with long curly brown hair and big green eyes came in.

"Is she all right," she asked, "I heard her screaming."

"She is under control," Dulce said. "Quiet, we put her to bed. Come see Aldo."

"Is Aldo here?"

"Yes."

Leticia went to Aldo and he stood up to embrace her.

"Merry Christmas," she said.

Dulce motioned for them to leave the dining room, and they went into the living room. Aldo sat in one of the armchairs in front of the television set. The women took the sofa by the wall.

"What happened? She's been doing fine."

"It's no major crisis," Dulce said. "She just got upset. It will pass."

"I got scared. I heard screams."

"She took her medicine. She'll be fine."

"What triggered it?"

"Nothing in particular. She just got upset."

Dulce was being evasive. Her neighbor was genuinely concerned, but Dulce felt she was being intrusive. She forgave it only because of the help she had provided at other times. But Dulce still remained a private woman.

"Will you stay the whole day, Aldo?"

Unable to obtain any information from Dulce, she had now shifted her inquiry to Aldo.

"Probably," he said.

Like his aunt, he knew a talker when he saw one. He, too, was set in not revealing his secrets. "Oh, stay. Stay with me if you don't stay here. How is it going?"

He answered her evasively as Dulce had. Then Leticia began to talk to them about the political situation and the speech she had heard the night before. Abruptly, she turned to Aldo and said she had heard they had killed someone in Rios. Dulce turned to Aldo. This was something she knew nothing about.

"Where did you hear that?" Aldo asked.

"Oh, I got my sources. Poor man, to die like that. Don't tell me you don't know."

Aldo gazed into her eyes and saw the look of someone seeking information by pretending to know more than she did.

"I know someone died in Rios but I did not know that he was killed."

"It was Patricio, a drunkard. Was he aiding the rebels?"

"There's no talk about the rebels in Rios. Everyone just minds his business, including me. Patricio was not into politics."

"Well, they must have had something on him to kill him like that."

"Who?"

"Oh, you know, the government. Batista."

Dulce had listened attentively. She did not want to discuss the issue in the presence of her neighbor but she later would question each of them alone until she was satisfied that her nephew was not in any danger.

The rest of the morning went by uneventfully. The medication had put Cecilia to sleep. After Leticia left, Dulce listened to Aldo's plans and made some suggestions. She could not force Aldo, but she could make him think. She wanted the best for him and would have given her life for a son like him. He was her pride.

It was late morning when Aldo left. He drove back toward Las Mercedes Plaza by taking General Gomez Avenue, a main drag, running parallel to Dulce's street. He turned right at a corner and parked the jeep alongside the curve. He entered the Aleman Center, a local bar where cattle-men met to drink and discuss business. The location was conveniently near most major connecting points in town, accessible to transportation, and yet away from the heavy traffic. It was a tavern with several wide entrances that remained open during most of the day and night. In the center was a long oval-shaped table with a dozen stools around it. It was artfully treated wood that shone from varnish despite its constant service. The place had a distinguished quality about it. One sensed that important things went on here.

As he entered, Aldo saw Pablo sitting near the end of the bar, next to another man whom he did not recognize. Aldo went straight to him and shook his hand.

"Merry Christmas, Aldo," Pablo said.

He was in his usual jovial mood. It went with the season.

"Merry Christmas," Aldo replied.

Aldo turned to Pablo's companion, a lean man with a brown Stetson pulled low on his forehead. Pablo introduced him as Angel.

"Sit down," Pablo said, "let's have a drink."

He whistled to the bartender. "Let's have a shot here."

"What will it be?" the bartender asked.

He came to Aldo and placed a round coaster in front of him.

"One Phillip, straight," Aldo said.

The man placed a shot glass on the coaster and poured the dark Brandy into it. Aldo took the glass, raised it, and clanked it against those of his friends.

"Prosperity and much health in the coming year, *salud*," Pablo said.

"Prosperity, *salud*," Angel and Aldo echoed.

As Angel turned, Aldo smelled the liquor on his breath. The man's eyes were red already. Aldo surveyed the bar. There were several patrons at the other end. Two were sitting on stools with others standing behind and leaning forward as they peered at something on the table. One of the men shook a round leather pocket in his right fist and cast two dice. The men looked as they rolled. Then they all roared with laughter.

"Mr. Pazos will be here," Pablo asserted. "I sent him a reminder last night."

"Why?" asked Aldo.

"I wanted to make sure he would be here."

"Don't make it sound like we are desperate," Aldo said.

"I'm not. I want him to know we are interested."

As they talked they kept glancing outside. The open doors allowed them a good view of the street, and they could see both pedestrians and cars passing by. Slowly, Don Fernando's Chevrolet pulled in front of Aldo's jeep, with Don Sanchez behind the wheel.

"Here they come," Angel said, "I'm leaving."

He got up and was going to lay a bill on the table but Pablo grasped his arm and stopped him.

"You don't have to go because he's coming."

"I don't want to spoil my holidays and yours. I don't want anything to do with that man."

"It's because of the holiday that you should stay. Ignore him."

"No, I'm leaving." He pulled his hat down even further and extended his hand to Aldo who shook it firmly. Then he tapped Pablo on the shoulder and quickly walked out. Just as Don Fernando and his driver were exiting their vehicle, he stepped out into the street and disappeared.

"What bugs him?" Aldo said to Pablo.

"Don Fernando did him wrong with a few heads, or so he claims. He says they made the deal, had the cattle weighing when Don Fernando stiffed him out of $5.00 per head. Angel needed the money and had no choice but to go through with the deal at that point."

"Hmmm." Aldo thought that if it were true, he would not be surprised.

It was one of the risks one ran in the cattle business. A man had to rely on his own instincts, his own knowledge that came from previous dealings with traders. There were no assurances, no written contracts among the traders except their word. Once two men shook hands, the bargain was sealed as if written on stone. If a man broke his word, it would get around and nobody would deal with him. Despite these dangers, Aldo loved the business. He had a gut feeling for it that, so far, had not failed him. But there was something odd about this Angel complaining of Don Fernando. Had it been Aldo, he would have confronted Don Fernando. After all, Angel was supposed to be the victim.

"Good morning, boys," Don Sanchez called. "Visiting town today?"

"A toast to you and Don Fernando," Pablo said happily.

He raised his glass and so did Aldo.

"*Salud*," Aldo and Pablo said in unison.

"Bartender," Aldo called, "give them a drink on us."

The two men sat in the middle of the bar on stools next to each other. Don Fernando was a shrewd old man who knew much about cattle. He had inherited his father's money but spent it all visiting whorehouses and living lavishly. The money went fast, and he had to take demeaning jobs as a cattle peon. Slowly, he had made his way back into the trade and learned his lessons. But he could never overcome what had caused his downfall. He loved to presume richness. Even at his age, he rode around with a driver, a luxury that his moderate purse could not afford.

Aldo knew of Don Fernando's faults but thought him a valuable acquaintance. Don Fernando knew how to evaluate a cattle head, and Aldo respected him for it. So he ignored the man's shallow ways by drawing upon his knowledge at every conceivable opportunity. But Aldo was cautious. There was a side of Don Fernando that could not be trusted. Would the old man steal a deal from him if he thought it advantageous? Aldo thought he would. Whatever he discussed with Don Fernando, he would never show him his full deck of cards.

"Want to join them?" Pablo asked.

"No," Aldo replied, "let's stay alone."

"Relax, Aldo, it's Christmas."

"Pablo, you just saw that man walk out of here complaining about Don Fernando betraying him and now you want to sit with him."

"Well, I'm not going to make a deal with him. I just want to have a drink with the man."

"We are. At a distance."

Aldo thought of Pablo as his best friend, the brother that Emilio might have been. Pablo's honesty and loyalty were incomparable, but he was not a leader. If left alone, Pablo would fall into a trap as a child into a dry well. And in this business, dry wells were the rule rather than the exception. They were both now waiting for a man selling a lot of calves. It was a golden opportunity for two young men who had done only sporadic trading at a low level. Aldo had obtained the backing of the Arapientos brothers who had vouched for him and Pablo. Aldo thought it was too good to be true. But if it happened, this could be the beginning of something very big for him and his friend.

They waited for over one hour. A patrol Army jeep pulled up in front of the tavern. Three soldiers dressed in full khaki uniforms and carrying carbines exited the vehicle and paced the sidewalk. One, a sergeant, left the others and came inside the tavern. He went to the far corner where the men were still playing and said something to them. One of the men took a bill from the table and placed it discreetly in the sergeant's hand. The sergeant turned from them and made eye contact with almost everyone behind the bar. Then he stepped out and joined the other soldiers. A tall man wearing a black

Texan hat now walked inside the tavern. He looked at the end of the bar table where the gamblers were gathered until he saw Aldo. He came up to him.

"Greetings," the man said.

"Merry Christmas, Mr. Pazos," Aldo said.

"Merry Christmas," Pablo repeated.

They both stood up to greet him and shook his hand. The man had a strong grip, light eyes, and an aquiline nose. His mouth was straight but his cheeks sagged. Poking from under the border of his hat was grey hair that gave away his age. He was dressed impeccably in beige slacks that hung over brown cowboy boots and a starched white shirt under a black leather jacket.

"Join us," Aldo said pointing to the stool next to him. "What will you have?"

"I'll call it," he said.

He whistled to the bartender who came from around the bar to lay a coaster before him.

"What will you have?" the bartender asked.

"Phillip II straight."

Mr. Pazos reached into his left shirt pocket, pulled out a Churchill cigar and lit it. It took him several seconds inhaling hard and fast to get the cigar burning. He let out several puffs of blue smoke and turned to Aldo.

"You boys must have real good credentials," he commented dryly.

"Who says?" Aldo answered him.

"Somebody likes you."

He took a quick gulp from his shot glass and let his cigar resting an ashtray in the form of a tire.

"That's good, but I don't expect it all the time."

"But you're not going to complain when it happens, right?"

They all laughed. Mr. Pazos looked straight at Aldo. "I may want to sell sixty-five heads. Can you handle them?"

"We can if the conditions are right."

"I'll tell you what the conditions are," Mr. Pazos said. "Thirty pesos a head. I will guarantee the weight of a calf, one hundred and fifty to one hundred seventy five pounds. It'll have to be before New Year's, or else there will be no deal. I will get the cattle to the weighing station, then you take over."

"Those are your conditions, Mr. Pazos?" Pablo asked.

He was going to continue but Mr. Pazos interrupted him.

"That's right. Those are my conditions, which means that if you want to do business with me, that's how it'll be."

"I'd say we have something to say about the matter," Aldo said jokingly. He smiled and lifted his shot glass as a toast.

"*Salud.*"

"*Salud,*" Mr. Pazos replied.

"We need to discuss price after we see the cattle," Pablo told him. "We can't promise anything until we see the cattle."

Aldo saw Pablo's point but knew what Mr. Pazos' answer would be.

"If I tell you what the cattle is, that's what it will be, boys. I know cattle, and my word is my word."

"I don't doubt your word, Mr. Pazos," Aldo responded. "But these are unstable times. We are willing to take a chance at a time when people are not exactly anxious to buy."

"Ahhh," Mr. Pazos interrupted. "This will all pass. I've seen this before. What do you think, that Batista is going to fall?"

"I don't know one way or the other, but whatever happens, it's got the traders scared."

"Anyway, what do you want to do? Do you want to do business?"

"We want to see your cattle," Aldo said.

"I need to know more than that. Seeing the cattle is only a formality. What I need to know is that you will buy."

"At the right price."

"I've told you what the price is."

"You are a businessman Mr. Pazos. Since you know cattle, you know that you haven't told us anything about your calves to fix the price. What you gave us was weight. That in itself does not say anything."

Pazos looked steadily at Aldo for a moment. Then he feigned surprise. "You can't tell what they are from what I've told you?"

"I can't tell whether we can pay thirty pesos a head."

"Let's see them, Mr. Pazos," Pablo said.

"I don't do business that way."

Aldo sensed that he was testing them. Like a pelican at sea, he was looking for his prey.

"Neither do we," said Aldo.

"Mr. Pazos," Pablo added, "what's the harm in letting us see your cattle."

"Not like this, no."

"Fine then," Aldo said, "better times are coming, hopefully."

Aldo lifted his glass again. He clanked it against Pablo's.

"*Salud*, partner."

"*Salud.*"

Aldo extended his hand to Mr. Pazos who shook it firmly. Pablo also shook hands with him and the two of them moved away and headed for the door. Aldo tapped his friend on the shoulder and pointed to where Don Fernando was seated. He walked to Don Fernando shook his hand and then Mr. Sanchez's. The two men had been drinking heavily since they came in.

"*Salud!*" Don Fernando grunted.

His face was red, and as he lifted his glass the drink spilled.

"Much prosperity in the coming year," Aldo said.

"Young man, let me tell you something," Don Fernando touched Aldo's right shoulder. "Don't ever hang out with trash like the man you were sitting with when I came in. And neither should your friend."

"Who's that?" Aldo inquired. Somehow he knew this moment would come.

"That man that was with you and left when I arrived. He's trash. And you know the saying, tell me who you hang out with, and I will tell you who you are."

"We barely know him, Don Fernando, who is he?"

"He's a scavenger, that's what he is. He's no businessman."

Pablo was curious but did not speak.

"I make a deal with him on a lot at thirty pesos a head, right? We shake hands on it, right? We meet at a stable near Santa Cruz.

The cattle is weighed and then he says to me, 'I'll pay you twenty five pesos per head.' I look at him and I say, 'that's not our deal.' He says, 'we had no deal until the weighing was done.' I almost nicked the bastard. I had to tell Sanchez to finish the deal for me. Unfortunately, for reasons that I could not help, I had to go through with it. But I tell you, he's trash, I will never forget it."

Aldo patted Don Fernando on the shoulder. His voice was strained from telling the story and his puffy cheeks had become even redder.

"Don Fernando, Merry Christmas to you and your family," Pablo said, stepping to him.

"Yes, merry Christmas," Don Fernando replied.

"Salud," Sanchez said, "much health."

Don Fernando was a real fox, Aldo thought. He must have seen Angel before he got off his jeep. How, he didn't know, but it proved two things. Don Fernando was not to be taken lightly. As for Angel, Aldo's suspicion was correct. The man was a sneak. Aldo believed Don Fernando's story.

They turned to go when they heard Mr. Pazos call them. Aldo looked back and saw him wave. He had loosened his hat and was drawing heavily on his cigar. He let out heavy clouds of smoke before he spoke. "When do you want to see the lot?" he asked, waving his cigar.

"Where is it now?" asked Aldo.

"Cimientos," Pazos said.

Aldo knew the place. It was a good twenty kilometers from town, off the Central Highway on the way to Santa Cruz, a port city on the southern part of the province.

"We could arrange to go tomorrow," Aldo said.

"Good," Pazos barked, "let's meet there in the afternoon, say 3:00 P.M. You can look at them then."

He extended his hand to Aldo. He had not really mulled it over and knew that he would do as they had asked. Aldo also knew it.

"You have peon help at Cimientos?" Pablo asked.

"They'll be brought up to you. You just show up, young man."

"Merry Christmas to you and your family," Aldo said.

"Yes," Pazos responded, "much health to you, *salud*."

He raised his shot glass up and drank.

Aldo and Pablo went outside. Pablo had walked to the tavern and had no car. The two stood outside for a moment, feeling the afternoon's dry breeze.

"You see," Pablo said, "motherfuckers like that are what have caused the mess we are in."

"Let's go," Aldo said, cutting him off, "come with me."

They climbed into the jeep. As soon as he sat down, Pablo began ranting in a voice filled with emotion.

"He was playing with us. He wants it all on his terms. It's them, people like him, that caused all this commotion. They are so greedy. They give a poor man no chance. There's just no way for anybody to get ahead with people like that, and there are many like him."

The jeep began moving slowly as Aldo turned towards Pablo.

"We are doing fine. He will sell to us at our price, don't you see? He's desperate to sell. No one, and I mean no one, is going to buy from him this week, or possibly next month, or the month after. He knows that, but thinks we are inexperienced, and he is trying to see what advantage he can gain."

"Mother fucker, *cabrón*," Pablo said angrily.

They reached Agramonte, a square similar to Las Mercedes, in the middle of which stood a park flanked by a church and a statue of Ignacio Agramonte, the region's patriot. The square was defined by two parallel streets running from Las Mercedes to the outskirts of town. Aldo passed the church, then turned right and entered the San Juan de Dios section, the historic part of town, filled with stately houses with terraces and red-tiled-roofs. He stopped in front of a brick house with two gigantic red clay pots in front.

"I'm going to take Amanda and the children to see my mother and aunt. Can you come?"

"No, I have to spend some time with Olga's parents."

"Then I'll meet you here tonight, and you can drive me back to the country. You can keep the jeep."

"All right. Be early. I don't want to be out late the way things are."

Aldo drove on, then turned into a side street leading back to Agramonte Park, in the direction of Guillermo's house. As he left town, he suddenly ran into a roadblock. One army truck and two jeeps were stationed at one side of the road and several soldiers had cordoned off the road. Aldo stopped behind a car whose driver had stepped out, and was surrounded by three soldiers. He waited. From the other side came a soldier, carrying an automatic rifle. He approached Aldo on the driver's side and pointed at him with his left hand as he neared.

"Where are you going?" he asked briskly.

"I'm going to pick up my family to bring them back into town." Aldo stared at him as he spoke. He was a corporal and wore a helmet instead of the usual military cap.

"Where does your family live?"

"They are staying with my father-in-law at his house in the Vista Hermosa suburb."

"Why are you picking them up?"

"I'm bringing them to my aunt's for Christmas."

"Get out of the jeep," the corporal ordered.

Aldo cut the engine and put the jeep in gear to prevent it from rolling. He opened the door and exited the jeep.

"Let's go, we don't have all day."

The corporal was only about 5'2", and as Aldo stood next to him, his head did not reach Aldo's shoulders. He stood back and looked Aldo up and down.

"What are you carrying in the jeep?" the corporal asked tersely.

"Nothing."

"No?" the corporal mocked, "you are not carrying anything for your family?"

"No, nothing."

"Don't you think that's strange? You're going to see your family on Christmas and you have nothing for them?"

He grabbed his rifle with his left hand and pushed the butt towards Aldo's rib cage. Aldo moved aside, causing the corporal to miss his target.

"I didn't tell you to move, *guajiro*," the corporal yelled. You move when I say you can move."

He stepped aside to face Aldo again. Hearing the commotion, another soldier drifted away from the group and came towards them.

"What the hell is going on with this one?" he said loudly to the corporal. His uniform bore the chevrons of a sergeant.

"This fool does not even know where he's going, Sergeant."

"If he doesn't have a place to go, then lock him up and confiscate his jeep," he said to the corporal.

The sergeant turned to Aldo.

"Where're you going, boy?"

"I told this skinny one that I was going to see my family."

"What?" The corporal yelled.

He raised his rifle, ready to strike Aldo with the butt of the gun. The sergeant smiled sarcastically and held up his hand as if to stop the corporal.

"Wise guy, ah? Tell me, boy, what is your name?"

"Aldo Ochoa."

"And the Ochoa family lives in this direction?"

"No, we do not live in this area, but my wife and children are at my father-in-law's home. He lives here."

"Who's your father in law?"

"Guillermo Diaz."

Aldo was sorry to have to mention the old man and to think that his name protected him. The corporal eased up somewhat but still had his rifle up.

"Of course, Mr. Diaz, the one who's got three daughters. Which of the three is your wife?"

"My wife is Amanda."

"Why didn't you say so before? The corporal here probably thought you were going out of town for some other reason. You know what I mean. Come on, get back in the jeep. Drive around this car and go on."

The sergeant tapped his shoulder. Aldo started to move on, then he turned to the corporal.

"Why don't you teach this fool here some manners?"

The corporal did not wait for him to finish. He thrust the butt of his rifle into Aldo's rib cage and would have hit him, had Aldo not turned quickly. The sergeant had enough.

"Ho!" he yelled, "boy, you're picking the wrong time to be talking, you know that? You are pushing your luck. I can easily teach you some manners. You want to spend the rest of the day away from your family?"

"Sergeant, I won't be abused by you or any of your men. I am not going to be pushed around."

"Well, today you might just have to, boy. This corporal here is my confidant, and what he does, he does under my orders. Whether you like it or not, I am the boss and I am telling you that you're not getting through this roadblock, no matter who you are or who your father is. How's that?"

The sergeant's face reddened, and he pointed at Aldo. The corporal smiled and looked triumphant. He made a vague attempt to go charge towards Aldo. The sergeant blocked him.

"Sergeant, do what you want to, but I won't let anybody push me around because he's got a gun and a uniform. If your corporal wants to get at me, tell him to take his uniform off. I'll fight him fair and square right here."

Aldo knew that he had lost it at that point. He thought about Frank and the twins and he was sorry he had not been man enough to endure their insults, but now it was too late. If he had to, he would go down fighting. He felt the urge to bust the corporal's nose, then take on the sergeant until he fell gasping.

"I am not going to have him do that," the sergeant said, "but I want you to get out of here, now. And you're lucky, boy, you're real lucky. You don't know it yet."

He motioned to the jeep with his left thumb, giving Aldo a way out.

"Go on," he said, "back up and get out of here. I don't want to see you around here for the rest of the day, you hear me?"

"They might still find him with his mouth full of ants tomorrow morning," the corporal said to the sergeant, loud enough that Aldo could hear.

"Shut up, corporal," the sergeant said.

Slowly, Aldo turned to leave. He didn't feel right about the episode and didn't like walking away from the abuse, although he knew it was the smart thing to do. It made him feel cheap. A car had pulled behind his jeep, and the driver remained inside waiting and looking at the soldiers. The corporal moved forward to meet the driver. As he did, he passed near Aldo who was entering his jeep. Very deliberately, the corporal let the side of his gun brush against Aldo's buttocks in an attempt to humiliate him in front of the sergeant. Aldo pivoted and struck the corporal in the face with his right fist. The corporal never saw it coming. He fell backwards and slumped on the hard pavement, belly up, his arms stretched out. His helmet rolled away, and his rifle shattered on the pavement. A stream of blood flowed from his nostrils. He was out.

The sergeant looked at the corporal on the ground, not quite believing what he was seeing. Then he looked at Aldo standing by the door of the jeep and began yelling at the top of his lungs. "You fucking idiot! You lousy idiot!"

"Shut up or I'll deck you, too, if it's the last thing I do," Aldo said.

He was ready to move towards the sergeant who saw it in his eyes and quickly pulled out his .45.

"You make one move, and I'll spill your brains on the ground, motherfucker. Turn around! Now!"

Holding the gun against Aldo's ribs, the sergeant grabbed Aldo's left arm. Then he called to the soldiers in the rear.

"Hey, Ramirez, over here, now! Move!"

A soldier jumped out of the truck and trotted towards him. The sergeant shoved the barrel of his gun hard against Aldo's ribs then pushed his head down against the jeep. He felt like breaking the cowboy's head, but the traffic was building up behind him. Too many witnesses.

"Handcuff him!" he said to the soldier.

The soldier seemed nervous and fidgeted with the handcuffs hanging from his belt. He unclipped them with his right hand. He yanked Aldo's right arm around his back and handcuffed him. Two more soldiers had rushed over to them, pointing their guns at Aldo's back.

"Throw him in the truck," the sergeant said, "and move this fucking jeep out of the way. Get somebody else over here, too."

Two soldiers pulled Aldo up by his forearms. The third one held his gun against him. They turned him with some difficulty. He was a big man, and they needed his help to move him. He did not resist but he did not help them either. The sergeant went to the corporal who was coming to. He knelt down and slapped him in the cheeks.

"Come on, corporal, it was only a fall. Wake up."

Just then, an Army jeep approached on the shoulder of the road, driving past several cars that had now lined up behind Aldo's jeep. The sound of the engine startled the sergeant, and he looked up, wondering if he was in for another surprise. The jeep stopped abruptly a few feet from him. The corporal had sat up and was bleeding profusely from the nose. A young sergeant jumped out of the passenger side of the jeep and approached him.

"What happened here, Sergeant Valdez? The road is getting clogged up."

Sergeant Valdez looked at him. He resented this young punk telling him his business. He had come up the ranks the hard way without help from anybody which was why he was still only a sergeant despite his many years of service. It rankled him to look at this young boy, who could have easily been his son, wearing three chevrons on his sleeve and having put in only a third of the time he had.

"I got eyes too, Sergeant. Don't tell me how to run my post, please. We had a minor incident here, that's all. Some punk got into a hassle with the corporal here, and we had to place the man under arrest. We'll get the traffic moving soon."

"Are you okay corporal?" the young sergeant asked.

"Yeah, I think so."

Sergeant Valdez held a handkerchief to the corporal's nose to stop his bleeding.

"Take him to the emergency room," Sergeant Valdez said to another soldier. He handed the corporal over to the soldier as if the small man was a package.

"Sergeant," the corporal said, "I want to get that bastard if it's the last thing I do."

"Take him to emergency," Sergeant Valdez repeated to the soldier. "Just go on and get well, Corporal. I'll handle that idiot myself," he added.

The soldier helped the corporal into one of the Army jeeps.

"Where's the guy," the young sergeant inquired.

"Sergeant Perez," Sergeant Valdez said to him patiently, "this is not your post. It's not your call. Let me handle my men, Okay?"

"Show me the man. I got orders to move this post further south anyway. We got trouble in Florida."

Sergeant Valdez looked angrily at the young sergeant. "Here we go again," he thought. They were going to move the troops, and the captain did not even have the courtesy to tell him. He had to hear it from a junior sergeant who wanted to make a name for himself. He was tired of the job, tired of the wealthy running the Army and pushing their sons up the ranks at whim. But he also needed to decide what to do about the crazy cowboy who had flattened the corporal. He wanted to look the man in the eye now that the soldiers had him inside. He would have never admitted it to his troops, but he was glad to finally see someone with balls. It had been a long time.

He began walking towards the truck and waived the young sergeant to follow him.

"Don't just stand there," he said to the other soldiers, "come on, keep this line moving."

He pointed to his left at the edge of the road where Aldo's jeep was parked.

"That's his jeep. Some pretty tough guy, I must admit. He knocked the corporal right out with one punch."

He climbed the truck and entered the cargo hold. They kept it closed to darken its inside, should they bring someone in. Sergeant Perez followed him. The soldiers had dragged Aldo to the end of the cargo hold and were taking turns hitting him.

"Stop," Sergeant Valdez said.

Despite the darkness, he saw that the man was unconscious, may be worse. He shoved the soldiers back. "Put that flashlight on him," he said to one of them.

The soldier flicked the flashlight on and shone it on Aldo's face. Lying on the floor, mouth half open, Aldo was covered with blood, his hands tied behind his back. The three soldiers had gone at him like vaulters. Aldo had put up a valiant fight, kicking and flopping them but they had knocked him cold by hitting him on the temples with their rifles. Then they had unmercifully worked him over by kicking him in the head, ribs, and face.

"You didn't cut him, did you?" Sergeant Valdez asked without looking at them.

"No," one of them said.

"Good, let's get this truck out of here."

"Wait," Sergeant Perez said, "I think I know this guy."

"Sergeant Perez," Sergeant Valdez said, "I just about had it with you. Why don't you mind your own operation?"

"Because I got orders from the captain, Sergeant," the young sergeant said, "that's why. I got orders to move this post."

Sergeant Perez took the flashlight from the soldier and shone it on the man's body. He immediately recognized the purple wool shirt from the night before and the man's light brown hair. He looked at his face. Despite the blood, he recognized it. He worried, wondering what this could do to his relationship with Aleida.

"Hell," he said in frustration, "Do you know who this is? This guy is Mr. Diaz's son-in-law. Are you fucking crazy, Sergeant? How could you let this happen?"

Sergeant Valdez hesitated for a moment. He knew he should have let this guy go the minute he saw him. He should have moved the corporal down the line and handled the bastard himself. But what the heck, these things happened.

"What do you mean, Sergeant Perez? The guy licked my corporal. What I'm supposed to do, kiss his ass?"

"I'm not worried about him. I am worried about my future father-in-law. How can I explain this to him? Hell, what do I do now?"

Sergeant Perez knelt down near Aldo's face. He saw the open gashes on his temples and hoped it wasn't that bad after all. May be he wasn't too late. Aldo was bleeding profusely, but nothing appeared to be broken. Yes, he had come in just in time, but what to do now? He turned to one of the soldiers on his side. "Go to my jeep and tell my men to come here right now."

The soldier walked towards the back of the truck and jumped out.

"What the hell are you doing, Sergeant Perez?" Sergeant Valdez asked.

"I'm taking this guy to the emergency room. As far as I'm concerned, he lost control of the jeep and went into a ditch. That's the story. Leave the jeep in the ditch."

"You can't take this guy out of here in broad daylight and in front of everybody out there!"

Two men came running. Perez ignored Sergeant Valdez's comments and looked up at them.

"Put the jeep over here by the back of the truck. We got to get this guy to the emergency."

The men ran back out. Sergeant Perez stood up and looked at Sergeant Valdez in the eye.

"You can have your men help me, or I'll have my own men do it," he said. "We'll put this guy in my jeep and I'll drive him to the emergency. Leave his jeep in the ditch."

He turned to one of the sergeant's soldiers.

"Take his bloody shirt off and leave it on the seat. Give me some cloth to cover him with. Come on, let's go."

The soldiers bent down and began undressing Aldo's upper body. They freed his hands from the handcuffs. Another soldier threw a heavy linen green sheet on him. Then they picked him up to bring him outside.

"Wait," Sergeant Valdez said, "wait for the jeep to pull over."

They heard the engine straining in reverse, then felt a slight bump as the rear of the jeep made contact with the truck.

"Now," Sergeant Valdez called.

He raised the truck's back cover and waived them to come. The soldiers bent down low while holding Aldo. The one in front handed the feet to one of Sergeant Perez's men in the jeep, then the other one pushed. Four more hands held Aldo and pulled him in. His arms sagged on the floor of the truck as he went in.

Sergeant Perez sat in the back and told his men to drive to the Spanish Colony, a private clinic that had been originally built by the Spaniards and catered only to private members. He figured Aldo must be a member and besides, this place was closer. He turned and tried to wipe some of the blood off Aldo's face. The bleeding had subsided somewhat but it was still flowing. "May be he'll be all right," he thought. Then he heard Aldo moan. That was good. He wiped his eyes clean and he saw them open. He'd been lucky they had missed his eyes.

"Listen, my friend, this is Roberto, remember me? I know you are hurt, my friend. You were in an accident, okay?"

Aldo's eyes fixed on him as he began to come to. Everything was hazy. Did he know this guy? It was somebody he had seen, yes.

"Listen, I need to know. Do you have a friend I can call instead of your wife? I don't want to scare her. Anybody?"

A friend. Yes, a friend. He had only one friend.

"Pablo, Pablo"

"Who's Pablo? Where do I find him?"

Where's Pablo? Where's Pablo. In Rios, a few huts over. No, no, no. San Juan de Dios, San Juan de Dios.

"San Juan de Dios Plaza, number 14."

Around 3:30 P.M. Olga was sitting at her parents' table, the chair next to her empty. She had scolded Pablo when he came in. He had taken so long at the Center with Aldo, and today was Christmas. Was it really all business or his way of getting away? Why did they have to meet at a club? She wasn't quite convinced.

Pablo had switched to drinking beer after Aldo dropped him off and he had been going to the bathroom every twenty minutes. Olga heard a knock at the front door. She was a little frightened at the sight of the two soldiers' khaki uniforms.

"Does Pablo live here?" one of them asked.

He was short and lean. He wore a helmet like the other man but carried no rifle.

"He's here." She said automatically shaking inside. What the heck did they want with Pablo?

"We need him, please."

She did not think to ask them to come in. She hastily went inside and passed the dinner table. She went behind the kitchen and knocked on a red narrow door.

"What?" Pablo said from inside.

"Soldiers are here looking for you," she whispered.

She began to cry.

"Soldiers?" Pablo said incredulously. He unbolted the door and zipped his pants.

"What do they want, Pablo?"

"I don't know. Let me see."

She briefly touched his face as he passed her but he did not stop. He wasn't really thinking. The alcohol had numbed his senses and he wasn't afraid. His father-in-law had risen from his chair and followed him. The soldiers addressed him first.

"Do you know Aldo?"

"Yes, I know him."

"He's at the Spanish Colony. He was in an accident. His jeep went into a ditch. We picked him up and took him to the clinic."

"Is he hurt bad?"

"I don't know. Better get over there and find out. We did our duty. Sorry. You'll find his jeep on the road to Santa Cruz. Make the arrangements to pick it up. Happy Christmas Eve."

The soldiers left without further explanation. Pablo saw them get inside an Army jeep and speed away. Pablo did not wait. He grabbed his black leather jacket and put it on.

"Can you drop me off at the clinic?" he said to Olga's father.

"Of course," the man said, "let's go."

He was a balding obese man of medium height with rugged face. He had lived in San Juan de Dios all his life and was a dental mechanic by trade. He and his wife had raised two daughters and had lived a peaceful life in the city. They drove his green Ford out of the plaza and onto the Central Highway and turned left into a wide avenue that led them to a large gray building. They drove back around the clinic and parked the car.

Both men climbed a wide stairway leading to the main entrance. They met a male nurse at a receiving booth and inquired if Aldo Ochoa had been admitted. The man, all dressed in white, looked at a chart. He told them to go check with the head nurse in surgery. She would have more information.

Pablo rushed through the empty hallways. He knew the place well and had been a member since he had married Olga. He went to the surgery section and spoke to the nurse. They were operating on Aldo right now, he would have to wait, she said. She could not tell him much about his condition except that he had received deep wounds to the face. She pointed to the row of empty seats. She asked him to wait and not to bring additional family members until Aldo was out of surgery when they would receive more instructions.

"Hell," Pablo said to his father-in-law, "what a way to spend Christmas."

"At least we know he is all right."

"We don't know that. They are not telling us anything. Listen, you should go back home. It's not fair to you and your family."

"I would not think of it, Pablo," he said. "We'll wait it out together."

It took over an hour for a man to exit the surgery room. Because he was dressed in white, Pablo assumed he was a doctor. The man went up to the nurse and asked if anyone had checked in.

"I'm here," Pablo said, interrupting them. "How is he?"

The doctor looked at him. "Are you family?"

"I'm his best friend, his brother."

The doctor looked the anxious man before him. He smelled the alcohol on his breath but thought it quite natural for this time of year and it had nothing to do with his patient. The man seemed genuinely concerned about Aldo, and, the doctor tried in simple terms to explain what must be done.

"He has severe gashes on the temples. He also has some deep cuts on his face. We have stitched most of them up, but we have a problem. He lost a lot of blood, and I am afraid that he is going to need a transfusion before we can finish. Do you know if anyone in his family has his blood type?"

Pablo listened attentively. Blood type. He wasn't quite prepared for this but he answered automatically.

"I'll give him my blood."

"Are you A positive?"

"I don't know. I could be."

"We can't do it this way. We'd have to test you. Anybody else in the family?"

"Yeah, I guess I could call several people."

"Well, listen," the doctor said, "this nurse can let you use a telephone. You can call his family and ask if anyone has blood type A positive. You understand? Do this right now, then come back here with the nurse, and we will draw some blood from you to test it. We have to do this right away."

The nurse took Pablo to a black telephone inside another room. Dulce's number was the only one that came to mind. Olga's parents did not have a telephone, and there was none in Rios. Aldo had made sure that his aunt and mother had a phone since the day it was technically possible. Pablo dialed and heard Dulce's pleasant voice at the other end.

"Dulce," he said, "it's Pablo. I'm at the Spanish Colony where Aldo has been admitted. He had an accident. We need to get someone here with blood type A positive. I am going to be tested right now to see if I have it, but do you know of anyone else that might have that blood type?"

She listened silently. She had lived through countless tragedies and could react rationally. The trouble was that it was her Aldo this time.

"The only one that can give him blood is me," she said. No one else in the family has A positive blood except me. I will be there in a minute. You wait for me at the entrance."

She hung up before he could answer. She ran next door and knocked on Leticia's door and told her that Aldo had been hurt and she needed to run to the clinic. She asked her to stay with Cecilia. Leticia saw her run and turn at the end of the block. Dulce suddenly realized she had brought no money. She went to the first orange car parked in the church's taxi stand and tapped the driver's arm.

"Spanish Colony," she said, "it's an emergency so go, fast."

The driver did not ask any questions. He raced through a short cut that only taxicab drivers knew. From the top of the stairway, Pablo saw the silver-haired woman leap out of the car.

"Pay that taxi, Pablo. Where do I go?"

"I am going with you, Pablo said." He motioned to his father-in-law to pay the fare. He and Dulce disappeared into the main corridor. The nurse took Dulce's name while another one went inside to check her records. As soon as they had confirmed her blood type, they led her inside surgery where she was placed on a bed next to Aldo and they proceeded to draw her blood. Dulce now began to realize what was happening and sobbed softly.

"Is he going to be all right?" she asked.

The doctor looked at her over the nurse's shoulder. He was busy sewing. The woman might be the patient's mother but he was not sure. She seemed too energetic, although signs of a breakdown were apparent.

"Thanks to you."

"What in the world happened?"

"Ah, we don't know yet. It's better that you don't talk right now while we do this, okay?"

He turned back to the table where he leaned over his patient and continued working.

It was mid-evening when Aldo was wheeled into a private room. He was asleep and an I V was hooked to his right arm. His face was completely bandaged. His eyes were puffy and swollen. He was unrecognizable. Around him were Amanda and Aleida who had arrived together, Blanco and Ana, Dulce, Pablo, Olga, and her parents. They had all been told by the nurse that Aldo was in serious condition due mainly to excessive bleeding and some blows he had apparently received on his upper body. His wounds would heal. There were no fractures and no evidence of internal bleeding but right now, his urine and bowel movements would have to be monitored. The nurse had given them instructions not to speak to him.

"What time does the milkman arrive?" Pablo said to Amanda.

"Oh, midnight," she said.

"It is now past eight. I think I should be going so I can take care of the milking tonight."

"No," she responded, "Alfredo is there. But can you please see about the jeep? Can you find out what happened?"

"Amanda," he said, "Aldo is my brother. His business is my business. The farm will run as if he was there."

He moved close to the bed and touched his friend's arm. They had been born in poverty and grown up together under miserable conditions. They had formed a strong bond and were closer than many blood brothers. Long ago, while they were kids, they had made a pact. Whatever each did the other would share it then they began living as if the pact was a commandment. They became business partners, friends, and brothers for life.

Pablo remembered that they had agreed to look at Mr. Pazos' cattle tomorrow. It was not something he was prepared to do alone and needed Aldo to deal with the old fox. He hesitated. What would Aldo say? What would he do? But he would have to go it alone. The venture would pay off in time. It was a calculated gamble, and he had never dreamed that he would have to execute it alone but fate had intervened.

"Make sure you're fine tomorrow, old friend," Pablo said, as if Aldo could hear him.

He said his goodbyes to every one in the room and left with Olga's father. The others would have a long night. Most of the women would probably stand watch in the room as was the custom among Cuban families at such times. He had much work ahead.

About three miles into the road to Santa Cruz, Pablo and Pedro saw the jeep in the ditch, facing in the opposite direction. They walked around it several times looking for signs of damage but saw none. Then Pablo went inside and saw Aldo's bloody shirt, which he found in the passenger seat. No blood stains anywhere, no broken glass. *Strange*, he thought. What was he supposed to do with the jeep anyway? He had no keys. He reached for the ignition but found none. He put his hand on the seat and felt the cold key ring with its two keys. He tried one in the ignition and it went in. He turned it, and the engine immediately roared to life.

"I'll be going from here," he said to Pedro. "I have to get to my place, and then to Aldo's farm. Take Olga with you. I'll come back tomorrow."

"You think he slid off the road?"

"I don't know," he said.

Pablo looked away from him and into the darkness, shaking his head. He turned the lights on.

"Aldo doesn't slide off roads."

CHAPTER SEVEN

THE FESTIVITIES OF THE NEW Year holiday were more elaborate than those in Christmas. In the city there were public dances. Some streets would be blocked off, with kiosks on the sidewalks that served food and drinks. Popular bands would play until dawn to the delight of the crowds. The more adventuresome would wake up in public places, not quite remembering how they got there. In the country, the peasants would celebrate at their parties, or *guateques*, as they called them, with the traditional roasting of a hog and the sound of their *décimas* to the beat of maracas. The festivities culminated with the arrival of the New Year at midnight when people embraced and wished each other a prosperous new year. Then the feast would go on.

The anticipation had grown during the week after Christmas. On New Year's Eve, the disturbances seemed to peak when the region of Santa Clara, located in the center of the island, fell to the rebels, implying that they would now control the eastern, more productive provinces. However, everyone knew that Batista's army had not really begun fighting. Many still did not dare side openly with the rebels, knowing that their skirmishes could vanish if Batista decided to strike a blow. But it seemed that with each passing day, the movement was gaining momentum. The rebels were noticed more often, even beyond the many roadblocks that tried futilely to contain them. It was now apparent that there were important forces propelling the rebel movement, forces that had, until now, been loyal to Batista.

Aldo returned to the country immediately upon his release from the clinic and told Pablo the true version of the events that had caused his injuries. Pablo convinced Amanda that Aldo was no longer safe in town. He was a marked man. Aldo had not recognized the sergeant who had kept him alive, but he understood that he had been saved by some lucky intervention. If he was ever stopped again, the corporal or Sergeant Valdez might remember him. Aldo was glad to leave the clinic early. He regretted being away from his children, but he knew it had to be. Besides, he felt more at home in the country. On the fourth day after Christmas, Amanda and Pablo drove him to the farm.

Alfredo was deeply shaken upon seeing Aldo, with his face mangled and eyes still closed from the brutal beating. He had learned the details from Pablo and was sure that it was a result of Aldo's involvement in Patricio's burial. He concluded that there was an informer in Rios, but not necessarily Tomas, who probably had told the government of what Aldo had done. Aldo's life was in danger, he thought. This had only been a warning.

At first, Aldo rested, sitting in bed to help bring down the swelling. He slept with his revolver underneath the mattress. Neighbors from Rios had come to inquire about his health and wished him a speedy recovery. Alfredo did not trust anyone and would, pleasantly but firmly, tell most visitors that no one was allowed to see him. Only Oscar and *el santero* were admitted. Amanda stayed with her husband during the day and tended to his wounds, but he would make her leave with Pablo as soon as evening set in. Aldo missed the children deeply and had not seen them since the day of the incident, but he would not have it any other way. Their safety could not be compromised. The question was, how long would the ordeal last. He could not stay away from town forever.

On New Year's Eve, Aldo sat across the table from Alfredo, having just seen Amanda and Dulce off with Pablo.

"Let's go to Rios tonight," Aldo said unexpectedly.

Alfredo looked aghast.

"Not even crazy. I would not stop in Rios now for any money in the world."

"Then I'm going alone."

"Aldo, are you crazy? It's too dangerous. How can you go to Rios after what happened?"

"It's New Year's Eve, Alfredo," Aldo said.

Alfredo shook his head in frustration. Aldo was just too daring.

"Is Pablo going?"

"Not that I know of."

Aldo's face was a mass of bruises. He had one big gash on each side of his temples, red and brown from the Mercurochrome and iodine. He had three long wounds on the right side of his face and one above his right eye that had been stitched because of their depth. His right eyelid was still half closed, and both eyes were ringed with black. As the swelling went down, he began to look as if he had been in a boxing match. His body was sore from the blows, and he still had difficulty raising his arms, but nothing was broken. He stood up and went to the kitchen to fetch some water. Alfredo made a move to follow him.

"I'll get it," Aldo said. "I feel much better. Freshen up if you want to come. I am going to gather some eggs for *el santero's* wife. I'll be ready in a few minutes."

"I don't like it," Alfredo said, again shaking his head. "Soldiers could be out on the road, Aldo."

"No soldiers are on this road, Alfredo. It's too peaceful here. The fighting is in Santa Clara and Oriente. Too much cattle here. They are afraid of scaring the cattle off, I suppose."

"Do you think the rebels will win, Aldo?"

Alfredo had been tormented all week by the thought of soldiers coming to the farm to finish Aldo off and do away with any witnesses who may be around. But he also worried about the bigger picture. What would happen if the rebels won?

"Anything can happen now, Alfredo," Aldo said. "I hear it's pretty tense tonight. I think we are in for either a long fight or a swift collapse of the government if Batista does not fight."

"I cannot believe the government will not fight, Aldo." "They really haven't until now. They are only picking on a few to make a show of force. But that could change."

Aldo reached into the bottom section of a wooden chest in the kitchen and unfolded a long paper bag. He took eggs from one of the drawers and placed them carefully inside the bag.

"I think Batista will fight now," Alfredo said confidently.

Aldo looked sympathetically at him. He had listened carefully to the news on the radio. He could read between the lines. The government had simply sought to ignore the rebels, believing them unimportant. Suddenly, the problem they created was out of control. Someone was now paying attention and decisions were being made. He could see that the government was readying for an offensive. The question was whether it would come. There seemed to be hesitation among the armed forces' upper echelons. Were they bribed? What then?

Aldo had also listened to the rebel station in the mountains during these past few nights. There was no hesitation from the rebel camp. The rebels were now pushing harder than ever. They were on the offensive, clearly looking to keep their momentum. A lot depended on the top people, Batista and his advisers.

"I'm ready to go," Aldo said to Alfredo, rolling up the bag.

Alfredo gazed at him and sighed. He could not let him go alone. "Let me put on some clean clothes."

"Yes, you might find your Juanita at the *guateque* tonight," Aldo said in jest.

He went with Alfredo into the yard and closed the door behind him. He unleashed Champ. It was a cool night, and the winter breeze felt good on his sore face. He had on a black Stetson, blue woolen shirt under a black leather jacket, blue jeans, and black cowboy boots. He felt happy going to Rios tonight.

The two men walked in the darkness of the road. All was quiet. As they approached the hamlet, the smell of roasted pork filled them, and the sound from the peasants' guitars surrounded them. They stopped at Oscar's home, passing dimly lit houses reflecting their shadows against the sparse trees. They passed a shallow ditch on the side of the dirt road and entered the garden of a thatched-roofed hut built from palm-tree bark. The door was closed, so they went around the side and stepped inside without warning.

As they entered, they found themselves among several men and women. Some were sitting on long benches, some were standing in the middle singing *décimas*. The room was lit by oil lamps. Some of the men recognized them immediately. The group stopped playing.

"Aldo, Aldo and Alfredo are here," one of the men hollered. He held a green bottle of beer in his hand and came forward to greet them.

Oscar appeared from the darkness and entered the room. He wore a white *guayabera* and a new white straw hat. He had been supervising the roasting of the hog. He shook Aldo's hand.

"I'm glad you came, Aldo. Let me get you and Alfredo a beer."

"I'll have one."

"Everything good at the farm, Alfredo?" Oscar said, reaching for his hand.

Throughout Aldo's ordeal, Oscar had been a loyal friend coming to the farm daily, inquiring if they needed help with the milking. Alfredo was glad that Aldo had chosen Oscar's house to visit tonight.

The other men also came to greet them. They all wore hats and had put on their best clothes tonight, simple but very clean.

Most of them had learned the details of Aldo's encounter with the Army. It had spread like wild fire in Rios. They were somewhat shy about socializing with him after what had happened but would never turn him away. One by one, each man sprung from his seat to shake Aldo's hand. The women hugged him and kissed him on the cheek.

"You are such a saint to come here tonight," a tall, dark woman with black bristles in her upper lip said.

"May God bless you."

"I want to give this package to *la viejita*," Aldo said. "Where is she?"

"She's inside. I'll bring her out," the woman said.

The musicians took their position at the center of the room. Two carried small guitars that were called *tres*, meaning the number three, a small version of the six-string guitar, much lighter in weight and smaller in body, capable of playing the same chords as a guitar, but in a higher tone. Another man was playing the *maracas* and another a set of *claves*. They began playing their instruments in unison, a slow tempo, rich in guitar chords. The man with the *claves* sung a verse that everyone knew, then, as he finished a line, he looked down for a moment as if in thought. He lifted his head and began singing a verse addressed to Aldo, which he would compose as he sang. This was the beautiful *décima* for which the peasants were so well known.

"And the *guateque* was lively. There were distinguished guests in attendance," he sang, "but there was something amiss, everyone knew. At that moment Aldo Ochoa entered the room and suddenly everyone realized what had been lacking."

The people sitting in the benches cheered as the singer finished this verse. Aldo sat with Alfredo on one of the benches. The singer went on with his story that he composed as he sang. Each line rhymed with the previous one. Then he turned his attention to Alfredo, calling him Aldo's loyal companion who would not leave his friend's side even on New Year's Eve.

The lady Aldo addressed as *viejita* came into the room. She wore a white dress with embroidered pockets. Her face was heavily powdered and her hair was combed in a short and slightly puffed style, with a comb on each side. She was small and thin.

"What have they done to you, my boy?"

Her pale blue eyes surveyed the wounds on his face. She became teary as she embraced him.

"I'm fine *viejita*," he said.

He returned her embrace, then pulled back and handed her the bag. "These are for you. Careful with them."

"Oh, thank you, my boy. May all the saints protect you."

Behind her came *el santero* with his crooked smile and yellow teeth. He, too, wore a white straw hat, that though not new, had been meticulously preserved. He took Aldo's hand in his.

"How are you feeling now?"

"I'm fine. I came to wait for the New Year."

"I'm glad you did. You are welcome here, always."

"How's Julia?"

"She's being taken in by the Arapientos. They are going to hire her as a maid, thanks to you and the saints, my boy."

"And the house?"

"Your old house is empty for now. Hopefully it will stay that way."

"He brought me eggs," the *viejita* said. "My sweet prince, you see? He doesn't forget."

"No, that he doesn't," he agreed looking at him, "and for that he'll be rewarded by all the saints. Pity on those who harmed him."

He poked his finger at him then reached for Aldo's shoulder, telling him to sit down. Aldo sat and drank his beer. He could sense the gaze of some of the others who had heard about the beating and visualized his injuries. But now that they saw him, they realized how ugly the episode must have been. This is what Patricio must have looked like. Death had almost knocked twice in Rios this year.

"I want to offer a toast to Aldo," the *santero* said, his voice rising over the singing of the men, "to the lucky man from Rios." He lifted a shot glass filled with rum and gulped it down. The others shouted back, "*Salud!*"

Then the *santero* took a step back and quickly jerked his right hand up and down, snapping his long fingers each time. "Let all the evil go, now!" he yelled. "Leave him alone now, I said!"

For a second, it seemed that he was talking to someone, and the musicians stopped playing. There was silence. But as he looked at the floor and shook his head, they all knew he had just performed an exorcism. "Let the party go on," he said, "let the party go on. The demons are gone!"

The musicians went on playing, and the men went on talking as if nothing had happened. Oscar came to Alfredo and asked him to join in and sing a *décima*. He stood beer in hand and went to the center of the room. The man with the *claves* moved aside to let him in. Alfredo looked down for a moment to concentrate and then sang in harmony with the others. They now let him sing alone, and he began composing. In his lyrics, he asked that his friend Aldo join him, addressing him as the great man from Rios. The men cheered. Aldo walked by Alfredo beer in hand. He strained to give it his best effort, and he sang to all the people in the room and how he loved being with them. The men did not let him finish the line and cheered loudly. Then others joined the band, which by now was becoming quite large.

It was past 10:00 P.M. when Pablo peered in. He was standing behind one of the porch's corner posts, hiding his body like a child would do. It was Alfredo who first noticed him and quickly pointed him out to Aldo. At that moment, someone else noticed him.

"Pablo is here," the man said.

Pablo laughed and walked forward.

"Yes, I'm here. I came to see my friends. Any drinks left for me? Any pork yet?"

"Now," one of the men said, "a peasant like you ought to know that pork is not served until midnight. Drinks, we got plenty."

Pablo laughed and began shaking people's hands. Someone handed him a bottle of beer.

"Here's to the New Year," he said lifting his bottle. "To my friend Aldo."

Immediately the musicians turned their attention to Pablo and they dedicated him a *décima*. They sang that Aldo had not been quite whole missing his best friend, but that now he was, having Alfredo and Pablo around him. He was better protected than the president of the country. Pablo took Aldo's left arm, pulling him aside.

"How did you know I was here?" Aldo said.

"Where else would you be?"

"Did you bring Olga?"

"No, she's at her father's. The roads are very bad. Soldiers everywhere. I am going to have her stay in town for a few more days."

"Listen," he added, "Aleida is in mourning. Her boyfriend, Roberto, was killed last night in an ambush."

"Oh," Aldo said. He remembered the stout young man from Christmas Eve night and was saddened. He would never know that he owed Roberto his life.

"How did it happen?"

"They said the rebels ambushed his truck around Cubitas. Poor Aleida. His family gave her the news this afternoon. I stopped at

Guillermo's to see Amanda and the children, and Aleida was at the funeral parlor. Amanda wants me to tell you that she is going there tonight with Guillermo. Ana will stay with the children."

"It's really too bad. After having her wedding set. It's a hard blow."

"That tells you how serious the situation is, Aldo. You should not be out on the road late. There could be soldiers anywhere."

"I'm waiting for the New Year here, Pablo. Besides, have you seen any movement of troops around here? I bet not."

"Still. It's too unpredictable, Aldo. With everything that's happened, you have to keep a low profile."

"And I have, Pablo. Anyway, thanks for letting me know. Go back to town. Stay with Olga tonight."

"I'm not leaving you. I'm waiting for the New Year here too."

It was this unwavering loyalty that had kept them together throughout their lives. It was a beautiful friendship born in Rios and now, after being put to the test one more time, it had come to full fruition. Aldo smiled at him.

"Come on, we're missing the party."

"It's going to be a good year," Pablo said as he followed his friend. "You will see, Aldo. We are going to sell all that damned cattle and make a bundle. We'll never have to milk another cow again."

Aldo said nothing but tapped his friend's back. Pablo had done well. He was proud of him. He had stood up to Mr. Pazos and made the deal, not on Mr. Pazos's terms but on their own. Pablo had gone to see the lot the day after Aldo's beating. Mr. Pazos had been surprised at Aldo's absence. At first, he suspected Pablo was undermining Aldo. He had thought Pablo to be that kind of a guy. But then, as they spoke, he became convinced that the two friends were still together. There was no other buyer. So he had sold Pablo the lot for twenty five pesos a head, believing it was too risky not to sell considering the present political situation. He thought these boys were fools for buying cattle during these turbulent times. But what did he care? The lot was now at the Arapientos' farm where they had been transported under Pablo's watchful eye. The two friends now had over one hundred heads of cattle. If their gamble worked and prices held out, they stood to make a good profit.

Some couples were now dancing the slow, angled steps of the *danzón*, the most popular dance among the peasants.

"Find yourself a partner, or I'll get the broom," Alfredo hollered at them.

He was dancing with one of the old women, and the alcohol had now made him uninhibited.

"I'm too ugly for anyone to dance with me," Aldo said.

"Who says?"

The *viejita* took his hand and led him near the other couples. The two danced once, Aldo taunting her to shake her hips while she took turns with her head up. Then he handed her to Pablo and he went outside where the hog was being roasted.

Roasted pork was a popular dish with the peasants. The hog was killed and its skin peeled off with boiling water. The insides were removed and the body cleaned. A wooden rod was then run from the hide of the animal and through its mouth. Its legs and body were either wired or tied to the rod with *yagua* strips. A shallow egg shaped opening, big enough to accommodate the whole animal, was dug. One short forked pole was placed at the end of each opening. Wood and charcoal were thrown on the bottom and a fire lit. Then the rod and hog were placed on the forked poles. In order to protect the meat from inclement weather and to make the fire hotter, the peasants used zinc tiles folded like a triangle, placing them over the opening. Someone would turn the rod over the forked poles and begin the roasting that took anywhere from three to five hours depending on the size of the animal, the weather, and the intensity of the fire. It was a long process, but while it lasted, the men would gather around the spot telling tales, drinking, and singing. In an atmosphere filled with excitement and anticipation over the main course of a meal that symbolized freedom and happiness.

Aldo peered inside the zinc covers near the head of the animal. A small fire was burning inside. The head looked yellowish but not dark, indicating that the meat was still not done. Someone had placed an oil lamp without its glass cover on top of a piñon tree at the boundary line of Oscar's property. The light it emitted made the faces of the men recognizable.

"Let me see your wire," Aldo said to Oscar.

He gripped a three-foot-long wire that Oscar was holding and poked the center of the pig a few times while it turned, and making a hissing sound as it hit.

"We still got some grease," Oscar said.

"Yeah, how long would you say?"

"Forty five minutes to an hour."

Oscar was known as a wizard of the fine art of hog roasting. His accurate predictions of cooking time had made him a virtuoso in Rios where many others could also claim a similar skill. But his estimates always proved right over any other man.

"I'd say the same," the man turning the rod at the other end said.

It was Rodolfo, the man who had come to see Aldo with Oscar the day of the shooting. He was sitting on a short tree stump, and his face reflected the flames of the fire. He had drunk quite a bit. A few older men sat behind him in wooden chairs while the younger ones leaned over them. Aldo handed Oscar the wire. One of the men stood between Aldo and Oscar, beer in hand.

"So, Aldo, how did it happen?" He asked.

"Ah," he said casually, "it was just an argument that got out of hand. Tempers flared. That's all."

"They were *casquitos*, right?"

Aldo and Oscar exchanged glances. Oscar was uncomfortable and waited to see how Aldo would handle the matter.

"Either that or regular Army. I don't know. It doesn't matter."

"Did you do anything to deserve that?"

"I wouldn't say so. I think they did not appreciate my yelling at them after they stopped me."

"Let's not discuss it anymore," Oscar said, cutting them short, "there might be others listening."

He looked at Aldo. He wanted no part of any gossip that might bring another tragedy. He did not trust the night and was astonished at Aldo's nonchalance about the subject. Was Aldo not afraid to lose his life? Pablo approached them and also grabbed the wire from Oscar, poking the hog several times.

"What do you say, master?" Pablo asked Oscar.

"One hour."

"Better get it done. I am hungry."

"You will eat. Have another beer."

"No. I want to talk to my friend, Aldo Ochoa."

"I saw your lot being brought in at the Arapientos," said one of the older men, "they looked like healthy animals. They'll be twice their size in three months."

"And then you'll sell," the first man who had been questioning Aldo said.

"I remember years ago," began the older man, "when Aldo's father and I used to sell our animals to the Arapientos. We had to because we could not afford to take them to the market. He paid us peanuts. Now his son rents land from the Arapientos children for his own cattle."

"Be careful on how you trade with the devil," Rodolfo observed, "those queers."

"Hushhh," another man said. "Don't bite the hand that feeds you."

"Like hell," he answered. "They're scum and they'll always be scum."

"I can tell you many stories about the Arapientos and how they got their money," added the old man.

"We all know how they got their money," Rodolfo said.

The old man ignored Rodolfo's comment. "Old Arapientos was a man who respected no one, stopped at nothing. He would go into the deep country with his hired hands at night and find cattle in wooded areas. This was cattle that belonged to people who rented land from landholders to feed their cattle, just as you and Pablo are doing right now. Imagine that! If the cattle was not branded, he would keep it. If it was branded, he would bring it right into the slaughter house to sell. That's how he started."

"And he never got caught," Rodolfo said. "Let's you or me try to do that."

"It was many years ago," the old man said.

"It's the same now," Rodolfo added.

"Your father always said that Arapientos had built his empire on mud. Sooner or later it would fall," the old man said.

"It remains to be seen," Rodolfo said.

"You remember when we used to ask Aldo's father to go into town with us?" one of the other old men asked.

"Yes, we were a wild bunch," the first man said, "but Aldo's father never left the house at night. When we went into town, we would always end up being run out anyway. We would tie our horses at the outskirts of town and walk to the carnivals. 'There go the peasants,' they would say. But no one would bother us. They were afraid of us."

"One day," began the other man, "we rode our horses into town during the carnivals in June. We rode as far as the Caridad Plaza, right into the heart of the carnival. We drank quite heavily and were wasted on our way back. Near Nadales, a shirtless man ran out from a shack. I said to myself, 'boy, I'm wasted but this sucker is more wasted than me' so I said to my friend, Pancho, 'let's get that sucker,' and he said, 'let's get him.' We swung our lassos and went after him. He ran so fast that we couldn't catch him. So we came back and lassoed his shack from our horses. We pulled and the whole thing came down."

"That was a rotten thing to do," one of the younger men said.

"One of the guys told my father, God rest his soul, and the next day, he made me and Pancho go back into town with a wagon full of palm tree bark and *yaguas* and we had to rebuild the man's hut. How do you like that?"

"And what did the man say?" Pablo asked.

"He was shocked to see us. He just took what we gave him, and we apologized. That was my father for you."

"I remember my father speaking about that," Aldo said.

"You guys didn't get into trouble?" Pablo asked.

"No. The rural guard would come around here from Christmas to St. John's day but they never even heard of that because we replaced the man's hut right away."

"You were lucky," Pablo said.

"Yes," the man agreed, "we couldn't get away with something like that now."

"Many times," the other older man said, "we would ride into town on a Sunday just to visit the whorehouses then we would end up getting in trouble if we drank because we would break something. But other than that, there was hardly ever trouble."

"We still visit the whorehouses today," Rodolfo said. "I might even visit them tomorrow."

"Hussh," the old man said, "here comes a woman."

You could not see her features, but when she spoke everyone recognized her. She was Oscar's wife.

"How much longer," she asked, "the salad is ready and it's past eleven."

Oscar examined the hog.

"You can set up," he said, "we'll be ready in a few minutes."

She went to the back porch and called some of the other women from the dance floor to help her. They quickly busied themselves by clearing the table of bottles and plates. Oscar's wife called out that the table was ready and that they should bring the *yagua*. They laid it on the table, and the women pressed it down to flatten the edges.

A few minutes later, Oscar said the hog was ready. He removed the hot zinc tiles from the top with a wooden stick. The fire flared up again. Then one of the men put on some gloves and grabbed the front of the rod.

"Stop turning, Rodolfo," Oscar said. "Pablo, take that end."

Rodolfo stepped back and Pablo and the other man lifted the rod and carried it inside. They placed the hog over the *yagua*. As they put it down, Oscar moved in between them and cut off the strings around the legs, allowing Pablo to pull back the rod until it was free.

Oscar went to work. He cut the skin, exposing the steaming hot brown meat inside. The room was filled with the rich aroma of seasoned pork meat. He had kept the fire low but steady, making sure that the deepest sections were cooked but the surface not burned. As he cut away, the animal turned into small pieces of meat with which the women filled the trays. Oscar handed Aldo a large piece of skin.

It was neither hard nor soft but it crunched as he bit into it. Aldo broke it with his teeth and gave a portion to Pablo.

"Hey, there is lots of it here," Oscar said.

"Let the music play," Pablo yelled.

He had drunk moderately but on an empty stomach, the alcohol had quickly affected him. He swayed his hips to the soft *décimas* that the band was playing. Aldo looked around for Alfredo. He was standing in the dark with the musicians, playing a guitar and singing. Aldo could not see his face but knew from his voice that he was happy.

"Let's get that pork on the table now," Pablo said happily.

"It'll get there faster if you lend a hand," Oscar joked.

"Not tonight, you do what you do best. I do what I do when I'm happy. Can we dance, Yolanda?"

She was a short dark woman with curly black hair and a lean face. She had come out onto the porch to help the other women carry the trays inside.

"I am busy, don't you see?"

"You'll be busy tomorrow too, come on."

He grabbed her wrist and led her to the end of the room near two other couples. She let herself be led onto the floor and then followed him. He was slow from the drinking but could still make a go of it. Aldo faced the dancers and watched Pablo in silence. If only Olga could see him.

The women emptied the pork slices into the trays as Oscar cut them. Then Aldo and Oscar moved the table to the center of the room.

"Bring the chairs near the table," Oscar said to the men. "Let's go. The food is coming."

The table now became a formal family dinner affair. There were no fancy tablecloth and candles, only the rustic wood planks, dark from years of use. Two women placed the plates and silverware in front of each chair. Others brought trays filled with pork, white rice, and *yucas* and placed them in the center of the table. Elena carried a large salad plate filled with avocado and pineapple, and a vinegar-

and-oil dressing sprinkled with sugar. There were also stacks of *casabe*, the indigenous bread that the peasants considered a delicacy.

Oscar was at the head of the table that sat only six and everyone else took their places on the benches. Elena and another woman moved about, filling everyone's plate with rice, pork, chunks of *yuca*, and salad. The ribs were usually a favorite but the soft inner meat with skin on top could be a substitute. Elena handed Aldo a full plate. It had been days since he had eaten a full meal. He had been on antibiotics and craved a good meal. Pablo sat next to him and tried to clean his plate but the beer had made his stomach queasy and he was forced to go to the outhouse to vomit. He dipped his hands in a basin then sat quietly next to Aldo again, face red and eyes watery.

As everyone finished the main course, the *viejita* brought in small cups of espresso. Some were chipped and others came without saucers. She poured the coffee and told them the sugar had been added. She also brought wet citrus shells with cream cheese on small plates. The musicians began to take up their instruments again and went on playing. It was almost midnight.

"May the New Year bring health and fortune to everyone," Oscar said.

"Yes," one of the singers said, "and let there be peace."

The musicians went on with their *décimas* singing to the memory of Patricio, treating his death as a legend that no one could quite explain. Then the lead singer added a verse at the end, which everyone knew because it referred to the death of a patriot of the 1868 war against the Spaniards. The singer, quite astutely, wanted to compare Patricio to a hero, something everyone in the room felt but dared not acknowledge.

"'And his majestic body they burned in Camaguey because the dead scared the king's soldiers,'" the man sang.

Aldo thought it quite touching and appropriate that Patricio should be remembered this way. He thought quietly for a moment then raised his eyes to meet Alfredo's concerned gaze.

"We have to go," Aldo said, "the milkman will be home any minute."

"It's only a few more minutes until twelve," Oscar said. "Stay."

"No, thank you," Aldo said as he rose. "You know our milkman. He would be terrified if he gets there and finds no one. Let Alfredo stay a little longer if he wants to."

"No, I'm leaving too."

"Pablo, then you stay."

"No, I'm coming to help you, friend. You are not milking any cows."

"Then let's go."

Aldo went to the table, shook everyone's hand, and kissed the women. It had been a good party. He hoped that he would always come back, that many years would pass and he would be still be coming but he was not sure.

The musicians began to sing them farewell and mentioned their names in their *décimas* and how much they would miss their presence. Their songs pursued them until they reached the jeep.

"Get in," Pablo said, "we'll get those damned cows done in no time."

"You are going to drive like that?" Alfredo said.

"Right now I'm safer than your boss. I don't have any black eyes, and I can see."

He turned the jeep around, leaving the larger part of the village behind where the poorest peasants lived and where Aldo and Pablo had grown. They both loved the place. It was their home.

Pablo reached the paved highway and turned left. There was no sound on the road, but as they passed the gate, they heard the barking of the dog, telling them that their arrival had been noticed. Pablo parked the jeep close to the fence then went immediately toward the outhouse again. Alfredo and Aldo got ready for the milking.

"No milkman yet," Alfredo said with concern.

Aldo looked at his watch and saw the time glowing in the dark.

"It's twelve now, Alfredo, happy New Year."

"To you also, Aldo."

"Get inside, old friend," Pablo said after coming back. "I'm doing the milking tonight."

"You have drunk too much, Pablo. Get some sleep. Alfredo and I will do it."

"No, no, no. I'm doing the milking."

"Well, you can milk if you want to but you are not keeping me from doing my share. Maybe it's not a bad idea after all. The three of us will be done faster than two, right Alfredo?"

They heard the soft rattle of the milkman's buggy who announced that it was now 1959, a new year. He moved his night lamp close to Aldo's face to survey his wounds.

"It looks like it's getting better," he said, "but you are going to get an infection out here."

"I don't touch the face," Aldo said dismissively. "Let's go, come on."

As he unhitched the horse, the milkman told them about the situation in town and how bleak the news were. The rebels were taking positions, and an attack was imminent. He didn't know if he could come tomorrow. There was talk of a strike. The roads could be closed and the situation was scary.

Aldo and Pablo started to sing, which irritated the milkman because he could not be heard. Pablo had to make a supreme effort to go on. He was very tired and only his devotion to his friend kept him awake. He had left Olga with her family on New Year's Eve night just to keep Aldo company. She understood how much it meant to him, and she had accepted it without hesitation. Now he felt guilty that he had drunk so much when he was supposed to guard Aldo.

Before they were done milking, Aldo told Pablo to go in the house and get some sleep.

"Go," he said. "We're almost done."

Pablo ignored him.

"Yes, it's all right. Just go on."

"If he wants to milk, let him milk," the milkman hollered. "He can take over my job if he wants to. Take the wagon into town. I'll drive the jeep."

Aldo milked the last cow and again told Pablo to leave. Pablo went to the milkman's cart and helped him hitch the horse while Aldo and Alfredo packed their milking gear and hung it.

"You take care in town, old friend," Aldo said to the milkman, tapping his shoulder as he passed him. "Happy New Year."

"Yes, let's hope this one won't be another miserable one around the fucking cows."

"Keep the faith, you never know." Aldo asked Alfredo to see him off as he walked towards the house.

Once inside, Aldo went into the living room and turned on the radio. They were welcoming New Year's Day and the events happening around the nation today. No war news. He switched the dial to Clock Radio, a national station that provided headlines by the hour. He heard the familiar tic tac, simulating a clock, but no news about the rebels. He felt tired and disappointed that nothing new had happened. He missed his children and his figurine. Tomorrow, roadblock or not, he would go into town to see his family.

"Sleep in the children's room," he said to Pablo. "I'm going to catch some sleep myself."

"Happy New Year, Aldo. It will be a good one. All this will pass."

"It will."

Aldo went to his bedroom and sat on the bed. It was pitch dark so he lit the oil lamp and adjusted the flame. He liked to sleep with a dim light on. Amanda hated it so he only did it when she was away. He undressed, keeping only his underwear, t-shirt and socks on and got under the blanket. He lay still for a long time, listening to the crickets outside and thinking about nothing in particular, his mind just floating, and then he was asleep.

He awoke when the first beacons of dawn began to filter through the cracks of the room. The herd had to be rounded and separated from their calves. He trusted Alfredo but wasn't sure he would rise after all the drinking last night. He dressed, gargled and went outside. It was foggy and cold. As he entered the cattle house, he heard a noise in Alfredo's room and knew he was up. Alfredo came out, fully dressed.

"You can go back to sleep," Alfredo said. "I'll round up the cattle."

"I'm already up. Let's do it."

"How's Pablo? Still sleeping?"

"I haven's heard him all night."

Alfredo did most of the work. Aldo saw him lead the cattle into the back trail and out into the pasture and the calves into another section. Aldo went back to the house, laid back in bed, and feel asleep again until after 9:00. There was a tap on the bars of his window.

"Aldo, Aldo! Wake up, wake up!"

Aldo opened his eyes without moving, recognizing Alfredo's voice.

"I'm coming," he said, "go through the back."

As he opened the door to the dining room he saw the excitement in Alfredo's dark face. His eyes sparkled. Something was happening.

"Aldo, there are many cars on the road cruising by at high speed, all full of people. I heard what sounded like shots. And then more cars, people waiving. Something's happened!"

"Any Army trucks?"

"Just regular trucks with people in the back. Come look, some are still going by."

They went outside and around the house. They now could hear the horns of cars on the road. They saw three cars drive by fast. They could see the occupants' hands waiving out of the windows and could hear their yells in the distance. Aldo didn't have to guess, something dramatic had happened for people to drive down to Rios on New Year's Day. The Army would have never allowed it.

"Let's go inside and listen to the radio."

They went back to the house and sat in the living room. Immediately, Clock Radio came alive, but it was too dull. Aldo switched to one of the more popular stations. Band music was playing. The excited voice of a commentator was describing the situation in Havana as "frenetic." People had gone out into the streets. Everything was paralyzed. Batista had fled during the night. An interim president was going to take over, but the rebels were calling for an immediate strike, refusing to recognize the new government. There was only one government, the commentator said, and that was one chosen by the people. But Batista was gone. The rebels had won.

"So that's it." Aldo looked at Alfredo. "Batista is finished."

"Oh, my God, Aldo. What now? What happens now?"

"I don't know for sure. But I guess I can go into town and see my family."

"Aldo, don't do that just yet. Maybe it's not quite over."

"It's over, Alfredo. The people want it to be over. You can't stop a whole country from wanting something. That's just it. That's why the rebels have won the war practically without firing a shot. Batista recognized it. He knew the war was lost, and he fled to save his skin."

"I can't believe it. I can't believe Batista would do that."

"It was coming, Alfredo. It was either that or total war. In a way, we have been saved from a big massacre. Let's see if this provisional government can restore order now."

"What's the matter, Aldo," Pablo asked from his room.

His voice, groggy and unsteady, filtered in through the curtains and over the voice on the radio.

"Pablo! Pablo!" Alfredo said excitedly, "Get up! Batista left!"

Slowly, Pablo got up. He was still light headed from last night. As he put on his clothes, he thought about what he had just heard. It was spectacular news, and he tried to recall the moment to make sure he had not dreamed it or had not been in jest. *What a way to begin the New Year*, he thought. He went to the living room and sat on the sofa, his hair still uncombed. The radio commentator kept describing the scenes in Havana. Mobs ran the streets in celebration. Shops closed.

"What's happened?" he said calmly.

"It looks like Batista left during the night," Aldo said. "We start the new year with a new government."

"Oh, my God. So who is in power now?"

"I don't think anyone knows."

"I can't believe the Army won't fight back," Alfredo said.

"If the leader goes, the generals are not going to fight, Alfredo," Pablo replied. "They let this thing get too far. If the people go out into the streets, then it's over. The Army can't fight the whole country."

Aldo went in the kitchen and built a fire. He heated up water to make coffee, then filled a pan with milk. He could hear the radio as he worked. He listened carefully to the details. Clearly, there had not been a take-over by the rebels. Rather, it was a desertion of power by the man who, for seven years, had ruled the island. The rebels had not taken the capital or put on a major struggle. In fact, it had been quite peaceful in this region. But things had been tense lately and Batista had apparently been boxed in. Either he fought, or he was dead. He had chosen to do as many other leaders before him had done: leave the country and save his skin. Probably emptied his bank accounts too. Aldo was no fan of Batista. He was no fan of any government. He was a working man. But how could a trusted leader run away during his people's darkest moment? In a way, he felt sympathy for the rebels who had stuck to their guns. The only trouble was, he did not know them and was not sure what they would do. Most people did not either. In that respect, he was not sure what the crowds were chanting about. They were welcoming something about which they knew nothing.

"Come and eat some breakfast," he said to Alfredo and Pablo. "We have all day to hear news, I'm sure."

He brought them some country crackers and milk and coffee in a cup. They all listened attentively to the voice on the radio.

"So the rebels do not recognize the new government," Pablo said. "How do you like that?"

"What happens now?" Alfredo inquired.

"I don't know. What do you make of it, Aldo?"

"Do you blame the rebels, though? If you fight you would want your prize after the victory. Of course the rebels don't want the provisional government. Why should they? They *are* the government. They won."

"The rebels are not associated with the provisional government."

"I think the rebels have one voice, and that is Fidel Castro. The people support him and not this provisional government, which is probably a left-over from Batista anyway. The people are going to listen to the rebels and the provisional government will go to pieces."

"This could lead to war."

"Or chaos."

"Someone has to gain control."

They kept listening to the radio until about 11:00. Aldo changed his clothes and got ready to go into town with Pablo. Pablo and Alfredo tried to convince him it was not yet prudent but he had made up his mind. The roadblocks must be gone, he told them, how else had all these people gotten here? He desperately wanted to see his children. He was leaving.

Alfredo saw them to the jeep. Aldo told him to take the day off and spend it in Rios if he wanted. It was New Year's Day, he said, and he might as well make the best of it.

As Aldo and Pablo drove to town, they saw scenes that would have been unimaginable the one day before. They could not recall ever seeing such hysteria among the people, not even during carnival season. Were they really sympathizers, or opportunists out for a good time? Men and women carried banners, and cars bore signs painted on the windshields. People stood in the back of trucks waiving red and black flags with the insignia of the movement and yelling victory. As they neared Nadales, Pablo slowed down. He expected to see the familiar military convoy of a truck and jeep at the side of the road, with soldiers waiving at them to stop but they were gone. A small crowd had gathered at the grocery store that served as the local bus stop, the last one in town on the road to Vertientes. The crowd cheered as they saw the jeep.

Pablo pulled up in front of the store where he would not block the buses, if any were running.

"Let's have a soda pop and see what's happening."

They got out of the jeep and walked through the crowd. A man stood in their path and began yelling, "Batista is gone! Batista is gone! The dictatorship is over. Long live Castro!" The man stood before them as if to block their way. He was short and fat, and his eyes gleamed with enthusiasm. Aldo and Pablo could smell the alcohol on his breath. The crowd echoed his chants as he spoke.

"Long live Castro! Long live Castro!"

For a moment, Aldo and Pablo felt claustrophobic. With the crowd circling them, they had no where to go. Then Pablo pushed him gently aside and moved past him with Aldo behind him.

"We just want to have drink, friend. That's all."

"Aren't you happy that Batista fell, eh? Or is it that you are Batista's sympathizers?"

"We're not anybody's sympathizers, friend. We're working people."

"Well, maybe you'll have to do us all a favor because we want to go to the Caridad Plaza, and we need your jeep."

The man kept yelling as if Pablo was a block away. He wanted to impress the crowd. Then he looked at Aldo. "And what happened to you? What happened to your face? Did one of Batista's *casquitos* get you, ah?"

"Maybe," Aldo replied.

He realized they had made a mistake in stopping here. The crowd was all around them, and the wrong move could mean a lynching. He and Pablo acted calmly. They moved by the counter and leaned over to ask the attendant for a refreshment, but the man behind them would not leave them alone.

"Tell me, tell me. What happened, ah?"

"Friend, leave him alone." Pablo said. "It's all right to have your fun, but that's enough, okay?"

"And who are you, ah? Are you his guardian? What did he do? Is he a *casquito* maybe, ah?"

"Hey, shut up," Aldo said. "Go and have your fun outside."

"Leave now," the storekeeper said from behind the counter. "You are looking for trouble."

"What? Are you going to keep me out of the store? Cuba is free now. I can be wherever I want to."

"Calm down," the storekeeper said. "Everyone is having fun, and you're spoiling it. Go outside. Do what you want, but do it outside."

"I want to know who did that to his face. Tell me, tell me." He got closer to Aldo, pointing his index finger at him. A truck stopped in front of the store, and the crowd immediately went outside to cheer the new arrivals. Two men remained, curious to see what the short man would do. Aldo saw the man was not going away. He was ready to tackle him for his insolence, but Pablo went first. He reached for the man with his open right hand as he came closer to Aldo, poking his finger at his chest. Pablo grabbed his collar and lifted him off the ground. The man flopped his arms, trying to get loose.

"I told you to leave him alone. What is the matter with you?"

"Leave him, Pablo," the storekeeper said.

He was about six four, with a lean body and although he looked well over fifty his stomach was flat. He had long arms and huge hands. He had run this landmark establishment in a tough neighborhood for years, witnessing many a brawl and knew just how to handle troublemakers. He dealt with all kinds of people who hung around the store to take the bus. He didn't mind waiting on them, but God pity anyone who dared challenge him. He knew Aldo and Pablo as well as the others in the crowd. They were boys that he had seen grow up over the years.

"Let him go," he said, waiving the four forefingers of his right hand.

Pablo loosened the man's collar. As he did, the short man anchored his feet then unexpectedly charged towards Pablo. But no sooner had he moved than the storekeeper stopped him cold, his long fingers spread flat against his chest.

"Now you're going home," the storekeeper said.

"I'm not going anywhere," the man said bitterly. "You don't tell me what to do."

"You want to bet? You choose how you want to leave, with teeth or without them. Now."

"I'm not going."

The storekeeper pushed him back with his open hand, then briskly and without warning, he took his hand away from him, placed it on the counter and swung himself. The next second he was standing before the man, towering above his head. The man looked up at him in surprise and blinked. Then he quickly turned and ran out of the store without a word. The storekeeper went back behind the counter.

"Happy New Year, Enrique," Aldo said.

"Enrique, much health to you," Pablo added.

"To you too boys," he replied. "What are you having?"

"Let me have a pineapple juice," Aldo said.

"A Pepsi for me," Pablo called.

The storekeeper reached into the store cooler, an old Westinghouse commercial model with four doors. He took out a bottle, then opened another door and took out another. He pried them open with an opener underneath the counter and threw the caps into a litter box.

"I won't ask what happened to you because I already know from talking with Pablo," Enrique said to Aldo. "It's too bad. I'm sorry."

"Thank you."

"Are you taking care of yourself?"

"Yes, I'm fine. I'm going to see my children now. I haven't seen them for a week."

"Good that you are seeing them. Be careful though. There's too much happening in the streets today. It's wild."

"When did it start?" Pablo asked.

"I woke up at about 5:00 A.M. from shots being fired in the air. Then cars started driving by with people yelling. I thought may be the noise was because of the New Year, so I started making coffee. I didn't think to turn the radio on until after some neighbors came in and knocked on my window. They said, 'Enrique, wake up, Batista fell.' I said, 'What?' I was hesitant because of the road blocks in front of the store lately, thinking maybe I was being set up or something. But they kept on knocking and wouldn't go away. Then my wife Yiya woke up with all the commotion and couldn't go back to sleep. So I went and opened the door for them. Before I knew it, there were twenty people in here, and it wasn't even 6:00 A.M. I still didn't believe it and was apprehensive, checking to see if there were any guards outside. Someone said: 'Turn the radio on, Enrique, you'll hear it yourself.' That's when I listened to the radio and heard it."

"What was it like around here yesterday?" Pablo asked.

"Well, you could tell that things weren't normal. But they haven't been for a while now. The road block has been erected out front for over one week until yesterday. They had been checking every car coming or leaving town. Sometimes they would make the passengers get out and search them. They searched the women's purses. They even stopped the buses going into Vertientes and making visual searches. It's been tough. But yesterday they kind of slowed down. I noticed it and wondered why. There was a roadblock in front of the store yesterday up until about mid-day. Then they left, and that was the last khaki uniform I saw. I don't know who'll be next. I guess we'll find out soon. I just hope I won't see anymore guards in front of the store, that's all."

He casually picked a small cotton rag and began wiping the counter in quick strokes over the smooth surface. He was not into politics. He enjoyed tending to the store and the public but resented uniformed men hanging around. Next to the cooler behind him was a narrow door, leading to his apartment. It opened, and a painfully thin woman appeared. She looked at him without noticing any of the patrons sitting by the counter.

"Enrique, can you come in for a minute?"

He placed the rag on the door handle and followed her inside, closing the door behind him. Moments later he reappeared again.

"How is she doing?" said Aldo.

"Ah, you know, same," he said shrugging, "the doctor gives her pills and more pills, but most of the time she is in so much pain that it doesn't matter what she takes. That's why I let her sleep when she can. Once she is up, all she does is suffer."

"Poor lady," Pablo said. "Well, I hope she gets better."

"God may hear you, boy. But she is not going to get better. I do not think she has too much time left," he said quietly.

His wife had been battling bone cancer for years, but in the past few months the disease had progressed. All that was left of her was a thin body that seemed to shrink away by the hour. She was often incoherent and would forget who she was. Sometimes she needed him to help her with the simplest of tasks. She was only a shadow of the woman she once was. Aldo and Pablo were silent and drank their soda pops.

"Well, we have to go," Aldo said. "It was nice seeing you, Enrique. Have a happy New Year."

"Happy New Year," Pablo repeated.

He came to them and shook their hands.

"You boys be careful in town today. Stay with your families. It's no good to be outside at times like these."

They went outside while the radio kept announcing the details of the strike being called by the rebels' leader, Fidel Castro, from the mountains.

"And Dr. Castro is calling for a total strike and does not recognize the provisional government...."

As Pablo and Aldo got into the jeep, several men from the crowd outside came towards them asking them to carry banners into town. Pablo was a little hesitant but told them he would take two of their group and drop them off in town. They couldn't carry any banners for them because they had work to do. Neither had any desire to cheer about an outcome which effects they did not yet fully understand. Better wait and see.

Two young boys that looked about seventeen climbed in the back of the jeep. They each held a red and black flag bearing the number twenty six and waived them enthusiastically as soon as they hopped in. Pablo drove onto the Central Highway, passing the cemetery. He went slowly into the center of town. A small crowd was gathered at the park and seemed to be having a meeting. A young man dressed in green fatigues and a red and black arm band stood on a bench addressing the crowd. Aldo and Pablo looked curiously at him. If this was militia, it would be the first rebel they had seen. They pulled next to the curb to let their passengers out. Other men on the sidewalk ran to the jeep screaming, "long live the 26th of July Movement!" They came near the driver's door, jumping frantically. They were students who, two days before, had been immersed in their finals. Now they expressed their content at Batista's departure and joined the wave of excitement that was gaining momentum by the second. There was no going back to the old regime, Aldo thought. The people themselves had let out a genie from a bottle. The rebels' biggest victory had been won by doing simply nothing. It was the people and their passion who had inflicted a mortal blow to the old government. There was no stopping them.

Pablo and Aldo waved at the group as they pulled out. They drove into the San Juan de Dios Plaza towards Olga's parents' house. Everywhere, they saw on the sidewalks waiving flags. Some gathered in corners and cheered while cars passed by. There was an air of genuine happiness in the air, something drastically different from the day before reflected in the people's smiling faces.

As they turned into the plaza, the noise dissipated. No crowds had yet gathered at San Juan de Dios and it was as lifeless. The place had kept as silent as usual. Aldo and Pablo went inside to greet Olga and her family. They were all gathered in the living room, listening to the radio. The room was beautifully tiled in sparkling turquoise mosaic. The ceiling was high with dark wood molding. The wall leading into the next room was arched on top, with columns at each side. It was an old house, as were most of the others in this neighborhood.

The family stood up to greet Aldo and tried to hide their surprise at seeing the scars on his face. The women kissed him, and Olga's father shook his hand.

"You are going to stay for New Year's lunch, I hope," Pedro said.

"I have to see my children, I'm sorry," he said politely.

"Well then, at least a drink, no?"

"All right, only one."

Pedro asked his wife to get him a bottle of brandy and some shot glasses. Aldo took a glass from Olga's mother and offered a toast.

"To everyone's health in the New Year," he said.

"Yes, and to a hopeful new beginning," Pedro repeated.

He lifted his shot glass and drank the dark-colored fluid in one gulp, bringing tears to his eyes.

"Did you sleep at Aldo's?" Olga asked Pablo.

"Yes."

"How was it on the way here? Did you see many people?"

"Are you kidding me?" Pablo said. "They're everywhere."

"Isn't it unbelievable?" She said excitedly, her eyes sparkling.

"Alfredo was the first one to know," Aldo said. "He noticed the cars driving by us with people cheering. Then we listened to the radio and heard it."

"So they are even in Rios?"

"They are there, too."

"I think that is just great. I am so happy."

"I don't know about all that yet," Pablo said, cutting in. "People are getting excited too quickly. Everything is happening too fast."

"Why, Pablo?" she asked. "This is what everybody has been waiting for. Batista's dictatorship is over. I think the rebels will do good. We'll all have a better life."

"Since when do you care about politics, Olga?" Pablo said sarcastically. "And what do you know about the rebels anyway? Are they going to put food on our table? For all you know, it might be just another tyranny. I wouldn't jump on any bandwagons just yet. Wait and see what happens. We'll have to work for a living no matter who is in government."

"Yes, but it's different now. There's freedom. It's better for everyone, a new beginning. Don't you see?"

Their normal closeness was gone. She was not speaking to him but lecturing.

"So you're going to go out into the streets and cheer like a fool, ah?"

"Forget it," Aldo said. "Let her be, Pablo. She is right to support whoever she wants. Leave her alone."

"This is already splitting up families and I don't like it," Pablo said angrily. "It's a bad omen. I hope your wife doesn't do the same to you. Until yesterday, Olga did not give a crap about politics. Now all of a sudden, she is a philosopher and a staunch supporter of the rebels whom she doesn't even know. What's come over her?"

"Pablo, you don't understand." She shook her head in frustration. She had wanted him to share this moment with her and felt genuine disappointment. Her father sat back on his rocking chair near the radio and soberly looked at his daughter. He agreed with Pablo. Pablo was her husband, and publicly disagreeing with him was disrespectful. And, like Pablo, he felt people were rushing. He, too, needed time although he felt a powerful urge to speak out for the rebels.

"Olga, why don't you give it a chance. Wait before you speak out, honey. Let's wait to see what happens."

Aldo stood up and tapped Pablo's shoulder. "Let's go, Pablo, drop me off at Guillermo's house."

Aldo shook everyone's hand and followed Pablo outside. In many ways, the two thought and feared the same things. They had grown up together and were used to each other's ways, and they thought alike almost intuitively. Whatever views they held about the present state of affairs, they would keep them in perspective, leaving others to rush into passionate declarations of support.

They drove quietly for a few minutes, watching the scattered crowds gathered at corners, waiving and cheering at them as they drove by. They felt as if they were at a theater, watching everyone perform. Finally Aldo spoke.

"You shouldn't argue with your wife about all this, Pablo," he said. "The whole thing may not amount to much after all. It will probably die out."

"I agree. So why in the world is Olga so uptight? She's not a politician. She's never been a politician. Why is she taking sides all of a sudden? I don't understand."

"Ah, well. I guess this is a little different. It's much more involved than ever before, and it's contagious, especially in town. She'll forget about it later, you'll see."

"I hope so. I don't want politics in my house. I always lived without politics and never got involved in anything, only work, like you. And I want to keep it that way. What has Batista, or Grao, and now Fidel Castro ever done for me? That's how I look at it. So why should I be on anybody's side? I am on my side and that of my family. But these political games? No way, that's for the birds. Let those who put Batista in power take him down and the same goes for anybody else who comes after."

He spoke in anger. Olga and he had a special marriage. They had no children, although they had tried. They only had each other, and they had grown accustomed to each other's ways. They had been married for seven years and had no secrets. Pablo felt disappointed. It seemed as if while he was in Rios looking after his friend, his wife had made up her mind about a lot of things. There had been no discussion between them. She had just decided on her own that she was going to support the rebels and that Batista was a dictator. He had never ever heard her use that term before. It bothered him. His ego had been deflated.

As they left town, they saw truckloads of people on the highway to Santa Cruz. They waived as they passed them in the opposite direction. People were coming into town from everywhere, anyway they could. Cars traveled in caravans with open windows with passengers hanging out and yelling that the tyranny was over.

When they entered the suburbs, the traffic subsided. They arrived at Guillermo's mansion. Aldo gazed up at it, thinking that his most precious possessions, the people he lived for, were inside. What would these changes mean for them?

Pablo parked the jeep in front of the house. The winter afternoon's breeze tugged on the weather bane on its pole. It swayed from side to side as if unable to decide where to point. The abundant sunlight and mild temperature made it impossible to ignore the mystical beauty of the first day of the year.

They went past the iron gate and reached the main door. Aldo gripped the door knob and tapped several times. Ramona opened, wearing a baby blue dress with a white embroidered apron and a small nurse's cap pinned to the back of her hair. They stared at each other.

"Happy New Year," Aldo said. "Can we come in, please."

"Wait one moment, Aldo," she said, going back inside.

"Doesn't this lady know who you are by now?" Pablo commented, "You can't get in without her checking in with someone? Gee, Aldo, I get in easier than you."

Aldo did not answer and stepped inside, waiving him to follow. He closed the door behind them and walked unannounced into the living room. The children were sitting in front of the television set watching cartoons and were momentarily surprised to see him and startled by his scars. Frank looked up after hearing his father's footsteps, hesitated, then quickly ran up to him with open arms. Aldo bent to hug him.

"Did you miss me?" Aldo said.

"Yes, plenty."

The twins were in their seats looking shyly at them and wanting to run up to their father. Aldo went to them while, his arm was around Frank's shoulders. They put out their arms and he kissed their cheeks.

"What happened to your face, Dad," said Frank.

"Didn't your mother tell you that I was in an accident with the jeep."

"She did. I didn't think your face was so hurt. Will those wounds leave scars?"

"Maybe some."

At that moment Ramona came back into the room. Behind her, Aldo heard rushing footsteps.

"Aldo, are you here?" Amanda called.

"I'm here."

"Mr. Aldo," Ramona said impulsively. "You could have waited."

"Ah, Ramona," Amanda interrupted, "he's my husband. Go inside, please."

"Very well, Ms. Amanda."

"How are you, Pablo?" Amanda said fondly. He had been her main support after Aldo's accident, running the farm while Aldo was at the clinic and taking on the added responsibility of picking her up every morning and driving her to the farm so she could spend time with Aldo, tend to him during the day, and bring her back to her father's at night despite the risk of arrest. He was truly a friend. The night before, Pablo had told her he would go to the farm and see Aldo, and she had not heard from him again. She had spent part of the night at the funeral home with Aleida, coming home early to be with the children. Like many others, she had been awakened by the beeping horns and yells announcing Batista's fall down. The celebrations were in sharp contrast to the solemn mood in the house. It was only a few hours ago that Aleida had received the terrible news of Roberto's death. Batista's flight had also been a hard blow to her father who had stayed in his room most of the day, refusing to see anyone and listening to his own short wave radio. She had been up since early morning, worrying about her family but mostly about Aldo. Was he alone at the farm? And where was Pablo? Why hadn't he come for her this morning? Had something happened?

She came up to Aldo and rested her head on his chest, then tightly embraced him, sobbing softly.

"Have you heard? Did you see what happened? I've been so worried."

"We have," Aldo said. "We left the farm as soon as we heard. How's Aleida?"

"Right now she's at the funeral home with Ana. She's destroyed. Imagine."

"I did not want him to leave the farm just yet, Amanda," Pablo explained, "but he insisted, and you know how he is."

"I know. But I have been so worried, Pablo. I thought something terrible had happened. Dulce has been calling every half hour. We must call her to tell her you are all right. Come."

"I'm going to go, Aldo," Pablo said, "I will see you tonight, Okay?"

"Yes, early. No later than seven."

Pablo left the room and headed for the front door. Ramona waited for him and politely bid him good-bye.

Amanda and the children went into the recreation room. Aldo sat on a wicker chair with the twins standing between his legs. They were still shy with him and stealthily looked at his face when he was not looking at them as if to study his wounds. He pretended not to notice.

"What can I fix you?" Amanda asked.

"Nothing," he said. "I'm not hungry."

"No, you must have something. It's New Year's."

"Isn't anybody here?"

"Oh, please, don't mention it. People have been stopping in all day, and I had to face them alone. My father has refused to leave his room, and then Aleida with the death of her boyfriend. It's been awful. Just me and Ramona, telling everybody to come back later and thanking them. I think tonight will be very bad."

"I won't be here tonight."

"Ah, the farm. I want to go back with you, Aldo. It's time."

"No, not yet," he said. "Let a few more days go by and see how these new changes turn out."

"I have to be with you, Aldo. Ah, that reminds me, let's call Dulce."

They went back into the living room and dialed Dulce's number. She answered, concern filling her voice.

"Aldo's here," Amanda said happily. "He's fine. Let me put him on for you."

"How are you?" Aldo said.

Immediately, Dulce began sobbing. She had been terrified that he might be in danger. The dramatic events of the last few hours made even Rios unsafe. Who knew what was happening among all this confusion?

They spoke for a few minutes, and he calmed her down, telling her he'd be over later with Pablo. He asked her if Cecilia had asked for him. She lied. Since the day of the last attack, Cecilia had been under heavy medication and had made a prisoner of her sister.

Aleida came in later, accompanied by Ana. She wore a black skirt and white blouse, and her face bore no make up. She looked composed but the redness in her eyes revealed what she had been through. She was twenty four years old and considered too old to be single. The death of her fiancé preyed heavily on her. She had been engaged to be married. Now what would she do? The society in which she lived did not allow for unconventional unions. It was either marriage at the right age or becoming an old maid.

"I'm truly sorry," Aldo said, kissing her. She held his face in her hands for a moment and wept.

"You are a saint to say that after what happened to you. Roberto was one of them. One of the ones who hurt you."

"No, he wasn't. He wouldn't have hurt me. He was a good man."

"Oh, yes, that I know. But now he's gone, and for what? The rebels have won anyway. He'll be forgotten. A wasted life."

She sat helplessly on a wicker chair, her face buried in her hands, crying softly. He stroked her black hair silently. There was not much he could say.

CHAPTER EIGHT

Epiphany was the children's holiday, its roots going back to Spain, and even farther back to the days of Jesus Christ. The catholic church was recognized as the official religion in the nation. Epiphany was celebrated on the 6th of January. It was the day when the three wise kings from far-way lands had reached the site of Christ's birth, bearing gifts and toys for the newborn. The legend went that the three wise men had continued to visit all children throughout the world on the same day each year to shower them with toys and other goods. There was a rush at the stores until closing time the previous night, and children were sure to be tucked into bed early that night, anxiously awaiting the arrival of their most important day of the year.

But by all measures, it was also the most ill-suited holiday for a society with significant disparities among its classes. For the wealthy, it was a welcome opportunity to reward their sons and daughters and another day to feast. For the poor, it was not only another day, one when they would have to hear their children's cries as they awoke and found their beds without toys, with an apology note from the three wise men. Whatever their elders' explanation was, it would mean nothing when the children saw others more fortunate than them showing off their new toys.

The peasants adjusted as well as they could. The popular ox team, made up of two empty bottles tied at the neck with a string, would be the traditional present for the boys. There was also a spirited horse made from a single thin branch of a pinon tree, with carvings to resemble a mottled mare. The girls might get a doll made with rags and a bottle. In the country, it was one more day to tell stories through *decimas*.

Aldo left the farm with Pablo early in the morning. As they entered town, they saw the first rebel soldiers, patrolling the streets. The caravan from the Sierra Mountains Range, with Fidel Castro at its head, had just passed the city. The rebel forces had devised a form of organization, badly needed to restore order in the disrupted local life. The last six days had witnessed unforeseen chaos, resulting in work stoppages and the breakdown of essential services. A large segment of the population was in the streets, drinking heavily and often rioting, with no authority to contain their excesses other than the first segments of rebel forces that were poorly equipped to moderate the crowds' revelry. Aldo and Pablo headed towards the Aleman Center to mingle with cattle the traders. Aldo had found it prudent to wait for a few days until the chaos subsided. They had not visited the Center since Christmas Eve. It was time to refocus.

"I'll stay with the kids for this morning," Aldo said to Pablo as he drove. "You go and do what you have to do and then pick me up later."

"All I have to do is see Olga," Pablo replied. "I can be back by 11:00."

"That's enough time for me. I want to stop over at the milkman's home. I am hoping to collect today."

"Why shouldn't you collect?"

"The way things have been, I wouldn't be surprised if he's unable to pay me."

"I don't think so. Milk is too essential in this country. People may run out of money to eat but for milk, they'll always find it. Besides, if he doesn't pay you, you don't let him milk anymore, that's all."

"It's not that easy, Pablo."

"Look at them," Pablo said, pointing with his chin.

They had stopped at the intersection of the Central Highway near the cemetery. Standing in the middle of the street were two rebel guards directing traffic. One faced them while the other one stood with his back to them, urging the highway traffic to move. They were dressed in green fatigues, their chests banded with ammunition, rifles on their shoulder. Each wore a red and black band on his right sleeve. But their most outstanding feature was the beard, bushy and frizzy, covering the bottom half of their faces. They looked shabby, and were it not for their green uniforms and weapons they could have easily passed for rugged mountain men. Their hair grew past their necks and they wore green caps sitting loosely on their heads. One of them waived Pablo to go.

"They've got some shaving to do," Pablo commented.

"It's a symbol," Aldo said. "That's going to be their trademark. Even Fidel Castro has a beard."

"Yes, but they can't expect to manage a country with that appearance. That beard has got to go."

"That beard is going to stay. In fact, I will bet you that you will now see half the men wearing beards."

"Monkeys."

As they reached the intersection before the park leading to the suburbs, two rebel guards stopped the jeep. Their appearance was not much different than that of the men they had just seen, but their beards were shorter. They wore large scapulars around their necks, two small pieces of woolen cloth joined by strings, a sharp contrast to their military bearing. A truck that had been parked sideways moved forward, and more rebels got out. They quickly formed a circle, pushing two men wearing khaki uniforms in its middle. The prisoners' hands were handcuffed in front of them, and they wore no hats. The rebels surrounding them pointed their long rifles at them, edging them on. The group began to cross the street. A crowd immediately gathered on the sidewalk. The people began yelling obscenities at the prisoners and moved slightly backwards as the group reached the sidewalk. The rebels made no attempt to contain the crowd and merely turned right, walking past the jeep.

The crowd followed them, clapping their hands in the air in unison and chanting, "*Paredon! Paredon! Paredon!*", meaning execute them at the wall. It was obvious that the prisoners were being paraded. The two men did not say a word. Pablo and Aldo were repulses by the scene and momentarily lost track of time until they were startled by one rebel's tapping on the hood of the jeep.

"Let's go," he yelled, "traffic is backing up. Let's go."

Pablo drove to the end of the circle then continued towards Guillermo's house. It was a long time until either one of them spoke.

"You know what that reminds me of?" Pablo commented. "You know that passage in the Bible where Pontius Pilate goes into the open gallery and asks the crowd what to do with Jesus? And then the crowd roars, 'crucify him! crucify him!' That's exactly what that was."

"Yes, you are right," Aldo said calmly. "I don't like this one bit. It is a bad omen. No matter who your enemy is, you don't treat him like that. Those guards were inciting the crowd. They took those poor men out of the truck in front of everyone as a show, just to stir up the crowd."

"What could those guards have possibly done?"

"That doesn't matter. They are using them to fuel the crowd. What they did is irrelevant."

"I felt like jumping out and freeing them."

"I know. Keep this to yourself, Pablo. Let's see what happens. This could be just overkill. Hopefully things like this will stop."

"You are not thinking of becoming a rebel sympathizer, are you?"

"No. I'm with neither side. You know that."

"It's a little scary, Aldo. I've never seen this quite like this."

"My aunt says that something like this happened during the Machado regime in the early thirties, but I think this is much larger. It seems that the whole world is out to support the rebels."

"They call it 'revolution.' It is the right word I guess. For one week, people have done nothing but drink and party. They have not worked nor do they care about anything other than celebrating. When is it going to stop?"

"What I see happening is that a lot of people are joining the rebel army, now that supposedly the war is over."

"Yes. Well I guess that's to be expected. It happens in every war. Everybody wants to be on the winning side."

"It seems the rebels really had not much of an army before. Their army is being formed now. They're picking them up as they pass, have you noticed?"

It was barely eight in the morning when the jeep pulled up in front of Guillermo's mansion. Aldo and Pablo got out and knocked on the front door. Ramona was already dressed in her usual attire.

"Wait here," she said, "I'll bring Ms. Amanda."

Defying her, Aldo walked inside with Pablo and sat on a rocking chair in the living room. On a glass center table in the middle of the room was the latest edition of *Bohemia*, a national weekly magazine. The front cover bore the picture of Fidel Castro, the leader of the rebel movement. His head was in semi profile, occupying most of the page, and printed in dark colors. He seemed distressed but as peaceful as Christ praying at the Mount of Olives.

During his many recent public appearances, Fidel Castro and his army had been presented to the media as deeply religious, wearing crosses and images of the saints around their necks, shaking the hands of those who came from miles away to see them. Some came on their knees, some on their bare feet, fulfilling their vows to the Virgin of Charity and other saints, made in exchange for the downfall of Batista. To them, the leader and his men were saviors. The rebel army was not only popular, but it also enjoyed the undivided support of the majority of the population.

Aldo picked up the magazine and leafed briefly through it. Gruesome pictures of the many killed by the Batista regime were depicted. Some of the bodies were in a state of decomposing. The articles disclosed in gruesome details the many crimes of the past dictatorship, how some of the victims had died, and the torture they had endured. For many, no doubt, it was a badly-needed eye opener but for neutrals like Aldo and Pablo, it was distasteful propaganda that only served to increase their mounting suspicions about the new order.

"Why are you sitting down in the living room Mr. Ochoa?" Ramona said from the loggia.

"It's not polite to make the family wait outside, Ramona," Aldo said pleasantly.

Despite her rudeness, he always managed to brush her off and refused to confront her, which made her even angrier.

"Right, Ramona, what's with your manners these days?" Pablo joked. "You're supposed to be a well-bred maid."

"There's only one person in this house to whom I owe any explanation and that's Don Guillermo. I do not answer to anyone else. And when he's not around, I rule. That's just in case you didn't know."

"Phew! Now I'm scared Aldo," Pablo said mockingly. "Aldo, let me see that magazine."

He took the magazine and, showing the cover to Ramona, he pointed to the figure on the front page with his index finger.

"From now on, Ramona, this is going to be your boss. No more Don Guillermo, no more bosses for anybody except him, Fidel Castro. Remember that."

"He won't last six months. Don Guillermo said so. Batista will be back."

"So, Don Guillermo has already made another prediction," Pablo commented. "And you believe that, of course."

"I do. He's never been wrong."

"He's never been wrong? I thought he predicted that Batista would finish Fidel Castro. What happened to that?"

"Anyway, Ms. Amanda is still sleeping, Mr. Ochoa," she said dismissively, "perhaps you ought to come back later."

Aldo stood from his chair as if to leave then turned to Pablo. "Pick me up around 11:00, okay?"

"Sure," Pablo said, also rising. "I'll see you later, Ramona."

She stood helplessly watching Pablo as he went through the front door while Aldo walked past her to go inside. She did not know where to turn. Aldo went to Amanda's door and opened it. "You are going to wake the children, Mr. Aldo," she said.

"The children should be up already Ramona," he said. "It's Kings' Day."

He went into Amanda's room and sat on her bed. She was still asleep, her head buried in the pillow.

"Do you want some coffee, Figurine?" he said softly.

She did not respond. The previous night had been long. She had been making last-minute toy purchases for the children. Then she had gotten up at 3:00 A.M. to place the toys by their beds. It had taken her over an hour to wrap them. Only Ramona had been around, supervising her, but Amanda had not let her help. She thought it was her job as a mother, regretting only that Aldo was not here. It was the first Epiphany Eve he had missed with the children.

Aldo quietly left his wife then went to the room where the twins and Frank slept on the canopied bed stacked with wrapped toys, the glittery boxes sparkling under a beam of sunlight. Aldo kissed each child and was going to leave the room, but as he turned Frank woke up.

"What did they leave me, Pap? What?"

"Go and look Frank."

The boy tossed the covers aside and jumped on the floor. He unwrapped the first box and gazed in amazement at its contents, then opened the next box. The rustling of the paper woke the girls who immediately climbed down off the bed.

"Daddy, Daddy, look what they brought me."

Aldo helped them unwrap their gifts. As they opened each box, they would look at its contents in awe, admire it for a few seconds, then move on to the next until all the boxes were empty. Each twin had received seven gift dolls, clowns, and miniature houses. Frank had received ten, mostly cars and revolvers. These toys would have been the envy any young child. Aldo's children had received a share from each member of the family. Aleida, Ana, Blanco, and Guillermo had all chipped in. Even Ramona had contributed by purchasing a toy for each.

Aldo left the children's room and went into the kitchen. He opened the refrigerator and took out three eggs. He took a bowl from a cabinet and cracked the eggs, whipping the mixture into a foam with a fork. Then he put olive oil in a shallow frying pan, emptied the contents into the pan, and let it sit on the burner for a few minutes, lowering the fire. He heated water to make coffee and milk in a separate pot. At that moment, Ramona walked in the kitchen.

"What are you doing, Mr. Aldo? I do the cooking around here."

"Making my own breakfast, Ramona."

"No. I will not have that in my kitchen. Please go. Let me work."

"No."

He placed a white cotton strainer in a wooden framework and poured several spoonfuls of coffee grains inside, then poured the hot water through the filter. The liquid ran into the cup.

"At least you could use our metal coffee maker, Mr. Aldo," Ramona said. "You are making coffee like a peasant."

"I am a peasant."

"Don't I know it."

"You should always keep it in mind, Ramona. Once a peasant, always a peasant."

"Nothing to be proud of, Mr. Aldo."

"It is for me, Ramona. Maybe you too should be proud of your heritage."

"How can you be proud of being a peasant?" she asked. "How can you be proud of something like that?"

"Easy. You are what you want to be, not what people say you are. They make the labels, you make the person. It matters nothing what they call it. It's only what you make of it."

She stood near the stove watching him. He mixed some milk and coffee with two spoonfuls of sugar in a tall glass and walked to the breakfast room. She followed him quietly, bringing butter and fresh bread.

"Thank you," he said. "Can you give me a small cup of coffee, please?"

He sat down and drank from his glass while Ramona returned to the kitchen. The children ran into the room, Frank chasing the twins with two silver-colored revolvers.

"Children, let me see what they brought you," Ramona yelled. "Frank, don't chase them, baby, you're scaring them. Wait until your friends come over later."

The twins came to Aldo and sat on his lap, flapping their dolls in his face. He giggled with them for a while until Ramona brought him a cup of espresso. He put the girls down and went into Amanda's room where she was still sleeping. He set the saucer and cup on the night table next to her and gently rubbed her cheek with his fingers.

"Figurine, I brought you coffee."

She opened her eyes at the sound of his voice. As she lifted her face, he saw the marks of the pillow on her right cheek. Her long hair shielded her forehead, and she pushed it back with her hand. She was wearing a pink night gown with a white lace tied with ribbons. She sat up on the bed and pushed the cover aside. She leaned over and kissed him on the lips.

"I didn't know you were here. When did you get in?"

"I've been here for a while. I woke up the children. They're out running around already. Get up and see them."

He handed her the cup. "It's hot. I made it."

"Thank you, Aldo. Where's Ramona?"

"She's out there running her mouth as usual. How was it for you yesterday."

"It was a long day. I had to leave the children with Ana so I could finish the shopping. I did not get back here until after 9:00 P.M. Would you believe it?"

"I believe it broke your heart to spend all that money on toys, right?"

"I didn't spend that much. Daddy gave me money, too."

"You shouldn't have taken it, Amanda."

"It's all right. It's for the children."

"You still shouldn't have."

"He hates to go shopping, Aldo. He'd rather I do it for him. Can you hold this?"

She handed him the empty cup and got out of bed. As she left the room with him, the children ran to her, showing off their toys. She went to the breakfast room and sat down with them and Aldo. The children ran back and forth, bringing their toys to them one at a time. Amanda played with them for a few minutes then went to the bathroom to wash up.

"You should have seen the people yesterday," she said. "Everybody was out shopping." "That means business is good."

"I think people are expecting so much from him. Castro, I mean. But my father says Castro is a communist, that this will all lead to trouble. Have you seen the new *Bohemia*?"

"I've seen it."

"And what do you think? Did you see all those bodies? It's awful. People being tortured, their nails being pulled out in cold blood."

"Don't believe any of that, Amanda," Ramona said from the kitchen. "No one has ever seen any of those people. Batista never tortured anyone."

Aldo and Amanda exchanged glances. For Ramona to admit what the previous regime had done would mean that her boss had failed in his predictions. And how could that be? They both knew that Ramona echoed Guillermo's sentiments. She was his maid and was expected to do so. She brought Amanda breakfast on a tray, placing the glass of milk and coffee, butter and bread before her on the table.

"And how is your father, Amanda?" Aldo asked.

"Still in seclusion. He's out working this morning. He has lost a lot of money over the past few days with the work stoppages and the celebrations, so he's probably going to try to make up for it in the next few days."

"How does he feel about what's happened?"

"Ah," she said, "he doesn't change. He thinks Batista will be back, that this is only temporary. He despises the rebels of course. And I have told him that he has to be discreet. I have to keep an eye on him."

"All he has to do is keep his thoughts to himself."

"But he'll never do that. You know it. And that's why I worry."

Frank brought the *Bohemia* magazine from the living room and showed his father a page with the pictures of bodies and comments underneath. Amanda snatched it from him.

"Don't look at those pictures, Frank. Don't let your sisters see them."

"Are they dead Mama?"

"Yes, they're dead."

"Who killed them? Batista?"

"I told you not to leave that magazine lying around, Ms. Amanda," Ramona said from the kitchen. "It's a disgrace for the children to see something like that."

"I have to agree with Ramona. They shouldn't print these gross pictures. That's insane."

"The press has been waiting a long time, Amanda. This is their chance to get even with Batista for all trying to gag them all these years."

"You know what I read here? The rebels are going to hold tribunals to try some of Batista's men. That's going to be a mess."

"I heard it on the radio. It's not going to be a pretty sight."

"No?"

"Of course, not. The people are in revolt. That could lead to lynching and to innocent people getting killed. I don't like it one bit."

Ramona asked them to move from the room as she began to mop the floor. They went to the recreation room and sat on chairs across from each other. Amanda was up to date on the local stories. Some were about neighbors who had suddenly disappeared because they had been members of Batista's secret police. She talked about others who had unexpectedly become revolutionaries and joined the movement. Everyone in the family had been shocked to learn that Blanco was now a militant. Ana was against it, but what could she do? Amanda went back to the national news and listened until Pablo came back for Aldo. She shook Pablo's hand and said pleasantly, "I am lending you my husband but I want him back early, you hear me?"

Aldo and Pablo drove to the Centro Aleman. Aldo was deep in thought as they drove through the busy streets filled with people. He wanted to be optimistic about the present. Perhaps this commotion was normal, but he could not recall anything close to it. Doubt was a sinister seed, he thought. One must always be sure in order to achieve. Being sure had been the key to his success; however, the dramatic events of the last few days had made him lose confidence. He did not feel comfortable owning so many heads of cattle. Perhaps he had misjudged. True, cattle trade men always moved fast. They bought as low as possible, then sold as quickly as possible at the highest price. The longer they held onto a herd, the larger the operating expenses would be and the lower the profit. But Aldo's plan had been unorthodox and a gamble from the beginning. He had counted on the political changes that had occurred as a factor in their strategy. Because of the rebel threat, traders had been scared to buy during the last days of the Batista regime, and stocks of cattle had been replenished. Those holding cattle had been anxious to sell, bringing opportunities to buy at a low market. That was when Aldo and Pablo had made their move. But Aldo had not counted on the situation changing so fast. They had now held their herd for twelve days. Arapientos was charging them a fee to keep their cattle. They had to be moved.

As they neared the Centro Aleman, they saw signs of the looting that had gone on in the last few days. Some of the stores sported cracked windows and litter still defaced the sidewalks. The crowds had feasted in the streets until some order was gradually restored.

"Good morning, boys," Mr. Sanchez said as he saw them enter the tavern. He was sitting on a stool next Don Fernando, wearing a Stetson, nibbling on a cigar.

"Boys, where have you been?" Don Fernando asked.

"How's that face coming along," Mr. Sanchez said.

He surveyed Aldo's right temple which still bore a big scab.

"It's coming along," Aldo said.

"You need some sun," Don Fernando said. "That will do it. Come, sit down."

He tapped the stool next to him. He was holding a shot glass in his other hand and his cigar bobbed up and down as he spoke.

"Pablo, sit down," he said. "Come on boys. Let's talk business."

Aldo and Pablo sat next to him. The tavern had escaped vandalism after the rebels' takeover. Other businesses up the street had not been so lucky.

"Did you hear about the shoot out in the hospital?"

"My milkman mentioned it. What happened?"

"I think it was nothing but a big show," Mr. Sanchez said.

"The rebels surrounded the hospital," Don Fernando said. "They claimed some of Batista's men were hiding inside. As you know, this is the hospital under construction in the Central Highway. Well, they began shooting and shot at it so much that the building now looks like it's had the measles. Of course, they found nobody inside. Drive by it when you have a chance. You'll laugh."

"Did any of the crowds come in here?" Pablo asked.

"No, this guy was smart. He was closed from the first of January. And he had his rolling metal doors down so they couldn't do any damage. But some places got hit pretty bad. The Gran Hotel, for instance. Chairs were thrown out in the street, windows broken, tables turned. It was all a big disaster."

"The whorehouse on the plaza was plundered and closed, the bitches were thrown out," Mr. Sanchez said. "That's what I regret the most. What's the use, I say? Those women make men happy. Why do they have to mess with them?"

"And how's business going?" Aldo asked.

"As well as can be expected under the circumstances. I haven't moved anything since before New Year."

"What have you been doing?" Aldo said curiously.

"Not much. Keeping a low profile. I tell you something, though. Around Christmas, there were people who wanted to buy cattle. I wonder how they feel now."

"What are you looking to do?"

"Right now, put deals together, but for me personally, nothing."

Aldo gazed at Don Fernando, then called the bartender for a drink. Don Fernando was playing it safe. There might be truth in what he said, but he was certainly looking for opportunities, too.

"What's in it for you?"

"I'll take one dollar a head of any sale."

"Do you have a buyer right now?"

"I can produce a buyer."

Aldo looked at him coyly. Did he really have one or was he setting him up? He decided to play along.

"Make that fifty cents a head, and we may be able to do business."

The bartender finally came over and slid a coaster in front of Aldo and Pablo.

"I'll have one Crystal beer," Pablo said.

"No, it's too cold still. I'll have a Phillip II straight."

"What do you boys have right now?" Don Fernando said, pushing the brim of his hat back. His breath smelled of alcohol, but he was not drunk.

"I have a nice lot," Aldo said.

"When can I see them?"

"Who's the buyer?"

"You want to sell or not?"

"I first want to know that you have a buyer."

"There's going to be a lot of cattle available right now, kid," Don Fernando said affectionately. "If you can sell, you're lucky, so I wouldn't be too demanding."

"I'm not demanding. I do not want to waste my time."

"Well, I'll tell you this. If I tell you that I can produce a buyer, I mean that I can. You're talking to a man. Tell me what you have, then let's talk price. I will then tell you if I can sell your cattle."

"We have sixty five heads available right now," Pablo said cutting in.

He knew what Aldo had in mind. They wanted to unload the heads they had bought from Mr. Pazos and make a fast buck. Then they would see.

"What's the weight?"

"I figure they'll make eight hundred pounds each. They are fattening up. All males."

"How much are you looking for?"

"Seventy nine per head."

"That's too stiff. Even if they're fat and healthy, you'll have to come down if you want to sell fast."

"If you have a buyer that can deliver, then you can see them at that price. We'll talk more about that once we have a serious buyer."

"Aldo, my point is that you're not going to get anyone to look at them at that price. Not now. The situation is too unstable."

"Not that unstable, Don Fernando. What's happened is a reaction to the change. That's all. On the other hand, a sense of security is building because of Batista's downfall. The expectation is also gone. Batista is gone."

"That's true to a point," Don Fernando agreed.

He turned to look at the tall man wearing green fatigues, black leather boots, and a green military cap who had just entered the tavern. He was showing the first traces of a beard. Don Fernando thought he recognized him. The man looked around, then focused on Aldo and walked over to them.

"Aldo, how are you?"

"How are you, Blanco?"

Blanco put his hand on Don Fernando's shoulder. Don Fernando shook it and so did Mr. Sanchez.

"Sit with us for a while," Mr. Sanchez said.

Blanco took a stool next to Pablo. He had been in Santa Cruz during the last few days and inactive in trading, and few knew what he had been up to.

"I haven't seen you since the hospital," Pablo said. "How have you been?"

"I've been all right. Helping the movement in Santa Cruz."

"Helping? What kind of help?" Pablo asked.

"I have been involved with the twenty six. So they sent me to Santa Cruz to help with some plans. I know the area well so that's why I was chosen. I will be going back."

"You are in the twenty six?"

"I have been."

"I did not know that. Did you, Aldo?"

The two exchanged glances. Who would have ever thought that the son of a rich cattle trader could be involved with the rebels? But then, wasn't that really what had happened? Wasn't it people like Blanco, rich and powerful, who had made the rebels' victory possible?

"I can't say I knew it but I had a feeling that you were up to something, Blanco."

"So you are giving up your father's legacy for this, ah?" Don Fernando said accusingly. He had known Blanco's father when he was nobody and knew how the old man had created an empire for himself. Would he have allowed one of his sons to join a revolution if he were still alive? He would probably turn on his grave, Don Fernando thought.

"My father has got nothing to do with it," Blanco replied.

He did not care what anybody else thought. He was in it for the principle.

"Well, Blanco, I hope you will still trade, ah?" Aldo said casually.

He wanted to soften the blow. Don Fernando did not care how he said it. He said what he felt, but Blanco was not a bad man. Whatever his intentions, they must be for a good purpose, a desire to do the right thing.

"Not for now. I haven't been doing anything at the farm. It might surprise you to know that my wife has been running all our affairs for the past two weeks. I just haven't been around except for the holidays. In fact, I came back today from Santa Cruz."

Aldo took a sip from his beer. Who would have guessed? Ana running a cattle empire? A delicate woman raised in Mr. Diaz's exclusive and aristocratic social circle was now involved in farming and cattle breeding? But was that really a surprise? Ana had her mother's inner strength. She could outlast even Rios if that's where fate placed her. She was tough when she needed to be. He had seen that in her. And that's what her situation demanded now. Guts. She found herself with a husband in love with a movement, and she reacted the only way she could. She had to take command of their affairs to save her family. Blanco had no idea yet the kind of woman he had married. Aldo could not help but wonder what Amanda would have done in a similar situation.

"With all due respect, Blanco," Pablo said. "It looks like my wife Olga has been hexed by the twenty six movement. All of a sudden, she has turned into a politician. She is a fervent sympathizer. I don't know what's come over her."

"You have to try to understand it, Pablo. It's a movement by the people and for the people. That's why so many persons with no political background join in. It's not really politics nor can it be compared to politics. It's the union of all the people coming together for once to form a true government. Everyone will eventually join. You too. There is no other way to fix this country."

"Can I tell you something?" Pablo said. "No matter how you slice it, it's politics. All I want to do is be left alone. I want to work, support my family, and live in peace. I want no part of government. And, I will say this to you meaning no offense, I have already seen things in the rebels that spell trouble. I won't say what they are. But I sure as hell hope that I am wrong, for the good of all of us."

"Yes, you may be a victim of your own prejudices. But just for a start, think about this. Could we have held this conversation here two weeks ago when Batista was still in power? No way. And what does that say to you? This is the start of a new beginning. Something that, deep inside, we have all been waiting for, something we deserve."

Blanco spoke with emotion. Don Fernando stared at the rows of bottles behind the bar counter and frowned. Nothing was worse than a rich man turned politician, Don Fernando thought. The bartender came to him and asked him what he was drinking. Don Fernando waived him aside. He was too involved in the discussion to need a drink.

"A better question is whether we can have a critique of the revolution six months from now, Blanco, without being persecuted for it," Aldo said. "But that aside, what exactly is it that the revolution proposes to do? How will it affect the average man like me and Pablo?"

"Well, first, I think you have to stop being suspicious. My God, give it a chance, okay?"

There was annoyance in Blanco's statement, as if Aldo's comments had cut into the meat of his beliefs. Aldo felt it, and it bothered him to think that Blanco expected no questions and that he presumed that his theories would be in perfect agreement with everyone else's. That was bad.

"No, no," Aldo said holding up his hand, "you said that this is about freedom, right? So let me ask you what else this is about. You want to lecture us about the ideas of the revolution, right? So I have a right to ask you what this is about in practical terms, not philosophical. You can't tell me how to feel or what to ask. If so, why are we talking?"

Don Fernando shifted his eyes to Aldo. Mr. Sanchez also looked at him, and Pablo stood erect on his stool. Clearly, the conversation had gone testy in a hurry. Or it seemed that way.

"I admire you, Aldo, you know I do," Blanco said apologetically, "but what I am saying is that you can't shut your mind. You have to approach this openly. Otherwise, it won't work."

"I should be able to state what I think, though," Aldo said. "If I have an opinion, it doesn't necessarily mean I am closed minded. I have a right to my opinion. You just mentioned freedom. So why can't I rely on my own thinking to judge this new revolution? If I can't, that would be a tyranny."

"But wait," Blanco said in near despair, "give it a chance. The revolution is about justice, about fixing a corrupt regime that is unfair to the poor and to all in general. The revolution is going to change our society. It is going to do away with injustice to allow us to live free."

"I think that what we are all asking is a very simple question," Pablo added. "How will the revolution affect me? How will it affect the peasants, the rich? What will happen to our work, our lives? Outside of freedom, what can we expect?"

"In the next few months you'll see what the revolution can do. You mentioned peasants. You know the misery that our peasants live under? Never mind a place like Rios. I am not talking about that. I'm talking about hard-core misery where children are dying of diphtheria, where they don't go to school, where they go to bed hungry. For instance, do you know how many kids woke up today without any toys? Yet you go to Havana as I have many times, and what do you see? Casinos, gambling, prostitution. You see people who are filthy rich and totally out of touch with rest of our population. That's what the revolution will change. What has to change."

"And how's that going to be accomplished?" Pablo asked.

"The wealth has to be redistributed. This country is so rich that there's no need for anyone to be poor. Our economy has to change. Our structure has to change. Everything has to change."

"You mean that the rich will give to the poor," Pablo said ironically.

"I mean that a restructuring of our society has to take place. Our poor have to be given the opportunity to learn, to improve their conditions. They have to be given a chance."

"But how?"

"By creating conditions that will let them have a better life. Building more schools. Giving the peasants idle lands to cultivate. You ever drove on the way to Rios and noticed the many acres covered with marabou, just sitting there without anyone caring? Isn't it a waste? Meanwhile, there are thousands of people who need this land to survive. This needs to change. If we only achieved a fair distribution in this country, everyone one could be fed."

"So I guess you're saying that the landowners will have to part with some of their land. If that happens you yourself will be affected, no?"

"I am not concerned in the least with my own situation," Blanco said, "and no one should be. It's not about that. It's about what's good for all of us."

"This gives a new meaning to our already-altruistic society," Don Fernando interrupted. "Ever since I can recall, our people have always been generous. The poor have been fed by the rich, and the rich have fed from the poor. But to say that there has been exploitation is not true. Besides, what are you going to do? Are you going to take a man's farm and break it in pieces to give it to poor peasants? You'll have a war."

"No, you won't," Blanco said. "The war has already passed. You'll have a transition, and it will be difficult, but it will be accepted. Many more people will support it than oppose it."

"Let me ask you something, Blanco," Don Fernando said. "How do you know so much about the revolution's plans? How long have you been involved?"

"Long enough to know what it's about."

"When did you join?"

"I have been involved since 1957."

Don Fernando was quiet for a moment. He gave Aldo a glance. He would have never known it, he thought. He had always been a

Batista supporter, and he had always expressed himself with impunity around everyone, including Blanco. Was he supposed to have been afraid? Was he supposed to apologize? Hell no, he thought. He was too old to care.

"Well, I got to tell you. I am not happy to see Batista go. We had a government by someone who knew what he was doing. It's true, not everyone was in his favor, but he ruled the country well and business was flourishing. This new wave of young people, inexperienced and immature, I don't trust them. I think this is like an experiment that's not going to last. Mark my words."

"Far from it," Blanco said. "This is here to stay, like it or not. There's no going back to the old order. You tell that to the people out there and see how they respond. You think anyone is going to ask that Batista come back? Forget it. Those days are gone."

Aldo agreed. At least for the moment, it would be insane for anyone to think that the Batista order could come back. The whole country had been gripped in the frenzy of the revolution and much of Batista's old Army had joined with the rebels, some even guarding Castro himself on his way to the capital.

"When is Fidel Castro expected to arrive in Havana?" Aldo asked.

"Probably tomorrow or the day after," Blanco said. "The whole city is awaiting him. A new president will assume command of the government, Dr. Urrutias."

"So I heard. Who is he?"

"He's an honorable man. He's not from the old order. He has been involved with the movement for some time and he has just arrived from the exterior."

"And what will be Fidel Castro's role in all this? From what I see there is little if anything to do for anyone else other than Castro himself. Do you agree?"

"Well, he's the commander of our armed forces, Aldo. We have never had one as charismatic before. The people are in love with him because he sparked the movement and he carried it through. That's why he seems to overshadow everyone else. But he's not a tyrant. He knows his role in history and he will not overstep it. A good form of government will be established. There will be elections, and Fidel Castro will be given a role to play if he accepts it. His real work, which was to lead the people to victory, has now been done."

"I doubt Fidel Castro would step down, Blanco. He's too popular. I bet you that a new president won't last. The real president is Fidel Castro. He's in charge, and he will remain in charge."

"I don't know why you are so cynical about it Aldo."

"Let's just leave it at that. Listen, in your travels, keep in mind that Don Fernando, Pablo, and I are still trading. So if you come across any opportunities, let us know."

"Well, there are going to be more opportunities now than ever before. I guarantee it. Cattle will move like never before. The revolution has brought security to our environment."

"If you run into anyone looking to buy or sell on your way to Santa Cruz, let us know."

"I haven't really been involved in cattle trading lately, Aldo. But I will keep it in mind. I didn't really know you were in a position to trade. Are you buying or selling?"

"Both."

"All right, I'll remember."

"Now have a drink on us for old times sake," Pablo said. "Let's put politics to rest."

"I'll have a Hatuey beer," Blanco said.

He pushed back the visor of his cap and streaks of long, bushy silver hair escaped from it. The bartender poured a beer from a red-brown bottle into a glass. Blanco lifted it high for all to see.

"*Salud*," he said, "to you, to the new year and to our revolution."

"*Salud*," they repeated.

The tavern had begun to fill. Men wearing hats were now occupying most of the stools. Some sat at tables. They had been away from this popular trade place for several days, and their business had suffered. Now they were back, commenting about the latest events and hoping that the future held better prospects for them. There was much enthusiasm in the air from the crowds in the streets but the men here were cautious. Most of them had grown up in the country and their lives had been molded by the past. They would make poor revolutionaries. They lacked the impetuousness and foresight needed in any change such as the country was experiencing. They were caught in a daily battle for their families' livelihood and support and their search for improvement that was their priority. Outside, young men and women could praise Fidel as a saint who had come from heaven to save them. But here, it was back to reality and work.

As the evening approached, Aldo and Pablo prepared to leave. They had agreed to show Don Fernando their cattle now at the Arapientos' ranch. Aldo had thought it best to stay in touch with Blanco, a man with important contacts who was obviously undergoing a period of insight and transformation. It did not seem all that good for Blanco and his family. The ideas he expounded were noble but incompatible with his way of life. Politics did not fit well within the world of cowboys and cattle trading. What would become of his wife? What would happen to his fortune? Aldo hoped that Blanco would return to his old self. He wondered if he had ever really known Blanco and if his present state of mind was not a projection of what he had always wanted to be. Blanco's future had been made for him by his father. Now he was setting his own, risking his reputation and financial well being.

The jeep turned into the narrow street of Padre Valencia where Dulce and Aldo's mother lived. Dulce answered the door at the first knock and let them in. Aldo hugged her and kissed her on the cheek.

"Where is *mama*?"

"In bed. She's asleep, not doing very well still."

"Has the doctor come?"

"We had Dr. Adan here today," she said sadly. "He prescribed some more medication. He wants us to wait a few more days, but if she does not come out of it, we may have no choice but to put her in a sanitarium."

The term had a strange sound to it.

"Hello, *mama*," Aldo said to Cecilia.

He bent down and kissed her face. It looked puffy and red. She was laying face up on the bed. A leather belt around her waist was clipped to another on each side and secured to the frame of the bed.

"She won't wake up," Dulce said. "She's sedated."

Pablo bent to kiss her. She had seen him grow up and had always considered him her own son. They went back into the living room. Pablo and Aldo sat at the table.

"I bet you haven't had anything to eat, ah?" Dulce said.

Her hair looked uncombed and she wore no make up. Her face showed the strain of caring for her sick sister. The last few days, Amanda had stopped by to help her watch Cecilia. It had served more as moral support than anything else since Amanda could not control Cecilia.

Dulce reached under the stove and pulled out a large tin can. Aldo got up to help her. He poured out some of the charcoal from the can into one of the burners. Dulce sprayed some alcohol over the charcoal then threw a match in. Blue flames leaped up then slowly died down. She opened the refrigerator and took out a pressure cooker, placing it on the burner.

"I am heating chick peas for you that I made this afternoon. I knew you two were coming today."

"That's great," Pablo said. "No one can make them better than you."

"How has she been acting?"

"Well," Dulce said from the stove, "she was violent and hurt herself a couple of times. And yesterday she got loose and struck me in the arm. Look."

She showed them her forearm with two black and blues streaks.

"She did that with her nails."

"Has she been tied all the time?"

"For three days now. But I don't know how much longer she will last. She is starting to get attacks like she did when Emilio died. I can't control her."

"Has Amanda helped you?"

"Yes," she said, "she came every day. But it's hard for her, you know. She can't control her either, and she gets very scared. I can't really leave them alone."

"Well, I hate to say it, but we have no other choice than to put her away for some time."

"I know," Dulce said. "What else can we do?"

Her eyes became teary. She had cared for her sister by herself. To admit that Cecilia would have to go with strangers, albeit professionals, meant that she had failed. When it first had happened, she had sworn that Cecilia would never come back to a sanitarium and that she would take care of her.

"And how is the farm?" Dulce said, turning to the stove.

"The same. Everything is normal. We were at the Center today, trying to do business."

"How are things there? Are the traders back?"

"Yes. They are back, but there isn't much going on."

"You boys just hang in there. You watch. I think business is going to profit from the situation with the rebels."

"May God hear you," Pablo said. "You are not going to believe this, Aunt Dulce. Blanco has joined the rebels."

"What?" she said incredulously.

"Yes," Aldo said. "He came to the tavern wearing his green uniform and cap. He started to preach about the revolution. Hard to believe. He implied something like that at Christmas Eve, but it was still a surprise to see him today."

"He's the son of a rich man. What does it matter to him? He can afford to be with whomever he wants. He's got the time and the money."

"It doesn't appear to be a whim, though, Aunt Dulce. He's talking like he's hooked. He says he's been in it since 1957. Can you imagine? No one knew."

"Ah, Olga is also hooked, Aunt Dulce," Pablo said. "She's so much into it that it's pathetic. All she needs to do now is wear the uniform herself."

"I guess she'll be in town to watch him on television on the eighth. That's when they expect Fidel Castro to arrive in Havana. Tell her she can come and watch it here, if she wants to."

"I think I may come and see it, too," Pablo said.

"Well," she said, "I thought you didn't care, ah?"

"Actually," Aldo said, "I think I would like to see what he's got to say."

"Yes," Dulce said seriously. "I think everybody wants to see him."

She removed the pressure cooker from the burner and set it aside on another burner.

"I am going to warm up the steaks and rice that I made. Then I'll fry you some plantains, all right?"

"Don't worry, Aunt Dulce," Aldo said. "The peas would be enough."

"Oh, no. You are not going to leave this house hungry."

They heard Cecilia sigh and move on the bed, and she began to moan. Aldo went in to see her. Dulce followed.

"How are you, *mama*?"

She glanced at him for a moment and pouted. She did not speak to him. She looked down at the belt restraining her and tried to push it away, straining from the effort.

"Leave it, Cecilia," Dulce said. "Leave the belt alone. Look, Aldo is here, and so is Pablo. If you promise to be good, I will untie you."

"Let's untie her. She'll be okay as long as we are here."

Aldo went by her side and removed her hands from the belt. He unclipped the buckle and she sat in bed without saying anything. Then with a swift movement that startled Dulce, she moved her feet off the bed and sat on the edge, pushing Aldo aside. Pablo and Aldo stood behind her as she walked out of the room. She went to the dining room without saying a word and stood near the stove.

"Cecilia," Dulce said, "Aldo and Pablo are here. Say hello to them."

Cecilia didn't respond. She only stood there, staring blankly at the stove in front of her. She made a swift move to reach into the stove, but Dulce stepped in quickly.

"No, Cecilia. Don't touch. Sit down. Talk to Aldo and Pablo. They came to see you."

"I have to urinate," she said suddenly.

She took a step back and lifted her skirt. She squatted on the floor as Dulce grabbed her arm. Aldo and Pablo went into the bedroom.

"Don't do it *mama*," Aldo said. "Stop. No."

"It's all right," Dulce said. "Come Cecilia, let's go to the bathroom. You don't go on the floor, remember? Let's go."

Dulce had a good grip on her arm and she walked her into the bathroom. Aldo and Pablo returned to the dining room and sat down. It was not the first time they had witnessed this, but they felt embarrassed nonetheless. Dulce was a saint, Aldo thought, and he wondered how he could have kept his mother at home without her. He walked to the stove and turned the steaks over. Pablo was quiet until Dulce came back, holding her sister by the shoulder.

"Sit with me, Cecilia," Pablo said. "Would you like some chick peas? Dulce made them."

Dulce shook her head, but Cecilia did not respond. She let herself be guided by her sister who pulled a chair out and sat her down. She was unfocused, unmoved by anything around her. Aldo sat at the table again and looked at her.

"Frank and the girls are coming later. They want to show you their toys."

She did not respond. Her eyes stayed fixed on the table showing no reaction to what was going on around her.

"Let her be," Dulce said. "For now it's all right."

She served each of them a plate of boiled chick peas and brought silverware from the pantry. Suddenly, she felt energetic again, happy to be serving her nephew and friend. The last few days had been hard. The political events that had taken place had been overshadowed by her sister's condition.

"You should have seen us with the shooting."

"You mean the hospital shooting?"

"Yes. It was scary. I managed to put Cecilia under the bed and I stayed in the room until it stopped. I could hear the bullets zipping by."

"We heard they found nobody in the hospital," Pablo said. "Pretty irresponsible, if you ask me. They shoot the heck out of an empty hospital and then find that there's nobody there. What were they shooting at then?"

"You have to realize," Dulce said, "that they are all young boys eager to prove their bravery and show off their guns."

"Exactly," Aldo said. "Most of them have never shot a gun before. I bet you the majority has just joined. So naturally they want to show off."

"You know that a man who was speaking to Margo was hit by one of the ricocheting bullets right in front of her house. Half a block from here. He had to be taken to the hospital."

"Amazing," Pablo said. "And this is the Army who's supposed to be saving us."

Cecilia shifted her body in the chair. She put her hands on the table and quickly pulled herself up. Dulce stood behind her.

"Sit down Cecilia. Stay."

She ignored the warning and walked behind Aldo. She took short quick steps toward the front door.

"No!" Dulce yelled. "Aldo grab her, quick!"

Aldo went after her and held her arm. She struggled briefly, trying to get loose but he overpowered her by grabbing her waist. Dulce brought in a chair and had Aldo sit her down. Then she strapped her to the chair with two belts, one over her lap and another around her chest under her arms.

"Stay, Cecilia, please."

Aldo went back to the table and went on eating. Pablo had cleaned his plate and waited for Dulce to serve him the second course. "So what time is Fidel Castro's speech expected?" He said.

"I don't know for sure. Probably afternoon sometime."

"Aldo and I will be here. Olga for sure. Maybe Amanda, too, right Aldo?"

"Amanda will want to see him I'm sure. We'll all come."

"Is Amanda going back with you tonight?" Dulce asked.

"She and the children. School starts tomorrow for Frank."

"Good. I'm glad to see things go back to normal."

Early that evening, Pablo and Olga drove Aldo, Amanda and the children back to Rios. The trip was nostalgic for Amanda, as it was always difficult to accept the fact that the country was her home. She already missed the hustle and bustle of the city and dreaded to think they would be replaced by the crowing of roosters in the mornings. It was no life, she thought. But there was hope. Aldo was smart. She had learned to trust him. She had sensed a tremendous potential in his latest dealings, something new that seemed to be happening around him. This would be the break she had been waiting for, their ticket to the urban life, away from the desolate prairie. She pitied the poor people in Rios. There was no hope for them.

When they arrived at the house Alfredo, was waiting by the gate. He came to greet them. He had not seen them since Christmas Eve.

"Let me look at you, Frank," he said. "I think you've gotten taller."

"Look what they brought me, Alfredo." Frank pointed to his revolvers.

The twins wasted no time in showing him their toys, too. Amanda told them to come inside. Alfredo went back around the house and met them in the small dining room. He sat at the table and began to examine their toys one by one under the dim light of the kerosene lamp.

"How was everything?" Aldo asked.

"I could smell the roasted pork coming from Rios today. I saw some people riding on the road, celebrating. But I didn't go. I didn't want to leave the house."

"Why don't you go and play dominoes tonight?"

"Nahh," he said.

"Yes," Aldo insisted. "Go tonight. I have to stay home. It's the family's first night back, but tell Oscar to come over tomorrow and bring Rodolfo. We'll have a match."

Alfredo was quiet for a moment, flicking the trigger on Frank's revolvers.

"I have not seen Tomas again, Aldo."

Aldo looked at him. Since the day of the murder, they had not spoken his name. No one had mentioned him in Rios either. Now that Batista had fallen, where would he go? He had been outspoken about where his loyalties laid. Everyone knew he had supported the previous government. He had gone so far as to say that he would squeal on anyone he thought was aiding the rebels. When Patricio disappeared, everyone suspected that Tomas was behind it. It was no surprise that he wasn't around now.

"He's probably hiding, Alfredo."

"Oscar says he thinks he is still in his shack but doesn't come out."

"It'll pass, Alfredo. The people in Rios will forget. They won't turn him over to the rebels."

"You think he did it? You think he told on Patricio?"

Aldo gazed at Frank's toy police car on the table. Some things were better unsaid.

"You know what I know Alfredo. Make your own conclusions."

"What do you think will happen to him?"

"Nothing. Like I told you. Think for a moment. Would you go into town and report to a rebel squad that Tomas is a rogue? Of course you wouldn't. And no one else will either."

"I think he deserves to be hung for what he did."

"Justice has funny ways to manifest itself, Alfredo," Aldo said, sarcastically.

He did not know it yet, but he would be living proof of this in months to come. He stood up and said to Alfredo, "Why don't you go to Rios and be careful what you say, ah?"

CHAPTER NINE

ALDO SAT ON A ROCKING chair in front of Dulce's television set. He had been watching the famous commander for almost an hour, having missed a good portion of his speech. The bearded man stood before a web of microphones, speaking articulately. At his side stood another rebel with a beard and black hair that reached his shoulders. At times Mr. Castro would pause and turn to the man at his side, asking, "Am I doing well, Camilo?" It was a pattern that was to repeat itself in many other speeches to come.

Aldo learned this was Camilo Cienfuegos, a man of humble background, a peasant who had joined Fidel Castro in the mountains and earned the rank of commander. The media had published detailed stories about the accomplishments of Commander Cienfuegos and his counterpart in arms, Commander Ernesto Che Guevara. It was said that the two men had delivered the death blow to Batista's forces when they invaded and took the city of Santa Clara by force. They were portrayed as military heroes who had fought a heroic battle and achieved victory against great odds. But if the country had fallen in love with their heroes based on their legendary victories, they were smitten by their presence on the screen. There was no doubt that Fidel Castro had reached the pinnacle of popularity, but the presence of his comrades in arms, especially Camilo Cienfuegos, was a force to be reckoned with. The crowds immediately adored Cienfuegos who appeared timid in comparison to the outspoken Castro. He stood quietly aside, occasionally turning his head toward the speaker as if he were presiding over his speech.

Despite his ragged appearance, Aldo liked him. He appreciated Mr. Castro's intellect but became suspicious of his rhetoric that seemed to go around in circles. But Camilo was no politician. He was a soldier, a simple peasant who had probably joined the movement out of sympathy for a good cause, sparked by the abuses of the previous regime. Aldo could not blame him. The question was what future would a man like that have in this new order? Could he survive along with Castro?

The crowd's screams reached a frenzy at times, making it almost impossible to hear. The speaker would lift his arms to appease the audience and then moved on, showing full control.

"That's true!" Olga said. "That is so true!"

She was sitting next to Pablo and excitedly pointed her finger at the screen.

"It's true that Batista stole the country blind," Pablo said, "but it's not true that the whole country is living in misery. Are you in misery, Olga?"

"There are things that you don't know, Pablo. Things that he is going to show us. You think that peasants in the country have a doctor to go to or a school for their children?"

"Maybe not, but we were making progress. And what is he going to do? How's he going to change it all in one day?"

"Maybe he has a plan," Amanda said. "Let us see."

"Too much control by one man, Amanda," Pablo said. "I don't like it"

"Yes," she said, "I understand that but don't you think he has good ideas?"

"Of course, he does," Olga said. "If Pablo would just listen for a moment and stop being so negative."

"And you should stop making such a fool out of yourself," Pablo said angrily. "It's sickening."

"Stop it, you two," Amanda said. "Let's see what he says."

"I've been listening, Amanda, and I am already tired. It's too much talk already. Everywhere the man goes, it's talk, talk and more talk."

"He's certainly a talker," Dulce added.

She went to check on Cecilia who had been lying in bed in her room. She was under sedation again after going through a violent attack.

"I'll go," Amanda said. "It's my turn."

"No, stay," Dulce told her. "I thought I heard her moan. Let me see if she's all right."

Amanda followed her into the second bedroom where they found Cecilia lying face up, eyes closed, her mouth foaming. Dulce noticed it right away and became concerned at the paleness in her face and the jerky movements of her right arm. She turned around and touched Amanda's shoulder as she went by her and ran into the living room.

"Aldo," she said excitedly, "we have to get Cecilia to the Spanish Colony. I think she's having a stroke."

Everyone got up immediately and ran after Dulce. Aldo told Pablo to start the jeep while he unbelted his mother. He moved her to the edge of the bed and was preparing to lift her in his arms when Dulce placed a sheet over her. Aldo carried his mother out the front door. The children yelled to their father that they wanted to go.

"Sit down," Amanda told them. "It's no time for nonsense. Don't you see your grandmother is sick?"

Aldo laid Cecilia on the back seat of the jeep. Dulce held on to her to prevent her from rolling. Aldo took the front passenger seat. They were off immediately. Pablo sped through the side streets and entered the Central Highway and parked by the hospital's front entrance. Aldo was out before the jeep had come to a full stop. He lifted Cecilia's body. Her face was ashen, and she was not moving. Aldo went up the steps, carrying Cecilia, holding her arms with one hand so they wouldn't hang. He was met by a nurse at the main door. She wheeled a bed in front of him and he lay Cecilia down.

"What happened?" the nurse asked.

"She's passed out."

"Since when?"

"It just happened."

The nurse pushed the bed, Aldo walking alongside it. The nurse moved the bed into an empty room. Aldo recognized the man in the white gown inside.

"What do we have, nurse?" he asked, as he stood.

A radio on a table crackled with Mr. Castro's voice.

"She's unconscious. There is some foaming and light shaking."

He placed his stethoscope around his ears and listened to Cecilia's chest. The nurse unwrapped the sphygmomano and wrapped it around Cecilia's right arm.

"We don't have much pulse. Prepare a serum right away. I'll take that."

The doctor took the instrument from the nurse. He pumped the black rubber ball at the end of the elastic hose then released the air slowly.

"Blood pressure is down. Sixty over thirty. We need a team here. Better hurry up with that serum and call for oxygen."

Just then the doctor noticed the stocky man at his side. The gashes on his temple had almost healed, but he never forgot a face he had worked on. He was about to dismiss him from the room, but after recognizing him, he quickly changed his mind.

"I will do all I can, son," he said. "But for now, I think it's better if you wait outside. We're going to be pretty busy around here. We'll call you."

"Thanks, doctor," Aldo said.

He looked at Cecilia's face before exiting the room. Her eyes were closed. She was no longer spewing foam and seemed perfectly at ease in her present state.

Aldo swung the door open. Dulce and Pablo were standing so close that he almost bumped into them.

"How is she?" Dulce asked.

Her imploring look reflected all her pain. For the last few years she had devoted her entire life to her sister. There had been no relief from her task. She had never dated a man or socialized with anyone, except when her sister's condition allowed it, and only for house chores. She had never been to a movie theater again. She felt as if the floor under her had caved in, and she was terrified.

"They don't know yet. They are working on her. But I think she'll be all right."

He lied, knowing the situation was serious, and he worried about Dulce. She was strong, as strong as Cecilia had once been, but if something happened, it could break her. He glanced at Pablo.

"Did they give you a prognosis?"

"No. I was only there a couple of seconds. They are working on her."

A male nurse dressed in white walked hastily by them. He pushed the door in and entered. A female nurse followed. Dulce retreated to the center of the hallway and peaked inside just as the door swung back. She caught a glimpse of her sister lying face up with an I.V. in her arm. A doctor and nurse were bent over her. She went back to Aldo and Pablo and folded her arms.

"Let's go, Dulce, sit down," Aldo said. "We can do nothing but wait." He pointed to the wooden bench.

"I can't sit down."

Pablo put his arm around her shoulders. She leaned her head on him and sobbed as he gently stroked her hair.

"Come, sit with us," he said.

It was already dark when Amanda's small figure appeared. She was puzzled for a moment. Aldo whistled to her and she turned. Aleida and Olga followed.

"How is she?" Amanda asked.

"They haven't told us much yet. She's in that room. The doctor has been in and out."

"The nurse told us to wait until the doctor could tell us more," Dulce said.

Aleida kissed Dulce. She shook hands with Pablo who stood up to give her his seat on the bench.

"Don't. Stay," she told him.

"No, I am tired of seating."

Aldo also stood and waived for Amanda to sit down. At that moment the doctor exited the room and looked briefly at the women. He recognized the older one with the long gray hair. She rose immediately, but he turned to Aldo.

"Is the patient your mother?"

"Yes," he said.

"All right. Well, she suffered a stroke. Her heartbeat was weak when she came in, so we have tried to bring it up. She is unconscious. We have now given her coramine and we will see how she reacts to that."

The medication was commonly known as a last resource to revive a patient. They all understood it.

"Is she going to live?" Dulce asked.

"Only time will tell," he said. "It depends how her body reacts to the medicine. The next few hours will be critical."

Dulce looked at Aldo and crossed her arms.

"I would recommend," the doctor said, "that you don't all stay here tonight. It might be a long wait before we know more. I understand that you want to be near her, but there is really no need."

He knew it was customary for the family to watch over sick other family members for days, a practice that had been carried on from home care to the advent of hospitals and clinics. On many occasions, it had proved helpful as the patient reacted well to having his family tend to his physical needs. But in cases of critical care, it could be a hindrance having family stand around watching his every move. He resented it and tried to repress it. The two men surely must have work to do, he thought. Why did they sit here? He could ease the situation if he could convince them to leave. He would have to tell them in front of the others or they would never leave on their own.

"Will it will be very long before we know?" Pablo inquired.

"It could be. Believe me, there is nothing that you can do by being here. If you have work to do, go. The others can stay. I will be around later. We are doing all we can."

He turned his back on them and returned to the emergency room. The women sat down, and prepared for a long wait.

"Well, Aldo, maybe you should go and tend to the cattle," Amanda said.

"Yes," Dulce repeated, "you go. There is nothing you can do."

Aldo took a few moments to reflect on the trend of events. He listened as Dulce related the afternoon events to the other women who gave their own prognosis about Cecilia's condition. Amanda thought it might be related to her mental state and that she would wake up normal. Olga compared it with one of her relatives' seizures from which he had fully recovered. Aleida concluded that Cecilia would be fine. After a while, Aldo asked to see the doctor. Since he had nothing new to report, Aldo explained that he would be leaving and would be back in the early morning. The doctor assured him that it was the right decision.

Aldo caught some sleep before milking the herd. When Alfredo knocked on his window, he felt refreshed and energetic again. He was silent as he made his way to the cattle house flanked by Alfredo. There was no deluding himself. He had seen it in the doctor's eyes. Cecilia would never recover, and if she did, she would be in a vegetative state. It was sad that a woman who had suffered so much on account of others would end up this way. He suddenly felt as if Cecilia was standing near him, watching him work with the cattle in this prairie where she had come to live as a little girl many years ago. It had been her downfall but the prairie was also her home. It was all she knew.

Aldo helped the milkman get his carriage ready. Then, without returning to the house to change, he buttoned his leather coat tight and he climbed on the buggy's seat.

"You can drop me at the Spanish Colony on the way into town," he said. "I know it's a little out of the way for you friend, but do me this favor."

"Sure, Aldo, it's no trouble at all."

Most of the milkman's customers lived near Nadales. He would deliver to their homes on his way in, then work his way into the metropolitan areas, past the cemetery. This morning, he drew his whip to spur his horse on. The animal intuitively slowed down to make the usual turn at Nadales.

"We are not going there today, friend," he said as if his horse could understand him. "Not just yet."

Nothing was more familiar to sleepy ears than the clanking of the horse hooves in the early hours of dawn. For some, it was a signal to rise. They went by at precisely the same time, but today they seemed a little earlier than usual and faster. Something was different.

The milkman turned at the Central Highway and upon reaching the intersection of the road into the clinic, he turned right.

"You don't have to drive me all the way in. Drop me here." Aldo told him.

"No," the milkman insisted, "what difference does it make to me? A few more minutes."

He let Aldo out in front of the steps and offered to wait, but Aldo insisted he should go. There would probably be a lot of waiting. He checked with the nurse at the front desk. It was a few minutes before 5:00 A.M. She looked at him and was about to say something, but he was already moving down the hallway. She followed him.

Aldo thought it strange not to see any of the women sitting on the bench where he had left them but he figured they had been allowed inside the room with his mother. He became aware of the footsteps behind him. He stopped at the door of the room for a moment and was going to push it open when the nurse grabbed his arm.

"Sir," she said, "no one is there."

He looked at her in surprise. Her face was so somber she did not need to say anything more.

"When did she pass on?"

"About midnight. We told your family to leave. I'm very sorry."

"Will you let me call a taxi," he said calmly.

"Sure," she said. "I'll call one for you."

She was a pretty, petite woman with black hair and black eyes and a chiseled face. She had been at the clinic since New Year. She had started her shift right at midnight and she had not seen Aldo before. But she had heard about him from the other nurses. He was a handsome man, she thought. And even in his dirty clothes and cowboy hat, he looked attractive. Too bad she had not worked at the Colony while he was a patient. She would have done all she could to comfort him.

"A taxi will be here in a few moments," she said.

"Thank you."

"If you would like to see the doctor, you can come back in the morning," she said. "The lady with the gray hair, is she your aunt?"

"Yes."

"Well, she made all the arrangements. The other ladies were in shock. Your mother will be at the Cisneros funeral home," she said, referring to a note from her chart.

Aldo thanked her. That was Dulce, always strong in the face of disaster, upright when others failed. Aldo smiled bitterly. He was now totally alone. He had no brothers, sisters, or parents. The people who had been responsible for his being here were all gone.

When he arrived at Dulce's house, she had already made coffee. She knew he would come. The two of them embraced in the kitchen for a long time without speaking. There was no need for words.

"She did not want you to box," Dulce said softly.

He did not let her see his tears. He went to the bedroom next to Cecilia's and undressed. Cecilia was no longer suffering. She had regained her sanity. He slept peacefully for three hours.

Funerals were a twenty-four hour ritual in this country during which families mourned their dead and accepted condolences from friends and acquaintances. It was a custom at odds with the Anglo Saxon tradition of showing the body over several days. Aldo and Dulce arrived at the funeral home at 9:00 A.M. The casket was wheeled into an empty room, and they saw Cecilia's pale face for the first time since the previous evening. They would spend the whole day and night in wait and would bury her tomorrow. It was a grueling process, allowing little time for the mourners to recover. In addition, because of the time constraints, many acquaintances would not find out in time, barely being able to attend the burial.

Aldo made the arrangements at the cemetery for the burial. He made sure that Pablo would be on hand to notify Don Fernando that they could not meet him at the Arapientos' farm, as previously agreed. It was a virtue among the cattle breeders and traders to be punctual and keep an appointment with one's business partners. In a world where communication was limited to word of mouth, the cattle trader's word was as good as gold. But there was no need to worry. That evening Don Fernando appeared at the parlor with Mr. Sanchez and offered Aldo his condolences. He did not mention business. Many other friends, rich and poor, peasants and town folk, stopped by to greet him and expressed their sympathies.

Early that evening, Alfredo arrived with Pablo. He had known Cecilia for many years. He took off his hat he had not cried during the night but the hardest moment had arrived. She clung to her nephew's shoulder, her last living relative, and looked at her sister's face one last time. Cecilia's ashen face seemed to be sagging a little but appeared peaceful as if she were asleep. Dulce's tears were silent. Amanda who was standing next to her, began crying. Her sister Aleida followed suit. The two men waited patiently for Aldo. Finally, he nodded, and they closed the coffin. The wailing among the women got louder. The two men slid the coffin on top of the cart and wheeled it into the street where the hearse and funeral car were waiting.

Aldo walked Dulce, Amanda, and her sisters to a waiting taxi. He told the driver to drive them to Padre Valencia, Dulce's home. He and Pablo and all the men began walking behind the slow-moving hearse loaded with flowers in a small, compact group that filled the whole width of the street. They gradually made their way into the cemetery. The designated pallbearers, Pablo and Aldo among them, reached for the side handles of the gray coffin and withdrew it from the funeral car. They walked through the entrance and made their way among the many sepulchers and white monuments with winged angels and large crosses.

They stopped in front of an open tomb, a rectangular marble structure whose cover had been removed. Each side was tiled with white ceramic to allow room for walking. At the head of the square were two small crypts used for storing the remains of the dead once they were gathered from the tomb two years after the burial, as was the custom. There was an oval framed picture of a middle age man atop one of the chambers. This was Aldo's father. The other unmarked crypt contained his brother's remains.

The undertakers climbed on each side of the vault, two on each side, holding wide straps over the opening. One of them stepped up and pulled the coffin as the pallbearers sought to guide it over the straps. One by one they released them, and the coffin descended. Aldo watched it until he could not see it anymore. Cecilia was part of a generation that was fading, brave people who had ventured into the prairie, overcoming its isolation. They had little education but high standards by which they lived. Their sons and daughters would inherit some of their indomitable spirit and would go on to conquer other lands, but their legacy would not be the same.

A slight thud told the men the coffin had touched the bottom. They loosened their straps and pulled them out. They moved past the spectators and lifted the heavy marble top by each of its gold handles, then carefully placed it on the opening, shifting it until it made a good fit. One man took what looked like a bucket of paint with white cement. He carefully spackled the edges with a spatula until all cracks were sealed. Some of the mourners made the sign of the cross and turned to leave. It was over.

Over the next few days, Aldo dedicated himself to the farm and stayed out of town. The day after the burial, he met Don Fernando and Mr. Sanchez at the Arapientos' farm, and he and Pablo rounded the cattle for him to see. Something told him that Don Fernando cold not move the cattle, but he did not care. He wanted to make good on his word, once Don Fernando said how fast he could sell the herd if the price was right, he excused himself and drove the cattle back leaving Pablo to handle Don Fernando. The time would come, he thought, when he and his friend would again go hunting for buyers. It was not yet to be.

In the evenings, some of the men from Rios came over to play dominoes and listen to the radio. Amanda would make them coffee and sit in the dining room, rocking the twins in her arms. She would later lie on her bed with the children and doze off, occasionally awakened by the flat, crude slap of the men's domino chips on the table.

The initial confusion after the rebels' takeover had now dissipated, but the wave of optimism among the people continued to grow. The enthusiasm for the new rulers, especially Fidel Castro, was immense. Castro and his deputies made repeated calls for vengeance for past crimes committed by Batista's government. Castro's speeches became more frequent and longer. He had taken the country by storm and now seemed to be reaching deeper into the island. In one of those fateful nights when he took the podium and spoke until past midnight, he emotionally announced the creation of revolutionary tribunals and revolutionary squads for the execution of Batista's criminals. It was new and speedy justice geared to even the scores with the previous regime. The decision, like all others so far, was received by the general population with tremendous enthusiasm. The media disclosed that some of the trials would be televised.

"He's certainly persistent," Amanda observed. "He will not stop until the prisons are cleared."

"So, you think it's the right decision?"

She looked at him. No matter how sure, if she noted the slightest doubt in his voice, it was enough to throw her off. She respected his opinion.

"No," he laughed, "I'm asking you. What do you think?"

"I think it has to be done. These people are murderers. I approve of justice."

"Now, Amanda, what would your father say if he heard you?"

"My father is not right about everything Aldo, you know it. But tell me, what do you think?"

"I don't like it."

"You sound just like Pablo, Aldo. Why don't you give the man a chance?"

"That's what bothers me. We're going back to him. Why him? I thought his work was done now that the revolution has won. I thought that President Urrutia would now make these decisions."

"I don't know that. I just think it's the right thing to do."

They had been listening to the radio early in the evening. The pleasant March weather of the tropics made this time of year ideal. Although spring was due to arrive, it had not rained yet. The night breeze was light, and a fresh smell lingered in the room. The men from Rios were due to arrive soon. The radio commentators described the anxiety of the crowd gathered in the plaza, waiting for Fidel Castro to appear and speak to them. It was expected that he would announce today his plan to distribute tools and implements to the peasants in the country. Aldo heard the sound of an engine getting close.

"Someone's coming," he said, rising.

He went out to the porch with Frank and the girls. An olive-green jeep was moving towards the house rapidly. Aldo saw it was military. Two uniformed men were inside. The passenger gripped the rim of the adjustable roof for support. The jeep made a wide turn as it reached the gate and parked in front of the house.

"Good evening," the man said, smiling.

He was tall. His face was hardly visible, covered by a bushy, grey beard. He wore a military cap and as he came forward, Aldo realized it was Blanco.

"Blanco, how are you?"

The bearded man extended his hand and smiled pleasantly, then ruffled the children's hair.

"How is everybody?"

"Fine. Come in."

"I bet you are surprised to see me this way, ah?"

"Well, yes, I am. I guess your image has changed somewhat," Aldo joked. "Tell the other gentleman to come in, too."

Blanco turned towards the jeep and waived to the driver to come out. He was barely twenty, swarthy and his face, too, bore a beard. He was dressed in fatigues with a tight green belt around his waist and a holstered .45 on the side that he patted lightly as he got out the jeep as if to make them notice it. He wore a green military cap and black army boots. He shook Aldo's hand.

"Come inside," Aldo said, "Amanda will be happy to see you."

"This is Corporal Antonio Mela," Blanco said.

They went into the living room. Amanda stood as they entered. She hesitated as she saw Blanco, hardly recognizing him, then hugged and kissed him.

"Hello, Blanco," she said.

She did not comment on his appearance, but she knew that she would not have recognized him without introduction. He was a changed man.

"Well, don't tell me you're not surprised, ah?"

"Yes, I am," she said casually. "But come in, sit down. Your friend too, please. Shall I make you coffee?"

"If you make it, we will drink it," Blanco said.

He took off his cap, and the other man followed. Amanda went into the kitchen, and Aldo dragged one of the rocking chairs into the room. The twins came and sat shyly on his lap.

"So you're listening to the speech, ah?"

"Yes. It's kind of a routine around here in the evening while we play dominoes."

"I'd like to think that you take some interest in it though."

"I follow it a little. Not much."

"Well, I didn't come to talk to you about that. I wouldn't impose it on you. I figure that you are a smart man, and soon enough, you will realize what the revolution is all about, and you will come around."

"How is Ana?" Aldo asked, ignoring the comment.

"She's fine. That's one of the reasons I'm here. I am devoted to the revolution, Aldo. I have practically abandoned my business. Ana has been making a go of it but it's too much for her. I came to ask you whether you will be interested in managing our cattle. I don't have the time to trade anymore."

"Manage your cattle?"

"Yes. Sell all of it. We don't want it anymore. What I would like to do is keep only a few heads, just enough to have a small milking business like you have. I am going to keep some of the land and donate the rest to the revolution."

"Are you sure you want to do this?"

"More than sure. I figure you can make the sales and I'll pay you a commission. You know cattle, so leave me the good heads that I need to build a milking herd."

"I don't think I can sell my own cattle right now. With everything that's happened, the trading has decreased. Very few people are doing business."

"Ah, no. You're not going to blame our revolution for this. Who said trading is down? I can sell all the cattle I want right now. Business has never been better. I just don't have time anymore. But you are not going to have a problem with that. That's a promise."

"Do you have some contacts?"

"Lots of them. I tell you what. There is a big need for cattle right now in Santa Cruz where I have been working lately. I will lead you to them, and you do the rest."

Aldo liked the idea. He had always thought that Blanco was honest. He didn't know what to make of his transformation. He was sure it would tarnish his previous reputation as a serious trader. Such things were looked down upon among cattle traders. And that was probably the reason why Blanco was asking him to intercede. Blanco knew he had lost credibility among the old conservative businessmen. The revolution must be really important to Blanco, so important that he was willing to do away with his reputation and fortune. He had sought Aldo to effect his plan for dismantling his empire. For the first time since his mother's death, Aldo felt the urge to work again. He was being given an opportunity. It was time to move forward again.

"I like trading. I think I can do well with it. But I have plans to sell my own cattle, too. If I meet buyers, I will probably end up selling them some of my own cattle, too."

"I know that, Aldo. And I expect it. It doesn't bother me. In fact, I welcome the opportunity to help you. I think it's part of my plan. not just a spill-over from it. I want you to get a piece of the action. And I appreciate your honesty in telling me. "

"I would protect your interests first and set your plan in motion before looking after mine."

"No, no. I don't want that. I want it to be an even venture. Trade my cattle as well as yours. And use these contacts wisely. Well,

I guess I don't have to tell you that." Blanco nodded as if to indicate the deal was sealed.

"You know my accountant?"

"No, I don't think so."

"Yes, you do. Gerardo Garcia. The little limping man on General Gomez Street."

"Yes."

"Well, see him for anything you need. He has my permission to deal with you directly, and Ana has authority to sign any checks that are needed. I'll make all the arrangements."

Amanda came back with two cups of coffee. She served Antonio first then Blanco. She stood before Blanco hesitantly and then said, "So, how is my sister? I have not seen her for weeks."

"She's fine. She has been working hard. I am hoping to make some arrangements so she can leave the farm and come with me to Santa Cruz."

"Santa Cruz?"

"Yes. I am going to be there for a while. The revolution needs me and I have been placed in command of that region. There is much to be done."

"But Santa Cruz is so far away. I never even heard the name until you started working there. I will never see Ana."

"You will see her. Actually, she is quite happy about it. It's a beautiful place, a beach town that has been exploited by unscrupulous traders and merciless landlords. We are going to change that and make it a true sample of revolutionary work with the people and for the people."

"I would like her to stay in Camaguey. We've always been a close family," she said sadly.

"She's not leaving you, Amanda. We have a moral duty to do our best for our people."

"Yes, I know," Amanda said tiredly. "But first comes the family. Without the family, there can't be anything. I worry about my family first. The rest of the people are not going to do anything for me."

"That's what the revolution is all about, Amanda, family. About a big family, all of us together. We are going to build something together.

To think of the family as just your own immediate family is heresy in this very important time of ours. We have to think of all of us as one."

"Heresy!" Amanda exclaimed. "I think it's more of a heresy to pretend that we are something we are not, Blanco. It may be altruistic on your part to think this way, but it's certainly not the norm but the exception."

She was holding her ground and was angered by his comments and his philosophies, which she thought fanciful, and she wanted to let him know. He refused to see it. He was in love with the revolution and could not get past that.

"In the old regime, maybe Amanda, but not anymore. This is the dawn of a new era, and we have to open our minds. The vices of the past have to go."

"Blanco," she said cutting him off, "what does all this have to do with political regimes? Batista did not tell me how to think. Why should someone else do so now?"

"No one is telling you how to think now. But you must try to see the light, to understand that you have been living a big lie. Batista did not tell you what to think, but his jackals went all around enforcing his despotism. You've seen it right here, didn't you?"

The implication was quite clear to Aldo, but to Amanda, who was not aware of all the circumstances surrounding Patricio's death, it was not.

"What are you referring to?"

"A man, an honest, humble peasant, was murdered by *casquitos* right here in Rios, almost across from your door, you know that."

"You mean Patricio?"

"Yes, I mean Patricio. You are not going to deny that the Batista government killed him. And why? For what reason other than he may have spoken out what was on his mind. So naturally, Batista did not tell you how to think, but had you dared to say what you thought, you would be dead. Now, if that is not control, then what is?"

Blanco wanted to be understood. But Aldo thought that Blanco was making a point that went beyond. Aldo felt there was something he wanted him to know. Something no one else knew.

"I am not defending Batista, but I don't know who killed Patricio," Amanda responded, "and no one that I know can make that assertion. Did anyone see it? Did you?"

"Don't worry," Blanco said cautiously. "Those who are responsible will be brought to justice."

"Will that be the revolutionary tribunals, Blanco?" She asked ironically.

"Yes. They will see justice done."

"Who are these revolutionary tribunals? Are they judges? Do they have any experience in the law? Or are they just people who have been hand picked because they are faithful to the revolution?"

Antonio shifted his weight uncomfortably in his seat. He looked at Aldo.

"They are people of high morals who have devoted themselves to the revolution. They are not part of the past bourgeoisie, so they don't necessarily have to be lawyers or judges. They are people who know right from wrong and who will judge those before them justly, that's all."

"You have to understand Amanda's point," Aldo interposed. "We are talking about taking people's lives here. That is an enormous responsibility. How can you be sure that these prisoners will get a fair shake?"

"But that's the thing, Aldo. Look at the crimes that Batista committed. We had judges and lawyers back then and supposedly, anybody accused was to have a fair trial. Now tell me this, did Patricio have a trial? Was he to go back to a rotten old system that served no purpose and totally abrogated our people's rights? I find it bizarre that you would even ask. We are not going to back to the old system. Never! We are going to try these pigs, and they are going to pay for what they've done."

Blanco had become emotional and pointed his index finger at Aldo and Amanda as he spoke. Aldo's senses were immediately on guard. He understood Blanco's point, but he was convinced that Blanco did not understand his or Amanda's, and he became alarmed at Blanco's reaction. He did not like anyone gesturing at him, no matter who he was, no matter what power he had.

"Easy, friend," Aldo said. "I do not want to discuss politics. And to answer your questions, I have always stood up for what I thought was right, and I have never let any man shake me, not during Batista and not now during Fidel. I have nothing to be ashamed of for what happened. I did what I had to do, and if it happened now with the rebels I would do the same. I merely asked you a question. That's all. You want us to understand you, but you don't want to understand us. Let's just drop it."

Aldo spoke without emotion, letting Blanco know that he was united with Amanda. He also wanted him to know that he would not tolerate being pushed around. He was sure that Blanco knew what had happened that night at the roadblock, but something told him that he had other ideas about Patricio's death. It just didn't figure, but he wanted to leave the whole thing alone now. He didn't care what Blanco thought. He realized that Blanco was a changed man, with ideas and hopes that only the wisdom of time could justify. To maintain Blanco's friendship right now would be a rather difficult proposition.

"Aldo, I understand, believe me I do. But you also have to understand that the revolution has the best of intentions, and to taint it with suspicion without reason is unfair…"

"Fine, fine," Aldo said, interrupting him. "Let's just not discuss it anymore. Understand something right now. I am not a revolutionary, just as I was not a Batista sympathizer. Neither is my wife. We just want to live in peace. If we are to be friends and family as before, then let's not discuss politics, all right?"

Blanco looked frustrated. He wanted to go on. He wanted to explain, yet he respected Aldo. There was something about his peasant roots that he had always found fascinating. He thought him the epitome of Cuban peasantry: humble, full of integrity, strong, and intelligent.

Blanco reached for Aldo's hand and stood up. His companion also rose.

"Let's work together on my cattle, all right? You won't regret it. I promise you."

"Well, as you know, I have a partner, Pablo. Let me talk to him and we'll both meet you somewhere. How fast do you need an answer?"

"I counted on you bringing Pablo in," Blanco said. "I will be in the area until tomorrow night. Why don't you and Pablo come to the ranch tomorrow? The man you need to see will be at my house tomorrow evening. He is from Santa Cruz. I want you to meet him."

Blanco turned to Amanda as he let go off Aldo's hand. They had always had a cordial relationship. He wrapped his arm around her shoulder and kissed her.

"Don't worry about your sister. She's well taken care of, and she's happy, very happy. Why don't you come tomorrow with Aldo and see her? She'll be happy about that."

"I will, but I want to see her more than just on occasion. I would like her to be around."

Blanco did not reply and merely smiled at her to make peace. Despite their differences, he wanted to remain a friend, although he could never hope to be part of the family as they once had been. He did not feel sad. He had liberated himself from old vices and a life of fantasy. This was part of the price to be paid. He was entering a new self, a new beginning. His life would never be the same.

"I will see you tomorrow then," Blanco said to her softly.

"All right."

Antonio shook Aldo's hand, then Amanda's. He had not spoken a word the whole time except to say goodbye.

"It was nice meeting you both," he said curtly. He walked behind Blanco, his right hand on the butt of his .45.

As the men got in the jeep, Blanco waived at them from the passenger side. Midway to the main road, they passed three men from Rios walking towards Aldo's house for an evening game of dominoes.

"I can't believe that man," Aldo said.

"What has come over him? My poor sister. How will she end up? What will happen to her? They are going to lose everything, Aldo. Please, you can't let that happen."

"But what can I do? Olga has become just like him. They are possessed. I am really surprised at Blanco, though. He fooled us all. He was one of them from way back, and none of us knew it."

"Truly? You think so?"

"Yes. He hid it from us because of your family, mainly. He has been working for the movement for years. How else did he rise so high so fast? One never really knows a person. He had it all, born into money, with a good education. He has traveled throughout Europe. He has lived in the United States. He had everything, but he chose to become a revolutionary. I say if that's his wish, let him be."

The next morning, Aldo rode his mare to Pablo's farm and the two discussed the events of the previous evening. Neither was opportunistic and would not have thought of using Blanco, no matter what the rewards. But they saw an opportunity to establish new contacts through him. Maybe they would not help him dispose of his assets, but they would pursue any chance to do business of their own if he offered it. That afternoon, after Frank arrived from school, the two families traveled together to Blanco and Ana's large farmhouse located at the edge of Blanco's estate, one hundred hectares, south of the city of Camaguey.

The high iron gate was kept open during the day. The property was fenced with wooden red posts and neatly tailored boards. The house was one of the area's landmarks. The path from the main gate to the house was flanked by beautiful dwarf coconut trees, and peacocks and ducks feasted on the low-growing grass. About three hundred feet from the road was the family colonial style brick house with an arched portico.

There were three military jeeps parked near the garage, which was detached from the house. Inside was Blanco's 1958 Buick, still as shiny and spotless as when new.

As Aldo parked the jeep behind the other vehicles, a thin old black man dressed in baggy clothes and a small straw hat came to greet them. Two barking German Shepherds followed him. Aldo and Pablo exited the jeep. The man made a squeaky noise, and the dogs sat down, still barking.

"Good afternoon, gentlemen. What can I do for you?" he said politely. He had not recognized them.

"I am Aldo. I am here to see Blanco."

"Ah, Mr. Aldo," he said surprised, "how are you? Yes, Mr. Blanco said you would be coming today. Ah, and you must be Pablo, of course. Please come in."

"Can I tell our families to get out of the jeep?" Pablo asked.

"Ah, your families are here. Forgive me. Don't tell me this is Mrs. Ana's sister and the children," he said, pointing to the figures inside the jeep. "Please come in."

He walked quickly towards the jeep, motioning for the occupants to get out.

"Please tell everyone to come in. I will get Mrs. Ana right away." He turned to the dogs: "Ah, Tato and Tata, come."

He pointed towards the bushes alongside the house, and the dogs obediently ran in that direction. Then he waived at everyone to follow him.

They entered through a foyer handsomely decorated with three oil paintings. There was an arched door on the right leading to a hallway, and on the left, a curtained opening to the living room. They were met by a middle-aged black.

"It is Aldo, Rafaela," the thin black man said. "Mrs. Ana's sister is here too. Call Mrs. Ana right away."

The woman looked aloof for a moment then smiled at Aldo. "You brought Mrs. Amanda with you?"

"She's right behind me."

The woman saw Amanda, Olga, and the children behind him and Pablo.

"Good, Mr. Aldo. Mrs. Ana really needs this now. Let me get her for you. She is in the garden. Go sit in the living room for a moment."

She pointed to the door on their left.

The room was paneled halfway up with smooth dark wood. The top portion was painted in baby blue. There was a large oak table supported by one single column shaped like a star and chairs of heavy dark wood with blue cushions. The floor was done with large beige ceramic tiles. A beautiful six-bulb chandelier hung over the table.

"Sit down. Make yourselves comfortable while I get Mrs. Ana."

She disappeared into the hallway as they sat down. The black man, who had remained by the front door, went outside. They could smell tobacco smoke and heard laughter from several male voices coming from another room.

"Whoever built this house knew what he was doing," Pablo said.

"Blanco's father spent a fortune building it," Aldo said. "Funny thing was that he lived in Cuba for most of his life yet he never lost his contempt for Cubans to the point where every mason who worked on this house was of pure Spanish blood."

"Truly," Olga said. "Did he ever go back to Spain?"

"He died in this house and is buried a few yards back from here. There is a small cemetery there. You can see it from the back porch."

"Aughhhh," Olga said, looking at Pablo. "That's a little grotesque, right?"

"I don't think I would like that. But that was his wish and Blanco fulfilled it."

"I know he never married, right?"

"He never did, and no one ever mentions Blanco's mother. Not even my sister talks about it."

"They say she was a maid in this house," Amanda added.

"You don't know that, Amanda," Aldo said.

"I am pretty sure," Amanda said jauntily, looking at Olga.

The footsteps in the hallway interrupted their conversation. Ana strode into the room, her long hair hanging down her back. She was wearing a man's shirt, its sleeves rolled up to her forearms, and blue jeans. She held a pair of gloves in her hand. She smiled at them, came quickly to Amanda and kissed her on the cheek, then kissed Olga and the children. She shook hands with each of the men. She stopped before Aldo.

"So you will come, then?" She asked him.

"I will come," he said nodding. She looked at him, hands on her waist and shifted her eyes to her sister.

"And how have you been, Amanda? How is our Dad?"

"Ah, he is fine. We all miss you. When are you coming to the city."

"I was in Camaguey two weeks ago to see him. But you know I can't leave the house with Blanco away. I am just too busy."

"Where shall I take them, Mrs. Ana," Rafaela asked.

"Oh, I'll bring them to the kitchen. They are family, Rafaela."

"Yes, ma'am. Mr. Blanco is using the living room, Mrs. Ana," she said coyly.

"It's all right. We'll stop in and see him. Come on, follow me," she said to them.

They followed her through the hallway into a large room, opulently furnished with a long French sofa and several armchairs, a glass table and matching end tables. Several bearded men in green fatigues were sitting down, puffing on long cigars. The room was filled with blue smoke. The filled ashtrays and empty bottles of beer covered the table.

"Blanco, Aldo is here," Ana said to him. The others looked up at her as she came in.

"Aldo?" Blanco said in surprise.

He rose from one of the armchairs. The other men stopped laughing for a moment, but then carried on as before. Aldo recognized Antonio sitting at one edge of the sofa, still holding on to his belted gun as he warily eyed him. Blanco set his cigar down in an ashtray and came forward to shake hands. The other men now seemed oblivious to their presence.

"It's good that you came," he said and turned to look at Pablo. "How are you?"

"I'm all right," Pablo said.

"Very nice to see you, Olga," Blanco said. "And you, too Amanda. I have a surprise for the children. But listen, if you adults want some coffee, help yourselves. There are no more maids in this house. Everyone helps themselves in the kitchen."

"No more maids?" Amanda asked. "I could have sworn I just saw one."

"That was but no more. As of today we have no more maids. That's for the elite. We are not elite here. We refuse to be. We are revolutionaries. Ask my wife."

Everyone looked at Ana who in turn, looked at Aldo and blushed. Her life had suddenly changed. Despite her background, she had always been a simple woman and could have done without maids. But hadn't her husband gone a bit too far?

"Well said," Olga added. "I'm with you. The revolution is for all of us, not just for a few, and we must be an example for everyone else. I admire you for doing that."

"Shall I wait for you outside?" Aldo asked.

"No. Get yourself a beer if you want one, or coffee, or whatever you like, and we'll talk in a few minutes. Here, let me introduce you to my colleagues."

He took his arm as he turned to the group of men. They were still immersed in their own conversation. Aldo thought he heard one of them mumble a prayer in ridicule.

"This is Captain Ramirez." Blanco pointed to each man. "This is Lieutenant Alvarez. This is Corporal Antonio Mazos whom you met yesterday, and this is my comrade, Lieutenant Ramos from Santa Cruz. Captain Ramirez fought in the Maestra mountains range so he has our respect."

Aldo and Pablo nodded to each man but it was obvious that their reception was cool. They were not part of their club.

"Olga, come meet the captain," Blanco said.

"It is an honor, Captain," she said, leaning forward to shake his hand. Olga was one of them.

Something in the corner of the room caught Aldo's eye. He noticed several submachine guns stacked against the wall. It appeared that Blanco was turning his house into an arsenal.

The man Blanco had called captain looked sternly at Olga and shook her hand without standing up. He radiated authority. Aldo thought him cocky.

"How are you, Olga?" the captain said. "I bet you and Ana will make a true home for our revolution in this house. You are her sister, right?"

"Ah, no," she said. "Her sister is Amanda, but I can be just the same."

"You probably have her heart," Captain Ramirez said. He looked at Ana above Olga's shoulder. Aldo noticed it. It was not an innocent look and bore something that smacked of deceit. Aldo didn't like it and noticed that Ana's faced remained cold and unreceptive. Aldo wished he were Blanco right now. Captain Ramirez's broad face was the perfect target for a good bare-knuckle punch. Blanco had lost his wits, Aldo thought. He would never have allowed these men in his house, let alone let one of them flirt with his wife. He tapped Amanda's shoulder.

"We will wait for you outside, Blanco," Aldo said.

He went out into the hallway with Amanda and the children, leaving Pablo and Olga in the room with the other men. Ana followed. They went into the kitchen.

"Can I get you a beer, Aldo," Ana asked.

"No, thanks."

"I am going to make myself some coffee," Amanda said. "Can I, sister?"

"Of course. I'll make it, you sit down. What shall I get the children."

She walked to a large refrigerator. It was a General Electric model that operated with kerosene. Electricity had not yet reached this part of the country. The electric lights in the house were powered by a portable generator.

"We have orange juice, coca cola, pineapple juice, ah?"

"I'll have a pineapple juice," Frank said.

"Me too, me too," the twins said.

She served them each in a Coca Cola glass and set the coffee pot on the burner.

"Ana," Amanda said, "don't you think this is going a bit too far? You are firing the maids too?"

Ana was silent. She was obviously embarrassed.

"Can we go out to the porch?" Ana said.

It had a brick floor and cement block columns and was enclosed with mash wire to keep the insects out. It was furnished with wick rocking chairs and a table. They all sat down, except Ana.

"What in the world has come over him?" Amanda repeated. "He wants to get rid of his cattle, his land, and now his maids? What's going to happen next, you're going to live under a bridge?"

"I think that's why you're here, Aldo," Ana said. "You are going to help us?"

"Well, I don't know that I can help you in that sense. Blanco asked me to sell some of his cattle for him. He wants to reduce the stock and leave a milking herd for the farm."

"Are you going to do it?"

"We are going to talk about it."

"But Ana," Amanda insisted, "what in the world is going on? You people are acting like kids. Giving away your possessions. And those men in the house with their cigars and their dirty beards. They look disgusting!"

Aldo stroked the twins' silky hair while looking at Ana. He didn't think it was Amanda's place to question her about her personal affairs, and he was ready to stop her. But Amanda cared for Ana, and she was looking out for her best interests in the only way she knew. Speaking her mind would probably clear the air.

"Possessions are not important to me, Amanda, you would not understand," Ana said calmly.

She went around the table to return to the kitchen. Amanda walked behind her, shaking her head.

"You know what I don't understand, I don't understand where our father went wrong with you. He always gave you the best and taught you to have class. Here you are acting like you came from the gutter. What's the matter with you?"

"Let's just leave it, Amanda," Ana said. "Leave it at that."

"But I don't understand you," she repeated, "I don't."

"That's right, you don't."

Ana looked serenely at her sister's angry face as she readied to serve her coffee.

"Here," Ana said, handing her a cup of espresso.

"I don't want any coffee," Amanda snarled. "I don't want anything."

Aldo entered the kitchen with the children behind him. He was not going to intervene. Ana could handle Amanda.

"Can you ask Blanco and Pablo to come here?" he said.

"Yes. I will be right back, Aldo."

Blanco, Pablo and Aldo went out into the yard brimming with rose bushes and flowers. They went down a winding pathway and passed a chain link fence. A few yards back was a cattle house big enough to hold twenty heads. As they entered it, the black man came out.

"Can you saddle two horses, Paco?"

"Oh, sure Mr. Blanco. Right away."

"Don't call me Mr. Blanco, Paco. Please, my name is Blanco."

"Yes, sir. Ah, well, it really is captain now, no sir?"

"No, just Blanco."

"Should I get a horse for you?"

"No, I'm not going. You show them around. Let them get familiar with the cattle and get an idea of what they'll be dealing with."

"Yes, sir. I'll get them two real good ones."

He went through the gate and into a small room adjacent to the cattle house. He came out carrying two bridles, opened a wooden gate, and went into the pasture, a four or five-acre section fenced with red corrals and immaculately kept. The grass was low, with some carob trees providing shade for the grazing horses. He bridled and saddled two horses and went back to where the three men awaited him.

"Tell me what you think can be done," Blanco said.

"I am sure you have fine cattle, Blanco. It's finding buyers that matters to me right now."

"I want you to meet a man this evening. His name is Adolfo Suarez. I'll introduce you, and you take it from there. He's from Santa Cruz and is looking to bring cattle there. He also can lead you to other contacts. He'll probably be here when you get back."

"Can I ask you why you are letting us in it?" Aldo said warily.

"I can't do it anymore, Aldo. I just don't have any use for it. I am a revolutionary at heart. Think what you want of me. Think that I am a lunatic and crazy. I don't care. I am done with it. I want to work for my ideals, not for money. I trust you, and I am letting you and Pablo pick up where I left off. I think you deserve the opportunity. Who better than you two? You are humble people who know poverty and have simple roots. You deserve to do well. People like you are the objects of our revolution. Its future is for people like you. Someday, kids will not have to suffer in this country like you did, when we will all be doing well, and when there is no class distinction."

Aldo and Pablo listened attentively. They could see that he was being honest. He was passionate about his ideas and would execute them no matter what.

"I don't think you are a lunatic at all," Aldo said. "Now, Pablo and I are going to take a ride and look at some of your herds so we can get a start. We're going to have to keep coming back for a few days to see all of it. I guess your man, Paco, can help us?"

"Well, he's going back to Santa Cruz with me tomorrow. I let him go. I told him he's free to go where he wants. He chose to join the rebel army, so he's coming with me."

"So who is going to be in charge?" Pablo said taken aback.

"No one," Blanco said. "You guys are. There are about twenty five hands at the farm right now. There used to be seventy five but that's all I know. You'll have to talk to Ana."

"Where do we go to account for the heads? Who keeps your records?" Aldo asked.

"I think Ana has been keeping them. My accountant, too. But honestly, in the last few months, I have been totally out of touch. I don't keep records anymore. I don't know what's on these lands anymore. I leave that to you. Report to our accountant. He'll help you wind up my affairs."

"You could be losing cattle and not know it. There has to be some control. We are going to have to survey all one hundred hectares. But I don't want really to be responsible for something that's not here, so before we do anything, we should count the cattle."

"It doesn't matter, Aldo," Blanco said, shrugging. "Do what you have to. I trust you."

Paco tied the horses to the top stake of the cattle house. They were beautiful standard-bred sorrel colts, with white spots on their legs and hooves about sixteen hands tall. They were clearly expensive. How many peasants had ever dreamed of owning a horse like one of these?

"Who bred these?"

"They were bred right here on the farm. My father imported the first ones from the United States thirty years ago. Paco has been breeding them since."

"They are beautiful," Pablo said.

"Yes, they are," Paco said. "Mr. Blanco's father, God rest his soul, knew what he was doing, Mr. Aldo. When he bought something, it was always the best. I'm going to saddle them for you now."

"Well," Blanco said, "I'm going to leave you with Paco, all right?"

"Wait," Aldo said, "we have to discuss money."

"Ah, yes," Blanco said casually. "You tell me what you want. How much do you want to make?"

"It's not that. You are being awfully generous to us and we'll be the same to you. How do you want to work it?"

"You want eight pesos on each head? Ten?"

"No," Pablo said, "of course not. We'll do three pesos on each head, all right?"

"I want you to take more than that."

"We'll take three pesos on each head," Aldo repeated. "That's how we'll work it. The rest is yours."

"Once you get going with the cattle, I want you to start working on the land, too. I want to sell most of it. And you'll get a commission on that, too."

He turned away before either could respond. Aldo walked by one of the horses and petted its mane. He could not make up his mind which one he liked best. They were exactly alike.

"Ride this one, Mr. Aldo," Paco said. "He's a little older than the other one and more broken in. Here, walk him."

He handed Aldo the reins. Aldo took them and pulled. The horse followed him. Pablo took the other one. They went down a trail towards the front of the property. As they passed near the picket fence surrounding the house, they heard the voices of the men inside. The laughter had gotten louder while Blanco was away.

"… and he begged for mercy. He said the Lord's Prayer twice and when we told him that if he said it again, he might not get shot, would you believe the scum bag began to say it again? That's when we shot him. It took the words right out of his mouth. He's in heaven…"

A roar of laughter from the other men drowned the speaker's voice. Aldo stopped instantly to look at Pablo. He had heard it too. They both knew what the men were talking about. The revolutionary squads had been active the night before. Over thirty men had been executed near the local Agramonte barracks. A short announcement had been made on the radio that the revolutionary squads had carried out execution sentences on several of Batista's hoodlums. The word in the street was closer to reality. The men had been executed in mass. And no one could confirm whether they had had a trial. A quick shift in the local command had prompted the swift executions, which apparently had been delayed by the previous commander. Justice could not wait, the radio claimed. The public approved.

The two friends exchanged a look of horror. Were these the men that were to govern them? How were they different from Batista? The attire had merely changed from khaki to green. The men were the same. Aldo brought the reins over the neck of his horse and mounted. He and Pablo rode their horses back towards the cattle house to meet Paco.

"Where is the most of the cattle?" Aldo asked Paco.

"I would say a good forty hectares inside the property. You would need a couple of days to see it all, Mr. Aldo?"

"What can we see today?"

"Some of the smaller herds are in the first twenty hectares. Many calves. But there are some full-bred cattle too."

"Let's see that, then."

"Well, I will gladly show you that, but you know, Mr. Aldo, after tomorrow, you'll be on your own. I am leaving for Santa Cruz myself."

Aldo remembered what Blanco had said about the old man. What could a man like Paco do as a soldier? He had been on this farm all his life. He was well over sixty. He had no military training and knew nothing about guns or discipline. He was curious to know what had prompted the old man to join.

"You are leaving for Santa Cruz?"

"I am joining the rebel army, Mr. Aldo."

"Why?"

"Well," he said rubbing his chin, "I like the revolution, Mr. Aldo. The revolution is going to help us all, you see. It's going to make our country free."

"You're going with Blanco, no?"

"Ah, yes, I'm going to be part of Mr. Blanco's guard. I will get to wear a gun and everything."

Pablo rode his horse back to the edge of the picket fence, dismounted, and entered the yard. Aldo watched him go in the house. A few seconds later, Pablo came back out, followed by Olga. They stood by the gate talking, Pablo gesturing with his hands. Aldo could not hear what they were saying but knew from the sound of their voices that they were arguing. Suddenly, Olga threw her hands up in frustration and walked back towards the house.

Pablo mounted his horse and trotted back towards them. "Let's go," he said shaking his head. "I don't know what's come over her. She might as well join the rebel army, too, and go with Blanco and the rest of them to Santa Cruz."

"Let's go, old friend, cheer up. It will work out in the end."

"I don't think so, Aldo."

That evening, Adolfo Suarez and his aid gathered in the back porch of Blanco's house, taking in the fresh spring breeze as they ate chunks of hardened guava paste with white cream cheese. The sky had clouded, and it finally looked like rain. They were seated in chairs facing the land extending far beyond the cattle house and waited. Adolfo Suarez was a burly man, muscular for his age, with wide biceps inside the short sleeves of his nylon shirt, which was always a size bigger due to his prominent belly. His large eyes and sweeping eyelashes had caused many a young woman to fall for him in his younger days. Despite the fact that he was sixty, he had remained practically wrinkle free. Beside him sat his driver and confidant, Federico Santos, who had been with him for most of his life.

Mr. Suarez took the Churchill cigar from the ashtray as he munched on his snack. He had been a close friend of Blanco's father and done a lot of business with him. He had admired the old man because of his no-nonsense style and his ability to get things done. Then he left Camaguey and moved near the island's southern coast where he bought some land and supplied cattle to towns near the coast. Despite the distance, he had kept in touch with Blanco's father and had bought a lot of his cattle. After his death, Mr. Suarez had kept in touch with Blanco. His father had done a good job with him, Mr. Suarez thought. And so Suarez had continued buying his cattle, at first cautiously and then as freely as before. Blanco had maintained the quality of the herds and in some instances, his attention to the weight and quality of the livestock had surpassed that of his father's. Near the end of last year, Suarez had decreased his purchases, worried about the instability in the country. He never liked to hold much stock at any given time. Then, after the change in government, he had seen a rise in the demand for cattle and was now ready to fill his empty lands.

He had sent his men to Blanco, only to be told that he was in Santa Cruz. He had then sent out a message for Blanco to contact him, and some rebels from Santa Cruz had come to see him. Mr. Suarez had felt uneasy about the presence of armed men in his property. In all his years of trading, he had never had to deal with men in uniform. He found it egregious that anyone could be a militant, and he generally distrusted all military men. He had been surprised when the bearded men had told him they had a message from Blanco. He could not imagine a connection between them and Blanco. Even now he could not understand how Blanco had become involved with their kind. Nevertheless, when the men told him that Blanco would meet him at his farm this evening, he had agreed to come. He never asked how they knew Blanco, or in what capacity they were acting but he was intrigued.

When he entered the house that afternoon, he met with Blanco and his young driver. He did not know it, but luck had spared him the presence of the other rebels who had left shortly before his arrival. But no matter, the dramatic change in Blanco's appearance was too much for his conservative ways. He was shocked to find his old friend's son in military attire and wearing a beard, and he could not hide his displeasure. He listened attentively to Blanco's proposal.

His friend's son had chosen to wrap up his business affairs. He had good cattle to sell him, but he himself would not be involved. In his place would be an agent Mr. Suarez was free to deal with from now on and who would be arriving soon. Mr. Suarez agreed to wait and meet him.

Blanco's attitude was different, Mr. Suarez thought. He seemed deliberately detached, as if the talk of business had suddenly become too good for him. His mood was almost dismissive, and Mr. Suarez resented it. He did not have to wait for anybody. He had come all the way out here for this? And where was this kid anyway? But he was a wise and patient man, slow to anger. He decided to wait. If anything, his agent could explain. After making small talk with the women, he sat down in the back porch and waited.

A flash of lightning lit up the grayish clouds in the far horizon. Behind it came thunder that reverberated on the walls of the house. Then came a wave of rain that traveled rapidly over the whole terrain, drenching everything. A strong wind bent the shrubbery in the garden. He thought he saw several figures in the distance. He got up and went to the side of the porch unobstructed by the plants. There were three men on horseback. His trained eyes recognized the first two riders as capable horsemen, galloping in the direction of the cattle house. The third trailing behind was surely a work hand. Mr. Suarez knew and appreciated good horsemanship.

The first two riders left their horses inside the cattle house, then ran out into the rain and onto the porch. The torrential waters drenched their clothes, and their hats dripped as they entered the room. Aldo looked at the two men sitting on rocking chairs side by side and greeted them courteously. The men's attire gave them away instantly. Aldo knew he was meeting cattle traders.

"Which one of you is Aldo?" Mr. Suarez said.

"I am Aldo and this is Pablo. It is a pleasure meeting you."

Aldo offered his hand to Mr. Suarez who gripped it firmly. Aldo turned to Mr. Santos and also shook his hand.

"The pleasure is mine, young man. Blanco tells me that you'll be helping him with his affairs. Can I talk to you about some cattle?"

"Sure. What are you looking for?"

"I need about one hundred calves right now. Nothing too big. Around seven hundred pounds. Can you handle that?"

Aldo thought about the herds he had just seen. The whole farm was in disarray. The animals were running wild. There were bulls pasturing with calves. Full-grown cows were mixed with large herds, which was a sin. And he found small calves in pastures that Paco told him had been used exclusively for holding young bulls that were ready for shipping. No one knew where the mothers were. The cattle had been practically abandoned and left to fend for itself. They would need time to sort things out, but he could not let this opportunity vanish. This man was ready to do business, and he would not disappoint him. It would be hell to round even fifty heads under the present conditions, but he would do it.

"Yes. We can do it."

"All right. I want one hundred young bulls shipped to me tomorrow. Now, let's talk price."

"Before we do that, Mr. Suarez," Aldo said, thinking fast, "I would rather not mix herds from different areas in one lot. But if you need them as fast as you say, I might have to bring some heads from another farm."

He was thinking about his own cattle. He had to. There was no way he could put one hundred heads together from this farm. He would have to rely on his own resources to make a good impression on this very important buyer.

"And why is that? Where is the rest of the cattle?"

"Well, only because I may need sometime to separate the cattle in this farm. We have some cattle of our own that we can use to fulfill your needs, but I really don't like to do that. Cattle raised in different areas can vary, even if they are of the same breed, as you probably know."

"Things are that bad here, eh? What in the world is going on around here, anyway? Let me ask you something, Aldo, how long have you been working for Blanco?" "We just came in this afternoon. That's why I am telling you what I might have to do. I do not want to mislead you."

"If the cattle is good, it is good, no matter where it comes from. I want muscled cattle that will stand out. I don't care if you mix them up as long as you know what you're doing. But I tell you right now. If they're not what I want, they'll be shipped back."

"You won't have to ship them back. The herd will be here tomorrow. I'll arrange for transportation. Now, can we discuss price?"

"We sure as hell can. You give me young bulls, no more than one thousand pounds each, good muscle, no diseases, and I'll pay eleven cents a pound."

"If I give you one hundred heads, one thousand pounds at point of arrival, will you pay twelve cents a pound?"

Mr. Suarez gazed at Aldo. He was an impressive young man, he thought. He knew what he was doing. Something had clicked between them. They were discussing business as if they had known each other for a lifetime. This was clean, old fashioned bargaining. The kind he liked.

"Why should I pay one more cent for something I don't even know you can deliver? I offer you a price, you either take it or leave it. There are many suppliers around right now."

"Not ones that will deliver the way you want it, Mr. Suarez. Besides, I am talking about weighing the cattle at your station."

"How the hell can you do that with the conditions you have here? Listen, you don't have to tell me. I can see it. Right now, this place is a mess. And I know why. Blanco has gone berserk, that's why. He's gone military. Even a man like you would need two whole months to straighten this place out."

"So," Aldo said, "will you pay twelve cents a pound?"

"Done," Mr. Suarez said getting up. He shifted his cigar to the side of his mouth. "Hell, now let's see if you can deliver."

CHAPTER TEN

DURING THE NEXT FEW MONTHS Aldo and Pablo achieved remarkable success. Their first sale to Mr. Suarez was accomplished with great speed. From that time on, the two friends split their roles in order to be more effective. Aldo chose the cattle and got it ready for shipment. Pablo hired the men and arranged for motorized transportation from one point to another. The men always spoke to Mr. Suarez together, but Aldo led the negotiations. Their first operation was especially difficult, but they knew it was a golden opportunity that would open other doors. To make the sale possible, they had to mobilize large resources that they did not have at the time. Pablo quickly gathered several peons from the Arapientos' farm and put together fifty heads of his and Aldo's own cattle, which Aldo had sorted out that morning. That was the easy part. Then Aldo went back to Blanco's farm to fetch the rest of the cattle they needed for the sale. It was a hectic day, but that evening, the three trucks loaded at the Arapientos' farm met with three more at Blanco's and drove in convoy to Santa Cruz. Aldo calculated the weight at the point of delivery by overestimating it by several pounds at the point of departure. The scheme worked.

That was only the beginning. Mr. Perez became the men's conduit to the province's entire southern region. The trips to Santa Cruz were first monthly, then bi-weekly, and then weekly. The two men had stumbled onto something very big, and they prepared for the future. Blanco's cattle would soon be depleted, so Aldo found other sources, including Don Fernando who became a new supplier. This is where real ingenuity had paid off. The price of the cattle Aldo purchased had to be sufficiently low to allow a profit when he sold it shortly thereafter. Aldo was forced to change his mind about maintaining a large supply of livestock. He had become a popular trader almost overnight. Other trademen recognized this, bringing him even more business. His reputation as a smart, sharp cattle dealer spread. He could no longer afford to be caught red-handed without enough herds, and began keeping a large supply of cattle. He and Pablo kept a careful eye on the sales, but to their surprise, they continued growing in quantity and frequency. Their biggest ally was Mr. Suarez who had grown fond of them, especially Aldo, as time went on. A friendship developed between them, and it became their practice to meet twice a week. At first it was only business, but gradually the discussions became more personal. Mr. Suarez enjoyed Aldo's wit, his intuitive perception, and most of all, his obvious honesty.

This inevitably led to changes in Aldo's personal life. He was hardly at his farm anymore. Rodolfo was hired on a permanent basis to do the milking and help Alfredo look after the cattle. Alfredo did not welcome this move. He was happy working alone. The idea of a stranger coming in made him uncomfortable. Aldo tried to soothe his feelings by assuring him that it was only temporary and that he would soon make up his mind about eliminating the farm altogether and bringing him to Blanco's place. Meanwhile, Amanda could not be happier. Aldo's long stays at Blanco's farm allowed her the opportunity to go to town, away from the hateful prairie. Frank was transferred to a city school one month away from his summer vacation. The family stayed at Guillermo's house temporarily but then rented a small home nearby.

Their lives seemed to be going well when Aldo and Pablo met with Suarez in the lobby room of the Gran Hotel during a misty afternoon in November. The room contained a bar table with stools in one section and several tables and chairs in another. Some traders were sitting at the bar, drinking their beers and talking. Mr. Suarez had called Aldo to a table for more privacy. Aldo and Pablo sat next to each other facing Mr. Suarez and his driver.

"One set of news overshadows the other, do you see?" Mr. Suarez whispered.

He was referring to the resignation of the local commander of the region, Commander Uber Matos, who had resigned his commission due "to incompatibility with the line of the revolution," as the papers had quoted. That was the first event. The second, immediately after, was the mysterious disappearance of Commander Camilo Cienfuegos who had last been seen boarding a small plane from the city of Camaguey during his return to Havana and was now missing and presumed dead. This had caused great distress among the population. Many idolized him, even more than Castro himself, and there were rumors that Castro had had Cienfuegos executed, thus ridding himself of someone who had eclipsed him as commander in chief. Speculations grew among the populace when it was learned that Commander Cienfuegos was leaving town after having met secretly with the deposed commander, Uber Matos.

"You mean intentionally, of course," Pablo said.

"Exactly. I bet you Huber Matos will be condemned to life in prison if he's lucky, or executed, but nobody will notice because of Camilo's disappearance. The devil could not have planned it better."

"The papers are calling him a traitor," Pablo said. "Of course, we all know why he's a traitor, right? Because he had enough balls to stand up to Castro."

"Sure," Mr. Suarez said, "then the opportunity presents itself for the elimination of Cienfuegos. A freaky accident. But what is ironical is the timing. He disappears just as the

news of Huber Mato's resignation came to light. That's what's strange. I'm telling you, Cienfuegos's disappearance was timed perfectly to drown the Matos affair. Now no one will care about

Matos because the focus is on Cienfuegos. Everyone loved him. So Castro is free to do what he wants with Matos without

creating too much of a raucous. He killed two birds with one stone."

"I agree," Aldo said. "I think we are all being manipulated."

"I tell you again boys," Mr. Suarez said, looking around to make sure no one could hear him, "this is communism, so make all the money you can now, but don't make plans too far into the future. Get out before the end comes."

"And where will we go?" Pablo said curiously, "This is our home."

"Think of your families and yourselves. You're still young. I'm old, so it doesn't matter to me anymore, but I don't want my daughter and grandchildren to live under communism. My older brother has been in Miami since the triumph of the revolution. I have asked him to arrange for their visas. I want them to be ready. When the time comes, I want them all out of here."

"I don't think it will come to that," Federico said.

He was a tiny man, with a thin, wrinkled face. He had small blue eyes, a hawk nose, and very thin lips and was in his mid sixties. His hair was totally grey.

"How do you figure that?" Mr. Suarez said, turning to him.

"If there's going to be a move towards communism, do you think that the rich in this country will put up with it? And don't forget, we are ninety miles from the United States. The Americans will never allow communism at their doorstep."

"Castro is going to fool everyone, Federico. He's already getting away with anything he wants. Tell me who in this country right now would oppose him. Ninety per cent of the population is infatuated with him. As for the Americans, I don't trust them. The democrats are going to lead the government now. If Castro plays his cards right, which up to now he has, he will fool them, too."

"I don't know about that," Pablo said. "The Americans have too many interests in this country. I know what you're saying Mr. Suarez, but I think the minute there is a hint of communism in the air, they will invade us."

"The hint has been in the air for months now, Pablo. Where have you been?"

"Nothing obvious, Mr. Suarez. We suspect and speculate, but we have seen nothing concrete."

"That's precisely the point. You are not going to see anything concrete until it's too late. What do you think all these militias and all this talk about arms mean? Why do we need all these soldiers and weapons? This is a small island. We are being militarized by the minute. Boys, follow my advice. Exchange some of the money you are making for dollars and send it to the United States. You are going to need it when you leave."

Aldo looked pensively at the table, picked up his beer, and drank. The last few weeks had been busy. He had not had time to reflect upon the latest events, but he could no longer ignore them. The latest political developments were being discussed at almost every gathering he attended. Here he was, ready to move another shipment of five hundred heads to Matanzas, a small northeast province. Such operations had suddenly been occurring frequently with and without Mr. Suarez. The profits were enormous. This particular sale had been arranged through a contact man to whom he had been introduced by Blanco. He and Pablo stood to make a handsome profit on the deal. Aldo had sold at one cent profit on the pound, leaving them with a net profit of $5,000.00. The cattle they were selling was their own, as Blanco's cattle had now all been sold except for a few heads they had saved as a milking herd. They purchased their cattle in remote areas during their travels, a heard here and there, and now this sale had suddenly come up. Now Blanco had proposed to sell them large portions of his estate. The opportunity was great but he was concerned. Where was this revolution going? What was the meaning of the huge militarization taking place? Time and time again in the past few months, he had heard Mr. Suarez's predictions that the revolution was headed for communism. Until then, he had hardly ever considered it. Now he suddenly began to hear many different versions of the word. None was encouraging.

The timing could not have been worse. He had, almost unexpectedly, bumped into success, and now it seemed as if it all might be snatched from him. But what could he do? The events surrounding them were totally beyond his control. Yet it seemed that one man with whom people had become enchanted would dictate the course of the future.

Aldo thought about his family. They meant everything to him. He had to protect them. Mr. Suarez's ideas were dramatic but not altogether off target. Precautions must be taken. Thinking about his children and how they would live under communist rule frightened him. He placed his empty beer bottle on the table and rose.

"Well, gentlemen, we must be going," he said. "I have to meet Blanco this evening."

"Ah, the captain is back home tonight," Mr. Suarez said sardonically. "What's he giving away now?"

"I don't know. I'm off to find out."

"Listen, Aldo," he warned, pointing his finger at him, "that land is like gold, but now is not the time. Do you hear me? Do you know what I'm saying?"

"I hear you, Mr. Suarez, I hear you."

"Listen to me. Five years ago, I would have given anything to buy that land myself, but now you couldn't give it to me and I know that's sad to say. But you can quote me on that."

"Ah, Mr. Suarez," Pablo said, "how can you say these things? That land is priceless. All that farm needs is cosmetic work, and it could be the best in the whole province."

"You think I don't know that?" Suarez said, "that's elementary. But you listen to this old man who's been around long before you were born. What's coming around the corner is a cyclone. You could have the best land in the country, and it wouldn't mean anything. Castro is going to take it all. Remember that I told you this on November 27, 1959, at 4:10 P.M. in the lobby of the Grand Hotel. Remember that."

He was still speaking in a low voice but stood up to make himself heard. He put his left hand on Aldo's shoulder.

"This young man knows what I'm talking about," he said, "I'll see you at my place on Sunday, Aldo, all right?"

He turned towards the bar to have his glass refilled. Aldo and Pablo shook Federico's hand and walked out of the lobby onto the sidewalk. The soft rays of the autumn sun bathed the sides of the street in golden light. They stood momentarily under the shade of the Gran Hotel's blue awning and then got into their jeep. They did not notice the military jeep parked some distance behind and the bearded black man dozing off behind its wheel.

They drove by San Juan de Dios Plaza and stopped momentarily at Pablo's in-law's house. Pablo went inside for a quick shower while Aldo stood outside, talking with Olga's father.

"How have you been, Pedro?" Aldo said.

"I'm all right," he said, rising from the steps to shake Aldo's hand. "Won't you come in and wait for dinner?" He wore a white Guayabera, beige pants, and slippers and his hair was still wet from a shower.

"No, thank you. We have to go to Blanco's farm now."

"Ah, you boys are always in a hurry. How's work. All right?"

"Yes. Things are moving."

Several minutes later, Aldo saw Olga's fat wrist as she unhooked the door.

"How are you, Aldo? How are things in Rios?" she asked, sitting on the bottom step.

During the past few months, Olga's stays in the country had become sporadic. Her marriage to Pablo was on the rocks as a result of the political abyss that had developed between them. Pablo had remained indifferent to the revolution from the beginning while Olga had become a sympathizer almost immediately, and her passion had grown with time. Pablo had become increasingly intolerant of her views, which he found fanatic and even stupid. On the other hand, Olga had become more determined in her support of the new regime. As more changes were announced and propaganda became more intense, she became more vocal about the revolution's support. To make matters worse, she was not a quiet sympathizer as most people, young and old, were, but an outspoken one. This angered and embarrassed Pablo. He refused to go out with her in public so she remained at her parents' home most of the time. Pablo kept clothes in their home, some bare necessities at first, then practically his whole wardrobe as Olga's mother now made it a habit to do his laundry. The relationship between Pablo and his in-laws had not changed despite his marital difficulties. They were borderline in their political views and quietly pressured Olga to amend her views and save her marriage, but nothing had persuaded her.

"All is normal. As always."

"We have gotten some of the people there involved now," Olga commented. "I know of three men who are going to join the militia."

"From Rios?" Aldo asked, somewhat incredulously.

"Yes. That's right, even from Rios. The revolution spares no region, Aldo. We have this man from one of the last rows of houses. His name is Juan Carlos. Then we have a young man who works for the Arapientos, Manuel, and this other man, Tomas."

"Tomas? Did you say Tomas?"

"Yes, Tomas."

"I know of only one Tomas in Rios. He's middle aged, dark complexed with straight hair. He lives alone near the end of the hamlet, is that who you mean?"

"Yes, that's him. He has been coming around to some of the meetings, and he is now officially a militia man. Why, you don't think he's capable?"

"No, it's not that. I just never would have expected him to join."

"But you see, that's the error. You cannot go by expectations, that's a vice of the past. You have to do what's right, not what's expected of you. The revolution is for everybody."

She had to stand so that Pablo could get through the doorway. He had changed into a blue, long-sleeve shirt and black jeans. He wore the same cowboy boots and hat and his hair was still wet.

"The revolution," Pablo said sarcastically, "the revolution is nothing but a bag of tricks."

"That's your problem, Pablo. That's why you can't appreciate it. You think of everything in terms of buy and sell. The revolution is not for sale. It is free. Leave your bourgeois ways don't…"

"Shhhh! I don't want to hear this crap. Let's go Aldo."

Olga's father had remained sitting, trying to remain oblivious to the exchange. Aldo was relieved by Pablo's sudden decision to leave.

"Until soon," Aldo said to them.

Again, they failed to notice the green jeep parked a few yards away behind them at one of the small streets that entered the plaza.

"The fucking revolution," Pablo murmured from behind the wheel as they drove away. He kept repeating the phrase as if trying to convince himself. In his frustration, he did not notice his friend's silence until far into the road to Santa Cruz.

"So what's the matter? What did Olga say to you?" He asked at last.

"Guess who joined the militia?"

"Who?"

"Tomas. You know, Tomas from Rios. Incredible, no?"

"Aldo, no?"

Pablo turned to look at his friend in bewilderment. He felt concern, a concern that had somehow been brushed aside in the past but that now had come back to haunt him. He pulled onto the shoulder of the road and brought the jeep to a halt.

"What's the matter?" Aldo asked.

"What's the matter? Aldo, do you realize that's the same fucking creep in whom you confided when Patricio was killed? What if he tries to implicate you?"

"I did nothing wrong. On the contrary, I am sure it was he who caused Patricio's death. The man is nothing but a coward. And now he joins the rebels?"

"I know what the fuck he is. That's my whole point. You were reckless by getting involved in something of that magnitude with that asshole. All to bury someone. Why didn't Tomas bury Patricio himself? Now he joins the militia. Of course, the man is nothing but a snake. That shows what this fucking revolution is all about. Letting a creep like that join them, ah? And of all people, my wife is one of them. I can't believe this. But what concerns me the most is that he now would be in a position of authority, capable of accusing you of involvement in Patricio's death just to gain favor with these idiotic rebels. I don't like it one bit."

"I wouldn't worry about that, Pablo. Besides, I have been thinking about what Mr. Suarez said. I think he is on to something."

"You mean that Castro is a communist?"

"That, and what might happen. I don't know, I guess I'm not sure yet. But you know, I think that we all ought to get passports ready. I don't like the way things are going."

"Well, I agree wholeheartedly that things are fucked up. This whole business of revolution stinks. But I don't think it will last. I think it's all going to crumble. What worries me is what might happen in between. And right now, I'm worried about you and that fucking idiot Tomas. Yes, may be you should get a passport, if only for that reason. May be you should stay away from here for a while."

"Ah, stop. Tomas means nothing. Come on, let's go."

Pablo pressed on the clutch with his left foot and shifted gear as he looked in the rearview mirror. Looking back, he saw the barely-visible outline of a jeep in the approaching dusk. *They must be having car trouble*, he thought, but then the vehicle began moving back slowly.

The spacious dining room at the ranch house seemed untidy. The chairs were scattered throughout the room. The three large ashtrays were filled with cigar butts and ashes, and the stench of cigar smoke filled the room. Blanco dragged the chairs to the table. He was dressed in full military garb but wore no cap. His beard had grown much longer and now reached the middle of his chest. His hair remained long but trimmed. Ana came behind them from the foyer and stood silently aside, apparently conscious about the appearance of the room. She wore no make up but her dark hair was neatly combed and fell around her shoulders. Aldo thought she looked beautiful.

"Come, pull a chair in," Blanco said. He waived at Ana to come forward. "Come, Ana, sit down."

Aldo took two chairs, placing one next to Blanco for Ana. He could tell rebels had been around and felt relieved they were gone. Since seeing them on his first day at the farm, he had made it a point to avoid them and had not spoken to them. But he could always tell their presence by the cigar smoke and the disarray they always left behind.

"How did you leave Camaguey?" Blanco said.

"Fine," Aldo replied, "We were at the Gran Hotel with Mr. Suarez."

"I bet Mr. Suarez told you about his misgivings with the Huber Matos's affair, ah?"

"It's politics, Blanco. I'd much rather not discuss it."

"Yes, I know," the bearded man said, chuckling, "you don't like politics."

"Anyway," Aldo said, "I have turned over all your accounts to your accountant. I do not think you need to sell any more cattle. You have seventy three milking heads and three bulls left, all Holstein. You have a fine milking herd there. I have assigned five men to them. It's up to you now how far you want to develop the herd but you really do not need us here any longer."

"Of course I need you," Blanco said reassuringly. "We all need you, now more than ever. Here's what's happening, I'm donating fifty hectares of land to the revolution. All I want to keep is five hectares. Now, you have the option of buying the rest. Forty five, that is. We can work out the price, and the payment arrangements will be in any form suitable to you. In addition, I will recommend you as an administrator to the revolutionary command that takes over the land because I think you two are among the best administrators that I have ever seen, and you can do a fine job for this country, too."

Aldo and Pablo remained silent for a moment. They knew this was coming. They had notified Blanco a few weeks ago that his cattle had been depleted. Aldo had dutifully turned all sale receipts to Blanco's accountant, but for some reason, he suspected Blanco was not keeping track and did not realize that they had completed the job he had assigned to them. They sent him four messages before they heard back from him.

"Assume that we buy forty five hectares from you as you propose," Aldo began, "we would then be bordering land that belongs to the government in view of your donation, isn't that so?"

"Yes. What's wrong with that?"

"What would the government do with this land? What would they use it for?"

"It would be put to good use. It would be given to small proprietors who would work the land. That's the idea."

"Are you sure about that? If that's so, why do they need an administrator?"

"Ah, the administrator would just be a temporary thing, Aldo. But it would give you a chance to do something nice for the people. You would maintain the property until all is passed to the peasants who need it."

"And wouldn't the government try to take the land we buy? I mean, if we are neighbors and are holding forty-five hectares next to small proprietors holding one or less, sooner or later it has to create friction, prompting the government to act. It's much like the Arapientos' situation in Rios. No?"

"Now, wait a minute," Blanco said shaking his hand, "the revolution does not take land from people. It only seeks to do justice. Why are you so suspicious of us? Haven't you seen enough already. I think it's been proven beyond a doubt that we are here to do good. You can't argue with that. I don't understand why you think like this."

"I'm not predisposed either way, Blanco. But it seems to me that the situation would be a little uncomfortable for us."

"Well, you could always improve it by donating some of your land later on."

Blanco smiled ironically. He thought it was unfortunate that such good men could not be on their side. He would love to recruit them!

"Yes, may be we would do that in the future and be Santa Claus, but right now we would want to know what we are getting ourselves into."

"You cannot compare this situation with Rios, Aldo. That's far fetched. The peasants in Rios have been victims of the Arapientos for decades. You, Pablo, your families, and the whole hamlet. It's totally different from what we are doing here. We are giving something away to people who need it. We are creating a community."

There it was, Aldo thought. Community. Communism.

It was a noble idea that Blanco gave his land away for a good cause, but was it wise to buy land next to a commune? Was it wise to buy land in a country that was turning into a commune? Mr. Suarez was right. The time was not to buy but to sell.

Suddenly Ana spoke.

"Please Aldo buy the land," she said, looking entreatingly at him. "It would be so much better having you here. You would be our neighbors."

"You two are still going to be living here?" Pablo asked.

"Well," she explained, "on and off. Blanco is in Havana a lot, so we would have to travel, but we would feel so much safer having you here."

"You see?" Blanco said. "It's a family decision, not just mine."

Aldo understood how Ana felt. She was apprehensive. She had bravely supported her husband until now, but she felt a deep concern that she did not dare reveal. Aldo saw it. She was looking for support, someone to lean on. She needed hope. She wanted Aldo to stay near, as if she expected that Blanco's actions would somehow come back to haunt them, and then Aldo would be there to protect them.

"I wish it was as easy as that, Ana," Aldo said. "There are many factors Pablo and I must consider. Personally, I have to think about my family. This is thirty minutes away from the city where I relocated them. And I have also my farm to think about. What would I do with it? Not to mention the question of price and payment. It's a great opportunity, and I am most appreciative to you both, but I need time."

"Don't worry about the terms of purchase," Blanco said. "That can be worked out. We want you here. I will help you with all the rest. You don't have to uproot your family. You'll have all the transportation you need."

"I feel as Aldo does," Pablo said. "I am most grateful for the offer, but I think we need to think about it."

"I wasn't expecting you two to decide this minute. But I want you to realize the potential, and most of all, I want you to understand that you are appreciated and needed."

"Aldo, please think about it," Ana said. "It would make us feel so secure knowing that you are here."

"All right," Blanco said, "you want a drink?"

"Well, maybe a soda pop if you have one."

"Sure," he said getting up, "I'll get it. Of course you noticed that we no longer have domestic help around here."

"It must be hard coming home and having to clean," Pablo commented.

"Ah, we don't mind it," he said from the hallway.

"I mind it," Ana said softly. "Tell me about Amanda and the children, how are they?"

"They're fine. Frank is going to private school, and the twins just started kindergarten."

"Which school is Frank going to?"

"Escolapios, right in the San Francisco Plaza."

"Of course. Remember? my school was across the street."

Aldo gazed at her olive eyes. He remembered the golden evenings as the sun set, when he as a young boy would meet the three sisters on the steps of the church on the plaza, waiting behind the columns to avoid being detected by the nuns. Ana and Aleida had always supported their sister. They had been accomplices to Amanda's illicit relationship with the young fighter, much to the chagrin and anger of their father. Much had happened since then.

"My dad is so happy to have Amanda and the children in town," she said.

"Quite right," Aldo said.

"Your father must not be very happy with the state of affairs," Pablo added casually.

"Please, don't even mention it."

Guillermo had broken relations with Blanco. He had never again spoken to him and refused to even see him. His views remained unwavering. He had been shocked to learn of Blanco's ideas and bitterly chastised his daughter for her devotion to him. The man he had admired most among his sons-in-law had turned out to be a Castro sympathizer. His name was now banned from conversations in the household.

"I have pine-apple juice for you," Blanco said. "No more coca colas. Those are foreign drinks. Let's drink what we make in this country."

"Don't we have a coca cola plant near here?" Pablo said.

"Yes. But the raw material is not ours. The pine-apple juice is ours, made with ingredients from this country. Big difference."

It was difficult to avoid discussing the revolution with Blanco, Aldo thought which made it quite uncomfortable for persons like him who preferred to stay neutral. The man was obviously possessed, and he was not letting go. For the rest of their stay, Aldo felt as if he was walking through a minefield of revolution rhetoric. What he missed the most was Ana's pleasant company. The soft-spoken girl of prior years now seemed withdrawn and almost afraid to speak.

The night had fallen as they stood up to leave. Blanco had pressed them for an answer, and Aldo had promised to get back to him. Blanco was due back in Santa Cruz in a week. They would meet again then.

Aldo and Pablo stopped at Aldo's new home in town. The house was in the suburbs but close to town, a modest cinder block ranch house with two bedrooms. The floor was beautifully tiled in off-white ceramic, and all the rooms were newly painted. Some of the furniture had been brought from their country home except for the dining room and the master bedroom set, which were new. The rooms were moderate in size but a big improvement over those of the house in Rios. The children were playing Parcheesi at the dining room table as Aldo and Pablo walked in.

"*Papa* is here, Mom," Frank said.

"And Pablo, too," one of the twins added.

"I hope neither of you ate. I had Ramona send us supper. White rice with fried liver in onions, and I will fry you bananas. What do you think about that?"

She seemed elated. She was standing by the door to the kitchen, fork in hand.

"What made you send for supper?" Aldo asked.

"These children have been driving me crazy, Aldo. I cannot do anything in this house. Nothing. As soon as they get in from school, I'm done for."

"Well, we are going to have a light supper, and then I'm going to Rios to see Alfredo."

"Oh, no. Why do you have to go tonight? Why not wait until tomorrow?"

"Because we have to get cattle ready tomorrow. We have a large shipment going in to Matanzas."

"You are not going to stay in Rios tonight, are you?"

"It depends. Only if Alfredo needs me."

"Please, *Papa* don't stay," one of the twins said. "It's too scary in Rios."

Pablo joined the children in their game while they waited to be served. Amanda sat with them, discussing the latest events and repeating her father's views that the revolution was headed for trouble. At one point, Aldo interrupted.

"I would like you to go with the children to see Mr. Acosta," he said casually. "I will go myself. We all should get our passports ready."

"Passports?" she asked in surprise. "Why passports? For what?"

"Just as a precaution, Amanda. That's all. We all need them. Pablo too."

"I don't believe Pablo is going to get a passport. Not with Olga he's not. Where are you thinking of going?"

"I just don't know. It takes a while to have it cleared, Amanda, so before we know where we are going, let's get it done."

"Has anything happened?"

"Nothing yet," Pablo said. "But Aldo is right. We may need them."

"Now you are beginning to sound like my father. We are not going anywhere, not now that we are doing so well."

"Not to worry," Pablo said. "Just a precaution in case the future gets any worse. I don't think it's a bad idea."

She studied them in silence. Did they know something new? Was there another emergency? Had Castro made a new announcement?

She was intrigued enough to want to keep asking, but the looks of the children's faces stopped her. They would go to school the next day and there was no telling what they might repeat to their friends. It was a shame that one had to think this way, but that's how it was. She would talk to Aldo alone tonight. She was now beginning to enjoy the fruits of his success. There was no way she would consider leaving.

Champ ran towards the jeep as it pulled up near the fence of the house. Alfredo had made it a habit to release him at sun-down, and the animal would run loose in the yard, smelling and poking the grounds with its claws. As he exited the jeep, Aldo looked towards the gate to the chute and saw Alfredo's face staring at them in the dark.

"I'll see you in the morning," he said to Pablo. "Don't oversleep now."

"Me, oversleep? I can't even remember when was the last time I had a good night sleep. See you in the morning, ah?"

Aldo watched the tail light of the jeep disappear in the distance as Pablo drove away. Pablo would also sleep alone in an empty house. His house had been practically abandoned since they had started to do business with Blanco. It was a price to pay for their success. Their old homes were dark and lonely. Deep inside, they both missed them.

"Is Rodolfo here, Alfredo?"

"No, not yet."

"Did you eat?"

"I made some supper, yes."

"Well, come in and have some coffee, no?"

Amanda had left a few chairs, but the dining room table was gone. Alfredo had quickly put together a makeshift table, and the room was livable. Aldo persuaded him to use what once was the children's bedroom to sleep, but Alfredo had refused. He thought it disrespectful to the family to use the house as his own, even if they no longer occupied it. He had used only the kitchen to cook his meals, but the rest of the house remained untouched. They sat together at the table and chatted while Alfredo had his coffee. Aldo withheld any comments about Tomas so as not to worry him, but he wondered how his joining the rebels might have escaped Alfredo.

Aldo heated some water in a bucket for a bath. He now had the comfort of a shower in the city. But old habits were hard to break. He still enjoyed the old peasant method of washing himself with luke warm water. After Alfredo left, he bathed, changed into clean undergarments, and went to the bedroom. He thought about listening to the radio but felt too tired. He lit the gas lamp on his night table with a match and turned the flame low. He fell into bed.

He couldn't have been asleep more than an hour when he heard a light tapping on the window by his headboard. He knew instantly it was not Alfredo. He heard Champ's restrained barking from afar, as if someone was holding it.

"Who's there," he asked as he lifted his head from the pillow.

"It's the rebel guard. Open up!"

Aldo sat on the bed and collected his thoughts. He shook his head to dispel sleep. There was more tapping at the window, now faster.

"We know you're there. Open the door!"

One year ago, a similar call would probably have caused Aldo to fetch his revolver and come out through the back door, prepared to meet his destiny. But since the triumph of the revolution, he had subconsciously relaxed. There was nothing to be apprehensive about. He had political stand. Automatically, he stood up, put on his trousers and shirt on. He walked to the front door and pulled the latch open. The door was pushed so fast it struck him on the chin. He felt something hard and cold on his face as he was shoved back. He saw the dark faces of men falling upon him like jungle gorillas. Luckily, his reaction was delayed by his drowsiness and lack of anticipation. He could have easily struck one of the rebels, but their guns were pinned to his face as he went down. They could have easily shot him.

"Don't move, mother-fucker. Don't move, or we'll kill you like a dog right here as you deserve."

More men came running from the back of the house and entered the living room where Aldo now laid face up on the floor with the two men stepping over him, pointing the barrels of their automatic rifles at him.

"We got him, we got him!" the other men began to yell.

The man who some months before had been ruthlessly beaten by Batista's soldiers was now kicked and butted by the fallen dictator's enemies. His olc were now reopened, and he began to lose consciousness. They rolled him gruffly on the hard floor and handcuffed his hands behind his back. Two of the soldiers grabbed him body by the shoulders and feet and dumped him in the back of one of the jeeps parked at the gate. Although he was not moving, they kept poking his ribs with the barrels of their guns. Other soldiers stayed inside and began to ransack the house, turning and throwing everything they could find.

Behind the house, two soldiers pointed their guns at Alfredo. They had made him sit on a stump inside the cabin. When they first came in, they had forced Alfredo to get Champ and tie him to a tree so it couldn't move. They held Alfredo at gun point, taunting him with threats. As the other soldiers forced their way into the house yelling profanities, tears rolled down Alfredo's face. They were tears for Aldo and what they might be doing to him, momentarily not caring about his own fate. He knew then he should have told him, about Tomas joining the rebel militia. If only Aldo had known, then maybe he would have had a chance. It had to be Tomas. Why else would these men be here? Why were they after peasants and honest working people like Aldo?

"What else do you know, peasant? We know about the gun. We know you have nothing to do with it but we know that you know where it is. We want you to find it for us. If you don't find it, we are going to bring you with us and then you'll be implicated for sure. Who knows what might happen to you?"

"Go on, peasant, tell us," the other soldier said.

"I know nothing," Alfredo said, shaking his head.

"Yes, you do, you fucking liar. You think we haven't been watching you? We know all about you. You're his fucking protector, and you're going to pay for it."

"Where's the fucking gun? Let's go, tell us now!"

"I know nothing."

For the last hour, Alfredo had been repeating the same words. They had counted on his being frightened, but they had never expected him to be so stubborn. They were learning something new about peasants tonight. They were not all as dumb and cowardly as they had thought. But now he became a problem for them. They didn't know what to do with him. At that moment one of the other soldiers came around the house and whistled to them.

"Let's go! We got him!"

The two soldiers looked at each other. Aldo was a valuable catch. They considered him a bourgeois, someone who made money off the poor, a parasite. But now they had him. They became excited about it. Forget this miserable wretch. They quickly ran towards the voice and disappeared in the shadows.

His years with Aldo had taught Alfredo how to handle a crisis. Don't let your emotions overcome you, just be rational and act in response to the situation. Do what's needed. But he had never before done it alone. He made himself ready. He heard the jeep move gradually away. When its engine reached the main highway, he knew they had go, so he quickly got up and released Champ. The animal quivered and jumped in anticipation as Alfredo untied him. In a second he was gone, leaping and barking at the dirt road as if somehow he could still reach his master's kidnappers.

Alfredo saw a small puddle of blood on the living room floor. He hadn't heard any shots and convinced himself that Aldo could not be dead, not realizing that the blows could have been just as lethal. He did not stop to think. He went to the back of the house and took a bridle, going into the section reserved for the small calves. He found the mare standing under one of the trees, slipped the bridle over her head, and mounted. There was no time to saddle her. The milkman would be here in another hour, but Alfredo would be back by then. He had never ridden her before. She was too high spirited for him. As soon as he was on her, she trotted along. Champ ran alongside them, still barking uncontrollably, and the mare began to gallop. Alfredo whistled at Champ and held the reins tightly to hold the mare back. Champ kept on. He motioned him back with his left hand. Then, he opened the gate and galloped in the direction of Pablo's house, leaving Champ behind.

CHAPTER ELEVEN

THE CITY JAIL WAS LOCATED near the railroad station. One block behind it was the street of Avellaneda, named after a prominent nineteenth-century female poet whose sharp wit as a small girl had so impressed the Spanish Crown that she had been summoned to recite her poems before the Queen of Spain. The street was uncharacteristically wide, which made it suitable for the busy bus traffic and its many terminals. Here one could find transportation for practically every destination within the province. Whoever had made the decision for the jail's location must have had travelers in mind.

When the revolution triumphed, the old prisoners were released immediately, but then the jail began to fill rapidly again. The old prisoners had been accused of sympathizing with the rebel movement. The new prisoners were being accused of being Batista's sympathizers. Many of them had been executed. Others had been transported to high security prisons after their sentences were issued. New detainees were constantly coming in.

As they heard the two jeeps pull up in front of the drab-looking structure, the guards went to a hole on the side and opened the grating. The man the soldiers brought in was big. He was barefooted and wore a bloody shirt and blue trousers. He had been roughed up, and one of his eyes was shut and swollen. Two soldiers held him up while a third pushed him forward with the barrel of his gun. The man limped and stumbled as he walked. One of the guards walked ahead of them, opened another grating, and let them pass. They moved down a corridor, not far from the entrance, stopped before a solid iron door and waited for another guard who quickly opened it. As the guard pulled the heavy door, they all shoved the man inside the pitch dark room.

"Get in, you piece of shit," one said.

"Yes, suffer for a little while until we kill you, fucking bastard," the other one added.

The guard shut the door tightly. It had a barred, two-inch square that was the only ventilation in the room.

"What do we have here?" the guard said.

"This is that fucking Aldo Ochoa. You know, the one from Rios who helped Batista's *casquitos* kill that other peasant."

"You finally got him? Good. I think the captain wants to talk to him himself. Don't fuck with this guy now. The captain will be here early in the morning."

Inside the cell, Aldo fell on the concrete floor. He tried to break the fall with his shoulders, but with his hands tied behind his back, he could not move, and the left side of his face struck the cold pavement, ripping the skin. He felt his head spin, and he lost consciousness again.

At about that same time, another of Aldo's friends had gone to work. After receiving Alfredo's detailed report, Pablo instructed him to ride back to the farm and not say anything to anyone. He jumped in his jeep and drove away. He knew his friend's life probably depended on him now. *What sons of bitches*, he thought. If something did happen to Aldo, his destiny was sealed. He would kill the fucking bearded clowns if it was the last thing he did. As he sped over the empty road, tears rolled down his cheeks. It had been a long time since he had last cried.

The gate to Blanco's farm was closed. The cressets had not been lit, which was a bad sign. But again, Blanco didn't particularly care about his home anymore. Pablo's heart sunk as he reached the end of the driveway and did not see the military jeep. He got out of the jeep and pounded on the door. Everything was dark. He pounded the door again, so hard that he hurt his fist. There was no one home. He closed his eyes. What would he do now? Who could he go to? He didn't know anybody in the rebel command. He was lost. What about Olga, his wife? Could she do something to help? Yes, he would go to her. He would cast his pride aside and beg her. He started to walk away when he suddenly heard a familiar female voice behind him.

"Who's there?"

He turned toward the door and saw a light coming from under it. He walked quickly forward.

"Ana, it's me, Pablo."

"Pablo? Is something wrong?"

"Yes."

She opened the door ajar. Her full figure was now visible under the light. She wore a blue velvet gown trimmed with white laces. With her pale face, olive eyes, and long black hair, she looked disarmingly beautiful. Even in his state of anxiety, Pablo noticed it. She looked at him, still unsure whether it was really him, then opened the door wide.

"Ana, is Blanco here?"

"No, he had to leave. Please come in. What's the matter?"

"I can't. I have to find him right away. Where did he go? Where can I find him?"

"He's driving to Havana. What's happened? Where is Aldo?"

"It's terrible, Ana. Some rebels came to the farm and arrested him. I know Aldo did not do anything. I am afraid they'll kill him. I have to find Blanco. He's the only one that can help me."

"Ay, my God. No, no."

She covered her face with her hands and lowered her head. She felt her heart break. She had seen up close what the rebels could do. All that was needed was for someone to dislike Aldo. Anyone could accuse him of anything. Under the pretext of justice, the rebels could arrest him and justice would be swift. A summary proceeding held by a revolutionary tribunal would quickly decide. She had yet to hear of anyone being found innocent by those tribunals. She did not know what grounds they had against Aldo. She knew him. Whatever it was, it wasn't true.

Something had to be done fast. It was really bad timing. She and Blanco had argued bitterly after Aldo and Pablo had left that evening. She had supported Blanco's ideology, but she couldn't help the way things were now. She didn't care for the casual way changes were being made by the new regime. It seemed as if the whole country was on a roller coaster. There seemed to be no rules, no standards to follow. And the speeches, oh, the speeches. She now disliked them so much, and she had told him so. She couldn't lie. She would support him because he was her husband and because Aldo had found him for her. But she was not a hypocrite and she had told him about her reservations and her unwillingness to participate in any of it anymore. She wanted to stay home and tend to the house, the garden, the farm, him. He did not take it well, and before she knew it, he had raced out of the house with his driver. Where was he going? She decided she did not care. She would do what she had to do to get her life back. But now she needed his help and she would go to the end of the world to find him.

"Come in for a minute," she said. "Let me get changed."

"No, no," Pablo said, "you don't have to come, Ana. I will find him if you just tell me where he is."

"You could never get through, Pablo," she said, already walking away. "They would never let you see him."

Pablo waited anxiously in the foyer. Despite his distress, he was thinking clearly. Once he found Blanco, and if he could set things straight, his next step would be to see Mr. Suarez. He would arrange for Aldo to leave the country immediately.

He didn't have to wait more than two minutes. Ana had put on blue jeans and a white blouse with red dots but had not fixed her hair or put on make up.

"Let's go," she said.

She told him to take the road back to Camaguey, and as they reached the Central Highway, she directed him toward Via Blanca where the local barracks known as Agramonte were located. They drove through the empty streets at high speed, passing only a few vehicles. Pablo kept checking his side mirrors. He told Ana everything Alfredo had told him, but he still wasn't sure if he could trust her.

As they reached the entrance to the military compound, they were stopped by two rebel guards. Bearded men carrying rifles whose faces they could hardly see walked slowly forward, one to each side of the jeep. The one at the driver's side of the jeep shone a flashlight inside.

"There's no admittance," he said. "What are you looking for?"

"We are looking for Commandant Blanco Salazar," Ana answered.

"And for what purpose, madam?"

"He's my husband. I need to see him right away."

"And who might you be?" the soldier asked Pablo.

"He is a friend who brought me here," she said before Pablo could answer.

"He can speak for himself, no?"

"Did you hear what I just said?" Ana shot back. "I'm looking for my husband, and I want to see him now! Either you get him or you show me where he is, you understand me? I have an emergency, and I don't have to tell you my personal business, so either you get the commander right now or I'll make sure that you get booted into a military brig for insolence."

She remained calm as she spoke. Pablo could not believe he was hearing the soft-spoken Ana talk so defiantly. He turned to look at her as to reassure himself of who she was. There was something deadly serious about the way she stared them down that made her look even more beautiful.

"Lady, first of all, we don't give information to the general public. This is a military base and…"

She didn't let him finish. She swung the door open and stepped outside. The soldier who had been speaking from the driver's window moved back and stared at his mate in shock. Ana walked around the front of the jeep past the other soldier. Pablo opened his door and got out.

"Don't you move another step," the soldier said to him.

He took a step back and reached for his rifle, not realizing his immediate problem was Ana. She came rushing towards him, standing inches from his face.

"You imbecile! Don't you have any brains? Are you the kind of garbage they let in this army now? No wonder your fort is so screwed up! You get the commander now! You hear me? Now! I want to see him!"

"Hey!" another voice yelled from the dark. "What's going on out there, men?"

The man came toward them, his face becoming gradually visible as he approached the dim glare of the spotlights. His beard was trimmed and he was in full uniform. His bars were not visible but it was obvious that he was an officer.

"This lady…" the soldier started to say, but Ana interrupted him.

"I'm looking for Commandant Salazar. I'm his wife. I need to see him immediately. This man doesn't seem to know his own name, never mind anybody else's. Do you know where the commander is?"

"Madam, I'm sorry. We need proof of who you are. We can't let just anybody in here."

"Well, you are going to let me in, sir! I did not bring any proof, and I am not about to go back home to get it, either."

"All right, what is your name, madam?"

"My name is Ana. If you know the commandant, then you would know his wife's name."

"Yes, that's right. I'm sorry madam. Now, would you mind telling me who this is?" He pointed to Pablo.

"He's our friend who brought me here. Why, you want him to show you identification, too?"

"Okay, sir," the officer said to Pablo, ignoring Ana's comment. "You can park the jeep over here." He pointed to the left of the small shack near the dirt road. I will take you and the lady to the commandant now."

Pablo got into the jeep while the soldiers went ahead to guide him. One of them pointed with the flashlight, directing him. Pablo drove the jeep onto the grassy area as Ana waited for him. As he went by the soldiers, he thought he heard one whisper to the other, "Looks like the commandant has got his hands full with that one."

They went by small cinder block buildings and reached a large open field where the road seemed to end. Then the officer walked towards one medium-size chalet that stood aside from the other structures. He went up one step, opened the screen door, and knocked. Except for a tiny reflection of light on the floor, the house was totally dark.

Pablo thought he recognized the bearded face of Blanco's young driver as the door opened.

"I have someone here who is looking for Commandant Salazar," the officer said.

"Ah, Lieutenant? Is that you? Who wants the commandant?"

"His wife," he said pointing behind him.

The young corporal stepped aside to get a better look. He made out the small waist and the silky long hair spread out over her shoulders that he had secretly admired.

"Ana? Is it you?"

"Yes. Is Blanco inside?"

"Ah, yes. Let me tell him you are here."

She would not wait and pushed past the lieutenant, holding the screen door and turning to Pablo.

"Let's go, Pablo."

"Madam," the lieutenant said, "may be you should wait."

"We are not in the army, lieutenant," she said. "We have to wait for no one."

They entered a small room and went down a small hallway and into a long rectangular room with a conference table and chairs. Blanco sat at the head of the table, speaking with another high-ranking officer.

"What are you doing here?" Blanco said, looking up. "Pablo? You are here?"

She walked towards the table and stood in front of him. The corporal stepped back in deference.

"Something's happened to Aldo," she said dryly. "Some soldiers went to his farm and arrested him without any reason. Can you help me find him?"

Blanco looked at the officer at his side, then at Pablo. He was silent for a moment. He addressed Pablo.

"Do you know where they took him?"

"Alfredo said they came in two jeeps. They drove towards town, so we think they brought him this way."

"Do you know why he was arrested? Has anything happened?"

"No, of course not. We have been together all day working."

"Corporal," Blanco said leaning back to address him from the chair, "can you call the detention center? Find out if any search units have been sent anywhere tonight. Ask if they heard of an Aldo Ochoa."

"Right away, Commandant."

The corporal went to the end of the room and dialed from a rotary telephone at the counter table.

"Ana, I find that very hard to believe," Blanco said to his wife.

Blanco was now more at ease. He had given the order almost automatically without realizing the extent of what had happened. At first he had thought his wife had come to see him, and he had enjoyed the moment, feeling vindicated by her presence. But no, she was here for another man. Then he regained his focus. The impact of the news was now dawning upon him. This could be a problem. Aldo arrested?

"Perhaps I should leave Commandant," the officer sitting by him said, standing up.

"No, you don't have to go," Blanco said. "Ah, I'm sorry Captain Moreno, this is my wife, Ana. And this is Pablo, a family friend.

"Madam, at your service," the Captain said. "Sir," he said extending his hand to Pablo. "Commandant, with your permission, I will go. I will be turning in for the night."

"Captain," Blanco said, "I will see you early in the morning."

"Yes, sir."

The captain strolled out of the room. Blanco pushed back the chair for Ana. They could hear the corporal talking on the telephone to someone, then calling another number.

"How could this happen? What has he done?"

"Nothing, of course. What has Aldo ever done? I just want to know who the clowns are that arrested him and who sent them. You know nothing about this?"

"Ana, how could you think...?"

"I don't think, Blanco. I came here to get answers. You tell me."

"Well, I am going to tell you," he said looking at Pablo. "You need to get your head examined if you think that I knew anything about this. I have high respect for Aldo. Something must have happened. We don't just arrest people for nothing, Ana."

"How can you say that, Blanco? You know Aldo as well as I do. You know he's not capable of hurting anybody. You're slandering his name by implying such things. You are going to put these filthy rebels up before Aldo?"

"Nothing's happened, Blanco," Pablo said. "I can assure you of that."

"Commandant," the corporal called from the kitchen, raising the receiver, "they want to talk to you from the jail."

"I'm not putting anybody before anybody else Ana," Blanco said rising. "That's where you're wrong, but what's right is right."

He took the receiver from the corporal.

"This is Commandant Salazar."

"Commandant, sir," the voice on the other end said, "this is Lieutenant Parrado. I just wanted to confirm it was you, sir. Yes, we do have that person detained. He was picked up this evening on orders from Captain Santana."

"Is Captain Santana there?"

"No, sir, he's not. I expect him in the morning."

"Do me a favor, Lieutenant," Blanco said slowly, "send someone over to the captain's house and tell him I want to meet him at your post."

"Tonight?"

"Yes, please, right now."

"It will probably take a couple of hours to get him here, Commandant. He is in Florida tonight."

"Get him."

Blanco put the receiver down and turned to the anxious faces waiting for him at the table.

* * *

The room inside the cell was pitch black. There was no toilet and no place to sit except the floor. The small opening cut into the door was shut tight. Aldo had laid on the floor for a few minutes then slowly came to. He dragged himself towards one end of the room and sat up. With his hands tied behind his back, he found it extremely difficult to rest. The stiffness in his arms and shoulders had now turned to pain. But that was nothing compared to the agony he felt in his head. His right temple was throbbing, and he could hardly see. He tried not to think, only breathe as normally as possible. He concentrated only on his physical condition and how to overcome the pain. He couldn't tell how long he had been in this position when he heard the heavy iron door being unbolted. He tried to open his eyes and saw a light in front of him.

"Move forward," a voice said, "let's go! Let's go."

A man shone a flashlight on his face and yanked his head forward. Aldo shrank from the pain at being touched. Every muscle in his body was sore. Another figure in the room moved closer and poked his chest. Aldo could not collect his thoughts but slowly he realized the object was a gun.

"Just remember, big boy, I've got you covered. You make a false move, and you're dead."

"Looks like the captain has taken an interest in you, pretty boy. We are going to have to un-cuff you, and you're going to clean yourself up for him."

"That's right," the other man said. "Let's go, get up."

Aldo thought about getting up but couldn't. As soon as he moved, sharp pain went through his left shoulder and arm like an electric shock. He closed his eyes. He knew from experience that muscular pain could be worse than a fracture so he decided no bones had been broken.

The first soldier came closer and tried to move Aldo away from the wall by pushing on his back. Aldo closed his eyes and recoiled in pain.

"He's done for," the soldier said. "He can't get up."

"Well, find a way," the other one said. "We have to get him ready for the captain. He's on his way here."

"Shit."

The first soldier now stuck his boot behind Aldo's back and pushed, clumsily moving Aldo's body forward. Aldo lost his balance and fell sideways.

"Grab him," the soldier said.

"I can't with my gun."

"Idiot. Don't you see he can't move. He's fucked up. Help me grab him."

The other soldier held Aldo with both hands. Then the first one placed the flashlight on the floor and fiddled with the cuffs on Aldo's hands until he got them off.

"You fuck," he said to Aldo in a whisper. "I hope you fucking die. If it was up to me, I'd kill you right here."

Aldo could see him kneeling next to him. He tried to move his head back so he could look the guard in the eye, and for a moment, he was able to get a glimpse of his face. Aldo moved his lips and slowly released a spat that landed on the soldier's left eye.

"Motherfucker!" the soldier yelled. He covered his eye with his left hand. "You fucking pig, I'll kill you!"

He grabbed the back of Aldo's neck with his right hand and quickly hooked his left arm around his throat.

"Are you crazy?" the other soldier yelled. "Stop! Stop!" He grabbed the other man's arm and pulled but couldn't get him away. The soldier kept squeezing Aldo's neck, trying to choke him in his fury. He pressed Aldo's throat against his own chest and as he did, Aldo's shoulders gradually squeezed out of the strangle hold, and his arms became free. Aldo closed his right fist and swung with all his strength. He struck the soldier on the right cheek, jerking him back. The soldier fell, and Aldo pulled himself up painfully but quickly and stood back.

"Don't move, motherfucker!" the other soldier said, pointing his gun at him in the dark.

"I'll die before I let one of you cowards touch me again," Aldo said.

"What the fuck is going on, here?" another soldier yelled from the door. "Are guys crazy? You gotta get this prisoner cleaned up for the captain. What are you doing? Bring him outside. Let's go."

It was only 5:00 A.M. when Aldo sat at the end of a table with an armed soldier guarding him as the captain walked in the room. He was a black man with a full beard. There was something familiar about him, and he quickly made eye contact with Aldo as he sat down. "So we meet again," he said.

* * *

Captain Santana had lived most of his life in the city's ghetto section. His father had been a *santero*, but Santana hadn't seen much of him. He only visited his mother and his five brothers sporadically. His mother had worked cleaning houses, and he and his brothers had gotten by on what they could. It had been tough to survive on a daily ration of sugar and water. So he had become a wise guy and learned to bully people. He was always a big kid, bigger than most, and he was fast with his hands, so he had learned to box. He wasn't disciplined as Aldo had been. He didn't work hard at anything. He boxed in the streets, his own way, but when he went into the gym, he felt he could do the same and did.

He was over six feet, tall for a Cuban. He developed wide shoulders and thick biceps. But he didn't lift weights. Rather, his favorite form of training was punching the bag at the gym. He began scoring bigger fights until he became almost untouchable. He visited other gyms and competed in them. One day, he heard about a kid people called the islander. He sounded like a white kid and Santana had laughed. No white kid could fight. But his gang insisted he must see this kid so one afternoon, he rode the tramway to El Casino, a private recreation club that held fights. Blacks were not welcome, but during competition days, the rules were sometimes bent. And he didn't care anyway. He would get in.

The seventeen-year-old Santana stood near the ropes with two of his friends, strolling up and down the floor and harassing people until one of the trainers threatened to throw them out.

They brought a tall white kid into the ring. The crowd was going wild. As they pulled his robe off, the kid seemed solid and strong but that didn't impress Santana. He looked at the kid's face and thought him weak. His face didn't bear a single scratch or scar. He looked like a prima donna.

The bell rang. The other fighter was black, heavier than the white kid. Santana slapped the canvass to get the black kid's attention.

"Break his face," Santana told him. "Get rid of that chump."

It was a short fight. Santana hated to admit it but he discovered why the white kid looked so clean. He went to work on the other fighter like a tornado, circling him, jabbing him. He was so fast that his feet barely touched the ground. The fight lasted two rounds. The black kid's face was swollen by the end of the second round, and he could hardly move. The white kid walked casually to him and pounded him with a combination at the head. The other kid fell head down on the canvas. Not once did Santana notice the white kid being hit. Then he noticed a short, stocky mulatto jump into the ring as they tried to revive the black fighter. The man rubbed the white kid's shoulder with a towel. The announcer got in the middle of the ring with a megaphone.

"…And the winner, by knock out, Aldo Ochoa."

Santana had been mesmerized watching this kid fight. He had not said a word. He never forgot the name of Aldo Ochoa or his face. For a long time, he avoided fighting that kid until his trainer made him fight him at the golden gloves. To everyone's amazement, he beat him. Deep inside, Santana knew it wasn't his win. Had the referee kept the fight going for a few more seconds, he would have been knocked out. But honesty wasn't one of Santana's greatest assets, so he felt perfectly comfortable with his victory. Besides, what better vindication of his triumph than Aldo's own refusal to fight again. Santana's reign was short lived. His next fight proved a disaster, and he lost by technical knockout. His boxing career never quite took off. He took too many punches, and six months later, he was out of the ring.

Years later, Santana and his gang were still plundering the streets in far-away neighborhoods and sometimes uptown. One afternoon, as they strolled by the Agramonte square looking for victims, Santana spotted two men leaving a saloon. They were dressed in country garb, cowboy boots, jeans, and hats. He thought he recognized one of them. They were not regular peasants. These guys had been in a saloon making big bucks deals. They probably carried a wad of bills right now. This could be his opportunity. It would be easy. These guys could not fight.

"Fucking cowboy," he yelled to the first one of them.

The man looked straight back at him, as if unsure he was being addressed.

"Yes, you, fucking stupid peasant. Ready to have your nose broken, asshole?"

Santana and his two companions crossed the street. The cowboy who looked familiar came to the edge of the sidewalk, stopped, and looked down as if too embarrassed to speak. Poor sucker, Santana thought, he didn't know that he was about to have his ass kicked. Santana came up to him first. "How much money you got, peasant?"

"I got plenty of money," the man said.

"Not anymore, you don't," Santana said. "Now it's mine. Here, give it here."

"You have to take it from me, buddy."

For the first time the man looked straight at him and he instantly recognized him. It was shocking to see him after all these years. That fateful night when he fought Aldo came back to him in a flash. Could he really beat him in a man-to-man fight?

"Break his fucking face," Santana said to one of his companions.

One of Santana's large friends walked up to Aldo. Pablo, who was at Aldo's side, moved forward, but Aldo pushed him back. One man came towards Aldo and pulled his fist back but never got to throw the punch. Aldo struck him on the mouth with a straight right jab. Teeth came flying out with a spurt of blood. The young man was so shocked he merely stood there covering his mouth, not realizing the danger he was facing. Aldo had stepped back and swapped him on the side of his head. The fat man fell sideways against the back of a parked car. Meanwhile Santana, now burning in anger after seeing his friend get mulled over, stepped onto the sidewalk. Aldo was waiting for him. He let him get into position to make it a fair fight. Santana threw him a combination of punches to the face but Aldo wove his head from side to side, evading them, barely moving his upper body.

Santana could not hit him. Then Aldo stepped back. As he did, he struck Santana on the left eye with his right hand and on his mouth with his left. The eye punch was so hard that it immediately blinded Santana. The punch to the mouth ripped his front upper teeth. He fell forward, missing Aldo by inches. The third man never got a chance to throw a punch. He ran past the square, disappearing into one of the narrow streets leading to San Juan de Dios.

* * *

"What a coincidence, ah?" Captain Santana said from across the desk.

He was twenty eight now. His left cheek was marred by a diagonal scar that ran from the bottom of his eye socket to the corner of his mouth where his beard began. His laugh showed the wide gap of his missing teeth. There was no doubt as to who he was. Santana mustered considerable effort to smile. He was angered at being awakened so early. He had made the trip to Florida, a small city about forty kilometers southwest of Camaguey, to sleep with his lover. He had told his men the night before not to bother him. He found it unsettling that Commander Salazar had taken an interest in this prisoner. What was there about this one man? For all he cared, his squad could have wasted him this morning. Who would have missed him? But now that he knew who he was, he himself took an interest in making him suffer. Killing him would be too easy. He was glad the soldiers had done their duty and worked him over. His turn would now come.

"I am glad we finally caught up with your sorry ass, peasant. The revolution will get justice through you."

For a second Aldo had a vision of himself standing helplessly before an execution squad. He wasn't afraid. It would be over in a flash. For his executioners, it would be a lifetime memory that they would have to bear. He remembered the bravery of one of Batista's colonels who had defied the rebels up to the last moment. Wrong as the man might have been for his past deeds, he had taught those animals a lesson. He had stood by the wall alone, facing them as he was allowed to speak one last time in front of the camera. He had looked at them and said, "Well, boys, I leave you with the revolution. Take good care of it." Then the guns had blown him away, his hat flying into the air from the explosion in his brain. Ironically, his taped execution, meant to disgrace him, had only served to immortalize him. His last words had been prophetic.

"Fuck you and your revolution," Aldo snapped back.

The soldier behind him shuffled uncomfortably and held fast onto his gun. The prisoner sounded demented. Santana abruptly got up, his eyes burning. Aldo also rose from his chair. The soldier behind him jumped back holding the gun with both hands.

"Try to touch me, and I'll bust the rest of your teeth," Aldo said.

Captain Santana stopped and hesitated. He badly wanted to hit him but was afraid to fail again. He went for his gun instead. At that moment the door opened.

"Captain Santana, back off!"

It was Blanco. He swung the door open, his driver close behind him. His grey hair was neatly combed but his uniform looked wrinkled. He looked full of energy as he walked into the room. As he looked past him, Aldo saw a man he had not seen in many months dressed in the olive-green uniform of the rebel army standing near the door. It was Tomas. Now Aldo knew how he had come to be here. Tomas, the stool pigeon who had sold Patricio to the Batista's forces he had once worshiped, had now joined the rebel army. The split second during which their eyes met told Aldo everything. This crafty creature could adapt to every regime and was a master of survival, totally devoid of morals. *People like him is what was making this famous revolution*, Aldo thought. Aldo burned with rage inside. What kind of a system was this which allowed the crooked to pass judgment?

"Sit down, Aldo," Blanco said, pointing to the chair behind him. "There's no need to stand. What's happened to your face?"

"I just had a little running with Batista's Army all over again," Aldo said sarcastically. "Only now they are dressed in green."

"Batista's Army is a thing of the past. Don't insult our rebels, Aldo. You should know better."

"Yes, you're right," Aldo said. "I know better. None of the men you have in this room is worth an ounce of shit."

"Shut up," Blanco said. "You are in no position to attack my men."

"I'm in as good of a position as I ever was. Don't waste your time with your philosophies on me. Get on with whatever it is you're going to do to me."

"That's where you're wrong," Blanco said, taking a seat in front of him. "People like you refuse to see what our revolution is all about. You just don't understand, do you? But let me tell you, despite whatever you may think, our revolution is not a murderous revolution. It is a revolution of justice. We seek to establish the rights of the people. Everybody's rights, from the richest to the poorest. That's what you don't see. Now, Captain Santana, what is this man accused of?"

"He's accused of murder," Captain Santana said looking over Aldo spitefully.

"Murdering whom?"

"Murdering a peasant. An innocent peasant in Rios named Patricio who was gunned down by Batista's *casquitos* right in front of his home. This guy here acted as a stool pigeon for Batista's forces."

"Those are serious charges, Aldo. What do you have to say for yourself?"

"If you're really interested in finding out, open that door behind you and ask your lackey standing there. He came to get me to bury Patricio after he was killed. Wasn't he a Batista sympathizer who complained to the government about Patricio? That's what really got Patricio killed. Now he's on your side. Amazing, isn't it?"

"What insolence!" Captain Santana interpolated. "You have the nerve to accuse one of our rebels?"

"Then why ask me? Ask someone else if you don't want to hear my answer."

"I tell you what we're going to do here," Blanco said. "We're going to have a speedy investigation on this. We're going to get to the bottom of it, and quickly. Now, if you are in anyway responsible for that man's death, then you shall pay the price. No more, no less.

If you're innocent, you'll be freed. But we are going to get to the truth."

It was hard to believe this was the same man who had cordially hosted him and Pablo at his home a few hours before. There was no memory of that on his expression. This new revolution was Blanco's God. When it came to that, he respected no one. No matter who one was anyone who came between him and the revolution would be eliminated without compassion. Blanco lifted his eyes to the soldier next to Aldo, indicating he was through with the prisoner. The soldier moved his gun, motioning with the barrel that Aldo should get up.

Pablo worked compulsively for his friend that day. He made two trips to the city jail, each time bringing peasants from Rios who knew Aldo and the circumstances surrounding Patricio's death. Despite the political situation, no one refused to cooperate. There was Rodolfo, the old man whom everyone called *el santero*, his wife, Oscar, and other men who knew Aldo from the village. But the best witness was Julia, Patricio's widow. She talked to Captain Santana and Blanco. The two men intimated that she was afraid to tell the truth, that she was a traitor to the memory of her husband for not reporting Aldo. Julia held her ground. How could anyone slander a man this way? she told them. Aldo had been her savior at a time when most had turned away from her. Then she told them about her own doubts. There was a man she had suspected. Why hadn't he been questioned? His name was Tomas, and he was a known Batista sympathizer. He had disappeared from the hamlet shortly after her husband's death, never to be seen again. Where was he?

By midnight, Aldo was brought back into the same room where he had been questioned by Blanco this morning. Captain Santana was sitting in the same chair as if he hadn't moved. Next to him was Blanco and, to Aldo's surprise, Pablo was also in the room.

The soldier came up behind Aldo, butting him in the back with the barrel of his gun. He led Aldo to the opposite side of the table to face the captain and the commander.

"I am going to give you and your friend here some instructions," Blanco said solemnly. "You're going to be allowed to go home tonight. But you're not free to roam around. You are confined to your farm. By that I mean your own farm. No more business for you. No more deals. You work the farm, and you are not to leave it under any circumstances. Is that understood? This investigation is by no means over. But while we conclude it, you're going to be allowed to work. However, the smallest deviation, and you'll be brought back here for violation of these conditions. And so will your friend here. You both have been warned. Now," he said raising his voice and pointing to the door, "get out of my sight."

Blanco's driver turned and opened the door for them. Pablo waited until Aldo was out of the room and then followed. Aldo was still weak and limped as he walked. The swelling on his face had gone down, but his left eye was still partially closed. There was a large blue spot on his right cheek. His hair was wet but uncombed. A soldier had doused him in water while three others held him. His clothes were tattered. They had tried to undress them to clean him, but he had resisted them.

"Go straight to the jeep," the soldier behind them said as another opened the gate. "No chatting with anyone. We'll be watching you."

Aldo stepped outside. It was dark out, and only the dim spotlights on the roof shone on the exiting area. Amanda saw her husband from the jeep. She ran to him and put her arms around him. Pablo urged them all to get inside and quickly pulled away from the building.

"We're going straight to Rios. Tonight we're getting you out of here," Pablo said excitedly, looking from Aldo to the road.

"Where to?" Aldo asked.

"Out of here. We'll talk in the house."

"I'm not leaving without my family."

"We'll be behind you."

The jeep sped through the Central Highway. When it reached the cemetery, it turned left into the Vertientes road. They soon left the town behind, driving through the open, dark road that cut across the flat land.

* * *

Pablo had not slept the night before. First, he had been busy trying to find Aldo's whereabouts. After leaving Blanco's barracks, he had paid Suarez a visit.

Mr. Suarez's mistress lived in an old section of town. Pablo had never actually been inside the house but had, on several occasions, waited for Aldo in the jeep while his friend conferred with Suarez. Suarez was strict about who he saw at this secret location. Only his closest acquaintances knew of its existence. One's presence there meant he was held in high esteem by the old man. This time, it was Ana who waited in the jeep. Pablo knocked on the large wooden door. The facade of the house appeared dull and unimpressive, like most other houses in this section. It was 4:00 A.M., and Pablo did not expect Sanchez to hear him the first time, so he knocked again. He stood back as the door creaked open. He saw a woman's face peer through the opening. He didn't wait for her to speak.

"I'm sorry to disturb you, madam. I am Pablo. I need to see Suarez. There's been an emergency."

"Who are you again?" she answered in a whisper.

Even in the darkness, Pablo could tell she was a beautiful woman, probably thirty, with long, unkempt hair. Despite having just been awakened she looked very awake.

"I am Pablo, Aldo's friend," he repeated.

"All right. I'll get him."

She closed the door again. Pablo stood on the narrow sidewalk for a few minutes, listening to the occasional far-away sound of a car engine. Then the door opened again.

"Come in," a man's voice said.

Pablo stepped inside a dimly-lit room with blue walls. Suarez, wearing a white under-shirt, pajamas bottom, and slippers, motioned for him to sit down. Pablo sat on a sofa next to the door. The only light in the room came from a lamp on a side table. The room was comfortably but simply furnished, two rocking chairs, a sofa, a center table and an étagère holding some porcelain statutes. The only modern touch was the television set across from the sofa. Suarez sat on the rocking chair in front of Pablo.

"What's the matter?"

"It's Aldo, Suarez. The rebels arrested him a few hours ago. I'm still not sure why, but I'm here for only one reason. If I'm able to win his release, I want him to leave the country immediately. You had mentioned that you had a brother in Miami."

Suarez looked thoughtful for a moment. He was a light sleeper and had been up on the first knock. It took him only a brief moment to think clearly. He liked Aldo but he had predicted that this moment would come. Aldo was only the first. Soon, they would all have to choose between being imprisoned and leaving the country. What happened to Aldo was only an omen of what was still to come.

"All right," he said after a few moments. "My brother cannot help us with this. This is an emergency. But I have somebody else. Write down all his information and leave it with me. We have to get him a passport. I'll call Havana in the morning. We'll get him a visa. It can be done."

"How fast?"

"Oh, a couple of days."

"We'll have to finish the paperwork in Havana, Suarez. If he gets out of jail, I want him out of here immediately."

"Yes, I agree. I have a flat in Havana where he can hide for a while. But you and his family also have to get out. You'll all be in danger."

"I know."

Suarez sighed and stared down at the floor. He dragged both hands across his head as if to comb his non-existent hair.

"Hilda," he called, "can you make some coffee?"

"Not for me," Pablo said. "I am on my way out. Look," he added, "Ana is with me. I'll have her contact you if anything happens."

"Ana?" Suarez said incredulously. "Blanco's wife?"

"You don't need to worry, Mr. Suarez, she's not with Blanco."

"We're all going to have to be very careful," Suarez said. "You can't trust your own family and friends from now on. That is the price we pay for losing our freedom. That's what's coming. What do they say Aldo did anyway?"

Pablo explained in few words what little he knew. Obviously, someone was after Aldo. And if Aldo was a suspect, it would only be a matter of time before his friends also fell prey to persecution. Suarez agreed to stay in town during the day. Pablo would stay in touch.

* * *

Pablo slowly drover over the dirt road to Aldo's farm house, skirting the bigger bumps. Half way there, they were met by Champ, Aldo's dog, barking incessantly until he confirmed the identity of his master. Alfredo met them at the gate. He and the milkman had been hard at work when he spotted the headlights of the jeep. It could have been a military jeep, so Alfredo had cautiously ran towards the house holding his machete. What could they want now?

"Alfredo!" Pablo called. "It's us. We're here."

"Is Aldo with you?"

"Yes, I'm here," Aldo said.

"Oh, thanks to our Virgin of Charity."

Alfredo came forward and shook Aldo's hand. He could see Aldo's damaged eye in the darkness.

"I can't believe what those cowards did to you," he exclaimed. "Let me tell the milkman," Alfredo added.

"No," Pablo interjected, "I'll talk to the milkman. Meet me at the cattle house, Alfredo."

Pablo went inside with Amanda and Aldo. He gave Amanda some instructions. He had a plan to get Aldo out tonight. It was their only option. If he stayed, there was no telling what Blanco would do. Aldo could be picked up again any minute without warning. Aldo silently agreed.

Aldo sat on the porch, waiting. He watched the dim lights of Rios across the highway. There was a new moon, and the night was clear. Aldo loved nights like these when one could almost smell the wet dew coming. He wondered if they had nights like these in America. Amanda came and sat by him.

"What are you thinking about?"

"I don't know. So many things."

She leaned her chin on his shoulder and held his hand. She cried for him and for herself. She had never wanted this place, but it was at least their home. Now they would have none. They were beginning a long and risky adventure, the results of which they dared not question.

Pablo joined them and stood behind them for a moment then told them it was time.

Amanda kissed Aldo, and Pablo hugged him. Aldo started down the dirt road with Champ running behind him.

"Stay back, Champ," Aldo said. "You can't come."

He petted him on the head several times, then, with wet eyes, he waived him to go back. The animal sat on the road watching his master disappear in the darkness, as if sensing that he would never see him again. Only once did Aldo look back toward the cattle house. He saw only one candle burning, which meant the men had finished the milking and were probably readying the buggy. Soon the milkman would be leaving. There was no going back.

Aldo opened the front gate cautiously, looking down both sides of the road. In the prairie, images blended with the darkness at night, and it was sometimes impossible to see a man until he was right up close, even on a clear night like tonight. He stepped to the right side of the ditch and went into the culvert. He laid there quietly, resting his head on the grass, waiting.

He heard the milkman's cart coming. After the buggy passed the gate, the milkman got off to close it. Aldo heard him walk back to the buggy and climb in. Then, almost as an afterthought, the milkman's deep voice called him.

"Aldo, are you there?"

Aldo pulled himself out of the culvert and, crouching, he looked around. Nothing moved but there was no telling. The rebels would never again leave him alone. He was a marked man. They would search for any excuse to imprison him and this could be the perfect opportunity. If caught, he would be hard pressed to explain why he was fleeing if he was not guilty.

"I'm here," Aldo said softly. "Start the buggy. I'll jump in."

The milkman allowed some slack in the reins, and the horse began moving. The cart was making the turn when Aldo grabbed its iron bracket and swiftly pulled himself up on its side, then huddled under the driver's seat in front of the milk pots. Pablo had made sure the milkman had made room for him. Aldo could not extend his legs so he had to curl against the bottom in a fetal position.

"I just hope like hell there isn't a road block at Nadales," the milkman said.

"Hush and drive," Aldo said. "You'll drop me off before we get there."

The carriage moved smoothly on the highway, meeting no one. There was only the sound of horseshoes, striking the pavement, echoing in the night. Aldo knew that sound. He had come to know it as a little boy when dawn began to set. It was the unmistakable sound of a milkman's carriage making its way into town.

Aldo waited a few minutes before peeking through the crevices of the boards. They were about mid-way to the city, he could tell, and the milkman had not spoken again. The poor man must be scared to death. He saw the reflection of light ahead, and he quickly put his head down. A car was coming, going towards Vertientes. Aldo stayed down and looked out again. He recognized the large houses near Nadales. He did not want to expose the milkman to any danger. He figured he could work his way into town through the lands, away from the road.

"Stop here," he whispered. "I'll walk the rest of the way."

"No," the milkman said. "I'm dropping you off at the station. That was my deal with Pablo. Fuck these bastards. I'm not afraid of them."

"No need to get you in trouble. Stop."

"I won't."

Aldo lifted his head and looked ahead. He could see the last curve before reaching Enrique's shanty store. He could see between the trees. There was nothing, just darkness.

"Don't worry," the milkman said. "They're not out there. They're fucking sleeping. Those bastards. Only Enrique is up, I bet you. Poor man. With his wife gone, he seems lost and so alone."

"Did she die?"

"They buried her yesterday. Poor lady was in so much pain she was already half dead."

Aldo gazed at the empty lot in front of Enrique's store as they passed by. He saw no light, but Enrique must be inside somewhere. The tall storekeeper had lost his best friend. He could see the frail lady tending to the rowdy crowds alongside her husband. She had been an iron woman, the kind that would support him no matter what his trade.

The carriage passed the store, then veered off the road to an Esso gas station at the corner of a local road. From here, one could reach the Central Highway without entering town. The station was a landmark for the out-of-towners. It was relatively modern, with a bright, multi-colored lighted archway over its gas pumps resembling a rainbow. The glare of the all-night lights made it an unlikely spot for a hiding, but this is where Pablo had told the milkman to drop Aldo off. The milkman didn't know what to expect as he pulled the carriage across the lot but got anxious when he saw no one.

"Turn around away from the lights," Aldo said.

Two cars were squeezed at the side of the station house, out of the range of the lights. One of them had been driven farther inside. Aldo recognized it as Blanco's 1958 Buick. Another man would have panicked, but Aldo's quick thinking told him who the driver might be. The milkman hadn't even noticed as he brought the carriage to a stop. Coolly, Aldo extended his right arm from underneath the seat to shake his old friend's hand.

"Thanks for the ride," he said.

"Are you sure I can leave you here?"

"Sure. Go deliver that milk now. I'll see you soon."

Aldo dragged himself out and slipped into the darkness. He watched as the carriage went back on the road towards Nadales until he could no longer see him and could only hear the horse's hooves tapping on the road. Slowly, he worked his way to the rear passenger door, opened it, and went quietly inside. He laid low on the seat. Behind the wheel sat Ana, the woman who had always protected him, even from her own husband.

"Are you all right?"

She turned her head towards him. She had not seen him since he was apprehended. She had prepared herself for this moment, knowing his face would show the torture he had endured, yet she was taken aback by his scars. Not too long ago, she had seen him go through a similar ordeal. Blanco had been on their side then.

"I'm fine. Can we go?"

She turned the ignition key then looked back at him once more, wanting to convey her thoughts.

"What have they done to you, Aldo?" she said, holding back tears.

"I can't seem to keep guards away from my face, no matter which government is in power."

"Yes. But that's enough now. Please lie down. We're going to get out of here."

She turned her headlights on, put the engine in gear, and went down the small road. She passed through a development that ended at the Central Highway. There she turned left, going north toward Havana. She drove at moderate speed, passing several military trucks going in the opposite direction. She traveled eight to ten miles before turning right through the middle of a mango grove. She drove the car towards the country cabin at the far end, and turned off the lights. She pulled up in front of the house and waited. The house belonged to a cattleman friend of Suarez. It was a small house located on fifteen hectares near the Central Highway. The land was used for holding cattle. Both Aldo and Pablo knew the place well. The house was empty most of the time and it was here that Ana had agreed to meet Pablo. Everything had happened so quickly that Aldo marveled at the ingenuity they had shown in putting such an intricate plan together on such short notice. He had let himself be led as a child. He had absolute trust in Pablo.

A few minutes later, the headlights of a vehicle shone from the road. Ana was startled. It was a jeep, but was it the right one?

"Lie down, Aldo, please."

"It's Pablo. Don't worry."

The jeep flicked the headlights on and off as a signal. Then, as planned, Pablo drove to the back of the house so the jeep could not be seen from the road. Someone would pick it up later. Out of the vehicle came Amanda, Frank, and Pablo carrying the twins. Amanda and the children went to the rear seat of the vehicle while Pablo sat in the front with Ana. No sooner were they seated when the car made half a circle in front of the house and headed for the road. Ana did not turn the headlights on until she was already on the highway. No one spoke. Aldo kissed the children. Somehow, he had thought this moment would never come, and yet, despite his excitement, he could not help but decry the absurdity of the present situation. Like a thief in the night, he had been forced to flee his own home with his family hidden in a car. What had he done to deserve this? Amanda took one of the twins, and he rested the other on his shoulder. Frank sat between them.

The car rode through the Central Highway at steady speed, stopping only once for gas. By the time the children awoke, it was late morning. Pablo calculated they were about one hour away from the capital.

Around noontime, they saw the scattered housing projects near Havana, pockets of cheap small houses on the outskirts of the city. Ana was the only one who knew the city well. During the early years of her marriage to Blanco, she had visited the casinos and the white sandy beaches near the capital. It all seemed like a dream now, but it didn't matter. She had made a decision. She now had a job to do.

The car drove down a busy avenue and then maneuvered a turn into a narrow street with high sidewalks. Ana stopped at a small hotel, barely visible from the end of the street.

"You take them in while I park the car," she said to Pablo. After they exited the car, Ana drove into a small lot parking far into the lot where she could not be noticed.

Pablo booked three rooms, two singles and a double. It was a cheap inn and Ana had picked it intentionally because of its location, away from the avenue and yet close to the other hotels. Pablo and Aldo used what little time they had to take a nap. They were due to meet Suarez at another hotel late this afternoon. The others also got some sleep. At 3:00 P.M., Pablo and Aldo entered the Capri, a local casino-hotel located at L Avenue and 21st Street. Pablo made Aldo wait at the entrance by the rows of potted palm trees that lined the passageway and went into the cafeteria, a large paneled room with round tables and a bar. At a table behind the pianist, almost unnoticeable, Pablo spotted Suarez with his eternal companion, Federico. He couldn't be happier at seeing the old man. Suarez had kept his word.

"Is he here?" Suarez said as Pablo approached, before greeting him.

"Yes, he's outside."

"Well, bring him in. We have a lot to do. Everything is in the works. If we can get him fingerprinted today, maybe by some miracle we can ship him out day after tomorrow."

"I'll be back."

Aldo came behind Pablo. His face was still swollen but his battered eye was now opened and was circled by a ring of dry blood. The most severe wound was on his right cheek where the skin had been broken into a wide gash. Because of lack of stitches, the wound had begun to heal itself and was covered with a hard crust of blood. He still limped a little. Suarez was touched by his friend's appearance. Suarez thought Aldo an honorable man, more typical of men from Suarez's own generation with whom you could shake hands and rely on their word. Men like that did not come along too often anymore. In deference, Suarez stood up to shake Aldo's hand. Federico followed.

"Look at what those scum bags did to you, eh?"

Aldo smiled and shook Suarez' hand then Federico's. "Thank you for helping us. I'll never be able to repay what you're doing."

"Never mind that," Suarez snapped. "You want a drink before we leave?"

"No."

"Then let's go."

Suarez put on his Stetson and grabbed his cigar. He was still wearing his cowboy gear, brown cowboy boots, beige pants, and large belt buckle. Federico, Aldo, and Pablo followed him. They went into the parking lot of the hotel to Suarez's blue 1958 Chevrolet. Federico got behind the wheel and they went off to meet Suarez's contacts and get Aldo's papers in order.

That evening the family had a quiet meal at a small restaurant a few blocks away from their hotel. The meal was somber since everyone knew that Aldo would be leaving the country the day after tomorrow. He had been fingerprinted. Pablo had provided the agency with two of Aldo's old pictures. A passport was promised to Suarez by tomorrow morning. The transit visa would be issued by the American Embassy tomorrow afternoon. A reservation was made for the early flight to Miami on the day after tomorrow. Everything was going according to plan. Amanda sat quietly, poking at the potatoes on her plate as she thought about the latest events as related by Pablo. It was all moving too fast for her. Aldo, too, was quiet. Ana, sitting across from the table, traded looks with them. Ana knew her sister and her moods.

"He must go, Amanda," she said. "We cannot let him stay here for a minute longer. His life would be endangered."

"I know," Amanda replied tersely.

"Forget everything else. Forget property, houses, everything. His life is what counts now."

"When would we go, Pablo?"

"We start our paperwork right after Aldo leaves. His case was so urgent that Suarez did not want to tie up his man here in Havana with anything else. We can wait a few days."

"But how many is a few days?"

"I don't know. Two weeks, three. It really doesn't matter. Once he's gone, I'll be breathing again. I don't care how much I have to wait."

"Can we go back to our homes?" Amanda asked.

"Of course not. No way," Pablo warned.

"You can never go back home, Amanda," Ana added. "They will look for Aldo, and when they can't find him, they'll look for you and Pablo."

"But Blanco is your husband. You can stop him."

"Amanda," Aldo spoke finally, "leave it alone."

She did not answer. She traded glances with her sister once more. Yes, she blamed her. She blamed her for a lot of things. At least for now, she could not afford to be mad at Aldo but some day, she would find ways to blame him too.

"I have asked Suarez to find out how things are going in Camaguey today without Aldo there. I just wanted to see if anyone already realized that we are missing."

"How would he find out?" Amanda asked.

"He's got ways. I don't know."

"Alfredo would never tell on us anyway," Amanda said.

"I gave him instructions. He is going to stay at the farm for a while. But then I told him to just go on his way after a while, and if they ask him, to say that Aldo just disappeared. He didn't see him anymore. He took it pretty hard, poor Alfredo. It was hard for me to tell him, too. It was like abandoning an old friend, you know what I mean?"

"Yes," Aldo acknowledged, "I don't want him to suffer on my account."

"He won't," Pablo said. "He's no dummy."

"Far from it. I would like to help him if I could."

They all remained silent for a moment. It was Frank who broke their thoughts.

"Dad, do you think Alfredo will go to jail."

"No, he won't"

Pablo spotted Suarez and Federico entering the restaurant. The two men had gone to their hotel for a bath. They both looked refreshed and wore neatly-pressed clothes. Suarez came to their table and then asked the waiter to move another table next to Aldo's. He asked for a menu.

"Now, under normal circumstances," he began, "I would go to the casino in my hotel and play for a couple of hours, but now I don't dare."

Ana's presence still made him feel uncomfortable He didn't like it. Who was to say that she and her bohemian husband would not get back together? He preferred to talk alone with Aldo. She had seen him with Aldo and he was more convinced than ever that his days on the island were also numbered.

"We'd better get the children to bed," Amanda said. "We've all had a long day. We'll leave you guys alone. Don't be too late now, Aldo."

"I'll walk you back to the hotel," Pablo said.

"No," Ana interjected. "Stay with them. I'll go with Amanda."

The children kissed Aldo and the women rose. There were few customers in the dining area. The room held about ten small tables. It was dimly lit but it had a good view of the street filled with pedestrians and slow-moving cars. Ana and Pablo had chosen it after roaming around several blocks. Strolling in public places was just too dangerous. The last thing they wanted was to run into someone who knew them. They decided that they would not go anywhere else. Aldo must stay at the hotel until it was time to go.

"After you go," Suarez said as the women left, "the rest of you can come to stay in my flat in the old Havana section. Right now, we need to be in the center of town because of everything we must do."

"How long before we can get Pablo and my family out of here?" Aldo asked.

"Probably a couple of weeks."

Aldo frowned at the thought of leaving them behind. He would have preferred to wait until they could all go together. But Pablo was right. He could pave the way for them in Miami. Besides, they all knew he was dead if he was caught again. He had to go.

"Let me tell you who you're meeting in Miami," Suarez said. "There's this man I know, Entrante. He is an old friend of mine. He spent time in the United States in the thirties. Then he came back here and made his fortune. Originally he imported liquor. He was a brilliant business man. Very aggressive. He did well with his importing business and later moved to the big league by going into banking. He had his problems with the bearded ones here since early on, so he's been out of Cuba now for a few months. He will receive you."

"All I need is to find a job."

"I suppose you have to start somewhere, but it's a whole different ball game in the United States. It's not like here, Aldo. Number one, it's a different language. You can make a living but doing what? Scraping pots at a hotel or cleaning the floors? I don't want to sound negative, but it's going to be rough. Let's see how you handle it. Just be strong, as I know you'll be."

"As long as he's out of here," Pablo said.

"Yes. He'll be out of here, all right. He'll be fine. We are the ones who will catch the heat. Listen, Aldo, this guy Felix, Entrante's helper, he'll wait for you at the airport. It's all arranged. He's a little guy, looks kind of wimpy. Don't underestimate him, though. He's as tough as they come. He'll show you the way. You'll do fine. I know you got guts. I'm not worried about you."

Suarez ordered dinner for him and Federico. The two ate a full-course meal while discussing the details of Aldo's trip. Then Suarez asked for the usual cup of espresso. The street noise had diminished somewhat, but the human traffic on the narrow sidewalks seemed relentless, even in this rather remote location. The people were still caught up in the wave of enthusiasm of the new revolution. Many carried red and black bracelets pinned to their forearms, signifying their sympathy for the rebel movement. The frenzy nurtured by the island's far eastern towns had taken hold of the capital like a windstorm, and there was no letting go. The rebels were here to stay. Military jeeps would occasionally drive by, brimming with uniformed men brandishing their long carbines as if they were toys. The ominous military presence was everywhere, a sign of the times.

Pablo walked out first, always concerned that someone might recognize his friend. The night was cool and breezy. Strolling was tempting, but it was out of the question. The wounds on Aldo's face were likely to cause suspicion. He and Pablo took the back seat in Suarez's Chevrolet.

"I would have loved to show you guys this town," Suarez said sadly. "This city was a hell of a place at one time, let me tell you."

"I am sorry I cannot see it," Aldo said.

"Take them past the Prado, Federico," Suarez told his driver.

"No, no," Pablo interposed. "It's too risky, Suarez. Let's not push our luck. Besides, Aldo needs time with his family. He's only got one more night with them."

"That's true. Back to their hotel, Federico."

The car pulled close to the curve at El Grande. The two street lamps at the front entrance shone faintly. The hotel was not known to many outsiders. Pablo felt comfortable with its location and found its quaintness most fitting to their purpose. Crowds were more likely in the more modern parts of town. He felt safe here.

They said their goodbyes inside. Then the two men stepped out of the car and disappeared behind the front door, taking the stairs to their rooms.

Late morning, Suarez came for them. He took Aldo to his notary in a busy section of the city. They waited until about noon when finally a secretary handed Aldo a passport.

"That's it," Suarez said joyfully. "There's no time to lose now. Federico, drive us to the embassy."

The large iron-gated building of the American Embassy was imposing. At his boss's direction, Federico drove past it once to look the area over and check for any military patrols. Suarez said it was well known by now that the embassy was being watched. People who entered it were fingered as possible counter-revolutionaries and sometimes questioned. They would have to be extremely careful not to be spotted. The difficult part would be entering and leaving. Suarez instructed Federico to find a spot a block away. Pablo could not accompany them as he did not have clearance to enter the embassy. Suarez and Aldo exited the vehicle and walked casually toward the embassy. Aldo walked on the inside protected Suarez's massive body to prevent detection. As they reached the building, they turned simultaneously and went up the steps leading inside.

"There are men across the street watching," Suarez said in a low voice without turning his head. "But they can't see you. Just keep walking and hand the guard your pass. I'll follow you."

Aldo handed the uniformed doorman his pass and waited for Suarez. Then they two went into a waiting room where Suarez spoke to a clerk. In a few moments, they were called in. Aldo was interviewed by an aide, completed some forms, and was sent back to the waiting room. The room was crowded. Most of the people appeared to be professionals or business men. About an hour later, he was handed back his passport, now stamped with a visa.

"Now let's check outside," Suarez said. "Let's see if the men are still there."

They approached one of the front windows and gazed past the American flag in the court yard. A gold Opel with two men inside was parked across the street. They wore no uniforms but it was obvious they were watching the building.

"Leaving is a lot more difficult than entering," Suarez said. "You are going to have to stay behind me."

"Yes, but what about you? If they detect you, they could follow you."

"We can shake their tail if they do. I'm not worried about that. Federico knows this town pretty well. I just don't want them to see you. Let's not give them any ideas."

The two men positioned themselves at the door. Suarez took the lead about two steps in front of Aldo. To make it seem more casual, Aldo walked at an angle behind Suarez, keeping his face blocked by his body. Suarez saw no reaction from the men in the car as they turned. He did not think the men had been there when they had first entered the building.

"Let's walk past the car and turn at the corner," Suarez said. "Then we'll look to see if anybody is following us. Federico will meet us a couple of blocks down."

They walked past Suarez's car and turned at the corner. They walked about three blocks, turning again at another intersection before Federico picked them up. After making sure they weren't being followed, Federico drove them back to the hotel. Suarez made a phone call and then sent Federico in a taxi to pick up Aldo's plane ticket. He returned with a yellow envelope which he handed to Suarez. Everything was now ready for Aldo's departure.

That night, the family had a simple supper at the hotel one last time. They talked about old times. Pablo did most of the talking and reminisced about their childhood in Rios and Aldo's boxing days as a teenager. Amanda clung to her husband, resting her head on his chest like a child as she listened quietly. She was overwhelmed with grief at her husband's departure. Despite all the assurances from Suarez, she did not feel secure. She feared that they would not see him again.

"I remember the first time I saw Amanda. It was an evening when I was in town from Rios for the weekend staying at Dulce's, and I went to the Mercedes Square with Aldo. He said he wanted to show me his girlfriend. The two of us were hiding at the end of the square, peering at the church entrance from the edge of buildings and waiting for the mass to end. When people began leaving church, we saw the uniformed girls from the St. Teresa School. They all looked the same with that uniform, the brown skirt, white-collared blouse with plaid vest, and black shoes. Aldo said, 'there she is.'"

Both Ana and Amanda laughed. Amanda rubbed her head on Aldo's shoulder.

"I just saw three girls coming our way. I did not know who was who. So I asked him which one was his girlfriend, and he said it was the middle one."

"That's right," Ana quipped. "She always walked in the middle. I was always on the side closest to the street because I was the oldest, Amanda in the middle and Aleida at the inner side because she was the youngest. We always walked like that."

"Those were great times," Amanda said. "The nuns from St. Teresa were so good. That was the best school for girls."

"The St. John School wasn't bad either," Pablo said.

"Never like ours," Amanda said. "St. Teresa was the best."

"They competed among themselves," Suarez said. "That's how it was. They each tried to be better than the other. My daughters went to St. Theresa."

"There was some arrogance at St. Theresa that you didn't see at St. John," Aldo said.

"And how would you know?" Amanda asked playfully. "Did you date any girls from St. John, eh?"

"That is true, Amanda," Pablo said. "You could see they were somewhat arrogant. The St. John sisters were humble."

"We were a better school," Amanda said. "That's so."

"Those schools are all going to fall by the wayside now," Suarez prophesied. "They are all doomed."

"What makes you say that?" Amanda asked.

"Amanda, mark my words, this is only the beginning. This is communism. The government is going to get involved in everything.

Private schools are finished. So is private enterprise, business, everything that is not controlled by the government. The next few months will be critical. You'll see. We've already started on the changes."

They all fell silent. They wanted to doubt him, but deep inside, they knew he was right. A storm seemed to be brewing in the horizon. The new government was talking changes, many changes. They talked about reform for the poor. Nothing wrong with that. In this country, the poor had been neglected for years as if they didn't exist while the rich got richer at their expense. But there was something suspicious about the way Castro was maneuvering into all aspects of life, commanding changes by the mere lifting of a finger during one of his heated, extensive speeches. The people applauded whatever he said, as if they were spellbound. Meanwhile, barriers were being torn down. Institutions were falling apart. Fear was setting in among the big capitalists, and those with resources were beginning to flee the country. If the exodus intensified, what would happen to the country when all its resources were gone?

A few minutes after eleven Amanda got up. She needed to get back to her room and prepare Aldo's luggage, what little he had. Suarez and Federico shook hands with Aldo and agreed to meet him downstairs by 6:00 A.M. They must be at the airport no later than 7:00. Ana had bought medications and worked on Aldo's face to make his wounds less noticeable. Suarez agreed that his cheek wound should be worked on more in the morning. After Suarez left, they went to Amanda and Aldo's room and talked for some time. Then Ana and Pablo left for their rooms. Amanda and Aldo put the children to bed. They laid in bed together for an hour, just talking about their questionable future and the uncertainty they faced. She fell asleep on his chest. He dozed off uncomfortably until about 5:00 A.M. when he got up to wash his face and brush his teeth. Someone was already tapping at the door. It was Ana.

"Let me work on your face one last time before you leave," she said. "Sit down."

She wiped the skin carefully with alcohol. Then she stenciled the wound on his cheek with a thin line of Mercurochrome.

"This really should have a gauze," she said. "But of course we can't put one on. It would make it too obvious."

By 6:00, Amanda woke up the children and dressed them. They went downstairs and waited in the lobby. Aldo carried one small black duffel bag containing an extra pair of shoes, underwear, a shirt, and pants. That was the extent of his luggage. Pablo had managed to exchange some pesos into dollars with Suarez's help and gave Aldo ninety five dollars. Aldo had folded the money into thin rolls that he placed under his belt. If they searched him at the airport, it would not show. He had been warned by Suarez that the most trivial discrepancy at customs could cost him his life. No formal announcement had been made, but the word was out that anyone leaving the country could take nothing with him.

They got into Suarez' Chevrolet. Federico took the Malecon drive by the City's piers. The sea looked beautiful, with the sun barely rising in the horizon. Aldo took a good look at it. It was a beautiful island, his home. But fate was causing him to leave and go somewhere unknown where he must start a new life. It was hard to understand but now was not the time to try, he thought. He had always been a practical man. A man of courage. He had raised himself from poverty and walked and dined with the rich. He had given his family a better life. He must do it again.

The car entered the airport parking lot. Federico headed for the terminal. Suarez instructed him to keep the car parked at a distance. They could see several turbo planes of *Cubana de Aviacion*, the national airline, parked on the runway. Suarez decided that Aldo must go alone inside and check in. The less they were seen together, the better it would be for everyone. It was more likely that one individual in a group would be recognized than someone alone. Besides, if someone saw them together, they could remember it during a subsequent investigation.

"Just check in and then come back to bid your family farewell," Suarez said. "Go into the terminal and check your luggage. You have time. Get your seat number. It's better that we don't go in with you. There are guards everywhere now."

Aldo turned obediently to his children and Amanda and smiled at them. For the first time, he was feeling the tension of the trip. He felt pressure on his chest. It was now inevitable. He was really leaving them.

He picked up his bag and opened the door. He heard the twins tell him to come back to say goodbye. He tried to respond but he felt a knot in his throat and didn't look back. He couldn't.

He entered the terminal through the double glass door held open by a wedge. He went into a hallway and followed a sign to Customs. He stopped at a small barred window and waited. A man asked him for his papers and looked at his passport and ticket. Then he told him to step aside and come through the door. He was then asked to open his bag.

"Aren't you traveling kind of light?"

"Yes. I don't expect to be gone for long."

"You don't?"

"No, I don't."

"All right," said the attendant, with obvious contempt, "leave your bag here and go through the aisle. Go to the next room and get in line."

Aldo pushed the door before him and entered the next room. It was small, with two rows of chairs and a counter at the far end. There was no other door except the one behind him. The room was enclosed on both sides by a glass wall. The one on the right faced the airport's runway. The other one faced the inside of the terminal. Several people had formed a line in front of the counter, waiting to check in. Aldo stood in line behind an elderly couple. As his turn came up, he walked towards the counter and handed a woman his ticket. She was a tall brunette dressed in the olive green uniform of the rebel army. She leafed through the pages and made a notation on a log.

"Window or aisle?" she asked.

"Window. Excuse me. Do you think I could get back out into the main terminal? I didn't realize this space was closed off, and I didn't get a chance to bid farewell to my family."

The woman looked maliciously at him, as if taking pleasure in his sudden discomfort. She was neither a stewardess nor airport staff. Her manner was too rough and detached.

"You can ask the guard back there," the brunette said.

She handed Aldo his ticket with the seat number written on top in red ink. Aldo went to the back of the room and approached the guard. He was about five foot four with an acme-scarred face. He, too, wore the green uniform of the rebel army and a .45 belted to his hip.

"Can I go back out for a few moments? I would like to say goodbye to my family outside.

"Don't you want to leave?" the soldier said sarcastically,

"If you go back out, you stay."

He had to tilt his head to face Aldo and assumed an arrogant stance as if to make his presence known. Aldo felt a strong urge to slap him. He turned away from him and went to the glass wall on the other side. He peered through it past the open door to get a peek at the Suarez' car outside, but he couldn't see it. He turned his head from side to side, trying to place the car.

"Stop that," the guard said to him. "Sit down."

Aldo turned towards the row of seats and sat down. He rationalized as best as he could that it would be in the best interests of his family not to say goodbye. He had to be strong for them. His leaving meant their salvation.

The room had quickly filled with travelers. They all entered empty handed, having left their limited baggage in customs, and stood patiently in line waiting to check their tickets with the attendant. More families began to gather in the main terminal, looking meekly at their loved ones through the glass partition. At one time, it might have served a useful purpose, but now, it seemed only to extend an agonizing moment. It was evident that all those in the room were leaving the country for good. Being unable to speak to their loved ones was painful and reminiscent of prison. It was yet one more degrading procedure aimed at humiliating those who, by their departure, dared to take a stance against the new government.

No one knew it yet, but it was only the beginning of a long and controversial exodus, unprecedented in Cuban history.

As the seats filled, people stood in circles conversing in low voices. Aldo gave his seat to an older woman. His view to the glass wall had been covered by those standing. He shuffled through them to look back, trying to get a glimpse of the car outside. Would they know that he couldn't go back? Somehow, he managed to see Pablo, who had strolled into the terminal to see if anything was wrong. He waived to him and Pablo waived quickly back. Pablo stopped, understanding what had happened, and indicated all was well. He would explain to Amanda and the others. Now he just wanted to see his friend get on that plane.

A man came in the room with a tray and offered them small cups of espresso. Aldo didn't know what to make of the gesture. Was it genuine courtesy or one last sadistic taunt aimed at increasing the travelers' pain? A cup of coffee was to Cubans like tea to the English or *mate* to the Argentines. Apparently, they were to be spared no punishment. A last act of cruelty toward those who dared leave the homeland would serve to remind them what they were forsaking, like a salt on an open wound. Aldo refused the coffee. Those who drank did so in silence with tears in their eyes.

A door opened on the side of the counter. A man dressed in fatigues announced that Flight 53 from Havana to Miami was ready to depart. Everyone was to form a single line and follow him to the tarmac. Aldo mixed with the crowd and followed people through a door facing the airport runway. He looked back one last time before leaving the room and waived at Amanda and the others. He couldn't tell how they felt, but as he turned, he felt a knot in his throat again. He didn't dare look back. Before him was a small two-engine plane. He went up the steps and boarded. He took his window seat and buckled his belt as soon as he sat down. He could hear the soft sobs of the couple behind him. They sounded like school children, crying without wanting to show it. The stewardess, dressed in an elegant navy blue dress with white stripes, gave them flight instructions. Then the engines roared, making the plane rattle. They taxied towards the main runway. The plane stopped, rolled, slowly picking up speed, then darted forward with a loud rumble and took off. Aldo closed his eyes for a moment, feeling the change in pressure. He looked through the small square window and watched the houses get smaller. He saw squares of green and brown like the patches on a quilt, then the contours of the beach line, and later the beautiful green water that extended into the horizon. He kept humming a tune he had once known as a kid. It was at that point that he noticed the person traveling next to him. He was an older gentleman in well-pressed clothes, wearing green-shaded glasses that kept fogging with his tears. A generation was dying behind them. A new one was about to begin.

CHAPTER TWELVE

The Miami tourist trade had declined by the end of 1959. Having achieved its renown in previous decades, it had now become a second-or third-rate vacation spot inhabited by thousands of retired elderly who relaxed in its comfortable block chalets. Despite its imposing high-rising hotels and wide express ways, the city had little to offer to a large influx of immigrants. Its lack of industry made it unlikely that it could help the wave of refugees seeking to relive the American dream. Yet, in many ways and despite the odds, it would become just that. No city in the United States had ever undergone such a dramatic transformation in culture, demographics, and economic structure as Miami was about to do. As his flight landed, Aldo sighed in relief. It was artificial relief nevertheless. His mind was filled with what was expected of him and what he had left behind. This was his first flight ever. It had taken the twin-engine plane forty-five minutes to cross the Caribbean waters into the Florida peninsula. Aldo smelled a freshness in the air as he descended the stairs and followed the other travelers into Customs. The airport was busy and noisy. Men in blue uniforms pushed carts indifferently. He entered a large room where he stood in line behind the others and waited for his license to be inspected. A wrinkled man with dishwater hair took his passport and mumbled something to him. Aldo merely looked at him. He didn't understand. The man stared at him, then called another who in very broken Spanish asked him where he was going.

"I am to meet a friend here at the airport," Aldo said.

"Friend?" the man said at a loss for words. "Friend? Where friend?"

"I don't know. Somewhere in the airport."

The other man now opened Aldo's bag and went through its contents. Again the other official spoke to him slowly with a pronounced accent.

"You visit here? Visit friend?"

"Yes," Aldo said swiftly, realizing that a long explanation would not help.

The officer said something to the other in English and handed Aldo his passport. The first man returned Aldo's luggage to him. He signaled toward a set of double doors in front of them. Aldo walked, not knowing where he was going or what he might find. He recognized some of the faces from his flight and stood with them at the entrance of an elevator. They went in and someone pressed a button. As the elevator stopped, the people walked out. He gathered they were now at the entrance to the terminal. He looked around and was surprised at the state-of-the-art airport. Everything looked new and sparkling. Big difference from the dull and antique terminal he had just left in Havana. He had no idea where he should go, so he walked down a corridor. He remembered Mr. Suarez's description of Felix, the man he was meeting, short and slim with glasses. He concentrated on the faces around him. People were grouped at each side of the hallway, waiting for their loved ones. Each passenger walked warily by, looking intently until he was recognized by someone who would leap into his arms. Aldo passed them and kept on until there was no one else to follow.

He turned and waited for the others as they went down a staircase. They entered the baggage claim area where four conveyors carried the luggage onto rollers for the passengers to pick up. Aldo took his bag and looked around. He stared at each face he saw, looking for Mr.

Suarez's friend but found no one fitting the description. Gradually, all of the familiar faces he had seen back in Havana began to disappear until the last couple gathered their belongings and left. The area was totally empty now. For the first time in his life, Aldo experienced that feeling of loneliness that overcomes those who suddenly discover they have no where to go. He was now in a foreign land, he could not speak the language, and he knew no one. He was truly alone.

Aldo went to the row of plastic chairs against the wall of the room and sat down. He thought about the conditions he had experienced in his homeland prior to his departure. Nothing could be worse than that. He had lost his freedom. He had been condemned by people who were his own countrymen. They would have willingly put him to death, and, had it not been for providence and his good friend, Pablo, he would have been executed. Strangely, he had become a foreigner in his own country, so what did it matter where he was now? Anything would be an improvement. At least men would not come looking for him in the middle of the night to kill him. His children would have a future without having to be political. He decided to think practically.

He assumed no one would be picking him up. Something must have happened. But no matter, he had some money. Discreetly, he felt the wad of bills under his waistline. He could get started. How many times had he heard cattlemen say that a dime well spent could last you for a hundred years? He would have to use the money wisely. The first thing he must do was to find work and then a place to stay. He must go where he could find people who spoke his language, but where would that be? He figured he would ask someone at the airport and go from there. He would sleep wherever he could tonight.

He was lost in thought, staring at the floor. From the corner of his eye he saw a pair of black-laced leather shoes approach. Intuitively, he braced himself to hear a question that he would most likely be unable to understand. To his surprise, he understood the words. For a moment he did not realize that the person had spoken in Spanish.

"Are you Aldo?" the voice said.

Aldo looked up at the figure in front of him. It was a man just over five feet and very slim. He had no stomach, and his shirt was neatly tucked under a tight belt. He wore wide-pleaded pants that made him look like a character from an old movie. His face, narrow and small, had deeply-sunken cheeks. He had bushy grey hair parted on the side and sprayed in place. He wore wide-rimmed glasses with green lenses.

"Yes," Aldo replied, standing up. He towered over the little man.

"Ah, finally, you are here, eh? I'm Felix Montenegro, at your service."

Aldo shook the man's hand. He couldn't decide whether he was genuinely friendly or a harmless charlatan. He had been so shaken by his arrival at the airport that he still felt off focus as if his normally-sharp senses had been somehow diminished by the experience.

"Aldo Ochoa, at your service," he responded.

"I am a friend of Mr. Suarez, the man who arranged for your trip. I am sure glad to see you. I've been looking for you all over the airport. How did you get here without my seeing you? I was standing right by the entrance near Customs. But I may have been a little late. Imagine, if I lose you in the airport after all that. What would I tell Mr. Suarez? But tell me, how is Suarez, ah?"

"He's all right. He's in Havana now."

"Did he tell you what he is going to do? Is he going to come or what?"

"I think he's seriously thinking about it now, with everything that's happening."

"Yes. All that's happened and all that's going to happen. I've been telling everybody about those bearded bastards. But as the Cubans say, no one learns from his neighbor's head, eh? But I hope he doesn't wait too long. Otherwise, he's going to end up like you. Well, let's go. You got your luggage, I see. Okay. Let's go, follow me."

Aldo picked up his duffel bag and walked alongside Felix. They went outside the terminal into a parking area. Aldo was struck by the similarity in climate. There were handsome palm and oak trees edging the sidewalk. Somehow he had expected a totally different environment and had to remind himself that he was only ninety miles from Cuba. Felix walked to the back of a 1956 blue Chevy and opened the trunk.

"Put your luggage inside," he said.

Felix turned on the engine and drove out of the airport. As they entered South Miami, Aldo surveyed the flat cinder block houses with louvered windows and neatly-trimmed gardens. The area looked like an updated version of suburban Vista Hermosa back in his home town. Felix made him give him a full account of his experiences in prison, trying to verify his own suspicions of the rebel regime. He had not been back to Cuba since March, he told Aldo, and then only to run an errand for his boss, Don Entrante, who had sent him there to put the finishing touches on the sale of some of his assets.

As they spoke, Felix told Aldo the high regard in which he held himself. He was a business man who had dedicated most of his life to banking on the island. He had started as a young man and slowly worked his way up within the tough hierarchy of the banking world. He had seen it coming, he said, and he had told Don Entrante. Before Batista fell, he had begun exchanging pesos into dollars and moving his liquid assets to Miami. Fidel Castro was a thief, and Batista should have killed him when he had the chance. Aldo got the impression that Felix was a braggart, the employee of a wealthy Cuban, who probably wished he was his boss. Aldo felt somewhat uncomfortable at being under the auspices of such a man, but at the moment he did not have much choice, so he decided to make the best of it.

"Where do you think I can find work?" Aldo said.

"Ah," Felix responded, "you are going to work and you haven't even arrived yet. Look at your face, for Christ's sake. You still look like you need to be in the hospital. Let's have you meet Mr. Entrante first. I am sure he can find something for you to do. Don't worry."

"Well, I can't just sit around. I need to start working today."

Felix looked at him and smiled. He was happy to hear his concern. This showed the stuff the man was made of. He had also heard rumors from Don Entrante about Mr. Suarez's star kid. Aldo had been a good fighter and was supposedly a shrewd business man, like Mr. Entrante had been in his youth. Felix had heard that Aldo had made a lot of money with Suarez. Maybe he, too, could make some money off Aldo.

"You know, Aldo, no offense, but you have to realize first that you do not speak the language. You would have to start at the bottom. What do you think you can do?"

"Anything," Aldo said, "I just need to get started."

"Let me tell you something about this town, Aldo. There is nothing here except some hotels and a bunch of old people. There is no money to be made here. And as far as work, you would probably have to go work as a dishwasher somewhere."

"I don't care what I do."

Felix reflected over the young man's confidence. Perhaps he was a little cocky. Time would show this kid. Too bad he couldn't have brought some of his wealth here. Felix could have guided him into the right investments. But to start cold, he couldn't do much for him.

They drove through 22nd Avenue in the southwest, passing Coral Way. They turned left on 18th Terrace. Before the events of the past decade, this area of South Miami had been nothing more than woods and shrubs. At one point this area had been considered by many the end of Miami. The boundaries had been redefined time and time again by sporadic construction. It was now a suburb with rows of modest houses and picket fences perfectly aligned. The area was prized because of its connection to affluent Coral Gables. Any of its homes would be the dream of a middle class family. A few of the most prominent Cubans had discreetly begun to settle here, a prelude to the large exodus that was about to begin.

The Chevrolet pulled alongside the cub of a handsome yellow ranch home. With its maroon clay tiles and white windows, it looked like a doll house. Amanda would have loved such a house.

"Let's go meet Mr. Entrante," Felix said. "He's waiting for you."

The house was beautifully landscaped. A row of gardenia shrubs bordered the sidewalk up to the front door. Behind them were rows of fragrant white lilies. The front yard on the right side was bordered by a picket fence and adorned by a multitude of tall rose bushes. Felix knocked and an older man wearing a shirt and tie answered. Felix' casual demeanor evaporated when he saw him.

"He is here, Mr. Entrante," Felix said, "safe and sound."

"You are the famous Aldo," Mr. Entrante said. "I heard a lot about you."

"A pleasure to meet you," Aldo said.

The two exchanged glances as they shook hands. Mr. Entrante's blue eyes were penetrating and made him look somber even when he smiled. There was aura of authority radiating from him. It was giants like him that had influenced and controlled the economy of Cuba in the past. They had been gradually tossed aside by the new order, sparking deep resentment and causing their emigration to the United States where they hoped to rally their forces and political strengths to return and reclaim their positions.

"Enter," he said. "We've been expecting you. We didn't know for sure whether you would get out this morning, but were ready for you anyway. How was the trip?"

He was over sixty but could have easily passed for a younger man. His skin was smooth. His perfect white shone as he spoke. The knot of his tie was perfectly aligned. He wore a dark jacket and pants and black leather shoes that shone like glass. He was of medium height and had short grey hair that was beginning to bald.

"It was all right. Short."

He offered Aldo and Felix a chair in the lanai, a small open room, adjacent to the dining room. In front of it was the kitchen, closed in by a wall of cabinets running the entire length of the room. There was a counter in between with two stools. Felix and Aldo sat on the love seats, and Mr. Entrante fetched one of the chairs from the dining room. He turned to the hallway leading to the rest of the house.

"Hortencia, can you come here for a minute?"

A young woman came in from one of the back rooms. She was elegantly dressed in high heels, short sleeve blouse, and pleated skirt. Her straight black hair was slightly curled at the ends and puffed up on top. Her eyebrows were neatly plucked and accentuated with pencil, probably a judgment error since it made her look older. Her face was heavily made up. She wasn't exactly pretty but her slim figure looked impressive as she entered the room and greeted them.

"This is Aldo Ochoa, Mr. Suarez's friend," Mr. Entrante said pointing to Aldo.

"A pleasure meeting you," she said, shaking his hand.

For only a fraction of a second, she focused on the purple patches on his face.

"Would you mind getting them some coffee?" Mr. Entrante said.

"If it's all right, I'll pass," Aldo said.

"You don't drink coffee?" Mr. Entrante said incredulously. "What kind of a Cuban are you? Give him some juice or something, then, eh? I'm sure he's hungry."

"Would you like some juice?" she said, turning toward him.

"Yes, that would be fine."

"And coffee for you, Felix?"

"Yes, of course, Hortencia."

"Aldo," Mr. Entrante said, "the wounds on your face, did that happen in prison?"

"Yes."

"So those bastards hurt your face, eh? Don't you hate them?"

"It's dirty politics, Mr. Entrante. I would just rather have none of it."

"Well, it's more than just politics, son. It's communism. You have to fight back."

"I have fought back."

"Yes, I know. Mr. Suarez made it clear that getting you out was an emergency. I want you to know I did it for him, not for you. I don't know you, but I figure that if Mr. Suarez recommends you, you must have promise. Mr. Suarez and I go back a long way. He's an able businessman and a good ally to have on your side. I guess you're finding that out."

Mr. Entrante glanced at Aldo and Felix, then went on.

"So, you wanted to live in America. Here you are now. What do you think of it?"

"I'm impressed by the newness of everything."

From the counter table, Hortencia looked up. The young man had just touched on a sensitive issue for her boss. An opinion about

America could get someone in trouble with Mr. Entrante, as the sly Felix knew. Hortencia waited for Mr. Entrante's response.

"Yes, new," he said, "but that's about it. Don't kid yourself, son. This is the land of slave work. You want to make this your home? Be prepared to give up the rest of your life to work and then, just maybe, you'll be able to afford a car and a home. By the time you own those, you'll be an old man ready for retirement. If you make it. I just hope the Americans don't forget us. We are going to need their help to get our land back."

Hortencia approached with a tray in hand. She handed Aldo a tall glass of orange juice and cups of espresso to Felix and her boss. Then she excused herself and went back inside, disappearing in the same room where she had come from.

"Aldo was asking me where he could get a job," Felix commented.

"Really?" Mr. Entrante said. "Well that's a good sign, Aldo. If you like to work, you will fit right in with this society. But I hope that's not all you do. Now, if I understand Mr. Suarez's correctly, you are a gifted businessman who's done well for himself, is that true?"

"I've done all right. I supported my family," Aldo said modestly.

He had begun to regain his confidence now. The worst was over. He could see Mr. Entrante was looking him over, probably deciding how good of an investment he had made in bringing him to America. Mr. Entrante had the rich Cuban's mentality. He had made it seem as if he had done his friend Suarez a favor by using his influence to get Aldo out of the country. In reality Mr. Suarez probably paid well for these services by looking after Mr. Entrante's investments in Cuba. Aldo did not think Entrante was the kind of man who would do something for nothing.

Meanwhile, Mr. Entrante was thinking that now that Aldo was here, he would have to find some useful purpose for him. He could pull the strings as he always did, but it had to be worthwhile. Perhaps Aldo would turn out to be a valued catch. He had the young man all for himself. Or so he thought.

"You've done more than just support your family. But I have to tell you something, Aldo, it won't be easy. First of all, you don't speak the language. Second, the business you know, which is cattle, does not exist in this area. Here, if you don't know how to wait on people, you're out of luck. There isn't anything but hotels around here. But something could be worked out."

"I will do what I have to. Most important for me now is to get my family here."

"Yes, I know you want your family. It's been arranged. They'll come. But now tell me something, you've left a good life behind, all because of the Castro regime. You are young. We need people like you to get what's ours back. There are several prominent politicians already here. And they are gathering some people together. I would like you to meet some of them. What do you think?"

Aldo realized what he was after. Mr. Entrante had found a purpose for him. Many of Batista's supporters had fled to Miami since the beginning of the revolution, and now that others were following, they were beginning to organize to strike back. People like Mr. Entrante had a lot at stake in Cuba. They wanted the old regime back so they could return to their kingdoms. It was people like him who, ironically had made it possible for Castro to win. Their insatiable craving for social status and their excessive greed had paved the way for Castro and his thugs. Now they were sorry and sought to rally their forces. They were calling on the peasants to help them win back their fortunes. But Aldo wasn't anybody's pet. As far as he was concerned, there was no going back to the island. He and his family had gone through enough. He was not going to get involved in any plot to bring down Castro. Mr. Entrante and others like him who had put the rebels in power would have to do it themselves. He disliked the thought of his family's fate resting in the hands of the man before him.

"Are these people organized?"

"They're starting to," Mr. Entrante said. "I figure it like this, Aldo. Castro is going to make some bold moves. I do not think he'll get very far with the Americans. You know, the proximity to this country will make it intolerable for him to try to deviate from the capitalist course. And I think he knows that. So he won't make too many drastic changes. What we need, then, is to get some resistance going. And I think it's starting to build here. I think someone like you would be interested in that kind of thing, no?"

"Well, right now my priority is to find work and bring my family here. The rest can wait."

Mr. Entrante glanced briefly at Felix. "I see," he said. "Well, we will have Felix take you over to meet some acquaintances later. May be we can do something to help you. Where can you take him, Felix?"

"I will take him to Puntiel's cafeteria later. It'll give him a chance to get acquainted."

"See, Aldo," Mr. Entrante said turning to him, "you are real lucky. And I mean that. At least you have friends to help you. Some of the folks that are starting to arrive have no place to go. At least now you know some people."

Aldo looked at him in silence. He was relieved to have gone through his arrival's shock, but for some reason, he did not feel as lucky as Mr. Entrante made it appear. There was something cold about his environment. Did this man have a family? Why was the house so barren?

Hortencia appeared in the hallway and called Entrante's name.

"There's a Mr. Paterson on the phone for you," she said. Mr. Entrante stood and followed her. One of the bedrooms had been converted into an office. He had been in the United States as a young man. He spoke English fluently and eventually had become a representative for an American rice company. Then he had taken his business to Cuba where he worked for the company selling their product. His aggressive and astute management had paid off. He became their number one man in Cuba by eliminating any competition and becoming the Cuban head representative with a dozen managers under him. He built an empire and became the director of two national banks. His position was secure before the rebels came into power. He was deeply connected with the Batista government, buying his way into any money market he fancied. His closest aides were government people who had left the country upon the triumph of the revolution. He had lived in Cuba for two months after Castro's victory. However, after being briefly detained by the rebels upon his return from a business trip, he had decided it was too risky to remain and had prepared his permanent departure by discreetly transferring large sums to the United States. He sent his family off to Miami and followed them, leaving Felix in charge of his business. He had hoped for a short absence, but after he left, his bank accounts had been frozen and his company shut down. Even Felix was no longer safe in Cuba after that.

Reluctantly, Mr. Entrante sought and obtained a distributing position in the Miami area from the same company he had once represented in Cuba. He kept active during the first few months, hoping that the situation would change. But he had now begun to accept the fact that the changes he had fervently hoped for would not be forthcoming for some time, and he sought to re-establish his position. He rented this house in the South West and hired a secretary. He immersed himself in work and tried to forget the fortune he had left in his native country. Not surprisingly, his business flourished in Miami. His aggressive selling techniques had not changed. In six months, he had built a clientele of small supermarkets that was growing almost on its own.

"And where is Mr. Suarez staying in Havana?" Felix asked.

"He was staying at a hotel, but now I don't know. I don't even know if he will be going back to Camaguey after this."

"You think he's a marked man in Cuba now?"

"He and I were doing a lot of trading together, so I'm sure that once the government realizes I'm gone, they will be asking him questions."

"Anybody who's got two cents in Cuba right now is compromised. And this is only the beginning."

Mr. Entrante appeared again. "Come in the office for a few minutes," he said to them. "I have to go to Miami Beach for a while. Felix, maybe you could take Aldo now and show him Puntiel's place."

"Sure," Felix said. "He might as well see what we have. It won't be like Havana, I promise you."

The office room was small but nicely furnished. Two desks faced each other. Their glossy surfaces were uncluttered, and two telephones and a note pad were the only objects on it. Mr. Entrante sat at the far end facing the door while Hortencia took the chair across from him. Felix and Aldo sat nearby.

"I don't expect to make this my home," Mr. Entrante observed as he put down the telephone. "I figure that this is a temporary set back. I am going back. Do you know what it means to give up your entire life? Leave behind everything you ever worked for? Those rebel sons of bitches. They've got it coming, I swear."

He shook his head in anger and looked toward Aldo as if in warning. He hated everything about this environment. Every phone call he took reminded him of how easy his life had been in Cuba, how much he missed his comfort and his plush lifestyle. Aldo thought him unreasonable. If this powerful man was as tough as he pretended, why not stay and fight for what he so believed was his. There was a real simple solution to his misery, and that was to leave America. Yet Mr. Entrante may have been gutsy, but not that gutsy.

"It will come, Mr. Entrante," Felix said. "It will come. Just give the Americans some time. Their feet have not yet been stepped on. When that happens, they'll jump. You'll see."

"I just hope Castro does that real soon before those sons of bitches destroy everything we ever worked for."

"That'll be Castro's next move," Felix commented. "He's real daring."

"What do you think?" Mr. Entrante said to Aldo almost tauntingly.

"I think Castro is too smart to do that right away. He'll bide his time and go about it gradually."

"I don't think he's smart," Felix said. "He's stupid, real stupid if you ask me."

"Because he's our enemy?" Aldo asked, drawing Mr. Entrante's attention.

"The man is an idiot," Felix repeated, turning to Aldo. "How could he turn against the upper class, the very people that put him in power? That's his demise. He's done for."

"I don't know about that," Aldo said.

"Why do you feel that way?" Mr. Entrante said.

He was hoping to draw on the young man's impressions. After all, he had just arrived. His anger towards the regime knew no bounds, but he wanted reality. He wanted a picture of the future. He wanted to know what to expect. Felix, on the other hand, was looking only to please his boss. And he knew what his boss wanted to hear. It was his job.

"Castro has the support of the majority of the people. Even some segments of the upper class are still on his side. He's working cautiously, whatever his plans are. I do think he's got crazy ideas, but he himself is not. He knows he's playing with fire, being so close to the United States, so he will move bit by bit, testing the waters without making anybody mad."

"And what do you make of his plans?"

"At the beginning I thought it would be just another fantasy, the kind our country has gone through in the past, but now I think that we are moving toward something more radical. Some say it's communism, and maybe it is. But, it is different from anything we have ever seen before. And it is all Castro's idea, of that I'm sure."

"So where does that leave us?" Mr. Entrante asked, annoyed.

"Something must happen to turn things around. Right now, they are on a steady decline. The press is being attacked, business is being cornered. And the resourceful people are starting to leave. So that leaves us where we are. Away from home."

Mr. Entrante exchanged looks with Felix. He couldn't hide his anger. What did Mr. Suarez do with this young boy? What the hell was he talking about? What did he know about Cuba? He was probably wearing diapers on with a dirty ass, as Cubans say, when Mr. Entrante was already a millionaire. He had seen it all since the days of Menocal. Cuba? Communist? That was the biggest joke he had ever heard. It was enough.

"All right," he said dismissively, "what about your capital. Were you able to get any of your money out of Cuba?"

"Not really. There wasn't anytime. I left prison one evening and left for Havana a few hours later. There was no time."

"You have bank accounts I suppose, right? Is there any way that your family can exchange the funds and wire them over here? It could be done, you know. I can have Felix help you with that. We have some people in Havana."

"I can't have my family involved," Aldo said. "It's too risky. By tomorrow, the rebels might be looking for me already. If they find my family, who knows what would happen. The money can always be replaced."

"Yes, but you are also going to need money to support your family. It's not going to be easy here. You need to get your money here. I sure hate to see any money going to waste. Felix, what can be done?"

"Well," Felix said rubbing his chin, "we could get a cable out to Ramirez in Havana. I take it that all your assets are in Camaguey, eh?"

"Yes," Aldo replied. He didn't care for their pressuring him, rushing to manage his affairs as if he wasn't even there.

"I don't want anything done for now," Aldo told them. "When my family gets here, then may be I will use your services." "By then it may be too late. Don't you understand that the government is going to freeze your assets? It's happening all over."

"I'll take my chances with that," Aldo said, "not with my family. I don't want them in any danger. They're more important. Money I can always make."

Mr. Entrante and Felix looked at each other. Not only did they think him ignorant but also cocky. Mr. Entrante could hardly contain his displeasure. He should not get personally involved, he thought. It was business. like everything else. Mr. Suarez had paid him to bring the young man here. He had done it. Now he must wash his hands of the whole thing before it got more complicated.

"Why don't you take him to Puntiel's restaurant?" Entrante said to Felix. "Show him around."

"Sure," Felix said, standing up, "let's go have a look."

Aldo shook Mr. Entrante's hand. He smiled at Hortencia.

"It has been a pleasure," he said.

"I wish you the best of luck," Hortencia said.

Felix drove back to Twenty Second Avenue and headed north. He turned right on 8ᵗʰ Street and drove down a few blocks. This street was still partially residential then, and there were only a few scattered stores in what was to become years later as "Little Havana." For unknown reasons, this section would attract a high influx of business, oriented immigrants who would transform the lethargic community into a vibrant string of shops. As they drove on, the street turned narrow and became one way only. Some of the glass windows displayed a modest assortment of clothes. The only two Spanish restaurants and bakery were most noticeable in this block. The narrow street and structures close to one another reminded Aldo of his hometown but he didn't mention it. Felix pulled the car over to the curb and parked behind a blue Chevrolet Impala. He put a nickel in the meter.

"Let's go meet Puntiel," Felix said. "That's a guy you might relate to. He was a captain in Batista's army but he was no dummy, let me tell you. He smelled a rat left Cuba even before the rebels took over. He brought a few pesos and opened this restaurant. People kept saying he was crazy, that soon the Castro government would change and he would have no customers. They still say that. But he hasn't been wrong so far. More Cubans keep coming and he's building a good business. He's a hard worker. He works from early morning until past midnight."

They were standing before a medium sized building with large windows. The place had gone from selling shoes to food. Felix walked ahead of Aldo, opened the door, and went inside. The room was small, containing only six tables and chairs. At the end was a counter with four stools. It was now lunch time, and all the tables were taken. Felix sat on a stool and waived for Aldo to follow. Three other men crowded at the end of the counter, sipping coffee. Felix waived at a man in white who peered from the open kitchen, trying to get a better look at them.

"Mr. Puntiel," Felix said loudly, "you have customers, sir."

"I'll be right there, Felix."

He was in his mid fifties, and his balding crown with sparse hair made him look almost comical. He dried his hands on his apron as he approached them.

"How are you?" he said, shaking Felix's hand.

He was of medium height and fat for his size. He had bulky arms and a very short neck. His face was chubby and his black eyes moved nervously about as he spoke. He gave Aldo a few quick glances as he talked.

"Look," Felix said pointing to Aldo with his right thumb, "just fished."

"No," Puntiel said incredulously, looking at Aldo.

"Just came. Picked him up from the airport this morning."

"I am Armado Puntiel," he said, coming over to shake his hand.

"Aldo Ochoa, at your service."

"Where are you from?"

"Camaguey."

"Oh, Camaguey, the land of the clay pots. Beautiful city, beautiful. I've been there many times."

"Aldo was a cattleman although I also heard he was a boxer."

"I can tell he is a boxer," Puntiel said, "but not because of the scars. He acts like one. And cattleman, well, everybody in Camaguey is a cattleman. What the heck."

"No cattle to raise here," Felix said. "There are lots of old people we could round up, though."

"Don't listen to him," Puntiel said shaking his hand. "Let me get you something to drink. A cup of coffee?"

"I'll have one," Felix said.

"Not for me, thank you." Aldo said.

"You have to have something, friend. Some juice? A refreshment, eh?"

"All right, whatever you offer," Aldo replied.

Puntiel moved quickly behind the counter and opened the Coca-Cola refrigerator behind him. He put a bottle on the counter, then turned to the coffee machine near the kitchen and operated the lever until a stream of coffee poured into a small cup.

"Puntiel, this man came straight from prison," Felix said. "He would have probably been on his way to the gallows if he had not been able to leave today. They had him incommunicado for some time, not to mention the treatment they gave him. That, I'll let him tell you. Mr. Entrante arranged for his departure."

Puntiel listened sympathetically as Felix spoke, a look of wonder in his face, but at the mention of Entrante's name he grimaced.

"How did Entrante get involved?" he asked.

"A mutual acquaintance, you know. Aldo traded with someone in Cuba who knows Mr. Entrante and he asked for his help."

"He didn't know Mr. Entrante?"

"No. They met today. Mr. Entrante was impressed. Quite a young man. We want to help him with some of his affairs, you know, set him on course."

"You came alone, Aldo?" Puntiel leaned forward on his elbows as he spoke.

"Yes."

"Is your family joining you?"

"Yes. I hope so."

From one of the tables, two men called for their bill.

"Where is your help today?" Felix inquired.

"Mario, the cook, had to leave early. I have no one until 3:00 when my boy comes back from school, and then only for two or three hours. My wife comes in the evenings to help me until closing. That's all the help I have for now."

He went around the counter and walked towards the men. They were sitting at one of the middle tables. They were dressed casually, having stopped for a quick sandwich. Puntiel told them the price and collected a five dollar bill. He went behind the counter and ringed the register.

"Puntiel, you know the first thing this man asked me this morning?" Felix said. "He wants to know where to find work. He hasn't even gotten off the plane, and he's looking for work. How do you like that?"

Puntiel smiled pleasantly at Aldo. He liked the young man. There was determination written all over his face. This guy was going places.

"Are you hiring, Puntiel," Aldo asked casually.

Puntiel looked aghast for a second. He hadn't expected such bold advance. The thought hadn't crossed his mind. But yes, he could use the help. But could he use him? He was probably inexperienced and did not have a clue about what was happening yet. Then, without really knowing why, he said, "Yes. I think I could use someone like you, gutsy and hard working. I cannot pay you much to start though."

"When do I come in?"

"Start tomorrow. Give yourself a chance."

"But you need help today. Why not start right now?"

"It's up to you and Felix."

"Why? Felix is not my father. All I have is one bag, can I bring it in here?"

"Sure."

"Wait a minute," Felix said, "what am I going to tell Mr. Entrante? Surely he wants to see you later."

"Tell him I thank him for what he did but I have to move on. Can I get my bag from your car?"

Aldo stood up. He seemed as ready for a day's work, as someone who had just awakened from a good night sleep. Felix gazed at him, rather bewildered by the quickness of his decision. What was he going to tell Mr. Entrante? Later he would learn that Mr. Entrante was deeply relieved to know he wouldn't have to look after Aldo. The two men went outside, and Felix opened the trunk of the car. Aldo took his bag and shook Felix's hand.

"Are you sure about what you're doing? This man is going to pay you peanuts. He's going to exploit you. Don't be foolish. A man of your caliber? Wait a while at least."

"It's like you said, Felix, I don't know the language. My prospects of finding another job are minimal. This is a start. I don't plan to make a living out of it. Don't worry, I know how to take care of myself. Thank you for everything."

With that, Aldo turned his back to him, crossed the street, and went inside Puntiel's restaurant.

Felix reflected quietly on what had happened. At first he considered the young man a fool. He had eavesdropped on Mr. Entrante's conversations and had heard that Aldo had done quite well. He had hoped to make money off him by helping him exchange his money in Cuba and transferring it to the United States. He was good at it. But Aldo had surprised him. He didn't seem to care about money. It was incomprehensible to Felix that a person could just walk away from wealth. It was a sin. But he recognized the young man's drive. Maybe he was part of that same breed of men like Puntiel and

Entrante. They had an inner drive for survival, something that drove them to succeed no matter what the price. Men like that could do anything. Maybe men like Aldo and Entrante could make something out of this barren place that he found Miami to be.

Aldo sat in Puntiel's kitchen on a wooden chair by the stove as he listened to Puntiel. He had brought his bag in and changed into more casual attire. He wore black shoes and a long white apron over his black slacks, a maroon shirt, and no hat. Suddenly, he felt relaxed. In less than one day, he had found a job. Who knew what he could accomplish tomorrow? He already liked America.

"I'll teach you what I can," Puntiel said. "Stay with me in the kitchen and see what you can pick up from me. I'll take the orders from the customers, but you'll bring them the food. Keep the floor clean, but don't get in anybody's way as you do it. Wash all the silverware and plates. That'll be a big help to me. I'll handle the cash register. If a customer pays you, bring me the money. I'll ring it up. Can you cook?"

"Yes."

"What can you make? Tell me."

"I can make rice any style. Jerked beef, fried or boiled vegetables. Mostly Creole food, really."

Puntiel laughed at his candor. He hadn't known that Aldo was a peasant, but that was all right with him. He thought him smart. He put his hand on Aldo's shoulder.

"No, I'm afraid that wouldn't sell here. Look," he said, pointing at the blackboard behind them, "that is our menu. I know it's in English but you have to memorize it. I don't have a full fledged restaurant here. We only make sandwiches, you know, fast food. We have a lot of Cuban customers that come in, so I do make them something special occasionally, but I cannot afford to lose the American crowd, so I have to stick with the menu in English. We will play it by ear. Now, the hours. I'll eed you here at 7:00 in the morning until about 8:00 P.M. I'll close the place afterwards by myself. Can you handle that?"

"Yes."

"You can work like that six days for now and see how it goes. Then you can come late on Sundays, let's say after 4:00 P.M., so you're here for dinner. That'll give you a day off. About your pay. I cannot afford to pay you much, but it will be a start for you. Twenty five dollars per week, how's that?"

"That's fine."

"You have to get your papers in order. You need that to work. I'll introduce you to one of the customers who may be able to take you to get your social security card. You need that to work. Then later you can apply for your green card. I assume you are going to get political asylum, right?"

"I don't know. I suppose."

"Yes, that's the same thing I did. I'll introduce you to the person who did my papers. You'll be fine."

It was late in the afternoon, and Aldo spent the rest of the day learning his way around. The surroundings were not much. There were the tables to keep clean and the counter. The most difficult thing was the espresso machine, which seemed to be going all day. He watched Puntiel fill the spoon-like fixture with grains and then turn the power on until the steam blew out like a train whistle, to let him know it was time to let the water run out. Then he made his first cup for a customer who grudgingly took it after Puntiel assured him he himself had mixed the grain in. Puntiel said it would take time. He could see that Aldo would learn fast. Aldo learned some of the items on the menu as he watched Puntiel make them. After the evening rush, he washed the floor and did the dishes and silverware one more time. When they were alone, Puntiel asked him about his incarceration, pushing him for details. He was deeply curious about the events in Cuba. Aldo was reserved. He wanted to put it all behind him. This was a new beginning. A fresh start. Besides, he had not forgotten what Felix had told him about Puntiel. He must have been deeply involved with Batista to have had to flee before Castro gained power. He wondered how many beatings Captain Puntiel had inflicted to become threatened by the rebel takeover. For all he knew, he could have been one of the officers responsible for his encounter with Batista's soldiers a year ago. But Puntiel had helped him, and he thought him a good man.

As Puntiel locked the front door and turned the lights off in the main room, Aldo thought for the first time about where he would sleep tonight. He had no relatives, no friends, and he did not know his way around. He began thinking about where to go as he let the warm water rinse the plates when Puntiel interrupted his thoughts.

"Have you thought about where you are going tonight?"

"No, not yet."

"Well, I have. Listen, you are a good young man, I can tell. I don't mind helping you. I have this friend who rents a house not too far from here. I am going to talk to her so you can rent a room from her. She'll give you one for the night. See if you like it, maybe you would stay."

"Better than sleeping under a bridge."

"You need money?"

"No, I'm fine. I brought a little money with me."

Puntiel's wife and son came in right before closing. Puntiel had called his wife earlier and told her about his new employee. Puntiel's son would be thrilled to know that he could spend the rest of the afternoon playing baseball. Puntiel let them in. His wife looked around as she came inside. She was a highly critical woman, as Aldo would later find out.

"Are you the young man who has been doing my job?"

"Yes," Aldo said.

He had placed all the chairs upside down on the tables while he mopped the floor. The stools were on the counter. This was a good sign.

She looked over him over her glasses as if inspecting him. She was tall, with shoulder length wavy brown hair. Her skin was very white, a mask of cream and make up.

"You just came over today?"

"Yes. This morning."

"And how did you leave Havana? How were things?"

"A little turbulent," Aldo said. "Many people are starting to leave."

"All the large capital holders are leaving," she said. "This is my son. He's awful mad because you took his job."

"Well, I'm sorry about that," Aldo said in jest. "Your father needed help, so I volunteered."

"That's okay," the boy said.

He had not yet reached his full growth but was almost as tall as his mother. He would be a big man some day. He looked impressed at Aldo's build and kept staring at his scars. He would have given anything to find out how he had gotten them.

"Listen, you guys, "I'm going to take Aldo over a friend. I want to see if I can get him a room," Puntiel said.

"Where are you taking him?" his wife asked.

"Lucrecia, the lady that lives near 4th Street."

"Oh, yes," she said. "She has a little house, but she lives alone and probably could spare a room. You will have to pay rent but it's cheaper than renting an apartment."

She went into the back and surveyed the area. She inspected the plates and silverware like a drill sergeant.

Puntiel lectured Aldo about the new world he had entered. He warned him on how to pick his friends. The south west was a peaceful area but not without traps for someone inexperienced like him.

"Take no wooden nickels," he said. "Be careful who you talk to about Cuba. This town is full of *fidelistas*. Just as many people are leaving the island, there are still some who are going back praising Castro. Best thing to do is not to talk about what happened to you in Cuba. You'll make enemies if you do, I can assure you."

"I don't intend to mention it," Aldo said. "I have no desire to discuss what happened."

"Good," Puntiel said. "Now let's go. I will drop you off at my friend's house. Tomorrow, I may have to pick you up. You don't know the area."

"I'll find my way."

Puntiel closed the main door and let Aldo and the others out. He went to a 1955 Dodge parked at the curb. He drove down a block where he made a right, heading for Flagger Street, then a left turn at S.W. 4th Street. The car stopped before a small white ranch house.

They entered a porch. Puntiel opened the storm door and knocked. An old woman stood before them.

"This is the man I spoke to you about," Puntiel said. "Oh, it's a pleasure," she said, extending her hand to Aldo. "My name is Lucrecia Pardo. Come in. Let me show you."

She led them to the back, passing a small living room with old furniture. They passed the bathroom on the right and she opened the door to a small room with a single bed, a chair, and a chest of drawers.

"It doesn't have a kitchen but you can use mine," she said, smiling. She seemed like a pleasant lady. She was rather slim, with a face heavily powdered, even at this late hour.

"It's fine," Aldo said. "Shall I pay you now?"

"Listen," she said, "I know Puntiel from Cuba. I've known him since he was a kid. If he brought you here, it's because you're a good man. I'm not going to worry about money. You'll pay me at the end of the week. Here, follow me." She walked out of the room and opened the bathroom door. "This is the bathroom. I'm sure you're tired and will want to take a bath. If you need a towel, take one from the rack."

"Not bad, eh?" Puntiel said. He had made his way in, leaving his wife and son standing in the doorway. He tapped Aldo on the shoulder.

"You think you will be able to find your way back to the restaurant tomorrow?"

"I think so," Aldo replied. "If not, I'll ask."

"Don't worry, Puntiel. I will show him the way."

On his first night away from home, an immigrant is likely to experience delirium. The most recent events become hazy. The mind is overwhelmed by the changes, and one loses track of time. After taking a warm shower, Aldo laid in bed with the lights off, his head on the pillow. He tried to collect his thoughts. He had to concentrate to follow the path that had led him here. He felt deep insecurity but convinced himself he was on the right track. Actually, he was very lucky. He had a roof over his head, and he had eaten. This, however, was not his most immediate concern. He did what he hadn't done in years: he closed his eyes and prayed. He prayed for Amanda and his children, for Pablo, Ana, Alfredo, and all his friends in Rios. And slowly his eyes filled with tears as he visualized Alfredo in the night waiting for the milkman. How long would he keep doing this? How long before he realized that his old friend was not coming back? Poor Alfredo. Where would he go now?

He kept falling asleep and waking up in a sweat. Thoughts of his family kept haunting him, and the image of Entrante's face flashed before his eyes. The fate of his loved ones was in his hands. Was it not a mistake to place them at his mercy? He did not trust him. He was another Arapiento. He had dealt with men like that, powerful men who once had controlled the lives of many. They acted only for their own benefit and sought profit for their actions. As long as Entrante was benefiting from the deal, he would go through with it. As much as Aldo hated to cater to such a man, he hoped he had not disappointed him. His family depended on him. He hated being in this vulnerable position. He would work day and night to never again be in such a situation.

The next morning, Aldo was up early. He brushed his teeth and met Lucrecia on his way out. She asked him if he knew his way to Puntiel's restaurant.

"I think so," Aldo replied.

"I will show you anyway," she said. She walked with him past the porch. "Look, Puntiel is a good man. He lost everything in Cuba. His family was all military. He had no choice but to leave when Castro was winning or they would have killed him. He was too involved. Now he's opened this restaurant, and he's made a go of it. But he doesn't know a thing about food. Maybe you can help him. I mean, really help him. He needs a real man behind him, you know. Someone who can protect him. He's too soft. I can tell you're that man. So do me a favor, watch out for him for me. I want him to succeed. If he succeeds, you will succeed too."

"Sure," Aldo said, surprised by this sudden revelation.

She pointed toward the end of the street. "At the corner you will look at the street sign. It will say Fourth and 12th Avenue. There, turn right. Walk up to Eighth Street and then turn left. You'll need to go up about three blocks. You will see the restaurant on the right. Tell

Puntiel to save me a loaf of bread tonight and bring it to me, okay?" Then she looked at him and said: "Don't worry about your family, they'll come."

Now how in the world did she know to say that? Aldo thought. He had seen the statue of Saint Barbara, the god of thunder, through the partially-open door of her bedroom before. And the way she carried herself, analyzing everything and everyone. She must be a spiritualist, someone who could read minds through the incarnation of spirits.

Aldo gave his new job his undivided attention. It was difficult to wait on some of the customers who spoke only English, but by and large, most were newly-arrived Cubans looking for a taste of their homeland. The menu was simple, and Aldo learned it quickly. As he tended to some of the American customers, helped by Puntiel who was not fluent in English, Aldo realized his greatest challenge would be to break the language barrier. No matter how hard he worked, he thought, he could only aspire to be successful if he spoke English. This was a priority. The second priority was to plan his schedule in such a way that he could work additional hours. He overheard some of the customers talk about work in the hotels at the beach. That's where the money was. Some of them were making as much in tips what he would make with Puntiel in one week. But for that he needed the language skills that he didn't yet have.

Aldo had not spent a cent since he had arrived but that afternoon, one of the customers took him to a nearby Western Union office where he cabled Amanda, providing her with Puntiel's number as their contact. On the way back, he entered a pharmacy and saw an English-Spanish dictionary. He bought it for seventy five cents and also bought some pencils and a notebook. He went back to work with a new focus.

"You're picking the language up very fast," Puntiel said to him that night after they were alone. "Keep it up, and you'll soon be able to do it alone. Maybe I can take a break. I have been working non-stop for a year, day and night."

"But you made a life for yourself, Puntiel. You have your own business."

"In Cuba I always dreamed of owning a night club. I thought that was the best business to have in a tourist town. I used to visit all those places in Havana where the money just rolled in. It was amazing."

"You were military?"

"Right," he said without looking up.

He was slicing the sandwich bread for the next day. Aldo was going to ask more about his leaving Cuba but then thought better of it. Puntiel appeared uncomfortable when discussing the subject.

"So let me ask you something, Aldo, if I may" he said cautiously. "What led you to leave Cuba? What problems did you have with Castro's government?"

"It wasn't that I had a problem with them," Aldo replied, "it's more that they had a problem with me."

"What happened?"

"About a year ago, some of Batista's soldiers came by our place and murdered someone. He was really harmless. Just a man who talked too much and said the wrong thing to somebody. Someone turned him in. I went and buried his body. After Castro triumphed, that same squealer switched sides and accused me of murdering the very person whose death he had caused. I became a marked man. I got out of prison two days before I flew here. They didn't know I left. They are probably looking for me now."

"Well, you've seen what the rebels are capable of. Tell me, what was wrong with Batista? He is a decent man. This crap about Batista's murders is nothing but lies. Don't believe any of it."

"Well, I have to say that at the eve of the change, there were just too many abuses going on. Something was bound to happen and did."

"But did you see any of those abuses? Did you see anyone missing finger nails or with cigarette burns on their back?"

"No, but I will tell you something. A sergeant and his soldiers once gave me a licking that almost cost me my life. So, yes I got to see some of it."

"Did you do anything to provoke them?"

"I would like to say no. I think I was as fair with them as they were with me. There was this corporal who tried to get cute, so I knocked him on his behind. Then the rest of them handcuffed me and beat me almost to death. I'll never know who stopped it. I was unconscious. Some other sergeant, I think. But I tell you, I owe that man my life."

Puntiel was silent for a few seconds. He was trying to open up to Aldo. The more he knew of the young man, the more he respected him. He felt ashamed that in his military career he could have hurt other young men like him or worse.

"Those things happen, Aldo. Tempers flare and people get carried away."

"They do."

Aldo understood. Short of saying that the Army had a license to kill, Puntiel had said it all. But the truth was that tempers didn't even have to flare, which was how innocent people like Patricio were murdered. The same thing was now happening again with the rebels. Wasn't it all a vicious, endless circle? He'd like to think that America was different, that he could forget about these things in his new home and live a neutral life.

"Is it true you boxed, Aldo?"

"How did you know?"

"Ah, you know that Felix has got a big mouth. Plus you can't hide it, Aldo. One can see it in you. You could probably make some good money in the black neighborhood here. They have matches sometimes. And they pay good."

"Where is this?" Aldo asked casually.

"Ah, there is a black neighborhood in Miami where I heard they still do that. It's prize fighting. It's illegal but they still do it for money, you know. Ask Felix, he'll tell you."

"I'm too old, Puntiel."

"Yes, sure," Puntiel jibed. "Kid Gavilan."

Aldo turned down Puntiel's offer for a ride. He wanted to familiarize himself with the neighborhood so he walked alone on 8th Street until he was out of the commercial strip. It looked pretty bare beyond this point. The houses were farther apart and the street was dark. Aldo stood near an intersection and watched the cars go by. Even this late, traffic seemed heavy. He appreciated and admired

America. It was a powerful country. What seemed most prevalent to him was the freshness of it. Everything seemed new, as if it had just rolled out of the assembly line. And the streets were so clean and tidy. Despite his recent misfortunes, Aldo thought that if his family was here, he would be the happiest man on earth.

That night Aldo had a terrible dream. He saw himself inside the ring again. And he saw his old trainer in the corner yelling out to him. Then he turned to the stands looking for his mother's face, felt a whopping blow to the side of his head. He was going down. When he awoke he found himself sitting on the bed, perspiring heavily. No, he wasn't fighting again. That was just Puntiel reviving old memories.

During the next few days, Aldo followed a rigid routine. He had now purchased a manual of basic English, and he spent at least two hours every night to read. He would go over the new words in the dictionary and check for phonetic. He would write down the pronunciation on a piece of paper that he carried with him. He would practice new words and broken sentences with some of the English-speaking customers at the restaurant. It was no replacement for a teacher, but he had a thirst for knowledge and he was setting himself on his own crash course. Puntiel was struck by Aldo's ambition and discipline and became convinced that his new employee would go places. It was men like that who had made America.

Puntiel's satisfaction with Aldo was obvious. For once, he felt, he had made the right choice. Aldo was a hard, honest worker. He seemed to have a way with the customers who were impressed by him. Puntiel only hoped that he would stay.

During lunch on Saturday, Aldo came back to the counter and rang up a customer's check. Puntiel's instructions about not ringing anyone had gone by the wayside as he depended more and more on Aldo. Aldo took some loose change from the open box and strode back quickly to the tables. He passed by Felix who sat on a stool, sipping his espresso.

"Do you have time for a word?" the little man said.

"I'll be back," Aldo said.

Felix put his cup down and took a cigar from his shirt pocket. He could hear a lot of talk from the tables nearby about conditions in Cuba. *More arrivals*, he thought. He had sat here for an hour surveying the new faces in hope of meeting someone he knew, but no luck.

"Do you have any news about my family?" Aldo asked.

"I tried to find out from Entrante, but it's out of my hands now. I finished all the paper work before you came, and he told me who to give it to. That's all I know. When I asked him this morning, he said that they should have their visas by now. Have you heard from them?"

"No, nothing," Aldo said. "It's difficult for them to contact me except by telegram. But what I want to know is whether Mr. Suarez has been in touch with Entrante. Has he said anything?"

"Not really," Felix said. "Mr. Entrante is very private, Aldo. He won't say."

Aldo looked at Felix. What did he care about Entrante's prima donna ways? Did it occur to Felix that he was talking about his family? If Felix was afraid to ask his boss a question, then he himself would ask. Obviously, Felix had no concept of what was at stake for Aldo.

Aldo took a check to a waiting customer.

"Aldo," the man said as he took his bill, "this is my brother, Ricardo. He just came from Cuba."

"A pleasure to meet you."

"He's started working at a hotel in Miami already. He's like you."

The man was quietly holding his cup of espresso. He was in his mid-fifties and heavily tanned.

"And how are you managing with the language," Aldo asked.

"Well, I'm surviving," Ricardo said. "There are other people who speak Spanish, so they help me."

"What do you do there?"

"I clean the rooms and bathrooms. I made some tips."

"If he learns a little bit of English then he'll be able to wait on people and really make good money." Ricardo's brother explained. "See, Aldo, you ought to think about something like that."

"Do they hire on weekends may be?" Aldo asked.

"They might," Ricardo said.

"May be you can ask for me," Aldo said, "I would like to work weekends if I can find a second job. Can you ask for me?"

"I can speak to a Cuban who works there. He can ask the manager."

"Leave me directions before you leave," Aldo said to Ricardo's brother.

Aldo went back behind the counter and rang the register.

"Well," Felix said behind him, "Mr. Entrante would like to see you Aldo. He told me."

"What about?" Aldo said without facing him.

"I don't know, his plans may be."

"I'm not interested in his plans."

Felix looked disconcerted. No one ever rebuffed his boss. On the contrary, people respected him. He thought Aldo was a little insolent.

"Aren't you forgetting already who brought you here?"

"I'm not forgetting anything."

"Then let me take you to him tomorrow morning, eh?"

"Pick me up here around 11:00."

That night Aldo received his first pay, a twenty and a five-dollar bill. He stashed them behind his belt. He owed a lot to Mr. Puntiel, and he showed it by staying with him until closing time. As usual, he turned down his offer for a ride and went back to his room on foot. He carefully lifted a corner of the linoleum floor in his room, took the two bills from his undershirt, and placed them with the other stash of bills. He counted one hundred and fifteen dollars. He had spent only five dollars since he came. Then he sat on the bed and began reading another chapter of his basic English course. As he went through it, he wrote down the new words and repeated them until he memorized them. He practiced pronunciation by reading the phonetics from the dictionary. He stayed up well past midnight.

On Sunday morning, Mr. Entrante was on the living room sofa as Felix and Aldo sat down before him. There was soft piano music coming from the living room record player. He resented to have to host visitors in his own living room. In Cuba, he had made sure that his private office had a separate entrance and exit from the house.

When he was home, guests were only allowed to see him in his office except for close relatives who would be quietly ushered through the main entrance. This had all changed when he came to America. Gone was his castle-like mansion and his maids and butlers. He now lived in a modest middle-class home, and his office was no more than a converted bedroom. Those who came to see him used the front door. On weekends, he had no secretary so he had to answer the door himself. He hated it all. Something inside of him kept revolting, and he felt so depressed sometimes he didn't want to see anyone. But he kept hoping and planning what he would do once Castro was gone. He had learned a valuable lesson late in life. If he ever got back what he had left behind, he would be merciless. Never again would he be charitable.

"How has your stay been so far?" he asked Aldo.

"It's been great," Aldo said. "I am working with Mr. Puntiel He's a good man."

Entrante looked at Felix. Aldo was not exactly what he had expected. From Mr. Sanchez's messages, it seemed that the man he had been asked to help was a money-making gold mine. At first, he had found that interesting. In this new and uncertain world upon which he had ventured, he would need any help he could get. And an able young man could be an asset for him which was why he had taken on the challenge of bringing Aldo to America. But his prejudices had taken hold. He found it repugnant that Aldo was from the country side, a *guajiro*. He couldn't see himself socializing with such a man, no matter how ambitious he might be. "That's good. But what are your plans. I'm sure you're not thinking of working in a restaurant forever, are you?"

"For now, I'm doing what I have to. I'll face the future as I go along."

"Well, look, the reason I asked you to come is that I may have a proposition for you. I want you to meet some of the other young men who are repatriating here. You know, men like you. I think you could be an asset to them. A substitute government will be formed here in the United States by the elders. These young men will be our army when the Americans decide to help us. They'll have to be trained, of course, but they will be prepared when we are ready to take on Castro."

Aldo's intuition was on guard. So this was it. Mr. Entrante already had a plan for him. Entrante probably saw him as mediocre but wanted to make good use of him. He wanted him as cannon fodder so he could regain his fortunes in Cuba. Had he been a general, Aldo thought, he would probably be the kind who didn't care how many men he lost to take a prized hill. It was too bad that he had to depend on such a man. He could turn around right now and walk away, but he had his family to worry about and their fate was in Entrante's hands.

"Have you heard anything about my family?" Aldo asked dryly. "What's happening with them?"

"I told you what happened?" Mr. Entrante said, rather annoyed.

"Well, tell me again, sir. I want to know how they stand right now. You seem to hold all the cards in your hand, don't you?"

The power of his words hung in the air. It was not what Entrante had expected, and Felix shifted uncomfortably in his chair. Entrante thought that for a man in his position, Aldo was quite daring. He could have brushed him off easily, but he admired a man with balls.

"Since the day I turned in their applications, I have not heard from the consul. Frankly, your family will hear before I do. My work is done. You just have to wait."

"Why is it taking so long?"

"It's not," Entrante said more kindly. "Yours came so fast only because Suarez made it an emergency, and it was treated as one. Theirs is going through the regular channels with little push, you know. But they will be here soon enough now. Relax."

"They're in a bad position," Aldo said. "My leaving has made it impossible for them to go back home. Right now they are living from hotel to hotel, just waiting for their visas. I cannot afford to have them floating around like this for too long. The government may wise up and arrest them. I must avoid that."

"I understand."

"Do you have a way of contacting Mr. Suarez?"

"There is a way. But why would you want to do that?"

"I want to know if he knows if they have received their visas yet."

"I know Mr. Suarez. If he told you he's looking after your family, then you can rest assured that they'll be safe. They're not in a hotel. They are with him in a safe place. I know him. He's an old fox. No one is going to catch him off guard. If your family is in danger as you say, then he'll keep them safe."

"I'm beginning to worry."

"You're not going to hear from them until they're about to board the plane. Trust me, that is how it will be."

"Can anything be done to speed up the process?"

"At this time, I'm afraid not. It's all out of hands. All we can do is wait."

Aldo stared him down. Entrante was being totally rational. He had come prepared to confront him. Whatever the enigma this man represented, Aldo did not care. People like him did not impress him. Right now, only one thing concerned him, and that was his family. But how could he argue with logic? Entrante was right. There was nothing to do but wait.

"You know," Entrante went on, "I understand you are pretty good with your hands. You were a boxer at one time, they tell me."

"Yes, somewhat."

"Too bad you didn't stick with it. Maybe you could have made a good living from it."

"Boxers don't make a good living, Mr. Entrante, they get ripped off."

"Not with the right manager they don't."

"Do you know the business?"

"I don't personally, no. But it's like any other business, you know, you run it right and it pays off."

"I could still fix Aldo for a match," Felix said. "There's opportunity for that in Miami."

"I don't want him to get hurt," Entrante grunted. "We need him as a liberator. He will make a good captain."

Aldo wondered at Entrante's blatant arrogance. This man thought of him in terms of property, and had already made plans for him as if he were a piece of land or cattle. He had probably lived and thought this way all his life and he was not about to change now. Aldo felt nothing but disdain for this absurdity. He would play along with Entrante's twisted philosophies and ultimately do as he pleased. He listened to Entrante's invitation. Several men would meet at a location on S. W. 8th Street tonight where the latest developments in Cuba's political life would be discussed. He was expected to be there.

"I'd like that number for Mr. Suarez now, please. I want to call him."

"All right," Entrante said impatiently.

He went to his office and came back with a sheet of paper on which he had scribbled a number.

"I don't know that you'll be able to talk to him there, but you can leave a message. Be careful, though. Your call may be monitored. You may be putting your family in more danger by doing this."

Aldo took the paper and started to leave.

"Wait," Felix said, "I'm not leaving yet."

"It's all right," Aldo replied. "I'm leaving on my own. I have to find a way to get to Miami Beach."

"Miami Beach?" Felix exclaimed. "Wait," he added, looking at Entrante, "let me tell you where you have to go."

"It's fine," Aldo replied. "I have directions."

"What are you doing in Miami Beach?" Felix asked.

"I'm going to see about a part-time job."

He sat on a bench and waited until a green and white bus pulled up near the curb. He got in and walked past the driver. He was used to the bus system in Cuba where the driver drove while the conductor punched the tickets and charged the riders as they came in. Aldo heard the driver say something in English which he didn't understand, but he guessed it had to do with money. He got up and went to the driver and asked him in English. "How much?"

Aldo could not be sure of the number, so he gave him a quarter. The driver put the quarter in one of the three nickel cylinders and gave him a dime and nickel back. So the fare was ten cents. He went back to his seat and took out a piece of paper from his pocket. A customer had marked the route numbers he would have to take. He got off at the downtown terminal and took another bus to Miami Beach. It was a sunny morning and the hotels rose smartly on Colleens Avenue as the bus made its way down the avenue. Aldo reached for the string to activate the buzzer. The directions were for Colleens Avenue and 14th Street, but he couldn't read the street signs from the bus. He would get off early and then walk to the hotel.

He saw the sign with the name, "Swank Hotel" from a distance. It was a tall pink building with wide front steps. The entrance was a horseshoe-shaped driveway where several cars were dropping off guests. It had a reputation as a love nest in the forties when movie stars and other celebrities frequented it. Aldo climbed the steps and walked past the marble-floored foyer. He went to a quaint wooden desk and asked for Ricardo in broken English. The clerk pointed to the back and said a few words, which Aldo took as a warning not to do something. He found Ricardo in the kitchen, washing pots.

"I'm here," Aldo told him.

"Ah, Aldo. I wasn't expecting you."

He turned the faucet and wiped his hands on his apron. He moved quickly towards the back and waived Aldo to follow him. "The manager doesn't like us to talk. Don't let him see you. How did you get in?"

"I asked. Who shall I speak to about a job?"

"Wait," Ricardo said briskly. "Stay here. I don't want them to see you. I'll get Raimundo."

He came back shortly with another man, also Cuban, who shook his hand. He was short and thin and had a pleasant, effeminate manner about him.

"If you want to work, the manager will give you work," he said, smiling. "But I warn you, it'll be hard work. They are busy now. What hours are you looking for."

"Saturday nights and Sundays," Aldo replied.

The manager was a large man with a red puffy face. He looked at Aldo and turned to Raimundo.

"We could use someone of his size for the heavy work here in the kitchen. But today we are shorthanded up front. Get him a uniform and set him up with the clerk to help you with the luggage."

Aldo worked until 5:00 P.M., mostly handling the guests' luggage. As a newcomer, he was lucky to get this position. Being exposed to the customers meant tips. Despite the language barrier, Aldo acted deftly, as if he was familiar with the entire surroundings. He smiled at the customers even if he could not speak to them. Then at the end of his shift, he was sent to the kitchen to move supplies from the pantry. He was happy with himself by the end of the day. He had made $7.75 in tips. The trip had been worth it. He took the bus back into Miami and reported for work at Puntiel's restaurant that evening.

Over the next few days, Aldo maintained the same schedule. No matter how late he returned home, he spent at least an hour going through his English lessons. By the end of the following week, he had picked up additional hours at the hotel for the weekend. His expenses were minimal. He had not yet bought any clothes, shoes, or even a meal. He ate at Puntiel's restaurant and spent nothing on himself. He counted the stash of bills under the floor of his room. He had $165.00 by the middle of his third week.

But Aldo was hugely worried about his family. Christmas was only a week away. What had happened? Why hadn't he heard anything from them? He had tried to contact Mr. Suarez in Havana, but there had been no response. He hoped for news every time he saw Felix. He was growing more and more concerned as the days went by. Then one night, he asked Lucrecia for permission to use the telephone. In broken English he spoke with the international operator and gave her Dulce's telephone number. She said she would call him back when a line was available. He waited in the living room for over an hour while he read his book. He laid his head back on the arm of the sofa and dozed off. About an hour later, the telephone woke him.

He picked up the receiver excitedly, heart pounding. He heard the ring on the line.

"Go ahead," the operator said. Aldo understood it.

"Dulce, it's me." He spoke in a whisper, as if afraid someone could hear them. He heard her sobbing on the other end and waited a few seconds.

"Are you all right, Aunt Dulce?"

"I'm fine," she said. "How could you not have called me? Do you know what I've gone through?"

"Someday I will explain. Have you heard from Pablo and Amanda?"

"No. Aren't they with you?"

Aldo was silent for a moment. Should he really answer that? What if someone was listening to this conversation?

"You haven't heard a word from them?"

"No. Where are they?"

"Are you okay? Is anybody bothering you?"

"They have asked me questions, that's all."

"Dulce, don't worry. I'll get you out of there soon, okay?"

"I'm fine. Can you please write to me?"

"No. Not yet."

"I miss you so much. Shall I look for them?"

"No. Leave it. Everything is all right. I'm doing great. Just missing you. Don't forget me."

"How can I? You are my whole life, my pride and joy. Don't you forget me."

"I'm thinking that I just got out of school and I'm training again. Remember?"

"Please don't say it. I always think about that. Be careful"

"I will, just for you."

"Just want you to know that your mother really loved you. Forgive her. She was doing it to protect you."

"I know. Love you always."

"Me too. You made me so happy."

Aldo put the receiver down and picked up his book. He went to his room and turned the light on. He undressed, leaving only his underwear and undershirt on. He got under the blanket and stared at the ceiling with tears in his eyes, thinking about Cecilia. He couldn't figure what had made Dulce bring her up. There had been no time for Cecilia and him. That was the tragedy of their relationship. She had lost her mind, and he had given up his dream for her. It was weakness that had made him call Dulce. He should have never done it. He was jeopardizing his family's safety. Dulce could not have known about Amanda, Pablo was much too smart for that. He was keeping them in Havana. He could rely on his old friend.

The next day was a Friday. That night, he took the bus back to Miami. He had been mopping the hotel floors late at night for a flat salary without tips, but he didn't mind. He took all the work he could get. He sat sleepily on the bus as it went through North-West Miami. He was sitting in the middle section and felt a vibration. It did not seem significant at first but then it became a rattle, and the engine faltered. It was past 1:00 A.M. The driver was struggling with the engine, shifting gears and giving it gas to make it go, but they kept losing speed and gradually came to a halt. The driver pulled off the road and onto the shoulder, and made an announcement to the passengers. Everyone got up and made for the exit.

Aldo walked out and stood by the railing at the edge of the shoulder. The night was chilly. Most of the passengers wore sweaters and jackets. The driver, too, came outside. They were a few feet from an exit off the main highway. The sign, barely visible, read N.W. 48th Street. Aldo thought he heard cheering in the distance. It was coming from the darkened streets behind them. He listened and recognized the noise. It was the sound of human competition. He buttoned his leather jacket and slowly wandered away from the group of passengers. He climbed over a railing, down into a ditch and into a side street. He followed the sound of the voices like a blind man in the dark. The street was desolate. The houses, from what he could tell, were shabby, some even looked empty and abandoned. The sound kept getting louder, and he noticed a speck of bright light coming from a large structure up ahead. Something pulled him to it. As he reached the door, he opened it and went inside. A crowd of mostly black men gathered around in a circle. He couldn't see well, but he knew instantly it was no cock fight. This was prize fighting in its crudest form. Some men turned as he entered. A black man came towards him. Aldo understood some of what he said. He wanted to know what Aldo wanted. The man signaled behind him, and two other black men came over. Aldo knew he needed to answer fast.

"How much…fight?"

The men looked at each other. He wanted to fight?

"You want to fight?"

"Yes. How much?"

"Call Murphy," the first man said to the others.

A tall, muscular white man with a balding head and a red face returned with the other two.

"You want to fight?" the white man asked, carefully surveying his face and upper body.

"Yes. How much?"

The white man smiled. He knew a fighter when he saw one. But here, this kid had no chance. Nevertheless, his business was not to judge the men who fought but the opportunity they offered. In the early hours of morning, after the local partygoers and drunks had had their fill of Friday-night boxing, there was no better chance at fortune than presenting the rowdy black crowd with a white contestant daring enough to make a go of it.

"You speak any English boy?"

"Little," Aldo said.

The white man held up a twenty dollar bill and smiled, testing him.

"I fight," Aldo said.

"Good," the man replied.

The two other black men stood around him and guided him through the crowd. Some moved as they pushed their way in. Most had to be shoved aside but paid no mind. Their attention was focused on the center of the room under the bright lights. The concrete floor had been covered by a thick canvas to cushion the inevitable falls, but it was still a far cry from a ring. Aldo felt a wave of excitement overcome him he hadn't felt for years. In the middle of the ring two large black men were slugging it out. One of them was bleeding badly, and the other clearly had the advantage. He kept pounding his opponent unmercifully.

A lean man wearing a fisherman's hat stood near the fighters, stepping back as the punches flew. He had to be the acting referee. He seemed to be moving faster than the fighters at times. His manner was loose but he clearly had good control of the men as he yelled at them to break.

The man they called Murphy raised his hand to the referee who came up to him. He whispered something in his ear. The referee moved back to the center and immediately raised his arms declaring the fight over and pulling the bleeding man away. The crowd roared. Some of them cursed, and money exchanged hands. Then the white man again whispered something to the referee. He turned and looked towards Aldo, pointing him out. The crowd saw it and jeered wildly.

"You're up, boy," Murphy said. "Move in."

"Let's go," the referee said.

The other fighter stood there with his big hands hanging by his sides. He was much taller than Aldo and had a build like a weight lifter with broad, tight forearms and a wide chest. His face was covered with sweat. He had no cuts or bruises that Aldo could see.

The referee motioned to the other two men who had brought Aldo in. They grabbed onto Aldo's arms. He jerked quickly away. "Your clothes! Take your clothes off!" they yelled.

"Take your shirt off," the referee said.

Aldo did not understand but sensed what they were telling him. He took off his leather jacket, then unbuttoned his shirt. He let the sleeves roll off his arms and then pulled his undershirt off in one quick motion, wrapping it all around his wallet. One of the black man tried to grab the bundle, but Aldo pulled back and placed it at the side of the canvas. His upper body was tight and naturally muscular, but much slimmer than the other fighter. He walked towards the referee standing under the bright beam of lights. He met the other fighter's blank stare. His opponent looked like a wild animal that had found its prey.

"No biting, no tricks," the referee cautioned. "You fight until one is down or until I stop it. Let me see your pockets boy."

The referee felt Aldo's pockets. They were empty.

"Let's go," he said, moving his left arm down in one sweeping motion.

The other fighter came at him, fists outwards like guns and weaving his head. Aldo got his right fist under the side of his jaw and circled his left in front of the chest. He stepped back, then out, outpacing his opponent. He had never fought such a large fighter before. His mind flashed back to the prison. He looked at his opponent and pictured the rebel guards raising the butts of their guns and Batista's soldiers kicking him. They were smaller men with guns. This fighter did not have a gun, only fists.

He continued retreating, tracing his steps with long strides, then quickly moving sideways and avoiding the other fighter's fast blows. The crowd began to boo. Then suddenly, someone pushed him and he fell on top of the other fighter's chest. His opponent reacted quickly and began to jab him in the ribs with powerful short blows. Aldo felt the punches and swayed with their impact as his old trainer had taught him. He placed both fists on the other man's chest, sticking his elbows outward, and pulled himself back while throwing a combination of punches at the man's face. His opponent had left himself wide open. Aldo stung him on the right jaw and the left cheek. The man took a step back, looking dazed. The crowd fell silent. But then he seemed to recover and in a fit of rage, he stumped the floor with both feet. He came forward again, weaving his head and shoulders. Aldo smelled the sweat dripping off his face. This guy was a sweater, Aldo thought. There were sweating fighters, bleeding fighters, and many other kinds. Aldo moved gracefully to the sides with quick jerky head motions, avoiding the punches. He had always liked to measure his opponent, see how far he could reach before he tried to hit him, but there was little time left in this fight so this was not the place. His opponent's movements were so powerful that they could be heard as he cut the air with his blows. Aldo lifted his left fist to his nose, then rotated his forearm as the punches landed. He felt their impact on the back of his arm and leaned his head back. As he blocked the blows, he quickly dropped his right hand and shot straight into his opponent's stomach. He heard the man groan. He tiptoed back, and as the man leaned forward, Aldo jabbed his face with his left hand and struck him on the other side with his right. Both punches landed. For a mere second, time seemed to stand still. His opponent looked frozen. Aldo knew that look, the awed look of a fighter who has never been hurt in the ring. Aldo moved forward and hit him again on the right cheek. Still, he wouldn't fall. So Aldo stepped back, weaving and now flat footed. With increased speed, he struck his opponent high on the bridge of the nose with his right fist, and even before pulling away, he hit him on the left cheek with the left. Then with his right fist again on the other cheek. The fighter had left himself wide open. He dropped his hands to his sides, and his body toppled over the canvass. Aldo stepped sideways to avoid being hit by his bulk. The man fell face down. The crowd was silent. It had all happened so fast that it seemed like a dream.

Aldo walked towards Murphy and laid out his open hand. The man was staring at him with a look of disbelief.

"Money," Aldo said.

"Boy, what is your name?"

"Money," Aldo said again.

"Yes, yes, here."

He gave him a twenty dollar bill. Aldo stuck it in his pants pocket. He took his clothes from the floor and began making his way through the crowd. The other two men who had brought him followed him, with Murphy yelling in the background. When he reached the door, he put his clothes on.

"Here is someone who speaks Spanish," Murphy said.

A mulatto dressed in a flowered shirt and dressy sil pants approached. His hair was short and bristled.

"Look," the mulatto man said, "he wants to know your name. Where can he find you?"

"Nowhere," Aldo said.

"Do you fight?" the man translated.

"No, I don't."

"Look, he says he knows you're a fighter. He wants to know where to find you."

"Tell him I'll find him."

Aldo pulled the door's rusty handle and opened it. The mulatto man grabbed his arm.

"No, wait, he wants to talk to you."

"Take your hands off me, friend," Aldo said, pulling his arm away. "Tell him I have to go. My bus is waiting."

"Look, don't be a fool. He'll give you a ride. You could make money, a lot of money. Talk to him."

Aldo stepped out into the street, with the mulatto man close behind him. The white man and the other black men stayed inside watching them.

"Look," the mulatto man, said. "You can't just come in here like that and leave."

Aldo looked at him. He realized the man wasn't Cuban. His idioms and style were rather crude and his Spanish Americanized, indicative of his many years in this country.

"Friend, leave me alone, all right?" Aldo said with a note of finality.

He stopped walking and faced him. He looked over his shoulder towards the door of the warehouse and saw no one. The mulatto threw up his hands in a gesture of surrender. "Look, you're wrong, man. You're wrong."

Aldo ignored him. He turned his back to him and disappeared in the darkness of the street. Slowly, he went back up the road. He spotted the flashing lights of a tow truck in the distance and walked in that direction. The passengers were still gathered nearby, watching the men fiddling with the engine in the rear of the bus. He hoped no one had noticed his absence and stood silently in the back of the group. He waited with the rest of them until the men got the bus running again. He had now had his fill, he thought. It had been a good fight.

The next morning, as Aldo rushed to tend to the tables, a man dressed in a uniform came inside the restaurant. He called the name of Aldo Ochoa with a heavy American accent to Puntiel. When Puntiel pointed towards him, the man gave Aldo a small envelope and left.

"It's a telegram," Puntiel said.

Aldo ripped the envelope open and unfolded the yellow sheet of paper. He read the single line of text to himself, then aloud to Puntiel.

"We arrive December 23. All is well. Pablo."

"Congratulations," Puntiel said. "You now have everything you want. You deserve it."

CHAPTER THIRTEEN

ONE MORNING AS HE WALKED to Puntiel's restaurant, Aldo wandered into another block parallel to 8th Street and noticed the for rent sign at the window of a duplex. He visualized his twin daughters running up the narrow walkway around the building and he would walk by, dreaming about the day when this would become a reality. The house became so familiar that he could describe it in detail if anyone had asked. But he told no one. Like most of his hopes and dreams, they remained part of his inner self.

The Saturday after receiving Pablo's telegram, Aldo went to the apartment and inquired about it. An American retiree owned it. He seemed suspicious of the young man who had come so daringly asking about the apartment. He studied him carefully before making a decision. What seemed to turn him off most was Aldo's broken English. He wanted to know how long he had been living in the States, the kind of food he ate, and the music he listened to. He also wanted to meet Aldo's family. After much haggling, he allowed Aldo to see it. It was a two-bedroom apartment with a bathroom, kitchen, dining room and living room. The rent was $40.00. No pets were allowed, and no music after 10:00 P.M. Aldo wanted to know where the man lived. When he pointed to the house next door, Aldo seriously considered forgetting the whole thing. The landlord might resent his kids, and they had been through enough. But the apartment was so modern and clean that he felt he could not pass up the opportunity. In what few words he could muster, Aldo told him that his brother would also be living with them.

"That's five people in a two-bedroom apartment. Not a good idea," the old man said disapprovingly.

"Brother never home."

"May be," the old man replied. "I'll think about it. Give me your number."

Aldo gave him the number at the restaurant and got ready to leave. "Have to know tonight," he said.

"I will come to see you at your job," the old man replied.

That evening, he walked into Puntiel's restaurant and sat down on one of the stools. He knew the place. He didn't like these newcomers in his neighborhood that, up to then, had been peaceful. But he had been impressed by their tenacity and perseverance. They were foreigners with a purpose, he thought, and he admired that. He sat quietly behind Puntiel's counter, listening to the chatter. He couldn't understand what they were saying, but he listened anyway. Out of the corner of his eye, he saw Aldo hurrying among the tables, carrying plates of food, and taking orders. Aldo walked past him and placed a coaster before him. He brought him a glass of water with ice cubes and, without looking up, said he would be back.

Joe Sorino was sixty-six years old and had retired a year ago after a long career as a salesman. He had come to Miami forty five years before and knew the city like the palm of his hand. There wasn't an establishment in Miami that he had not visited. He had worked for a flour company in the northeast that had sent him to the Miami area before the depression to promote the company's product and test the southern market. Joe Sorino had all the attributes of a good salesman. He was not easily discouraged and his persistence knew no bounds. That was the reason for his success. He had built a window of opportunity for his employer by selling paper flour to the small grocery stores when nobody was buying them, then to the restaurants, and eventually, to the chain supermarkets. But at the end, Joe had felt betrayed. He was never properly compensated for his efforts and never held an important position in his company. More importantly, despite his obvious self-assurance, he never accomplished the one thing he had wanted the most, which was to own his own business. What had happened during all those years when he had battled to build his company's good name? What had he gotten for it? He didn't even have a decent life insurance from his employer, and at his age, he and his wife had to pay for their own health plan. He had put his life savings in two duplexes, anticipating his retirement, and he lived off the rent and his social security. It really wasn't much for a man who had built a market for his company single handedly.

Life's hard lessons had taught Joe to be careful. His apartments were the apple of his eyes. He had nothing else to live for, and he would make sure that he didn't rent to deadbeats or trouble makers. After all, who better than him to tell them apart. He had been dealing with them all his life.

He waited for a chance to speak to the older man in the kitchen who he knew owned this business. He had seen him open up shop about a year ago and work long hours. Although the man was a foreigner, he respected him as he respected anyone who worked this hard to make an honest living. Before the waiter returned for his order, he whistled to Puntiel and waived for him over.

"Your waiter over here," he said pointing towards the back with his left thumb, "is he a good man?"

Puntiel looked into Joe's fading blue eyes. He wasn't sure why the old man would be asking about Aldo but thought nothing of it. It was probably just general talk. He had seen him hanging around at times and knew him just as a local who probably had nothing better to do than to watch what other people did.

"Very good man," Puntiel responded, "very good."

"He works for you, right?"

"Yeah," Puntiel said in broken English, "work here, yeah."

"Is he honest? Hard working?"

"Yeah, very good," said Puntiel, now somewhat puzzled.

"Does he owe anybody money?"

"No. He don't buy nothing. No spend nothing. Good man."

At that point Aldo came around the counter. He was going to take the man's order and had book and pencil ready when he looked up at him and recognized him.

"Hello," Aldo said, "what do you like?"

"Oh, I think I'll just have an orange soda and French fries."

Aldo went into the kitchen, passing Puntiel. He set the fries in the deep fryer, went back behind the counter, and got an orange soda bottle from the refrigerator. He uncapped it and put it in front of Joe with a glass filled with ice. Then he went back to tending the tables until he returned with the fries. As he gave Joe the bill, the old man looked pleasantly at him.

"Listen, young man," he said, "you got the apartment. Come in tomorrow with a deposit and the rent for the first month, and I'll give you a key, okay?"

"Okay," Aldo said. It was a good American word, Aldo thought. It was such a simple, practical word that said so much.

The reunion with his family at the airport was an emotional one. Although they had been apart for only four weeks, it felt like years. These had been hard times for Aldo's family and the strain showed, especially on Pablo. He had kept Amanda and the children in a hotel under an assumed name without any contact except with Mr. Suarez as he waited for their visas. The most difficult task had been to stay calm in the face of the unknown. Amanda had lost her nerve several times and wanted to go to Camaguey with the children. It had taken considerable effort on Pablo's part to keep her under control. By the time he had received word from Suarez that the papers were ready, he had ran out of stories to tell them. He was mentally exhausted, tired of waiting in shady corners and watching his back and missing sleep. He had been so devoted to his friend's family that he had neglected himself. He had lost a lot of weight, and his face looked gaunt. His appearance was untidy, a far cry from the usually-neat businessman who, with Aldo, had brought about the largest cattle deals that their hometown had ever seen. But the minute he entered the airport with Amanda and the children and saw Aldo standing near the turnstile, it all seemed worthwhile. He waited while Amanda and the children, teary eyed, ran to Aldo, wrapping themselves around him. Then he walked up to him and embraced him with tears in his eyes.

"I'll never be able to repay for what you've done for them," Aldo said.

"Forget it. Now that I see you, I see heaven. I can go back to being myself again. Whatever I did back there was not something Pablo would do. It was someone else."

"No, it wasn't. Back there was the real Pablo. But now it's over. We're all together again. You're coming home with me. You need rest."

Aldo turned to Puntiel who had driven him to the airport. Although it wasn't his family, he, too, had become emotional at the reunion. He had had the luxury of leaving the island with his family.

"This is my family," Aldo said. "And this is Pablo, who is my friend and brother."

"I'm so glad to meet you all," Puntiel said. "Madam, you are a lucky woman."

He looked at Amanda. She was a small woman, but he found her very attractive. Dressed in a sky blue dress, she looked like an actress. Her tears at reuniting with her husband had streaked her make up, and she took a white handkerchief from her purse to wipe her face. Puntiel noticed the well-behaved young boy with the freckled face and the two beautiful little girls standing next to each other looking like dolls. He was instantly smitten.

"Don't tell me they are twins, these two," he said.

"Yes," Aldo replied, "this is Clara and this is Teresa. In a little while, I'll ask you to see if you can tell them apart."

They all laughed and followed the crowd of passengers to the baggage claim area. After picking their luggage, Puntiel drove them to their new home. Upon renting the apartment, Aldo had realized that he had four rooms of empty furniture. What could he do in the little time he had left before they arrived? But in two days it had all been filled. Lucrecia had given him a couch and Puntiel had sent a double bed. Two customers in the restaurant heard about Aldo's plight and they too pitched in with odd pieces of furniture. As the family entered the apartment, they found a comfortably furnished home. Amanda felt as if she were in a dream. To be away from the hotels and the dull-looking rooms, and, best of all, to be able to move freely without fear of being followed was the greatest relief. She had brought very little luggage. One valise with the children's clothes, and the blouse and skirt she had worn every day since the day Aldo left. As for Pablo, he carried a single hand-bag with some underwear garments, having had no time to fetch any of his clothes the night he had taken Aldo away from Camaguey. All he had was five dollars in his pocket that Suarez had given him.

From Havana, Pablo had tried desperately to withdraw some of the savings he and Aldo had hoarded in their joint ventures, but it had been impossible. Through Suarez and his contacts he learned that the rebels were hot on Aldo's trail. As soon as word got out that he was missing, Aldo became a wanted man. His family and friends were the focus of a detailed investigation. When they discovered that Pablo was also gone, he too became a fugitive. Pablo learned how Dulce was interrogated on several occasions and even detained at one point. All of Aldo's acquaintants, including those who had barely known him, became the target of irrational searches and harassment. As the days passed, Pablo came to believe that he, Amanda, and the children would be apprehended and forbidden to leave. Up to the last moment as he sat on the plane with his eyes closed, waiting for take off, he firmly believed that an armed guard would burst in and drag him to prison. It was only when the plane landed and he saw the airport signs in English that he felt safe. It had been an odyssey that had tested his nerves to the limit. As he and Amanda told the story of their stay in Havana, there seemed only one link missing.

"Where is Ana?"

Pablo and Amanda gazed at each other as if they had been keeping a secret but they knew it wouldn't escape Aldo. They had merely wondered how long it would take him to ask.

"She did what you would expect of her," Pablo said. "She stayed with us for a few days, but when we got word of how hard they were looking for us, she went back to Camaguey to try to diffuse the situation."

"But how could you let her?"

"We didn't. She left one night while we were sleeping. She left us a note. What could I have done?"

"Did you hear anymore from her?"

"I tried to find out, but it was just too dangerous, Aldo. Especially with the kids. It was horrible. I couldn't do anything. I asked Suarez to see if he could find out from his people. He asked someone but couldn't come up with anything. We were pretty much shut from the rest of the country, Aldo. I was afraid to make a move."

Aldo stared at his wife for a moment. Thinking about her older sister, he realized how unselfish she had been. She must have known what she was about to do from the beginning. She couldn't stay. She would not have jeopardized Amanda and the children. One thing was to have the wife of a convict hide, another to have the commander's wife aid and abet her. So she went back to Camaguey to face the wrath of her husband and to quiet things down, even at the risk to herself.

What could he do for her? In his present situation, he could not send for her. He felt an enormous sympathy for the beautiful lady who had always thought of others before herself. There was only one way he could help her, and that was through Entrante. But Entrante, the wealthy bureaucrat, would never lifted a finger without payment. And what could he possibly offer him for Ana's freedom? There was only one way out. He would have to work day and night to buy Ana's visa and those of the rest of his family. That could take years. Quietly, he swore that the day would come when he could bring Ana to the United States and pledged that this day would not be far.

"I would like to make everyone coffee," Amanda said rising from the sofa. "It's been a long time since I have been in a home. You want to show me how to use the stove?"

"Yes," Aldo replied, "you will need some instructions. This is not like Rios."

She did not respond at the mention of the name. For her it was almost a forbidden word. *Let there be peace in this house*, she thought. Hell was behind. So she waited for her husband in the kitchen while he took a pressure coffee maker from one of the cabinets, unscrewed the bottom and filled it with coffee. Things were sure different here.

She had never seen a pressure coffee maker before. Then, as he turned on the electric stove, she was even more impressed. It had taken her years to get an electric stove in Cuba. Here, it had taken Aldo four weeks. Not bad.

After coffee was served, Aldo hugged the children and kissed Amanda. He told Pablo to rest and went back to Puntiel's restaurant. As he turned into the busy S. W. 8th Street, he felt rejuvenated. It would be a nice Christmas after all. Just a year ago, he had ran into the biggest challenge of his life. Had Patricio not been killed that morning, the odds were he wouldn't be here today. But that was history. He was happy about America. He was happy that he was here and that his children would grow up free without having to join one political party or another. For him, that meant a lot. The future looked bright in America for those who were willing to work hard. He was one of them.

At the hotel, Aldo spoke to Raimundo about a position for Pablo. He wanted Pablo to rest for at least one week, but he knew that Pablo would be looking for a job, as he was not the type to be idle. Raimundo promised he would do all he could. He could always find room for a hard worker, he said.

Christmas Eve was different in America. Nevertheless, the new waive of immigrants would not let go of their customs. So this Christmas Eve, men and women entered Puntiel's restaurant asking him to roast their pigs. What would Christmas Eve be without that? Puntiel, always the entrepreneur, had seen it coming. So he had brought in an extra stove for the roasting.

"I know you know how to season the meat," Puntiel said to Aldo. "So you do that and I'll roast."

"I'll help you with both, Puntiel."

"Good morning." They were interrupted by Felix.

"Good morning," Aldo and Puntiel responded.

"Roasting pork for Christmas Eve, eh?"

"Some," Puntiel said.

"Well, Entrante would like you to do his pork. Can I have it brought to you."

"I don't think I can, Felix," Puntiel said. "I can't do a whole pig. I can only do a leg. I don't have an oven large enough. He should take it to the bakery."

"He'll be disappointed."

"I'm sorry. I just can't do it."

"Here he comes now," Felix said.

Mr. Entrante had been outside speaking to someone. As soon as he entered, Felix went to meet him. The pair sat at one of the middle tables. Entrante raised his right arm, signaling Aldo to come to serve him. Aldo took two menus and carried them to the table.

"Good afternoon, gentlemen," Aldo said, handing each a menu. "Anything to drink?"

"Just bring us water," Felix said.

Entrante did not acknowledge him. He put his menu down and began studying it. Aldo came back with two glasses full of ice and water.

"I'll have one fillet mignon, white rice and ripe bananas. But the filet has to be well done. Understood?"

He looked at Aldo with an air of command. Aldo acknowledged him with a nod and did not respond. He had planned to thank him now that his family had arrived but instead, he thought how thrilling it would be to bust his teeth.

"By the way, friend," Entrante said as Aldo turned, "you owe me a big one."

"And what is that, Mr. Entrante?"

"Your family has arrived, haven't they?"

"They have."

"Well? I made that possible, didn't I?"

"Mr. Entrante, if I owe you for your services, why don't you tell me how much?"

"You mean you have that much money, eh? You're a little cocky, aren't you?"

"Oh, not at all, sir. But I do not want to owe anyone money. I pay my debts. How much do I owe you?"

"Let's just say that you are indebted to me, eh? May be I will need a favor from you one of these days."

"But I don't want to be indebted to you. You just tell me what I owe you. and I will pay you."

"No. Let's bank on it."

Aldo returned to the counter and gave Puntiel the order.

"He wants his steak well done," Aldo said, "the obnoxious son of a bitch."

"I know," Puntiel said and held his left index finger up, remembering something. "By the way, Aldo, I forgot to tell you there was an American here this morning looking for you."

"An American? What did he look like?"

"He looked like an American, tall and red."

"Hmmm."

People were now coming in for late afternoon coffee. Puntiel's place was not yet the full-fledged restaurant that it would someday be. It was best known for its friendly atmosphere and good espresso. That's what this community looked for and he never lacked for customers.

Aldo took care of the men at the counter, serving them coffee and cigars. Then he took an order for a couple at the table next to Entrante and Felix. When he came back to the kitchen, a man sitting on a stool called him.

"I'd like some coffee, cream, and sugar in it, friend."

Aldo thought he recognized the voice. There is no man that can memorize a face like a boxer. He may forget his name. He may forget where he saw him, but not his face. He remembered the man when his rooster face with the deep-sea blue eyes. He had rolled down his baseball cap over his head, revealing his baldness. Aldo could not help but smile at him. What was this old creep doing here?

"How have you been, young man?" Murphy said.

"Good. Want American coffee?"

"Yes. I also want you to sit down next to me. I want to talk serious business. I need to get you into the ring."

Aldo filled a cup with black American coffee and set it on a saucer before Murphy. Then he brought him cream and sugar.

"Listen, kid," Murphy said, "you got some talent and one thing I know about is boxing. You can make a lot of money. And I can make it happen for you."

Murphy was talking with his hands as he spoke. He seemed intent on making sure Aldo understood. He knew Aldo needed the money. A man like him working in a restaurant was a sin.

"Me no fight no more," Aldo replied in broken English.

"Kid, are you crazy? You know what you're saying? That's like throwing away a million dollars."

"No, no fight."

Murphy had still not taken a sip of his coffee. Now he took his cap off and wiped the top of his head with his right hand. He had put his best men on Aldo's trail, and he was not going to let him go that easily.

"How much do you want to fight? Tell me, how much?"

"No money to fight. No, I don't want to fight anymore."

From the kitchen, Puntiel had heard them and took an interest in their discussion. He leaned back without moving to get a look at the American. Yes, that was him. Was Aldo in some kind of trouble?

Aldo left Murphy and went into the kitchen to pick up Entrante's order. He took clean plates and silverware for their table.

"What's his problem? What does this guy want?"

"He is looking for someone to box. You want to box? This guy will give you a job."

"How do you know this guy?"

"I've seen him once near Miami Beach in a prize fight. That's all."

"Be careful, Aldo. This guy could be some kind of mobster."

"This guy is harmless, Puntiel. He's probably hooked into the ring like an alcoholic into booze. There are people like that, you know. The ring does strange things to you. It's like a bad habit that gets into your blood. I can tell he's got it."

"How do you know so much about it, eh?"

"I used to box. I've seen it happen."

Aldo went into the dining room. He set the table for Entrante and Felix and then took an order from another table. Each time he passed Murphy, the American had something to say, trying to lure him anyway he could. But Murphy had obviously been drinking and soon crossed the line. In one of Aldo's runs, he stood and blocked his way.

"Get out," Aldo said to him, jerking his head towards the door. "Out."

Entrante had come out of the kitchen and was now standing behind the counter, watching Murphy.

"I'll get out if you come with me," Murphy said with a slur and put his cap on.

Aldo laid his tray on the counter and grabbed Murphy's left wrist with his right hand. Murphy did not resist. He let himself be led outside like an unruly child. Suddenly, everyone in the restaurant was silent. Puntiel followed the men to the door. Aldo and Murphy were now on the sidewalk with Murphy in front of him, gesturing with his hands. Aldo looked past Murphy's shoulder and saw two men moving towards them from the other side of the street. He recognized one as the mulatto he had seen at the fight, still wearing his dark glasses and spiked hair. The other was a tall black man, taller than Aldo, no doubt a prize fighter. They stood next to Murphy, listening to their boss pleading with him.

"I guarantee you," Murphy went on, "you will own this restaurant in a couple of months. There is a lot of money out there for you, kid. Tell him, Dardo."

Murphy had spoken to the mulatto, ignoring the black man who was now also standing near him giving Aldo a menacing look.

"Look," Dardo said in Spanish, "he's offering you a steady position. Man, are you crazy? Look, you know how hard it is to get that? You have to be really good. Look, none of those big guys have that. Man, you're crazy. Look, let me tell you…"

He took a step forward and reached towards Aldo. But Aldo swiftly drew back and looked at him.

"Don't touch me, friend or I'll knock your head off."

"Look, man, don't be stupid, ah? I just want to help you. This guy is a big man. You don't understand."

Dardo took another step forward, but no sooner had he moved when Aldo whacked him on the upper lip with his right hand. It was a fast, light jab, hard enough to stop Dardo but light enough not to do any serious damage. Dardo stopped and wiped his bleeding lip. He bent forward and covered his face. Aldo's eyes were now on the tall black man, waiting to see what he was going to do. The black man looked at his bleeding companion and slowly moved forward. Aldo walked back and sideways as if he was in the ring.

"Stop, you fool," Murray scolded the black man, "don't you see he'll kill you."

"Like hell he would, Mr. Murphy," the black man said, looking intently at Aldo.

"You don't know what you're saying," Murphy said impatiently. "This man is a boxer, a real boxer. That's why I want him."

Murphy grabbed the black man's left arm and yanked him towards him. "Enough," he said, "let's go. I'll see Aldo some other time. Come on."

He patted Dardo on the shoulder and waived for him to follow. Dardo straightened up. He and the black man followed Murphy. They were walking across the street when Murphy turned to Aldo one last time.

"Anytime you want to stop by my ring, Aldo, just come, okay? I'll be there. We'll set you up."

"That was great," Puntiel said as he held the door open for Aldo. "I was ready to start shooting at any minute."

"Shooting?"

"Yes," Puntiel said, patting his bulging waistline hiding his .38.

"That was a good show," Entrante commented to Aldo later. "We must find you a place where we can put your talents to good use, eh?"

"Can I get you guys anything else?"

"Coffee for both," Entrante commanded. "No sugar. I'll pour my own."

In the evening, after all the customers were gone, Pablo, Amanda, and the children came to see him. Pablo had taken the family for a walk in the hopes to find Puntiel's place. They were all eager to be together on this Christmas Eve. It was the first one that Aldo could recall in his years of marriage when they had not been at Guillermo's house. He wondered how it would affect Amanda.

"Those little girls are adorable," Puntiel said. "Will you give them to me, Aldo? What do you say, eh?"

Teresa and Clara came running to their father. They looked more like each other each day. Their hair was light brown, falling straight down over their shoulders. Their eyes were green like their grandmother's, and they had little round faces like Amanda. Amanda came over to her husband and kissed him on the cheek.

"Ask them if they would go," Aldo dared Puntiel.

"Will you?" Puntiel said to them, "will you come with me?"

They shook their heads, smiling at him while they held onto their father's leg. Aldo showed them and Frank around the place. He showed them what he did and how he spent his day. Pablo's only question was the one that Aldo had asked several weeks before when he had first arrived.

"Where do you think I can find a job?"

"I have spoken to the manager at the hotel. You can one down the street from us. Not a problem, but not right now. I want you to rest for at least one week."

"I'm already rested," he said.

"Good, then you can help me take our leg of pork home."

Aldo took a tray from one of the kitchen shelves and placed it on the counter. Puntiel had let him cook his own pork to his own liking. He had done a good job with the meat, and it looked well done inside as he cut it open. He set the whole portion of a hind leg on the tray, then covered it with foil. Aldo had seen to it that his family would have their dinner. He had given Amanda some money, and she had purchased rice, sweet potatoes, lettuce and bananas. Lucrecia had come over the apartment and showed her where to shop. Amanda seemed overwhelmed with joy at the abundance that prevailed in the markets. Only one thing kept her from getting everything she wanted, and that was money. Gone were those days when she could buy almost without limits. Their funds were limited, and Aldo was only a waiter in a restaurant. This realization finally came home when she saw her husband mopping Puntiel's floors. She was a little scared about the future.

Aldo picked the tray and bid Puntiel goodbye and wished him happy Christmas Eve. Puntiel promised to stop at their place for a drink. In the same block where Puntiel's restaurant stood, some of the store fronts were undergoing renovations. Slowly, new people were moving in and converting empty spaces into cafeterias and a variety of stores. They crossed the street at the corner of 12th Avenue and headed for home.

As Aldo cut the pork, Amanda served the salad, rice, potatoes, and plantains. After they sat down, Amanda asked them to wait while she said a prayer aloud, thanking the Lord for their blessings and asking Him to remember the relatives they had left behind. It was a somber moment that shadowed the evening. For Aldo it was mostly his aunt. For Pablo, it meant the end of his marriage to Olga. For Amanda it was her father, her sisters, and the life that she had been accustomed to. Only the children, through their infinite innocence, could escape this sad moment. After dinner, Aldo put a record on the record player Lucrecia had given them. The family did not yet own a television set. They stayed up past midnight, remembering stories from their hometown.

The next morning, Aldo awoke Amanda as he left for the restaurant. He had purchased five small toys at a variety store near Puntiel's restaurant and surprised Amanda with the little bags as he headed for the door.

"These are for the children, you and Pablo. You will find out that they do not celebrate King's Day in America. Christmas is now the day."

"So I have heard," she replied, opening her eyes. "Thank you for being so thoughtful, Aldo. Even now, you find the time to think about us. I know I don't deserve you."

"Yes, you do, Figurine. I'll see you later."

That week, Pablo began working at the Sea Breeze, a hotel a block away from Aldo's work, frequented mostly by senior citizens who came south during the winter. It was a full- time job as a janitor since the waiters' positions were only available to men who spoke English. Aldo persuaded his friend to read his English books as he was doing. But Pablo was much less. He would work endlessly and found it impossible to read a book. He would learn the language by ear.

For New Year's Eve, the family visited Lucrecia where they greeted the new year with a simple dinner. The news from Cuba seemed grim. There were rumors f nationalizing big enterprises. The population was still in favor of it, still infatuated with the green revolution. Meanwhile, the executions were getting more frequent and intense. The crowds boarding the flights from Havana to Miami kept getting bigger.

With these thoughts in mind, Amanda kissed her husband and wished him a happy New Year. Then, she whispered in his ear that she hoped they would celebrate their next New Year's Eve at Guillermo's house. Aldo smiled. He had his own ideas about what was taking place. Castro's rebels had now ceased to be rebels and had gained a foothold a year ago. Now they were a government solidly in power, enjoying the support of most of the country. Who could fight such a thing? He would think of America as his new home. Dreams and hope one could always have, but one must have plans for the future, and right now, his plans were in America.

The months of January and February were sluggish for business. The post-Christmas season left shoppers rallying to recover their losses. As a result, all business, including tourism, was affected. And so Miami, a city heavily dependent on it, was no exception to the torpor that prevailed during that time. This was something Aldo had not expected. By the end of February, his hours at the hotel had been decreased to three a week and even at Puntiel's he was not working a full day anymore. He kept his ears open for an opportunity.

Late one morning, he saw Ricardo take a table with his brother. This must be more bad news, he thought, Ricardo worked long hours at the hotel during the day. If he was here, it meant he had lost his job.

"Taking it easy today?" Aldo asked.

"I was laid off from the hotel last night," Ricardo said.

"And," his brother quickly added, "he started working in the fields this morning picking tomatoes. Can you believe it?"

"I need a job like that," Aldo said. He was dead serious.

"No, you don't. When are you possibly going to do it? They start at 5:00 A.M."

"I'll fit the time. Ricardo, how do I go about getting a job there. Who do I see?"

"Oh, it's easy. They need people right now. We can ride with this man who picks people up in his truck at 4:00 A.M. If you want to work, you can meet me at 22nd and 8th Street. We can ride together. I'll get you in."

"Can I bring Pablo? He has worked only one day this week."

"I'm sure they'll take him."

"What are the hours?"

"We start picking fruit at dawn, and we go until 10:00 or so. Then we stop and ride back. They want us to do it early when the ground is still fresh and it isn't too hot. It's hard work, though."

"But what about Puntiel?" Ricardo's brother said.

"I'm not leaving Puntiel. I can come here after coming back with your brother."

"You're going to work three jobs?" Ricardo's brother said incredulously.

"You can't really count the hotel as one."

The next morning at 3:30 A.M., Aldo and Pablo were up. They began walking the twelve-block stretch to the corner of 22nd Avenue and 8th Street where Ricardo had agreed his man would pick them up. They walked quietly in the stillness of the unborn morning, both wondering what challenges they would meet. Aldo was in good spirits. Wearing his country shoes, long sleeve flannel shirt, and blue jeans, he felt as if he were back in the country. While someone else might feel dismayed about the prospect of leaving his bed in the middle of the night to pick up tomatoes, he sensed that this would be a new beginning.

The blue Chevy pickup approached the curb and tooted the horn. There were four men sitting in the back. Ricardo stood up as the vehicle stopped and opened the rear door to let Aldo and Pablo in and they sat down next to the other men.

"Where are you from," one of the other men asked.

"We are from Camaguey," Pablo replied.

"Camaguey, the city of jugs," the man commented.

His face, barely visible in the dark, seemed to belong to an older person. His eyes seemed to want to tell a story. With his small hat, he could have easily passed for a juggler on his way to a performance.

"I was out in Camaguey…"

"No," one of the other men interrupted him. "No stories this morning, Armando. We have enough dealing with our misery. We don't want to hear any stories this morning."

"Well," Armando added, smiling at Aldo and Pablo, "welcome aboard anyway."

He leaned forward and shook their hand. The other three men did the same and introduced themselves.

"He's right," Armando went on. "This is misery, boys. This is as miserable as it can get. Don't let anyone fool you about that. But just keep the faith. One of these days, the Americans will wake up and kick that bastard Castro out of Cuba."

"Don't be so sure about that," one of the other men said.

"I heard the CIA is training some men."

"The CIA has always trained men," Armando said.

"That's what it does, it trains spies. What's new about that."

"No, this is different," Ricardo explained. "They have them in Central America somewhere. They are being trained right now for an invasion."

"Ahhhh," Armando smirked. "Don't you believe it."

"It's true," another of the men said. "I know someone who's there, Armando. It's happening."

"Rafael," Armando said, "the Americans don't need to train anyone to go into Cuba. They can do it right now with a snap of the fingers. That's it. Why would they have to train anyone?"

The truck stayed on the expressway for a good half hour. After passing Holmestead, it turned onto a local highway and then a dirt road. It went through a gate into an open field, stopping near a small shack where other vans were dropping people off. Aldo and Pablo followed Ricardo who had them check in with a foreman. He was a tall, slim American wearing a baseball cap and carrying a clipboard. Ricardo looked at him to get his attention, then pointed to Aldo and Pablo.

"New men?" the foreman asked. "Is that what you're trying to tell me?"

"Yes, new," Ricardo spoke in broken English.

"Okay guys. I need your names. Here, sign here." He pointed to a paper on the lectern that he used as a desk under his tent. "Now, you guys go ahead. He'll show you what to do. Come on." He pointed to a large bodied man standing a few feet away.

The ground was marshy at the bottom of the furrows. The spring rains had arrived early this year. The men's feet would sink deep into the puddles as they picked the soft, pulpy tomatoes.

"There is an art to it," Armando said from a distant row. "Pull hard but fast so as not to break the branches. That's the secret."

Aldo laughed to himself as he heard Armando. He had been born in the country and knew its hardship. Picking tomatoes was nothing compared to what he had known as a kid. Most of these men were professionals who had never in their wildest dreams seen a plant, let alone pick its fruit. It was hard work but Armando's advice was correct. This was a different kind of operation. The Americans did everything on a large scale, and there was a method to everything. One did not pick tomatoes to feed one's family. The idea was to comb the field quickly, scoop the tomatoes in one hand, slip them into a shoulder bag, and move on to the next plant. One was paid to do, not to think.

Next time Aldo looked up, there was sunlight all around him. He had been absorbed in his work and had by now filled and emptied his bag at the end of the furrows several times. Pain ran down his back as he straightened up from his crouched position. He grabbed a cup of water from a bucket at the end of his row and kept on. Pablo worked next to him on the next row.

A few minutes after 10:00 A.M., the men quit. Aldo and Pablo sat with the others near the gate until the 1949 pickup came for them. At 11:00, Aldo was at Puntiel's restaurant where he changed clothes in the bathroom and tended tables until late evening. This would be his life from now on. On Friday evenings, he still worked at the hotel. By mid-March, Aldo checked the small nylon bag he kept hidden inside the crack in his mattress. He had $325.00 saved up.

"You see that man, Aldo?" Puntiel asked him one night. "He was an architect in Cuba. Can you believe it?"

"And now he's got himself a route delivering bread," Aldo observed.

"His wife helps him. He's been doing it for a year now. He started with an empty truck, delivering one loaf of bread here and there. Now he delivers to the whole neighborhood."

"Not a bad business, Puntiel."

"I don't particularly like it. Think about it. You have the expense of the truck, maintenance, gas and you're dealing with a product you cannot re-use. If he doesn't sell his bread in one day, he's done for. He's got to throw away the left overs."

"Not the way he runs it, Puntiel. He knows exactly what he has to bring. He takes the orders for the next day when he delivers."

"Yes, that's true. He runs a tight ship, that guy. But his exposure is too high."

"I don't think it's a bad business at all, Puntiel. You have to do it on a large scale to make money. It's the same with your vegetables and your eggs and the rest of your supplies here."

"Ah, no," Puntiel said shaking his index finger, "that's even less predictable. Look, you get a couple of cancellations on your orders for one day, and you're in trouble. What are you going to do with vegetables in the summer? They go bad in one day. You could lose a fortune."

"That's why they have refrigeration, Puntiel."

"Yes, but then your costs go up. That's the problem. The only way you can run a business and make a profit is if you're big. The small guy could never survive."

"In any business you have to be small before you get big, Puntiel," Aldo philosophized.

"I don't know, Aldo. I think it's too risky."

It was late and they were alone. Aldo was mopping the floor. They were interrupted by someone tapping on the front door. It was Aldo's landlord, Joe. The old man had taken a liking to Aldo and took any opportunity he could to see him. There weren't that many since Aldo was working day and night.

"There's your friend Joe, Aldo," Puntiel said. "Go let him in."

Aldo went to the door and turned the key. Joe, dressed in his usual short-sleeve shirt and summer pants, stepped in.

"I need you to stop over my house on the way in," Joe announced. "Bring your friend Pablo. There's something I want you to pick up."

"Your coffee is ready my friend," Puntiel said. "We wait for you."

"Gee, thanks, partner," Joe said merrily. "I can use a cup, that's for damned sure."

He sat on one of the stools while Aldo served him a cup of American coffee. The old man and he had had long discussions about stores and prices, with Aldo asking most of the questions. What was going on, Puntiel couldn't tell, but he was sure that Aldo was up to something. He knew Aldo had little money, and this American guy was only a crazy retiree with nothing better to do. Puntiel thought Aldo was wasting his time. He feared that Aldo might get hurt in the process. Whatever Aldo was cooking up, he was bound to lose what little money he had and he wished he could advise him and stop him from making a mistake. But every time he got ready to speak, he stopped himself. Aldo had a certain aplomb, a self-assurance that radiated from him as if there was no doubt about what he was doing, no way he could be wrong. Puntiel did not dare question a man like that.

"The Food Fair on Coral Way is buying tomatoes at five cents the pound, believe it or not," Joe explained. "Now, why in the world the prices are not the same in all stores I don't know. They have different suppliers, I guess, and I suppose that is their decision. But I don't really understand it. Anyway, they will buy from me, I can assure you."

Aldo leaned on his elbow, listening intently to the old man. His English was by no means perfect, but he had made considerable progress, and he could catch almost every word now. The long, tedious hours of reading and repeating phrases to himself late at night had really paid off.

"How much will they buy?" Aldo asked.

"A good ten pounds to start," Joe said. "May be more. I have to see."

"Hmmm."

The floor had now dried so Aldo went around the counter, picked up the chairs and put them around the table. Then he went back and gathered his clothes from his field work. Later he would be up by 3:30 A.M. There was no time to talk.

"I'll see you tomorrow, Joe," Aldo said.

"Wait, I'll give you a ride. Good night Mr. Puntiel."

Joe drove his 1956 Chevy down 8th Street then turned right on 12th Avenue, down to 4th Street. He pulled into his driveway. "Come in," he said to Aldo, "I got something for you."

Aldo followed him inside. They went into the living room where Maureen, Joe's wife, was sitting in her reclining chair, watching television. She turned her head as the men came into the room. She was fair and she had a small face and hair that must have been very blond in her youth. It was now a mixture of gold and gray. Her eyes were pale blue and sparkled when she spoke. She smiled broadly at Aldo.

"How are you?" She asked.

"Fine, thank you."

Joe pointed to the General Electric television set in the middle of the room with its chord wrapped around it.

"That's for you, buddy. I want your kids to have a T.V."

"How much?"

"You'll pay me later. We'll talk later. Those kids need a T.V. Come on, I'll help you with it."

"How much?"

"Oh, you'll pay me later, come on."

"No, how much?"

"How much you want to pay? Ten dollars?"

"You tell me."

"Ten dollars, okay?"

"Okay."

They carried the set into Aldo's apartment. The children were sitting on the floor in the living room with their school books. They seemed startled as their father and Joe walked in and placed the set against the wall.

"This portable antenna will do for now," Joe said. "But we really have to get you a stationary one. I'll work on that tomorrow."

That was the first television Aldo's family had in America and it was a blessing for Frank and the twins.

The next morning, as Aldo sat on the grass with Pablo, waiting for their ride, he found himself wondering whether he could do business with his present employer. Not that he hadn't wondered about it before. But this morning he was thinking more clearly than ever. Too much was at stake and he could not afford to be wrong, but he always thought better under pressure. He watched the men load the vegetables into a large van which read "Vanderbuilt Distributors." Aldo saw the foreman, clipboard in hand, as he marked something on his papers while counting the boxes. Aldo walked towards him.

"Where's Aldo going?" Ricardo asked.

"He wants to practice his English," Pablo said.

"How much the pound of tomatoes to Vanderbuilt?" Aldo asked.

"You've really taken an interest in this, buddy. I'm not really supposed to discuss it, but this guy gets a break. They don't really tell me why. My guess is because he buys in large quantities. Every day, four or five vans. Sometimes more. And that's just in this field. I'm sure he picks up a lot more from the other fields. You understand?"

"Yes, I understand. If I buy sixty pounds per day, how much?"

"Sixty pounds is nothing, buddy. Probably the same, three pennies per pound. You really have to check with the head office."

"Can I have the number?"

"Yes, you can." Without taking his eyes off the loaders, the foreman gave Aldo a business card. "Give them a call. Good luck buddy. I hope it works out for you."

Aldo took the card and slid it in his pants pocket. He went back to his friends as their ride pulled into the field.

"I wish you told me what the heck you're up to, Aldo?"

"Ricardo," Aldo said. "Is our driver still selling the truck?"

"Yes. He wants to get himself a big van."

"Good. Find out how much he's asking for it."

"Why? You want it?"

"I don't know yet. Don't say I asked you. Just find out for me."

"Now I really wish you told me, Aldo," Pablo repeated.

As the pickup pulled at the corner of 22nd Avenue and 8th Street, Ricardo displayed three fingers from the window of the cabin where he was riding. Aldo and Pablo went toward Puntiel's restaurant.

"You want to buy his truck? What for?"

"We will need one, Pablo."

"I still don't know why. You haven't told me."

"I will. Let's hurry up. Joe is going to be waiting for us at the restaurant today."

"Again? That's no surprise."

Aldo held the card the foreman had given him for Joe to see. The name was Smith and Sons. It bore an address in Northwest Miami and a telephone number.

"I know the place," Joe said. "I'll call them."

"No, I will call them. We"ll talk later."

"Wait, buddy. Look, I've got a new deal worked out at S. W. 18th. I can get them to order ten pounds per day to start. See that? That's a great start. And wait. Wait till the real manager gets back. We will have a picnic."

"I'll see you later," Aldo said as he went tend to customers.

Today was Friday, which meant he would work at the hotel. It would be a hard day, but he had rested last night. As he got back to the counter, he reached under and took a gym bag. He took it to the bathroom, locked the door behind him, and unzipped the bag, checking its contents. Then he went outside and asked Puntiel if the operator had called.

"No, she hasn't. You placed a call to Cuba?"

"Yes, last night. I'll pay for the call."

"Don't worry. You'll get it," Puntiel said and laughed.

It was past 5:00 P.M. when the operator called. Aldo took the receiver from Puntiel and spoke into it.

"It's me, Aldo."

"I miss you so much my boy. How is Amanda? And the children, how are they?"

"Fine. I miss you too."

"I've gotten your letters. Don't worry about me. It's no good for you."

"I still do. I love you."

Dulce's voice hesitated for a moment. "Don't do it my boy. She wouldn't want you to."

"I know."

"Please?"

"Don't worry. I love you."

"Me too. And I know you're the best. That's why I don't worry. But she wouldn't want it this way, remember?"

"I know."

"She loved you. Please forgive her."

"I do. I love you always."

"Will you call me again?"

"I will."

He put the receiver down and went into the dining room to tend to the tables. The late-night crowd was now coming in, but he would have to go in a few minutes.

"Pablo just called," Puntiel said. "He said he and Joe are picking you up at the hotel tonight."

"They are?" Aldo said surprised.

"That's what he said," Puntiel replied, studying him. "Why? You got something going tonight, Aldo?"

Aldo smiled at him, took his gym bag and bid him goodnight.

Aldo's shift at the hotel was scheduled to end at 11:30 P.M. But he would have liked to leave earlier if possible. None of his friends were working, and he still needed the money. Badly now. So he waited on the vacationers as they came in and sat down. The manager had been impressed with his language skills, so he now worked the floor serving the customers. The tips were good. It was where everyone wanted to be. But tonight, Aldo was somewhere else. There was a lot on his mind. He had decided to start a new venture. Joe wasn't crazy. He saw Joe as an asset. He believed Joe could sell and he had the contacts. He had watched Joe as he walked into food markets, chatting with everyone. Everyone liked him.

So Aldo had worked out this scheme where he and the old man would go on the road. He would buy vegetables and sell them to the supermarkets. He had studied the prices carefully. There was a small margin for profit, but the margin grew wider with higher volume. He would start from scratch. He would buy the 1949 pickup from the driver who took him to the fields every morning, and he would fill it with tomatoes. He would hit the markets with Joe and sell them. What did he have to lose? But he couldn't use the money he had saved. That was his cushion so he needed to make $300.00 and had figured out how. He thought about his aunt. Dulce was a wizard and she could read him like a book.

He left the hotel through the back. The smell of salt water filled the air. He turned into the parking lot and saw Joe's Chevy parked out front, facing the street. He walked over and tapped on the passenger window. Pablo rolled it down.

"Let's go?"

"Yes, let's go," Aldo said and sat in the back.

Joe started the engine and headed for the expressway out of Miami Beach.

"How was the hotel tonight?"

"Busy," Aldo said. "Very busy."

"I had to drop Maureen off at our son's, so I told Pablo to ride with me so we could pick you up on the way back. You get home faster that way."

They went past the airport and were headed for the southwest when Aldo asked Joe to veer the opposite way.

"Why?" Joe asked.

"I have to go somewhere. You don't have to come. You can leave me."

"No. I'm not leaving you. Where are you going?"

"I'll show you."

"That's a laugh. Come on."

Aldo bent his head to get a better look at the signs and told Joe to get off the highway.

"Do you know where you are?" Joe asked. "This is a tough neighborhood. What are we doing here?"

"Don't be afraid, Joe."

"I'm not afraid. I worked all of these neighborhoods. That's how I know them. But at midnight, I tell you, coming here is a crazy idea. What in the world are we doing here?"

"Turn here," Aldo said.

They went up a narrow street crowded by small wooden houses. Two or three blocks down, Aldo asked him to stop. It was pitch dark. Joe stopped and looked both ways. He didn't recognize the place.

"Where the hell are we?"

"You don't have to wait for me," Aldo said. "I have something to do."

Two men were coming toward the car. Joe could see them.

"Where are you going?" Pablo said in Spanish.

"I'm meeting someone here."

Aldo grabbed his gym bag and opened his door. He stood by the car and spoke to the men.

"I want to see Murphy," Aldo said.

"What for?" one of the men asked.

Both were big black men and looked unfriendly.

"I want to fight."

"You know Murphy, man?"

"Yes."

"Okay. Tell your friend to park out here."

The other man walked up to Joe's window and signaled him to turn the car.

"Park there, behind those other cars."

For the first time Joe noticed the cars on the side of the road. There were lots of them. Behind them was a building that looked like a warehouse. Where were they? He parked behind an old Chevy, leaving room to avoid being boxed in by another car, and followed the men inside.

One of the black men opened the door and held it open for them. The place looked like a barn inside. It was dim out here, but the center was flooded with lights. A large crowd was cheering. Another man came towards them.

"Who are they?"

"He's looking for Murphy. Wants to fight."

The man took a good look at Aldo. He showed very white teeth and laughed.

"Bring him up."

They waded through the crowd, elbowing some and getting elbowed by others. Murphy was sitting on a high chair watching the two black men in the center of the ring as they blasted each other. He looked back as one of his men got his attention. Upon seeing Aldo his face lit up.

"I knew you'd come, kid. Once a boxer, always a boxer. Welcome. What do you want to do?"

"I want to fight. Fifty a fight. I fight until the end."

"Good, but I tell you what the price is. Fifty is too much."

"Then I don't fight."

"Easy kid, easy. We'll work it out. You want to change?"

"Yes."

"Okay. guys, take him to change."

Aldo followed the men while Joe and Pablo sat near Murphy.

"Now," Murphy said, looking at them, "you want to see your friend fight, right? Then you must bet. Everyone here must bet. This guy will take your bets."

He pointed to the man who had led them through the crowd. He looked at them and put his hand out. Joe felt like he was dreaming. He felt his pocket for change. Pablo did the same.

"We'll wait until Aldo fights. We don't know these fighters."

"That's all right," Murphy said. "Here he comes now."

Dressed in gym shorts and sneakers, Aldo walked towards Pablo and handed him his bag.

"You take the money for each fight," Aldo said to Pablo in Spanish, pointing to Murphy. "Pay him," Aldo told Murphy.

"Don't worry kid. I won't let you down. I want you to keep coming."

Murphy pulled two twenties from a stack of bills from his pocket and handed them to Pablo.

"Now, I'll have to weigh each fight, okay? I have some tough fighters here tonight, so you might do very well. Just box for me, okay."

Aldo waited until Pablo had the bills, then he stretched his arms and twisted his neck several times. Murphy whistled to the acting referee in the center of the ring. He was the same skinny man Aldo had seen before. He looked at Murphy, then at the two fighters. One of them had taken a beating and was bleeding profusely from a cut in one eye. The referee lifted his arm and closed fist to the other fighter.

"Come on," he yelled, "let's get some real fighting going on here."

He had not finished talking before that fighter went at the other as if he was a punching bag. Aldo saw that he punched wildly in every direction. The other fighter merely dropped his hands and took it. The referee stepped forward, put out his hand, then moved back quickly. Another barrage of punches, and the other man was down. The referee lifted the winner's arms. The crowd hollered then bills were exchanged back and fourth. The referee pointed to Aldo.

"You're up, kid. Let's go."

The men who had greeted Aldo at the door stepped into the canvas and brought the other fighter. The crowd fell silent as Aldo walked slowly to the referee. The fighter was big and slightly overweight and was about an inch taller than Aldo.

"No biting. When I tell you to break, you break. You fight until one of you falls. Got it?"

Someone tugged on Joe's shirt. He quickly turned. A black man with gold front teeth held a five dollar bill to him. "Come on, man," he said. "Five against your one, ah?"

Joe wasn't sure. He saw Aldo, standing almost casually near the black fighter. Not in his wildest dreams had he ever imagined that he would visit a place like this tonight. Even more astonishing was to see Aldo in the ring. Although he had wondered about Aldo's physique, Joe had no idea that he was a fighter. He looked about thirty pounds lighter than the huge black fellow. Joe feared that Aldo was going to get the licking of his life. In fact, it would be a miracle if they all got out of here alive tonight. With much trepidation, he took out a dollar bill and held it. Another man behind him tapped him on the shoulder.

"I'll double that, man."

The referee clapped his hands and stepped back. The black fighter charged forward as the crowd roared. Aldo took several steps back, keeping his eyes on the fighter. Joe sensed that the man in the ring was not the Aldo he knew.

The black man kept moving forward, faster now. He threw a right that swept the air, but Aldo wasn't there. He had taken a step sideways and leaned his head back. With his right hand at chest level, he jabbed the other fighter on the right side of his face. He pivoted with the punch so that when it landed, he was facing the fighter. He jabbed him with his right, then with his left, then with the right again. It was happening so quickly one could not count the punches. The black man fell flat on his back. There was an awesome silence. After a few seconds somebody in the back spoke.

"Hey, Murphy, get us some good fighting, man. What kind of shit is that?"

Murphy smiled and couldn't hide his thrill. "That you just saw is real boxing," he replied. "In case you haven't seen it before."

The crowd murmured. The men paid each other's bets. Aldo stood back while the men helped the fallen fighter to his feet and out of the ring.

"Bring the next guy," Murphy yelled.

The next fighter was a black man, bigger and more muscular than the last one. He had long legs and took big steps on the canvas as he moved to the center. Again, Aldo retreated, arms down and weaving his head slightly. Suddenly, he moved aside as his opponent almost passed him. The man turned. By then, Aldo was on him, jabbing him with his left hand on the nose, then quickly moving back. The man was suddenly bloody and took a wild shot at Aldo. Aldo bent and struck him with two hard body punches. The fighter seemed to stop moving for a second, and Aldo came from under him with an uppercut to the chin, then a left jab that turned the man's head. He fell sideways with a big thump.

Again a deep silence permeated the crowd. Two fights had taken place, and Aldo hadn't been touched. He had dropped both fighters in less than five minutes.

"Get him a real fighter," someone yelled from the back.

"He's had real fighters," Murphy said. "Come on," he waived to one of the black man standing at the edge of the crowd on the other side. "Bring in the next fighter."

That fighter also went quickly. The fourth fighter was more difficult. He was a huge black man, an inch taller than Aldo, with hard, round biceps. He was a fast puncher and came in moving and sticking him from the side and middle. He was faster than any of the others. Aldo blocked his punches. In his unique style, he slowly paced back, tiptoeing, making the other fighter think he could hit him. Whenever his opponent charged toward him, he would jump back quickly, punching away. But still Aldo couldn't stop him. They had been going at it for ten minutes, and the other fighter's face was now a mass of blood and cuts, eyes totally shot. Aldo connected three quick jabs to his midsection and jumped back as the man tried desperately to hit him. The man couldn't see him and wobbled. Aldo pointed to the referee with his left hand. The referee waived him to go on. Aldo strode towards his opponent. The man did not see him coming. Aldo struck the right side of his face with a right jab, then caught the left side with his left, took a step back, and hit the pit of his stomach with a left, right, left combination that doubled his opponent. He caught the tip of the man's jaw with a right hook, strode back as he saw him stagger, then punched the man's right temple with a right. His opponent's hands were down. He was defenseless. Blood oozed from his right eye. Aldo stepped back and the crowded booed.

"Stop the fight," Aldo said to the referee, "he cannot fight anymore. Stop the fight!"

"No," the referee replied, "I won't stop the fight. He's got to go down."

"I won't hit him. The fight is finished. Bring the next fighter."

Aldo turned away and walked to the far side of the mat. The referee looked hesitantly at Murphy. Murphy gazed at the black fighter standing in the middle of the mat, arms down, head slumped forward. He waited as the fighter's legs slowly gave out and he fell on his knees. He put his arms forward but couldn't keep them under him as his upper body hit the floor. The crowd fell silent. Aldo walked up to his fallen opponent and raised his right arm. The crowd cheered wildly. For the first time tonight, they recognized him as a true fighter.

"Bring the next fighter," Murphy said.

"We have him," one of the men who had brought them in said.

He was a tall mulatto with a crude hair cut. As soon as he stepped onto the canvas, he began circling, moving cautiously and gracefully. Aldo could tell he was a good boxer and not just a slugger like the others. The man began jabbing at him with long, straight punches. Because of his long reach, he could afford to stay back. Aldo first strode away from the punches. When his opponent gained confidence and got closer, he quickly moved in with a combination of punches to the mid-section. He then threw him a left and a right hook. They were perfectly timed and both punches landed on his jaw. The crowd cheered Aldo. Then the mulatto went after Aldo, taking full advantage of his longer reach and using a steady barrage of jabs, which Aldo blocked with his arms as he retreated. Then the punches caught Aldo lower on the rib cage. He blocked them with his elbows, then opened them wide as he pushed himself toward him. His adversary locked his arms with Aldo's and pushed back. He managed to get to Aldo's kidneys which was the quickest way to get to a fighter by hurting him and wearing him down. Aldo let his body go limp to minimize the punches as his trainer had taught him to do. He covered his ribcage with both arms, face down. His opponent was struggling to get inside him. Then Aldo shot at his midsection again with powerful blows that shook the man. As he had done before, he pulled quickly back, hitting him in the face with a left, right, and left jab. One of the punches immediately opened a gash in the fighter's face. Aldo came quickly forward again and jabbed him fast and hard. His opponent was stunned, but he managed to get into Aldo's face. He struck a blow to Aldo's right side. Aldo sensed his opponent's shock and kept pounding him and getting closer to him. The crowd was going wild. Then he suddenly changed direction and threw him a left uppercut, a shot of lighting that struck his opponent's jaw. Sending him staggering back. Before he could regain his equilibrium, Aldo pounded him again, this time with a right jab that turned the man's head sideways. His face was now beyond Aldo's reach, so Aldo punched his midsection repeatedly. Then Aldo jabbed him with all his might, again and again. There was no need for anymore. The man slumped backwards, hitting the canvas with his bare back.

The crowd loved it. It didn't matter now that the fallen fighter was black and Aldo white. Aldo had shown them real valor and the courtesy of a true fighter. The whole place shook with shouts and cheers.

Aldo took his gym bag from Pablo. He knew there weren't any more fighters. He walked out of the canvas and went to change.

"That was incredible, Aldo!" Joe said inside the car. "Unbelievable. Unbelievable."

"Why in the world did you do it?" Pablo asked.

"We needed a truck," Aldo said.

CHAPTER FOURTEEN

"How many tomato heads tomorrow, Fred," Joe asked the store manager.

"Get me one more box than today, okay? Is that fair?"

"Yes. And that's all I ask Fred. Be fair."

"I'm sticking my neck out for you, Joe. I hope I don't get it cut off."

"Anybody gives you any flack, you let me know. I'll straighten them out myself."

Fred looked at him. At times like these, he could almost believe that the old man was getting senile if it wasn't for the young man who always traveled with him. He figured that Joe was merely tagging along. He felt sorry for old Joe but now he seemed to have found a way to be useful again. Good for him.

"Like they're gonna care what you say, Joe. May be your friend Aldo could stick up for me and pop my boss' nose."

"Oh, you don't want to get into that, Fred. You've never seen a star until you see this guy in the ring. He could beat Floyd Patterson."

"Stop, Joe," Aldo said. "Come on, let's go. Fred, I have it." Aldo wrote down something in his pad. He stuck the pencil behind his right ear and turned away.

"See you tomorrow, Aldo," Fred said. "See you, Joe."

The old man folded his body into the truck's passenger seat next to Pablo. Aldo sat behind the wheel and headed for the expressway. It was past eleven, and they were behind schedule with two more stops to make in the southwest Miami area. They had been making six to seven deliveries per day and attempted to get least one new account daily. Aldo drove while Joe id most of the talking. Pablo and Aldo loaded and unloaded. All had been hard at work for the past four weeks. Aldo and Pablo's day began at 3:30 A.M. They drove two hours to pick up the vegetables from the farms up north. Then they stopped to pick up Joe on their way back to town. By early afternoon, Aldo would work at Puntiel's. But he doubted that he could go on working at the restaurant.

Everything had happened very quickly. Aldo got his driver's license as he purchased the pickup. The three hundred dollars had come from his earnings as a prize fighter. Only one thing was wrong. The orders had grown so fast in the first two weeks that the new pickup had already become obsolete. There was not enough room in it to bring all the orders in one day, so their credibility with their customers was now in jeopardy. Joe kept stressing this point to the young men. A salesman's stock in trade was his word, his credibility, how fast he could deliver the goods but most of their deliveries had yet not been paid for, something Aldo had not anticipated. He had not realized that the big markets took delivery but paid within thirty days. This put him at a disadvantage with the other suppliers who had been in the market longer. Of course, he could do the same with his own suppliers by stalling them for thirty days.

Aldo wanted a bigger delivery truck, but it seemed that he would have to wait until he was paid for his first monthly deliveries.

"I told you buying this thing was a mistake," Joe said. "This truck is too small. I could fill this sucker with orders in one day. And you saw it happen, didn't you? Did you doubt for a minute that I could make the sales?"

"No," Aldo said. "But it is a new business, Joe. How do we know that the stores are going to buy?"

"Oh, come on buddy. You have to have faith. This is America."

Aldo laughed. At times Joe sounded out of touch with reality, but he delivered what he promised. Aldo's instincts had been on target once more. The old man had been a great help. Nothing could have been accomplished without him. All he needed was someone to keep him under control and that someone was Aldo. The old man had found the person who would listen to him and believe in him. Aldo felt that the he, Pablo, and Joe could take Miami by storm. There was no stopping them now.

"I got a solution for this whole freaking problem," Joe said. "After we finish the deliveries, let's go to Hialeah. I'm gonna talk to a friend of mine."

They went on Highway 826 and later exited by Flagger Street. Both deliveries were within a commercial area of Miami that divided the Northwest and Southwest. Gradually, new businesses owned by Cubans had sprung up in this area, but Aldo had not yet sought their patronage. He had been too busy with the supermarkets.

They backed the truck into one of the rear gates. While Joe went to the back of the building, he and Pablo proceeded to unload the boxes.

"I will deliver," Aldo said to him.

He was going to explain but thought better of it. The trouble was money. He needed money to get this business going.

"I told you," Joe said back in the truck. "We need a real truck now."

After their last delivery, Joe had him drive to Hialeah. The city was still a quiet suburban area flanked by deep canals where boys tried their luck with fish. There were few commercial enterprises, but Joe seemed to know the right place. They stopped at an old body shop where he was greeted by several men.

"What are you up to, Joe," a tall red-haired man said. He wrapped his right arm around Joe's neck. "Didn't think you lived in Miami anymore, ah?"

"I'm back on the road with these guys," Joe said, pointing to Aldo and Pablo.

"Who are they?"

"They're friends of mine. I travel with them now. We sell vegetables."

Lost Generation

The man greeted them with a hand gesture. He looked to be about fifty, with bushy eyebrows and sunken cheeks.

"You guys want a beer?" he asked Aldo and Pablo.

"No, thank you," they both replied.

"We're working, Red," Joe explained. "We still got things to do this morning."

"What the hell are you guys up to?"

"I'll tell you why we're here. I'm helping out my friend Aldo over here," Joe said pointing to Aldo. "He's got this great idea about a distributing business, and he's made a good start so far. But what he needs is a freaking delivery van, Red. I figured you must have something that runs."

Red eyed the two strangers leaning on the pickup's hood. He had been around a long time, working in Miami's humid summer afternoons, dragging himself under a smoky engines or rolling on the shop's floor, tightening bolts. He didn't trust strangers and did not care for shyness in a man.

"What kind of a truck are you guys looking for?"

"Something that will drive," Aldo answered.

"No kidding. One that has four wheels, too. Okay. Look, I have known this man for a long time. If he brought you here, it must be for a reason. I got a couple of things in the back if you want to look."

"Yeah, they do," Joe said promptly. "They're riding around in that pickup, Red. But they need something bigger. What they need is a van. Let's see what you got, come on."

"Come guys, follow me."

He waived them to follow. Then turning towards them he asked, "Hey, are you guys Cuban?"

"Yes," Aldo replied.

"Well, if you will pardon my expression. I think we're getting fucking invaded. What the heck is going on in that island?"

"These guys are good Cubans, Red," Joe observed. They're hard working guys. I want to help them out."

"Oh, okay."

They went around the side of the shop past a wire fence. The lot in the rear was crowded with old cars and rotted frames. Red walked

411

past several engines lying on the ground. He pointed to a large six-wheeler van.

"How does that suit you, fellows?"

"That is good," Joe said. "How's the engine?"

"The engine is from that other baby over there," Red said, pointing to a partially-disassembled van.

"I took it apart myself," he added. "That one won't do anyone any good anymore, but I was able to save the engine."

Aldo climbed inside the van and took a look in the back. It had two shelves on top that probably would not hold more than three vegetable boxes. There was plenty of room to serve all the supermarkets. It just had to be restructured.

"How much do you want for it?" Aldo asked.

"Well, I don't know. It's gotta a new engine, and the body is in good shape."

"Listen buddy, these guys don't have much. Is there a way you could finance?"

"Hell, no, Joe," Red said briskly. "Do I look like a bank?"

"I want to help these guys out, Fred. Let's give them a break."

"Break is four hundred, Joe. That's it."

"That's not a bad price. but they can't give it all to you now."

"Well, no money, no truck."

"Wait," Aldo said. "Can I start the truck?"

"Sure you can. Wait, let me get the keys for you."

He went back into the shop and called out for someone to bring him the keys. Aldo started the engine, and it roared to life. He spent several minutes looking under the truck to check for oil leaks. Then he asked Red if he could take the van for a short drive and drove around the block.

"Joe told you the truth," he told Red. "I don't have much money. I can only give you two hundred now. More later."

"No," Red said. "You bring me four hundred dollars, and the truck is yours. Nothing else to say."

There was a finality to his words, and Aldo did not insist. Business was business. Why should the man give him a break anyway?

Then Joe said, "You guys wait for me in the truck, okay?" he told him and Pablo. "I'll be there in a minute.

"Listen, Red," Joe began.

"No," Red said. "I don't know these guys from apple, Joe. And let me ask you, what the hell are you doing hanging around with them anyway? For all you know, they could be a couple of thieves. You don't need this at your age. What are you, nuts, Joe?"

"Listen to me for a second, Red. I am asking you for a chance. Not for them, but for me. I'll sign a fucking note if that'll make you happy, ah? I'll guarantee the other two hundred."

"No. Bring four hundred dollars, and the truck is yours."

"I'll have that beer now, Red."

"Like hell you will."

"Bring me a fucking beer," Joe yelled towards the shop.

It was a good half hour before Joe finally joined Aldo and Pablo. They were not expecting good news, but as Joe got in, they heard him laugh.

"Let's get that damned thing registered now. You're going to need plates to drive it tomorrow."

The next morning, Aldo drove the van and Pablo took the pickup. From then on, he and Pablo would work as a team, but on separate routes. The new vehicle proved to be a tremendous advantage. They took on larger orders and in less than a month, they were again looking for additional transportation. Aldo paid Red the balance of the price in less than two weeks and used his shop to maintain the vehicles. The next van that Aldo purchased was through Red's trained eye. In Red, he had found another piece of the puzzle that he needed to build his business. He now had a trusted mechanic on whom he could depend. If his trucks broke down, he could count on Red's shop to tow him and find him a replacement fast.

"Joe," Aldo said one morning. "We now have transportation but we need a place to store our goods. It is time to get a place. Let's look for one."

"You're damned right," Joe said.

They looked at different locales every afternoon. Joe's inclination was to have Aldo rent a small warehouse where he could store goods for a short period of time. Aldo, looking at the future, thought better of it. He looked for a medium-sized structure with electrical capabilities for refrigeration. He was counting on growing and using the extra room. He had plans for major trading that not even Joe could imagine. The old man was just happy to show that he could do it but had little ambition. They found an empty cinder-block structure with a roof in need of repairs and no partitioned walls, over ten thousand square feet of room for one hundred and twenty dollars per month. Aldo thought it was a steal. He liked the location adjacent to Route 826. From there, he could connect to all points in the City of Miami, Miami Beach, and Hialeah. Joe thought it insane.

"You don't see what I see," Aldo said to the old man.

"I see four decaying walls and a broken down roof. That's what I see."

"We can fix it, Joe."

"But that will cost you more than if you get a decent location in the southwest," the old man protested.

"Not the way I plan to do it."

First, Aldo negotiated a long-term lease with the landlord through Joe. The building had been empty for so long that the owner was happy just to find a tenant, even if only temporary. He was shocked to learn that the man was actually asking for a fifteen-year lease with an option to buy, which Joe had suggested to Aldo. He was again taking a gamble, but he always had before. Much work would have to be done inside. Aldo went back to Puntiel's restaurant looking for masons and carpenters who could help him convert the slummy-looking structure into a warehouse. It took a team of four men to build him what he wanted. He rebuilt only those portions that he needed, but as the weeks went by, the workload increased so much that the remodeling seemed to go on forever.

By the end of summer, Aldo was forced to stop making deliveries. The business was growing at such fast pace that he needed to devote his time to selling, so he concentrated on going after new accounts. He and Joe would travel together still in his pickup, always finding some remote market in a corner of the city that only the old man knew about. They almost always got a sale, even if minimal.

They operated under the theory that once they had a customer, they would keep him.

"They'll buy one box from you today," Joe always said, "Tomorrow they'll buy two, then three. The important thing is to have them. Once you see them everyday it's just a matter of patting their back, like a puppy, you know. They need attention but you'll have them, believe me. Always remember that."

Aldo followed this technique, and it paid off handsomely. Not once did a customer leave him. On the contrary, just as Joe said, the accounts grew once they came in.

At first, Pablo became the lead driver, but as the orders continued growing, he began supervising the others. He was now delivering a light load, and his main role was to oversee the loading and serve as backup in case of a breakdown or emergency. He made it a point to visit each store daily to check on the deliveries. His English was improving, and although not as fluent as Aldo's, he could now hold a conversation, albeit in broken sentences. In the afternoons he would work with Aldo at the warehouse where the two would analyze their accounts and look for ways to increase the volume. Aldo had hired a bilingual secretary to handle most of the paperwork and telephone calls. He insisted on quality service and routinely called customers himself. Customers always found an opportunity to complain when called, but it had the effect that Aldo wanted. It made them realize that, unlike anyone else, he cared.

By the end of the year, Aldo's success was unquestionable. The once dilapidated building he had rented was now a warehouse that housed four trucks, and the next step was delivery of refrigeration equipment.

On the evening of December 23, 1960, Aldo entered El Lazo, a new Cuban restaurant in southwest Miami. It was a call he regretted to have to make, but he needed the man's help.

He stood by the waiter as he surveyed the tables.

"There," he said in Spanish. "Those gentlemen are waiting for me."

"Follow me, sir," the man dressed in coat and tie said. "This way."

Aldo stood before Mr. Entrante and Felix. Entrante looked up and smiled, feigning surprise. Felix was the first to speak. "Aldo, what a pleasure to see you." The man who had once met Aldo at the airport now reached out to greet him. His demeanor was different. He looked subservient, probably after hearing of Aldo's successful business ventures. Aldo was now someone to look up to.

Mr. Entrante, too, had changed. Respect showed on his face as he greeted Aldo. "A pleasure to see you, Aldo," he said. "How have you been?"

"Good," Aldo said, meeting his eye. "Shall we?"

He pointed to his left. He was a peasant at heart but knew the manners of the rich. He sat after them.

"What will you have?" Entrante asked.

He snapped his fingers to the waiter who approached quickly. He was a man accustomed to service and demanded it with much fanfare.

"Sir?" said the waiter.

"Get him a drink," Entrante said, pointing to Aldo.

"Sir, what will you have," the waiter asked humbly.

"One brandy straight," Aldo said.

"We have Duke de Alba, Phillip II…"

"I'll have a Phillip," Aldo said. "Some ice in it, please."

"How's business," Felix asked. "I've been to your place a couple of times but didn't see you. It's coming out beautifully, ah?"

"We're working on it," Aldo replied casually. "There's still much to be done."

"You could have fooled me," Felix added. "I think it looks great as it is. You've brought that place back from the dead."

Aldo glanced at the shrewd little man. He wondered whether Felix had been watching his operation from afar. And why his interest, he thought. Had Entrante ordered him to spy on him?

"The reason I chose this place to meet is because it is classy. Look at those chandeliers, eh?" Mr. Entrante eyed the ceiling with satisfaction. The owners were old entrepreneurs recently arrived from Cuba. Entrante knew them from the island. They had used the space where two stores had previously been and renovated it. The room was wallpapered, the tables covered with spotless tablecloths, and the lights were dim. A piano player caressed the keys of his instrument in a corner, crowded by several baby palm trees and artificial ivy. It was a quiet atmosphere with a night club touch. It seemed far away from the lively, casual cafeterias that had sprung up all along S. W. 8th Street in the past year. Aldo got right down to business.

"I asked for a meeting because I need your help," Aldo said, looking straight at Entrante.

"And what can I do for you?" he asked somewhat surprised by Aldo's bluntness.

"I'd like to know if you still can manage to get people over here as you did with me."

"I may," Entrante said importantly. "What's on your mind?"

"I have several members of my family that I need to get over here," he said.

"Are they in danger?"

"One may be."

"Well, if they're in danger that's another thing. But I tell you, I wouldn't put too much effort into it. Things may go back to normal soon."

"I doubt it," Aldo said.

"Do you hope that it will be?"

"Of course."

"I thought maybe you found it more prosperous over here now."

Aldo was stricken by this remark. Entrante was referring to his humble roots, saying that he now made money in the United States and was finally living like a human being and not like a peasant that he was in Cuba. *Screw him*, Aldo thought. Who needs him? He might just get up from the table and walk away.

"Here it is, sir," the waiter said handing him a glass containing a dust-colored liquid.

Aldo took it and toasted Entrante and Felix. "*Salud*," he said.

"*Salud*," they repeated.

Aldo's thoughts went back to the old house in Padre Valencia. Dulce must be so lonely, probably cooking for herself right now, not going out except to the cemetery, and waiting for the mailman. Ana must be at her father's, keeping it all inside. Or perhaps she was at the farm house with her husband, if there was still a husband. He had to try. He owed it to them.

"That has nothing to do with it, Mr. Entrante. I have personal reasons. Can you do it?"

"It could be done. You and I could work something out. How many are they."

"Four. One man and three women."

"Old, young, or what?"

"The man is my wife's father, and he is in his sixties. One woman is my aunt, and she is about sixty. The other two women are my wife's sisters, and they're in their late twenties. Why does that matter?"

"It doesn't, really. But your relationship to them may. In any event, we go over that, you know. Now," he said after a pause, "how soon do you need them here?"

"It's not an emergency right now, but it could turn into one pretty soon."

Aldo had received letters from Dulce. The situation in town seemed to be deteriorating. The police was now openly arresting people. There was talk about an agrarian reform which was in reality nothing more than a drive towards utilitarian rule and government control. Dulce spoke of Ana as if she was her child. She pitied the young woman and what she was going through, but she wasn't specific.

"Well, then maybe we ought to something about that, right?"

"What do you need to get started?" Aldo asked, ignoring his sarcastic tone.

"First, you have to have your family contact a friend of mine in Havana. Can they get away?"

"They can if need be."

"Felix here will give you the name of the person and his address. Your family contacts him in Havana and gives him all the information. We'll get them visas, and they'll get out."

"How much is this going to cost?"

"Why, Aldo," Entrante exclaimed, "we're friends. Let's just say you owe me a favor."

"No," Aldo said, "I want your price. It's a valuable service, and I'll pay it."

"We'll put it in our mutual account. We're going to be doing business in the future."

"What kind of business?"

"Sales, of course. You're a salesman, right? I'm a salesman. Two salesman can sell together."

"Give me your price."

"You just don't take no for an answer, do you? Felix will handle it."

Aldo did not like it. He glared at Felix who was sipping his drink. The little man would probably milk this opportunity to the end and use it as an excuse to show up in Aldo's warehouse. Or perhaps he would call him for months, reminding him that he was indebted to the great and influential Entrante. But even that was better than having Entrante consider him as a partner.

"All I want to know is that I will be charged for the services. When can I get the information on your contact?"

"You'll have it before you leave here," Felix said. "You must caution your relatives to be very discreet. After all, there is no middle man this time, so one of them will have to make the contact."

"What happened to Suarez?"

"Suarez is in prison," Felix said.

"Since when?" Aldo asked in shock.

"We don't know. He's disappeared. All we know is that he is in prison."

"Anything I can do to help?" The news had hit him like a bolt of lighting. Suarez had been his savior.

"I'm afraid not. None of us can."

"What happened?"

"He was hesitant about leaving. He took too long so they got to him."

"Do you know where he is?"

"In Havana somewhere."

"His family?"

"His children came. His wife is still there, waiting."

Aldo would have done anything to help him, and now worried about his old friend.

"What can you do to help Suarez, Mr. Entrante?"

"I'm afraid not much while he's in jail. Castro's regime is out of control. Once they have you, they have you."

"Maybe I can help," Aldo said, thinking aloud.

"And what could you possibly do, friend?" Entrante said mockingly.

"I'm not yet."

The two exchanged silent glances. Entrante was somewhat overwhelmed by Aldo. He now felt that he had underestimated the young man. He could never admit his prejudice towards his kind. He motioned the waiter over without taking his eyes off Aldo.

"Take his order first," Entrante said to the waiter, pointing to Aldo.

"Sir?" the waiter asked. "Would you like a menu?"

"No."

"An appetizer? We have oysters, shrimp…"

"From the main course only," Aldo said. "I'll have *congrís* with an onion steak, and green bananas."

"Very well, and to drink?"

"One Coca Cola."

"Sir?" the waiter said turning to Felix.

He took their orders, spending most of his time with Entrante who became exceedingly demanding. He described each item in detail, ordering it to be cooked in a certain way. The waiter apologized. The rice was already cooked but they would add some red peppers to it. No, Entrante insisted, they had to be simmered with the rice. The waiter said he would see what could be done. Aldo hoped for a fast meal.

"Can you make a request for me to the pianist, Felix," Entrante said.

"Sure," his aide replied. "What shall it be?"

"Ask Aldo. Let it be his."

"Thank you," Aldo said. "I'll ask him myself."

Before Entrante could protest, Aldo stood up and went near the piano. "Can I make a request?" he said.

"Sure," the man replied.

"Can you play *La Paloma*?"

"A pleasure." He began playing a soft melody that soon had everyone humming, including Entrante.

"So tell me about your business. You're doing good, I hear."

"I'm surviving."

"Let me ask you this," Entrante said, "what gave you the idea? It's vegetables, right? You've never done that before, so how did it occur to you?"

"I saw a need for that business, so I took a chance at it."

"Yes, but it's a money intensive business. By that I mean that it requires much investment to start. How were you able to put it together?"

"Well, first of all, it's not totally put together yet. But the answer is that I started without hardly any investment. Only a truck."

"So how did you get your customers? If you don't have equipment to start with how did you convince them to come to you?"

"I hustled them," Aldo replied.

"Well, with a language handicap, that's quite an accomplishment, Aldo. I'm proud of you."

"His language skills are good now, Entrante," Felix observed. "You ought to hear him. His English is better than mine."

"I bet it is, Felix."

Dinner was pleasant but awkward. Entrante kept asking about Aldo's plans. Aldo could sense his interest, and his desire to somehow be a part of it. But Entrante was too proud and would never concede that, despite heavy odds, Aldo had surpassed him. Despite Entrante's contacts, his experience, and his superb abilities in business, Aldo had left him far behind. Entrante had seen a huge potential in Aldo since the young man had arrived at his house. But he had let him go. Perhaps he was persuaded by what he saw as obstacles. Perhaps it was something else, but deep down, he now knew that he should have listened to Suarez more carefully. Suarez was a great judge of character but the damage was now done. Aldo had escaped from his grip. He must get him back. Maybe it wasn't too late.

Felix gave Aldo a business card with a name and address on the back. He also gave him some additional instructions. Aldo got up to leave.

"I must go now," Aldo said. "I have somewhere else to go tonight. It's been a pleasure."

"The pleasure has been ours," Entrante said. "Listen, I should have told you, it there is anything you need, all you have to do is call me. You hear?"

"Thank you," Aldo said shaking his hand and then Felix's.

"Good night."

"Good night."

Aldo drove the pickup past Puntiel's restaurant and saw the lights. There were still a few people inside. He wanted to stop, but it was past eight thirty. He had to pick up Joe for a meeting, so he turned right on the next block and went to S.W. 11th where he made another right. He pulled alongside Joe's Chevrolet in the narrow parking space. He saw the twins looking at his headlights from the front window of his unit. He walked past Joe's car and went inside his apartment.

"Aldo, you're home early," Amanda said. "Pablo is not even back yet."

"Hello, girls," Aldo said to the twins. "Where's your brother?"

"In his room. Daddy, you want to see what we did today? Look."

They each held a sheet of white paper with crayon scribbles on it. They had started kindergarten in September. The transition was easiest for them because they were young.

"It's beautiful. Do you speak English now?" Aldo asked in English.

"Yes," they both replied.

"And what are you doing peeking at me from the window?"

The two giggled while Aldo went to the bedroom to check on Frank. He knocked on his door and went inside. The boy was lying in bed, pillows stuffed under his head, reading a comic book.

"How are things, Frank?" Aldo said, sitting on the edge of the bed.

"Good, Dad, good."

There was a knock on the front door, loud enough that Aldo and Frank could hear it from the bedroom.

"That's Joe," the two said in unison.

"We have to go to a meeting. I'll be back early."

Joe gave each of the twins a lollipop. He wore a light blue Eisenhower jacket, jeans, black shirt, and sneakers.

"Ready?" he asked as Aldo entered the room.

"Ready."

Aldo kissed Amanda and the twins. He got inside Joe's car. The old man was particular about the Chevy and would not let anyone touch it, not even Aldo.

"This guy we're seeing is the head honcho," Joe said as he backed out of the driveway. "He's got the say for the whole chain, and I know him. I've known him for twenty years."

"How many stores?"

"Listen, buddy, if we hit this one, we're talking about Hollywood, Fort Lauderdale, Tampa, all the big cities. We're going for the big fish. If we get this guy, that means we don't have to go ask any store manager. We'll do in one deal what normally would take us months."

It had been difficult to talk the district manager into a meeting. At first, it seemed the man had agreed to talk to them only out of courtesy to Joe. Joe had been so insistent that it was a miracle they had not been barred from the stores altogether. But Aldo knew that Joe could get away with it because of his age and charm. Up to now it had worked.

Joe followed the Miami Beach signs. He got off near the airport and went into a Grand Union supermarket. He parked and they went inside through the front door. The place was empty. They went towards the booth in back of the store. This is where they usually met the managers and where they pitched their product. Tonight, they were playing in the major leagues.

Ralph Schwartz was dressed in suit and tie and sat behind a small desk next to the store manager, going over some records. He seemed to be glad to see Joe and Aldo come in.

"Hello, Joe," he said, getting up, "nice to see you."

"Well, Ralph, I'll be darned if you're not looking good. That suit and tie look better than an apron. Yes, sir, and you sure deserve it."

"Thanks, Joe. Well, what do we have here? This is the young man who's been stocking some of my stores? What do you say, Aldo? Is it?"

"Yes," Aldo replied. "How do you do?"

"Oh, I'm fine. You guys sit down. Want some coffee?"

"I'll have some," Joe said. "I'll get it myself."

"Okay, Joe," Ralph said, shaking his head in amusement. He was a mild mannered man but Aldo did not underestimate him.

He got right to the point. "Joe's asked me to give you guys an opportunity. I'm sure Joe's told you that I've known him since I was a stock boy in this company. I've heard many good things about you, and I'm satisfied that you have a quality product. But the decision is not just mine. It's a big company. However, I have made some recommendations on your behalf because I like what I've seen so far. Now, let's talk about prices. How do you want to treat us if we buy big?"

"We'll give a discount for anything beyond fifty pounds daily per store. We can scale, too."

"What he means," Joe said, butting in, "is that we can work up a scale in terms of price per weight as the orders go up beyond a certain amount."

"And what scale do you have in mind?"

"Half a penny less for every extra hundred pounds," Aldo explained.

"Well, that's not too bad, but it's not much either."

"But Ralph," Joe protested, "you haven't told us what you have in mind, have you? How can we commit ourselves to any price without knowing what we're dealing with?"

"It goes both ways. How can we commit our orders to you without knowing your price?"

"I understand that," Aldo said, "but we have to start somewhere. We, too, have our suppliers that we need to talk to."

Ralph was focused on Aldo. He thought him smart despite the accent. "Okay look," he said. "We have to start somewhere. I like your proposition. Let's say we start with fifty pounds. What will be your price?"

"For what product?" Joe asked.

"Oh, let's say tomatoes."

"Eight cents a pound," Aldo replied quickly.

"And then what?"

"A penny less after one hundred pounds," Joe added.

"Not bad," Ralph noted. "But you could do better. Is that your best price?"

Both Joe and Aldo knew that right now the market was paying more than that for their produce. It was a question of how badly they wanted to gain entry but they also could not show weakness. That could be fatal. So they both nodded.

"I tell you what," Ralph said, "you give me seven per pound, and I'll make it happen. You then give me a scale that we all can live with and we may have something here."

"Rock bottom is seven," Joe said.

"Good," Ralph agreed, "want a beer, guys?"

"No. I'll finish my coffee. You Aldo?"

"No, thanks."

Around midnight, Aldo was sitting in bed in the dark. He had called the international operator and asked for a line to Guillermo's house in Cuba. Amanda was too excited to sleep and sat in the living room sofa in her night gown, watching television.

Aldo leaned back on the bed, stretching his neck. He then pounded the pillow and laid down. He was used to interrupted sleep. Amanda would probably stay up all night. He had not slept for more than five minutes when the telephone rang. He picked up the receiver and he heard the operator.

"We're on," he said to Amanda with his hand over the receiver. "Here, you can talk to them first. Tell Ana to get on. I need to speak to her."

Amanda cried as she spoke briefly to her father and Aleida. She then gave the telephone to Aldo as Ana came on the line.

"How are you?"

"Aldo, how are you?" Her voice quivered.

"I'm sending you a telegram with the name and address of my friend in Havana. Can you go there?"

"Yes, I'll go."

"See Dulce. Read my letters to her."

"I already did. I know."

"Yes. But there's something else. Remember my friend in Havana?"

"Which friend?"

"Mr. Suarez."

"Yes?"

"He needs your help. Wait for my cable."

Aldo waited a few seconds then spoke again. "What are you going to do?"

There was a short pause then she said, "I'll see you and Amanda soon."

"Good. Here's your sister."

Their conversation was guarded to prevent detention. The next morning, Aldo sent a telegram with a name and address. His letters to Dulce had explained the rest.

The family's Christmas Eve no longer had the same significance. The children were now influenced by American culture. No one talked about it, only Christmas day. The children expected their toys as American kids did. So dinner was, for the most part, nostalgic as they remembered what had once been a sacred gathering in their homeland. Amanda missed it the most and was heartbroken to be away from her family tonight. She hoped that they would come soon. The unrelenting apprehension and unrest made her tired. For the past three years, there had been only worry around the holidays waiting for something to change. Now the reports talked about Castro's fall as if it were a certainty. She just couldn't listen to it anymore. All she wanted right now was to be reunited with her family.

They sat at the table talking and drinking. Pablo had brought half a roasted pig. Amanda had prepared a lavish meal of typical Cuban dishes. Everything was almost perfect except for the absence of family members. Amanda remained quiet while Aldo and Pablo discussed business, biding her time until the opportunity came. Aldo was telling Pablo about last night's events at the Grand Union supermarket. The deal was on and they would deliver to four new locations starting next week. It was good, but they had a logistic problem. How would they meet the increased demand?

"I think that is the least of your problems Aldo," Amanda said.

She wore a pink dress with an open collar and fake pearls. Her hair was wavy and only a touch of make up on her white skin. She looked quite beautiful. Aldo wondered what she meant.

"Why?" he asked.

"The important thing is that you have the orders, no?"

"Yes. But now we have to figure how to make these deliveries. We don't have enough trucks right now."

"Why do you accept new deliveries, then?"

"Because we want to grow, Amanda. We can't grow if we don't take new orders. We just never figured that if would happen so quickly, and we cannot invest in new trucks until we have the orders."

She remained silent for a moment. Pablo looked at her. He was always respectful of her but felt at times that her thinking was askew. She reminded him of her father.

"We don't want to drive empty trucks, Amanda," Pablo said teasingly.

"I guess. I don't know about all that stuff. All I want to know is when we are going to have a decent house for these children to live with a yard for them to play. I see you guys talking about renovations and purchasing new trucks, but we ourselves don't seem to make any progress."

"It hasn't even been a year since Pablo and I started this business, Amanda, and you complain?" Aldo said. "Look around you. There are so many people who have been here as long as we, and they don't have enough to eat. Be thankful. Everything will come in time."

She looked into her plate like a scolded child embarrassed to face her elders. "I don't know," she said. "I just don't know about that. All I know is I hope to see my family soon."

"Oh, I'm sure they'll come," Pablo said.

"It's been a year. Did you send that wire today, Aldo?"

"Yes. Your sister should have it already. She'll know what to do."

They were joined by Joe. Aldo brought a bottle of red wine for him. The old man loved wine. Aldo poured him a glass and served himself and Pablo.

"To a good night, or whatever it is you celebrate today," Joe said.

"Yes. To you," Aldo replied.

Joe was happy. They had quadrupled their orders yesterday and they had a lot to celebrate.

"From now on, we concentrate on the big ones," Joe announced.

He was a changed man. Ever since he had teamed up with Aldo, his life had changed. His retirement had been reversed, and he felt needed again. And he had been lucky. Aldo was honest, and he appreciated him. At first, Aldo had wanted to make him a partner. It was the only fair thing to do, but Joe did not want it. He was a salesman and wanted to stay a salesman. So Aldo had proposed an arrangement that would treat him fairly while preserving his independence. He would be head of sales with a basic salary and a ten per cent commission on everything he sold, which was more than Joe had ever gotten from his company. In the few months they had been together, he had made more money than in the last ten years before retiring. And that was only the beginning. They stayed up until almost midnight. Joe and Pablo walked the stumbling Joe home to the face Maureen's wrath.

Aldo got up at 5:00 A.M. before the children were awake. Their toys had been stacked under the Christmas tree, their first since leaving Cuba. Pablo was up already, and they drove to the warehouse. They had planned a short day because of the holiday, but with the latest developments, there was much organizing to do. Aldo spent the morning moving skids and clearing space. The drivers had already taken their loads, and he was alone when Joe appeared. "Shall we take a ride?"

"It's Christmas, Joe," Aldo said. "Take a break."

"What are you going to do about trucks?"

"I'm going to see Red," Aldo said.

"I'll go with you."

They drove to Hialeah and met Red at his shop. This time, Red couldn't help. Aldo needed at least three more trucks and some trailers. He had some decisions to make. But Red said he would see what he could do.

It was about 10:00 A.M. when Aldo and Joe returned to the warehouse. There was no one there, and Aldo had asked an answering service to take incoming calls. He called for his messages and found one call from Amanda. He dialed his home number and Frank picked up.

"What's the matter Frank," Aldo said without saying hello.

"Oh, Dad. Mommy is real upset. Grandpa died."

Aldo remained silent for a moment. It occurred to him that his son was fast becoming a man. Soon he could watch after his family.

"How do you know, Frank?"

"They called Mom. Aleida called."

"Where's your mother now?"

"She's in the bedroom, crying."

"Where are the girls?"

"They're here with me."

"Stay with your sisters until I get home, Frank. I'll be there soon."

Aldo drove with Joe without saying a word. He wanted to gather his thoughts before seeing Amanda. Then, as they neared the house, he told Joe what had happened. Guillermo had always opposed him. Since the time Aldo was young, the old man had done everything in his power to fend him off and had made no effort to hide his contempt for him. It was not the man he hated, it was what he represented. Fortunately, Francisca had stopped him, and Guillermo had gradually been forced to accept his daughter's choice, but he had done all he could to poison Aldo's relationship with Amanda. Even while infatuated, Amanda never ceased to be influenced by her father. There were secret conversations to which Aldo was never privy. Yet, despite everything, Aldo had not held any grudges. It actually amused him that Guillermo disliked him but he never tried to understand why.

But things had now suddenly changed. Aldo knew how irrational Amanda could be. Among her sisters, she was the one closest to her father. Ana and Aleida had understood what their father was. Ana especially, was ashamed at his behavior, although she never mentioned it. There was no telling what Amanda would do who or what she would blame for this tragedy. Surely the fact that he was now gone would make her regret the time she had missed with him. As Aldo entered his apartment, these thoughts crossed his mind and he felt suddenly apprehensive about his future with Amanda.

Clara and Teresa were seated on the sofa, dressing their new dolls. Frank sat quietly on the floor, his toys put aside as if waiting for someone.

"Where is your mother?" Aldo asked.

The girls interrupted him and jumped from the sofa as soon as he entered, each showing him their dolls. He took the time to kiss them and admire their toys.

"Mom is in the bedroom," Frank said.

Frank appeared aloof, as if this morning's events had thrown him into a state of confusion. Aldo knew that look and bent down to hug him.

"It's reality, Frank," he said to his son. "People have to die. We all die."

"I know," the boy said, now sobbing. "But I was just going to see him now. How did he die?"

"I don't know. Don't be sad. When people die they don't suffer. They rest. So cheer up."

He wiped the tears from Frank's face and hugged him. Frank was no longer the innocent boy who had once played at their small farm near Rios. He was beginning to know the world.

Aldo entered the bedroom and found Amanda laying face down on the bed, crying uncontrollably. She hadn't even noticed Aldo.

"I'm sorry, Figurine," Aldo said. "I'm really sorry."

He stroked the back of her head and then ran his hand up and down her back. She gradually stopped crying. She rolled toward him, sat up, and held him with both arms.

"Ah, Aldo," she sighed, "I feel like the sky came down on me. Do you believe it? He was about to come to be with us."

Aldo stood silent for a few seconds before he spoke. Yes, it was a tragic twist of fate. What would Guillermo have wanted anyway? Would he have been happy in the United States? Probably not. He was too attached to his fortune. Been deprived of his money and possessions would not let him appreciate the wonder of this country. He could never have been happy here. Perhaps this was for the best.

"How did it happen?"

"She said he died at home last night. When they took him to the Spanish Colony, he was already dead."

"Had he been sick?"

"Aleida said that he had been very depressed. The government has been appropriating his clients' property and he was losing business. Everything had been changing, and that affected him. They also froze some of his bank accounts. It was just too much for him, seeing everything he worked so hard for go to pieces. Those bastards killed him, Aldo."

"Where is Ana?"

"She's been in Havana. Aleida said she reached her last night, but I don't know if she'll be able to make it back in time for the funeral. Can you imagine?"

Aldo knew why Ana was in Havana. She was the motivating force in this family and had wasted no time. He had entrusted her with Suarez's fate. Just one more favor from that giant of a woman, as if she had not done enough already. What Aldo didn't realize was that there was nothing in this world that the brave Ana would not do for him. He hoped that he would see her and Dulce soon.

"Ah, Aldo, what am I going to do without my father?" She rested her head on his chest and began weeping again. She started to lose control, and her voice faltered. Then she began to scream. The scene was troubling to Aldo because it reminded him of his mother.

He grabbed her shoulders and shook her.

"Snap out of it, Amanda," he said.

Frank came running in and stood bewildered by the door, watching his father shaking his mother.

"What's wrong with her, Dad? What's the matter?"

"She'll be all right, Frank."

He slowly put her down in the bed. She didn't fight him. She squeezed her temples and stretched her neck. Aldo watched her to make sure she wasn't convulsing.

"Frank, watch your mother. I am going to make her some linden tea."

He went to the kitchen and poured tea into a small pot. He filled it with water and placed it on the burner. Then he lit a match and turned on the gas. He waited a few minutes and filled a cup with the greenish liquid. Just then, there was a knock at the door. It was Pablo.

"How is she?" he said. "I heard what happened."

"She's hanging on."

"How did it happen?"

"I don't know much yet. I am going to put a call in to try to speak to Dulce."

"You're giving her tea?"

"Yes."

Aldo went in the bedroom and made her drink. She did not lift her head, but he made her sit up and drink.

"My poor father," she said a few times. "He was never the same after my mother died. My poor father."

Pablo came into the room and silently hugged her, wanting her to know that he was thinking about her. It was a hard blow for Amanda to lose the one person she trusted most in the world. Even if they ever went back to Cuba, things would never be the same now.

Aldo and Pablo sat in the living room for most of the day, discussing the problem of transportation. Life had to go on. Aldo kept checking on Amanda who remained in her bedroom the entire day. In the afternoon, Aldo sent Pablo to Puntiel's restaurant for some food while he chatted with Joe about the business. He was waiting for a call, but his mind kept going over the things that were worrying him.

In the evening, Puntiel came to pay his respects. Amanda still did not come out, but Puntiel said he understood. The telephone rang about 8:00 P.M. Aldo heard the operator and then a familiar voice sounding cautious but firm.

"How is she taking it?" Ana asked.

"Pretty hard," Aldo said.

"She has to try to go on. You have to anticipate that she may turn on you."

"I know. I expect it."

"Be patient, though."

"I will. How did it happen?"

"Depression. All the doors were closing in on him. No business. Everyone is pretty much being shut down. He couldn't take it. He had a heart attack last night. I barely made the funeral. He will be buried tomorrow."

"I'm really sorry."

"I know you are. We will see you soon."

"Have you taken care of everything?"

"Yes. I'll bring them with me, even he."

"Really? You did it?"

"Yes."

"I can never repay you. Well. Be strong now. I know you carry the heaviest burden. But there's light at the end of the tunnel. You will find happiness here, so don't lose it now. How's Aleida doing?"

"Probably like Amanda. I am going to have to keep an eye on her."

"Do that. Do you want to say hello to Pablo?"

"Yes, that would be nice."

"Here he is. Take care now."

Aldo passed the receiver over to Pablo and thought he noticed some tension on his friend's voice. He wondered about he and Ana.

The first few days were hard on Amanda. She was in a daze, and he was left with both the responsibility of looking after the children and overseeing the business. The trouble was that there was no one he could trust at home, so he had to rely on Frank to watch the twins and keep an eye on Amanda. The next few days were difficult until New Year's when Pablo gave him a telegram that had arrived for him at Puntiel's restaurant.

"We arrive on the 15th. We are all fine. Ana."

It was the break he needed. He showed it to Amanda, hoping it would lift her spirits. She read it and cried. She was finally going to be reunited with her family but she was devastated knowing that her father was not with them. She would never see him again and she would never recover from it. She now sifted through evidence in her mind. Anything or anybody that might have been a cause of her father's pain was in danger of being accused. To her, he had been a great man.

"I am going to move to a single room next week," Pablo said to Aldo the next morning.

"Over my dead body," Aldo replied.

"But think for a minute, Aldo. Where are you going to put your two sisters-in- law? There's no room. It's all right. And besides, I wouldn't feel right. There is no need to be uncomfortable. We are doing well now."

"I don't like it," Aldo said.

"I'm not being put out, but it's got to be done."

"No."

"Yes. I have the last word."

Pablo turned and walked toward the main entrance. The warehouse had now been partitioned. One large refrigerated room filled half the space. The rest was for deliveries. Pablo walked through the rear door and went outside to look for his truck. Aldo and Joe had coordinated rentals with a trucking company. It was a short-term solution to a recurrent problem. They were now handling trailers, and both he and Aldo had been forced to learn to drive the eighteen wheelers. Their philosophy, which was not shared by Joe, was that they had each had to know the details of the entire operation.

"Let me at least talk to Rebeca," Aldo said as Pablo climbed into the cabin of a truck.

"All right. You do that."

Rebeca was a young, attractive woman who spoke Spanish and English fluently. She worked for Pablo and Aldo and was married to an older man who had been a doctor in Cuba but was now was hoping to validate his degree in the United States. His young wife had worked two jobs to put him through school. The next morning, she answered the telephone at the warehouse.

"Where is Aldo?" a familiar voice on the other end said.

Rebeca hesitated for a second as she recognized the voice. She was going to say hello but stopped.

"He's right here." She handed Aldo the receiver as he came through the door. He was holding a clipboard in his right hand and Joe was talking behind him.

"Have you heard anything else from Ana?" Amanda asked.

"No. I think you would hear before me."

"That's not true and you know it. You would hear first."

"Well, then maybe you should call Puntiel and ask him. It's the only other place I would get to hear other than the house and here."

"I wouldn't call that dirty place. Why should I do that? I guess my father was right about you after all."

Aldo waited for the words to sink in. What he had feared was already happening. The question was, how was he going to handle it.

"Then don't call," he said softly, and hung up.

He turned back to Joe and continued their discussion. Aldo said nothing as he listened to Joe ramble on. He now was sure that Amanda would never be happy with him. She had never been. Emptiness overcame him. He had given her so much. He sat down on a chair in front of the other desk and waited until Joe finished talking, listening to him as he collected his thoughts. The door opened and he recognized Hortencia, the young woman who had received him at Mr. Entrante's house over a year ago.

"Hello," she said as she strode in.

Her hair was longer but still curled under as before. Her plucked eyebrows still appeared painted on her forehead. She was heavily made up and her perfect figure could not be ignored.

"I don't know if you remember me," she said, looking at Aldo with her big black eyes. "I'm Mr. Entrante's secretary. He asked me to ask you to come to the office today. Since I was in the neighborhood, I decided to stop by."

"Good. You are welcome. Hortencia, right?"

Aldo waited for her reply, then spoke in English: "This is Joe, my partner."

Aldo pointed to Joe who was standing next to her. The old man was all smiles, and he took her delicate hand to shake it.

"And this is Rebeca, our secretary. Would you like something to drink? We don't have much, but we can get it."

"Oh, no," she responded in perfect English. "I am surprised how well you can speak the language already...Mr. Ochoa."

She hesitated, and Aldo interrupted her. "You can call me Aldo. It's okay. Joe here taught me how to speak."

"That's half true," Joe said. "Let me get you some coffee though, please."

"Fine."

"When does Mr. Entrante want to meet?" Aldo asked.

"He would like to speak to you today. I have this note for you."

She handed him a sealed envelope and hesitated when Aldo placed the envelope inside his shirt pocket.

"I'm sorry. Mr. Entrante instructed me to bring back an answer today," she said.

"Your boss is demanding, isn't he?"

She did not respond but took a sip from her coffee, staring at him mischievously. Aldo took the envelope and opened it. Whatever the old fox was up to, he was thinking, it must be for his own benefit. He opened the folded sheet of paper inside and read the hand-written single line in Spanish: "We must meet as soon as possible. Call me. Entrante."

Aldo folded the paper and placed it back inside the envelope.

"Tell him I can meet him tonight. About 8:00 P.M. His house?"

"Yes. That would be fine. I will tell him." She took another sip of coffee. "Your place is so big."

"Big with problems," Aldo said. "Joe, you want to show her around?"

"My pleasure," Joe said.

"Why is she here?" Rebeca asked as they went out of the room.

"Beats me," Aldo said. "She could have called. It was probably Entrante's idea. She's spying on us."

"I don't know about that. Why would he? What's he after?"

"You have to understand some of these old power houses Rebeca," Aldo said, handing her the envelope. "They're used to power, and when somebody else makes waves, it eats them up. He's looking for control, some way to make his way into this operation."

"You wouldn't let him, would you?"

"Of course not. We don't need him."

"I think she likes you," Rebeca said.

"Now whatever makes you say that?"

"A woman knows that look."

"Too bad I'm married."

"That won't stop her. The question is whether it will stop you."

Aldo and Rebeca had a good relationship. Rebeca found him easy to work for. He treated her as family and she liked her new job. She was an insightful woman who sensed Aldo had problems at home, although he said nothing about it. She also knew he was a good man. There was no stopping him in business, but what would happen to his family life?

"It's splendid," Hortencia said as she returned with Joe. "You have turned this place into a palace. I've been watching it as I ride by here everyday."

"You live around here?" Rebeca asked amicably.

"I live in the Southwest but I take the expressway to go to Hialeah every so often."

"I see."

"Rebeca gave me a lot of ideas," Aldo said.

The telephone rang and Rebeca went back to her work.

"Joe and I are leaving for Holmestead in a few minutes and we have to get a truck ready. You are welcome to stay in the office if you like."

"No," she said. "I must be going. I left the answering service on, but I can't be gone too long. The boss doesn't like it."

"It was nice seeing you again."

"Yes. It was nice seeing you. You must stop by one day."

"I will."

She left the office and disappeared. Joe was the first one to speak. "Wow, what a doll. Where do you know her from?"

"You know that guy Entrante? That's his secretary."

"With a secretary like that, who needs work?"

"What about Rebeca? You forget her?"

"Of course not. Rebeca is Doll Number 1. That other one is Doll Number 2."

They laughed. Aldo stood up and got ready to leave.

"We'll be out on the road for a good three hours," he said to Rebeca. "After Holmestead, we have to go see Ralph."

"Yes. We're picking up some new markets in Hollywood," Joe added happily.

Rebeca shook her head as she watched them leave. There was something about these two, she thought, something she couldn't describe but which she had never seen before. Everything was flawless, smooth, automatic. They made things happen right before one's eyes. The new accounts with Grand Union were coming in such massive quantity that they simply could not keep up. She had been forced to come in on Saturdays to maintain order in the office. She would have quit her other job and work more hours for Aldo. He had told her he would give her more hours, and he had agreed with her decision to come in on Saturdays.

"You guys think you can handle Hollywood?" Ralph asked from his chair. They met only once since their meeting on Christmas. But he had given Aldo and Joe plenty to do in the last few days. They had struggled but they had made all their deliveries. He wondered how they had done it and what they were doing. He liked their determination.

"We can handle anything," Aldo replied.

"We will see about that. Three busy markets in Hollywood. I'm talking busy now. At least half a trailer every day for each. How do you like that?"

"Not a big deal," Joe said. "Gee, Ralph, I thought you were going to give us a large number. Half a trailer a day? That's a joke."

"That would be for a week. If the managers are happy, we'll give you the rest. All Hollywood. Now, let's talk price."

He waived the men to sit down, and they all looked at the paperwork Ralph spread in front of them. Ralph could finagle his way through any tough bargainer and had not made way up the bumpy ladder of success easily. He was pushing Joe and Aldo pretty hard, knowing they were still new, and what he offered them was pure gold. They would not pass up the opportunity and would sacrifice profit just to get in.

They came up with a complicated price scale that allowed for reduction for every one hundred pounds, then for five hundred, and so on. After they had negotiated their way through most of the issues, Ralph offered them coffee. Only Joe accepted. Aldo drank a Coca Cola. They agreed to meet in Hollywood two days later.

* * *

Aldo knocked at the door of Entrante's home. Pablo was behind him. It was a breezy night and the wind was fanning the leafs of the coconut trees on the opposite side of the street. It was chilly but it felt good.

A woman answered the door. She was small with rosy cheeks and she smiled at them.

"Good evening," Aldo said. "We're here to see Mr. Entrante."

"Yes," she said. "He's waiting for you. Come in. You must be Aldo, ah?"

"Yes. And this is my friend Pablo."

"It's nice meeting you both. Come in and have a seat. He will be with you in a second."

"I guess you must be his wife?"

"Yes. I am Nelida. I heard much about you. I am glad to meet you. Sit down."

She took them to the small living room and then disappeared down the hallway. Entrante came in wearing a white *guayabera*. His hair was combed over his head to hide his baldness. Felix was with him.

"I'm glad you were able to come. How are you?"

Aldo stood and shook his hand. Pablo followed.

"I'm fine. This is my friend, Pablo."

"Good to meet you, Pablo."

Felix also shook hands with both men. He wore his usual attire, short sleeve shirt and dark slacks.

"I got a message that you wanted to see me as soon as possible," Aldo said to Entrante.

"Yes, I did. Sit down."

Entrante pointed to the sofa behind the men. He pulled the loveseat forward and gestured for Felix to sit down.

"Would you like a drink? Some coffee for you, Pablo?"

"No, nothing. Thank you."

"Your secretary came by and gave me your message."

"Yes, I know. How is your place running?"

"It's running. We're making it."

"Are you able to get the transports you need for your goods?"

"Well, yes. We are working on it."

It was a double-edged question, Aldo thought. It was obvious that Entrante had spent time studying his business. He had probably grilled his secretary after her visit this morning. Aldo was disappointed knowing that Hortencia had spied on him. But it probably was what she was paid for.

"I can help you with that."

"Thank you. We are not yet at a point where we need help. We're making it."

"Well, I want you to remember what I said the last time we met. Anything you need, just call."

"I know, I know."

He turned to Felix. "Tell him," Entrante said.

"Yes," Felix said, shifting his body uneasily on the chair. "Mr. Suarez is out of jail."

Aldo smiled and faked surprise, but it did not fool Entrante.

"And now we must figure how to get him over here, shouldn't we?" Entrante said.

"You mean you haven't yet arranged his visa?"

"He just got out. He contacted us today."

"So what have you done so far to get him papers?"

"I started to work on it today. "He's safe. Staying with some friends," Entrante said. "You don't know who they are do you?"

"No, not exactly," Aldo said. "Wherever he is, he cannot be too safe. Get him over here, whatever the cost."

"There's no cost," Entrante said. He rose from his chair and went to the kitchen without saying a word. He missed not having a maid, so he clumsily took two glasses and poured cognac into them. He took ice from the refrigerator and put some inside each glass. He poured ginger ale into another and carried the glass into the living room. He gave one to Pablo and offered the other to Aldo.

"Suarez is a lucky man," he said as he sat down. "He has many friends."

The rest of the evening was spent in casual conversation, with Entrante making his pitch for a partnership. Aldo saw what he was after and was on guard. Entrante was biding his time. By now he knew Aldo's potential and was waiting like an attack dog for that moment when Aldo would need him. He was only afraid that the moment had already passed. He could kick himself for having missed this young man.

Aldo had anxious moments for the next eight days. It seemed like a dream as he stood at the airport among those waiting for the wide doors to open and reveal their loved ones. The first thing he noticed was her beautiful long jet black hair curving softly around her shoulders. She looked deeply into his eyes and hugged him, putting her head on his chest. Then, Aldo saw Dulce who rushed to greet him. Behind them came Aleida, Mr. Suarez, and his wife.

Aldo's entire family was now out of danger. His biggest mission had been accomplished.

CHAPTER FIFTEEN

"IF NOTHING HAPPENS TODAY, THEN it's over," Puntiel said gloomily from the kitchen.

"It's only the beginning," Felix replied. "You really think that the Americans will let this happen? Before the week is over, Cuba will be invaded. Just watch."

"I can't believe they would let it happen," Pablo echoed.

The two sat drinking coffee at the end of the counter while Puntiel remained inside the kitchen, fidgeting with pots and pans. Aldo sat next to Felix, deep in thought. The last three days had brought turmoil to the growing Cuban community of S. W. 8th Street, or Little Havana, as it was now known. It was April 20, 1961. On the 17 a group of armed Cuban exiles, trained by the Central Intelligence Agency, had successfully landed on the southern coast of Cuba. The move had been widely

anticipated by most emigrants, as was the inevitable American invasion that everyone thought would follow. But Castro's regime had rallied and fought back the invaders, corralling them into the area's swamps and virgin jungles. The news stations had not yet broadcast what everyone knew. The invading force was done for. Without reinforcements, food and ammunition they had no alternative but surrender. The question in everyone's mind now was where the Americans were at this decisive point. Defeat was hard to admit, but Puntiel spoke about that everyone saw but dared not discuss.

"You're not going to see an American invasion. It's over. This is Castro's biggest victory, don't you see? This is his hour of glory. It's bigger than when he gained power from Batista. The Americans are not going to interfere. They've done what they were going to do. They trained the men, gave them supplies, and sent them on their way. That's it."

There was a silence among the men. It was now past eleven. The small radio on the counter vibrated with the high-pitched voice of the announcer, angrily denouncing Castro and his men, idly mentioning the sleeping American giant that had just witnessed the biggest upset of one group of brave men. The curtain had started to come down.

"Do you believe that, Aldo?" Felix said.

Aldo did not respond and merely nodded. He was tired tonight, not physically but mentally. The last four months had been relentless. His business had grown exponentially and kept going as if on a wild roller coaster. He had a routine now. He and Joe concentrated on bringing additional business, and they always seemed to score. He couldn't explain his success. It was almost second nature. He was happy for his family. He had bought Amanda a beautiful white home in the Southwest Miami area, not far from Puntiel's. His children were in private school, and Amanda drove her own car. It was more than he had ever hoped for but despite it all, Amanda's irrational behavior had now bordered on the unbearable. Last night had been particularly difficult. So before dawn he had arisen, gathered his clothes, and placed them in a supermarket bag. He had gently kissed his children and gotten into his pickup. He wasn't coming back. The news from the island had stirred his emotions. But he was too distressed to form an opinion. He agreed with Puntiel. Puntiel was intuitive, one of the early dinosaurs. One of the gutsy men who had come to a dead town with nothing and opened up shop. One had to trust a man like that.

Aldo's thoughts drifted back to his family. Could a man really fall in love twice? He had loved Amanda like no other. Where had he gone wrong.

He glanced at Pablo who still sought to make a point with Felix. Things had taken on a different course ever since the rest of the family had arrived. Pablo had now divorced Olga. Ana had divorced Blanco. Aleida was still single and worked with them at the warehouse. He knew Pablo had a special interest in one of the two women. At first he thought it was Aleida, the logical choice. But gradually, he discovered how wrong he had been. It was Ana. It had always been and he found it disconcerting. Inside, it saddened him deeply. Somehow it seemed strange to see his best friend with Ana. He had never expected it but he had to show his friend that it was a good choice. Were he in Pablo's shoes, he would have done the same. There was no better woman than she. However, he felt very hurt about it although he told no one.

He looked at his watch and got up. It was now near midnight. "I will see you in the morning, Pablo," he said.

"Wait," Pablo said. "I'm leaving with you."

"No, I'll see you at the warehouse tomorrow."

"I'm leaving right now. Let me walk you."

"Stay, stay. Let me know what happened tomorrow."

He turned towards them and shook their hand. Puntiel came from the kitchen and followed Aldo to the door.

"Stop for lunch tomorrow, ah?"

"I will, for breakfast."

"Sleep a little late tomorrow. You need it. I'll save you some milk and coffee the way you like it."

"Okay, friend."

Aldo drove his pickup to S. W. 2nd Street and stopped by a duplex. He parked on the dirt shoulder and took out his bag. He went to the unit on the left. A dim light shone on a modest single door. Aldo knocked twice. He could hear the low sound of a television set inside. He heard footsteps by the door and then his aunt's cautious voice.

"Who is it?" She said.

"It's me, Aldo."

"Aldo?"

She fumbled a bit with the double lock. She took the chain off its groove and turned the knob.

"What are you doing here? What happened?" She said as she opened the door.

"I would like to spend the night. Can I stay?"

"What a question? Come in. What happened?"

"Nothing much."

She wore a white night gown, and her grey hair was unpinned. The only light in the room came from a ceiling fixture in the kitchen. Her face was barely visible, but Aldo could see her expression of concern. He closed the door behind him.

"Are you all right?"

"I'm fine. I want to take a shower. You're listening to the radio, ah?"

"It must have been pretty bad for you to leave, Aldo. Are the kids okay?"

"They're fine. I talked to them this evening."

"And how is she?"

"Upset."

"Did you eat?" she asked, changing the subject.

The years had taught her that husband and wife problems must be handled like glass. The less one said, the better. So she decided she would let him tell her if he really wanted to. But she knew him well enough to know he wouldn't. She would have to surmise on her own. She went through the small hallway, passing the kitchen on the left, and stopped at the bathroom where she turned the light on for him. She took a towel from the cabinet and a new bar of soap.

"Bathroom is ready. Go take a bath. I'll make some soup for you."

He didn't answer. He went into the bathroom bringing his bag. She watched from the kitchen as she filled a pot with water, peeled two potatoes, cut them, and placed them inside. Then she added some noodles and chicken breast. She emptied the mixture inside a pressure cooker and placed it on a burner.

She wanted for nothing. Aldo had rented this unit for her as soon as she had arrived. She had no income except what he gave her, and give her he always did. He had bought her new furniture and all the amenities she could ever want: telephone, television, radio, clothes. As she thought of these things, she suddenly began to cry. If he was hurting, she was hurting. too. But she must remain neutral. She pulled herself together, wiping her tears on the lapel of her gown. As the hissing sound of the pressure cooker came on, she took a large plate from one of the cabinets and brought it to the table. She placed a spoon and knife next to it. She cut up some bread in thin slices and put them in another plate. This was how she had made Aldo his supper years ago when he lived with her. That was when he had met Amanda. She had never approved of the wedding, but of course, she had kept it to herself.

* * *

Aldo was barely seventeen, she remembered. It was late, and he was still not back from the gym. She kept her front door closed at all times, unlike some of the neighbors who kept theirs ajar. She was boiling some water to make coffee when she thought she heard a knock and stopped for a moment. She heard it again. Whoever was there must be very timid, she thought. She wiped her hands on her apron and went into the living room. It was dark, so she turned on the light, and opened the front door. Two young girls dressed in the brown uniform of St. Teresa Catholic School stood on the sidewalk, looking up at her. One was taller than the other. She was an astonishingly beautiful girl with sensuous lips and long, wavy black hair. The other one was and wore her hair in a pony tail. She had a small round face and a tiny nose. She spoke first.

"Is Aldo home?"

"No, not yet."

"Are you his aunt?"

"Yes. And who are you girls?"

"I'm Amanda, and this is my sister Ana."

"What is your last name?"

"Diaz."

"Where do you girls live?"

"Vista Hermosa," Amanda said.

"That's very nice. Well, you're welcome to come in if you like."

"No, we can't" the other girl said. "We have to be home by 6:00, and I'm not sure which bus to take back."

Dulce liked her at once. She sounded mature and she smiled when looking at her. She hoped that if one of them was involved with her nephew, it would be her.

"Ah, I will show you where to go."

"Can you give this to Aldo," the girl named Amanda said, taking an envelope from inside her book.

It would have been improper for a young girl of that era to drop off letters in a man's house. Anyone else might have thought ill of her. But Dulce was not priggish, and she took the envelope, somewhat disappointed that the other girl had not given it to her.

"Please don't tell anyone we were here except Aldo," Amanda said.

"How old are you?"

"Fifteen. Well, not really, almost."

The other girl smiled at Dulce and rolled her eyes. Dulce liked her even more.

"Let me show you," Dulce said. "You go down to the corner and make a left. Then walk to the next corner by the back of the church, and there you will see the bus stop."

"Do you know which route goes to Vista Hermosa."

"Maybe I should take you girls there. It's getting dark."

"Oh, no," Ana said. "Really, it's not necessary."

"No, wait," Dulce said. "Let me call someone."

"Please don't. We'll be all right," Ana insisted.

Dulce ignored her and went to the house next door. She brought a boy of about ten by the hand.

"Show them the bus stop and stay with them until they get on it. Make sure they get on the right bus. Ask the attendant at the shop at the corner which bus goes to their home."

The boy nodded, eager at the prospect of showing two older girls around in his neighborhood. Dulce bid the girls goodbye and watched the three of them go around the corner. She went inside and placed the envelope on the dining room table. She looked at the handwriting on the envelope. It read: "To Aldo Ochoa, E.S.M.," meaning "in your hands." They were small letters, and she could visualize the younger girl writing them. She would let Aldo see it and wait for him to tell her who she was.

* * *

Her thoughts were interrupted by Aldo. He stepped quietly into the living room, wearing a white undershirt and black shorts. His hair was wet and combed back.

"So you're listening to the news, eh?"

"It's terrible, Aldo," she said. "I can't believe those poor men. I cannot believe the Americans will do nothing."

He sat on her rocking chair and tiredly leaned his head back. She watched him. He showed no signs of aging despite the rough past two years. He was still very muscular and could have passed for a weight lifter. She saw a lot of his father in him.

"I'm afraid it's bad," Aldo said. "I'm not sure the Americans will interfere."

"Come and drink your soup. It's ready. Or do you want me to bring it to you?"

"No, it's all right. I'll come."

He went to the kitchen and sat down at her small table. There was no dining room in the apartment. She sat across from him and watched him.

"I guess you are wondering why I'm here. Amanda has gotten unbearable since her father died. She lives in the past and is miserable most of the time. She blames me for her father's death. She blames me for having had to come here. I guess she blames me for everything, even Castro. I left this morning after a long night of hearing her whine. I need some sleep. I am going to miss Frank and the girls though."

"The children can come to see you here," Dulce said.

"Yes, I guess you're right. This soup is great. Just like you used to make it when I was a kid."

She looked at him and said nothing. What could she do to help? Probably not much, but inside she seethed. How dare Amanda blame Aldo for her wretched father? Aldo was a saint to have stayed with her all these years. She didn't deserve him. As far as the old man was concerned, he should have died years ago. She controlled her anger and waited for him to speak but he said no more about it.

"You can sleep in my bed tonight," she said. "I'll sleep on the sofa. I want to listen to the news."

"No. I'll sleep on the sofa. I am not going to kick you out of your bed."

"It's a sofa bed, you know. It's all right, believe me. You go and sleep inside in the bedroom. You need it. I'll be comfortable here."

He quietly ate his soup. Some things just didn't change. They listened to the speaker on the radio forecasting what he viewed as the inevitable fall of Castro. The reason, he said, was that the Cuban people would rise. They would now recognize the sacrifice of their compatriots from Brigade 2506 who had come to set the example, and they would take to the streets. It didn't matter that the Americans hadn't come. That was another issue for another day. But now was a decisive moment. The people must act. He went on to issue a call to the people of Cuba to rise and fight for their freedom.

"Do you always listen to this station?"

"Yes. La Fabulosa. It's a new Spanish station. It has good programs."

"What about the television? Do you watch it much?"

"No, not really. Only some of the evening programs."

"I think one of the guys behind this station is a man I know. Entrante."

"Who is he?"

"A businessman. Probably involved with some of the exiles who are behind the invasion too."

"What did he do in Cuba?"

"He was a banker and a politician. An unscrupulous, wealthy wretch, but a shrewd one."

"People like him are what caused us to be here."

"I agree."

"You want to go to sleep? Go. Can you sleep late tomorrow?"

"Pablo and Joe are going to be looking for me early. I have to call Pablo and let him know where I am. Let me use your telephone."

"It's in the living room by the television."

She stood near the radio while Aldo made his call. The speaker's oratory was now a high- pitched, emotional speech appealing to the masses to support the invasion. Aldo dialed. The voice on the other end sounded drowsy.

"Did I wake you?"

"No. I'm listening to the news."

"I'm over at Dulce's. I am going to stay here."

There was a long pause at the other end. Pablo had expected it but did not ask why.

"I'll see you there in the morning then. Go to sleep. You need it."

"All right. Good night."

He hung up the receiver and went back to the kitchen. Dulce had gone inside to make his bed. He drank a glass of water and went to the bedroom. She had turned on a small lamp. A blue lay over the right side of the bed. She turned the air conditioner on as he came in.

"Thank you, Dulce. This is great."

She came over and hugged him. She still thought of him as a young boy.

"Sleep well, my boy. Don't worry. Everything will be fine."

"I guess," he said and went to bed.

She closed the bedroom door. He could hear the static of the radio dying down as she lowered the volume. His legs ached. He had been up since 5:00 A.M. It had been a day of tribulation during which he had thought about his life and family. It was not like him to debate issues as he had done today. For the most part, his decisions had always been quick and accurate. If asked to what he attributed his success, he would have said intuition and luck. The energy his mind had expended had left him weak, and he was exhausted and ready for sleep. He thought about the next day. He could probably sleep late. Pablo would be at the warehouse early. He relaxed, thinking about his old friend and Joe.

Aldo lived on 15th Terrace S.W., which was lined with neat ranch homes, kelly green lawns, and chain link fences. His house was in the middle of the block. The garage was shrouded in ivy, setting it apart from the rest of the houses. There were three bedrooms and two bathrooms. Half the backyard was taken up by an in-ground swimming pool, fenced for privacy. The family had moved in just a month ago and they couldn't seem to get enough of swimming and watching their new big screen T.V. The sun was setting when they heard the sound of a car pull into their driveway. The twins craned their necks from the water to see who the visitor was. They gave up and called Amanda.

"Mom, someone's here," one said.

"Let me see who it is," Frank said.

As the boy opened the sliding glass door open, Amanda got up from the reclining chair in the house's recreation room from which she had been watching the children.

She looked through the peephole and saw Ana's face.

"Hello," she said as she opened the door.

"Hello," Ana responded.

Ana and Aleida had lived with them until Aldo had purchased this house. The two sisters had since rented a unit in a duplex near Dulce's apartment and were both working for Aldo. Amanda had been told about Ana and Pablo's romance. She first had seemed indifferent about it but then seemed to develop a coolness towards her sister.

"Where are the kids?" Ana asked.

"They're in the back swimming. Come in. Want something to drink?"

"No."

"Did you just leave work?"

"Yes. Aleida still had things to do," Ana said.

"And how are you?"

"Good."

They went inside. Although the house was not still fully decorated, it was attractive and comfortable. There were wooden figures of old men displayed on shelves in the hallway. The kitchen was open and flanked by counter. The Florida room, which connected with the kitchen, was paneled in oak. Ana opened the sliding door to the yard and went outside to greet the children. Amanda laid back on her reclining chair. Ana came back, looking grave.

"Well?" Amanda said as she pulled herself up. "You've come to talk about Aldo, I'm sure. Aren't you happy?"

Ana gave her sister a wooden look and walked toward the sofa but remained standing.

"What do you have to complain about Aldo, idiot? Tell me, what?"

Amanda now stood up and smiled ironically at her sister. "Of course," she said, "you find no fault in him. That's because you've always been in love with him. You think I don't know that?"

"Who cares what you think? The reason that he is not here is because you don't know how to treat him. You've never known how. I've come to warn you that you better you had get him back before it's too late then you regret it for the rest of your life."

"Oh, yeah? And who's going to take him, I wonder? Could it be you, by any chance? You don't think I believe that little farce you cooked up with Pablo, do you? You want to make Aldo jealous, don't you?"

"Shut up and listen to what I'm telling you. You bring Aldo back to this house now. You know what burns me about you is that you are so stubborn and never learn. All those years that have gone by, and you haven't learned a thing. What has he done to you? Tell me, what? You don't seem to realize that he's put up with you all those years when nobody else would."

"I can never forgive him for hurting my father."

"Aldo? Hurt our father? Give me a break. Our father had no right to treat Aldo like an outcast as he did all his life because Aldo was from a farming family. Our father was lucky that Aldo still spoke to him afterwards. You just never saw it because you were blinded by him and still are. You are just like him."

"How dare you blaspheme my father?"

"I'm speaking the truth, and you know it."

"You, you hurt him too. You did nothing but hurt him after you and your crazy husband gave up your possessions. You think that didn't hurt him? I'll never forget that."

"God rest his soul," Ana said and paused, "but all he cared about was money. And you're just like him. This is your downfall."

"And you don't care about money? You, who are supposed to be so humble? Why is it that you married a rich man then, ah? And how about now? You're only after Pablo because of money. You don't love him. You love Aldo. That's who you're really after. You've been after him all your life. Well, now it's your chance. Go get him, go!"

The two women stood perilously close to each other. Ana had remained calm listening to her sister, but her face was now red with anger. Angrily, Amanda shoved her sister back. It wasn't a hard push, but it was enough to fuel Ana's fury.

"Shut up," Ana yelled.

Her silky hair swayed as she slapped her sister on the cheek with her open palm. Amanda flinched, covering her face with her hand. Her mouth hung open as if she couldn't believe what had just happened. Neither said a word. Ana turned away and walked out of the house. Hearing the car engine outside, the children rushed inside to look for their aunt. They found their mother sobbing on the sofa.

* * *

Joe was sitting in the office, trying his jokes on Rebeca. Pablo had just exited the cabin of an eighteen wheeler. He came in the office and put his clipboard down.

"Where's Aldo?" He asked Rebeca.

"He's somewhere in the back. Shall I page him?"

"No, I'll get him."

Aldo was standing by a desk, in the rear of the building. A man on a forklift was unloading large crates from the trailer as Aleida sat behind the desk, reading the orders to him. Pablo approached and tapped him on the shoulder.

"Are you going anywhere else today?" he asked.

"No," Aldo replied. "Joe and I are going to Tampa in the morning so I've got to leave early."

"Will you be at Puntiel's later?"

"If I need to be, I can."

"Can we meet there for dinner?"

"I'll see you there. Where are you going now?"

"I've got to back for a run."

Aleida looked at the two men as they spoke. Despite everything that had happened, she had remained neutral between her sisters and hoped they could be a family again but when Ana refused to return to work at the warehouse, she knew why. As she watched Pablo rush out of the building to catch his next trip, her heart sank thinking about any possible friction he and Aldo. The two men had been like brothers and comrades in war. Nothing could break that bond. Maybe, it was time for her to have a talk with Amanda.

South west 8th Street had changed considerably since Aldo's arrival in Miami. The neighborhood had gone from a few sparse, tiny stores to a busy strip of large variety shops and restaurants operated by Cuban entrepreneurs who had defied the odds by moving in. The neighborhood was undergoing dramatic changes, moving, for the most part, from a quiet residential community to a thriving business center. Homeowners like Joe were on the way out, seeking peace and quiet in the high rises of Miami Beach or other suburban areas. Joe himself had put his duplex on the market after Aldo moved out and no longer needed to rent Aldo's old unit. He had hit the jackpot with Aldo and now looked forward to quiet evenings at home, which was no longer possible in the southwest area.

Aldo and Joe sat on one of the stools of Puntiel's restaurant. Aldo looked at his watch and turned to Joe.

"You should leave. We have to go by 4:00 A.M."

"I think I will, Aldo. I have to look after Maureen. She's not feeling well again."

The old man put on his baseball cap and took one last sip of his coffee. His wife's health worried him. She was the only reason why he went home, and he regretted being away from her for so long during the day, but he needed it for his sanity, too.

Aldo asked the waiter for an orange juice. He drank only fruit juice now and ate moderately. Dinner had been particularly difficult for him over the last two days. His aunt pampered him and always cooked him a big meal that he could not turn down. She kept his plate warm in the stove, no matter what time he came home. He compensated by not eating anything after 4:00 P.M.

"A damned shame for the Americans," the waiter said, "a damned shame."

"It was Kennedy," another man at the counter said.

The waiter was new. After Aldo had left, Puntiel took his time hiring someone else. His wife began coming in the afternoons, and his son returned to work for him part-time, but it again got to be too much, so he had hired Arturo who had just arrived from Cuba.

"He really surprised me," Arturo added. "He really has no guts. How could he leave those men stranded in Cuba? I don't understand what happened. I go over it in my head, and I still don't believe it."

Aldo listened to them in silence. Everyone had a different theory as to what had happened. Most people believed that there was a sinister American plot behind all that had occurred and that in the end, the United States would invade Cuba and wipe Castro from the map which was everyone's belief and hope. Only few realized the truth, but they were widely unpopular and were not heard. Puntiel was one of them. He came in from the kitchen and leaned on the counter while a beep on the radio announced the upcoming news bulletin.

"...and Havana said today that the invaders will be put on trial..." the announcer said.

There was a deep silence in the restaurant as everyone strained to hear the announcement. It was a matter of profound concern to all. Everyone, even Puntiel, hoped that the news had changed in the last hour, that something had happened to cause a change.

The announcer went on describing how most of the men had now been apprehended. It was a huge embarrassment for Washington. President Kennedy had declared that the invasion had been his full responsibility. The question in everyone's mind was, why not go all the way and let other waiting Cubans land in the island. But everything seemed to be at a standstill right now. It seemed incomprehensible that the U. S. government would accept defeat and not take further action. Something must happen.

Puntiel turned away and went back to the kitchen. Aldo saw his frustration. He himself had not had much time to follow the invasion, and most of what he knew he had learned at Puntiel's restaurant.

"Anything new?" Pablo asked, sitting next to him.

"No," Aldo replied. "It sounds like it's over."

"It's hard to believe, isn't it?"

"It's a shocker. But it's clear that the Americans don't want to get involved. One thing is to send Cubans to fight there. Another is to shed your own blood for them. I guess that's the reason."

"There is still something odd about it."

"Yeah, you're right. There is. So, tell me what I already know."

"I know you know," Pablo said, smiling, "but I want to tell you first."

"You don't owe anyone an explanation, Pablo. Do what your heart tells you."

"She's a great woman, Aldo. Doesn't get much better than her."

"You're right," Aldo said brightly, hiding the distress he was feeling at hearing him confirm the news about his wedding to Ana. "You're lucky and you have my blessing. It should have happened many years ago."

He did not recall ever having lied to his friend before, but he must.

"But that's just it, Aldo. I think certain things are meant to happen at certain times in life, eh?"

"Probably," Aldo said.

"I want you to be my best man."

Aldo was not looking at him. He was afraid that if he did he might reveal his feelings.

"Is there going to be a reception?"

"No, only a ceremony."

"When?"

"Next Friday."

"So soon?" Something suddenly told Aldo that the relationship was older than he thought. Perhaps it had been born in Cuba before anyone became aware of it.

"We both want it this way. Will you be there?"

"Of course. Why wouldn't I?"

"Because of Amanda."

"It won't stop me from going."

"Besides, I don't think she'll be there."

"She won't?"

"There's been trouble between them."

"Too bad. What kind of trouble."

"Ana went to see her yesterday, and they argued."

"What about?"

"About you, I think."

"About me?"

"I think Ana was trying to talk some sense into Amanda, trying to get her to understand that she's been wrong. It probably wasn't a good idea to begin with, but she did it. She did it without telling me, and the whole thing got very ugly. Ana stormed out of the house, and I think she and Amanda are no longer speaking. It's a real shame. She did not show up for work today. She doesn't want to go back."

"Why?"

"I think she feels uncomfortable."

Aldo gazed intently at the coaster in front of him. He wondered what was going through Ana's head right now. Was she really in love with Pablo? He shunned gossip and chatty talk, but he wished he could have heard the two sisters' heated encounter.

"Tell Ana to come back," Aldo said. "There's no reason to feel uncomfortable about anything. Don't you agree?"

"Why don't you talk to her? She'll listen to you."

"Bring her in tomorrow."

"No. You'll have to come over her place."

Aldo hesitated a moment, but it was no use, he would have to face her sooner or later. "Then I will," he said quickly. "And, make sure you are off for after the wedding. Honeymoon is on me."

Aldo rose and left two quarters on the table. He leaned forward to make himself heard in the kitchen and said good night to Puntiel. The poor man's spirits were down. Then he turned to Pablo. "I will follow you."

"In your antique?"

"Yes, in my antique."

"Hey, Aldo," Arturo said from behind the counter. "Will you sell me your old pickup? Surely you can afford something better now."

"It brings me luck. The day I get rid of that truck, I'm done for."

Arturo laughed and said good night. As Aldo and Pablo left the restaurant, Aldo saw the Thunderbird he had bought his wife. He did not mention it to Pablo but walked slowly to his pickup which was parked a short distance from the restaurant. If she was going to make a move to talk to him, she would probably do it now. She did not.

Aldo followed Pablo. Pablo's car was a beautiful black 1958 Buick that Aldo had helped him pick out. The car was so polished that it shone under the street lights. They both shared a passion for vintage cars. Aldo had grown attached to his 1949 pickup. They teased him wherever he went, but those who knew him understood the reasons. Aldo was a peasant at heart. Despite his driving ambition, deep inside he was humble and could have happily lived his entire life in Rios. But his ambition had double-crossed him, and he now knew that he could never go back to his roots, so he would drive his old pickup and dream about it.

Aldo waited for Pablo to pull out. He looked at the rear-view mirror and saw the T-Bird's round headlights. Amanda was right behind him. He wondered who was watching the kids. The three-car caravan drove by Little Havana. They turned left going north and left into S. W. 2nd Street. Two blocks from Dulce's duplex, Pablo parked on the road's dirt shoulder. Aldo followed. The lights of the T-Bird were still behind him. The car slowed down, then abruptly gained speed and overtook them.

Pablo was already standing in the driveway when Aldo got out of the pickup. Ana's car was gone.

"Is she not here?" Aldo asked.

"She's here. Aleida took her car."

Pablo knocked on the louvered door. The moon was out and the night fresh and breezy. Aldo stood quietly behind his friend, waiting. A light came on, and they saw Ana's face peer out. As she opened the door, the moonlight shone on her face, and she looked more beautiful than ever.

"Hello, I didn't expect you this late," she said to Pablo. She had not noticed Aldo.

"Aldo is here with me."

"Aldo? Ah, Aldo, hello." She was startled to see him.

"Come in, come in," she said to both.

They stepped inside. It was a standard unit with two bedrooms. The small living room was furnished simply with a sofa, two chairs, and a recliner. The only light in the room came from a pole lamp. There was a small television set on the far wall.

"What a surprise, Aldo, I did not expect you."

"I heard the good news, and I came to congratulate you."

She paused for a few seconds, caught off guard and her face reddened slightly.

"Pablo told you?"

"Yes. And I'm very happy for you. I want to tell you that you have no business being uncomfortable about anything. Why should you? Come back to work, all right?"

"All right," she said softly.

"I plan to be at the wedding next week, so you better save a seat for me."

"It's just you and Aleida."

"We'll have a good time just the same."

She stood before them, hands crossed, looking at the floor. Then she lifted her head and fixed her eyes upon Aldo. "I'm sorry," she said.

A tear rolled down her cheek. Aldo put his arms around her and patted her shoulder. Her words had a double meaning that Aldo caught instantly.

"No need to be," he said. "Just be happy. You should be happy."

Then he let go off her and shook Pablo's hand.

"This is the best news I've had in years," he said walking away. "You guys really know how make one happy."

He turned the pickup around and drove a block to Dulce's duplex. He noticed the Thunderbird parked at the edge of the road and parked two car lengths from it. As he closed the driver's door, Amanda came walking towards him, her face hidden by the darkness.

"Aldo, it's me," she said gently. "Amanda."

"I know," he answered.

He could see Dulce's oak door, bathed in the porch light she always left on for him. He wondered if she might be watching them.

"Aldo, how could you?" Amanda asked passionately, her voice breaking. "How could you leave your home and your whole family without even a warning?"

"Everyone has a breaking point, Amanda. I reached mine. Where are the children now?"

"Aleida is home with them. But how could you? How could you leave us like that?"

She was now sobbing gently. She came closer, looking intently into his eyes.

"It's the best way, Amanda. I will see the children as often as I can, but it all has to stop somewhere. You can't go on blaming me forever. Make your own life from now on."

"But I can't. I never could without you."

"Amanda, that's what you say now. That's what you always say. But you're not going to change. I am the target of your frustrations, Amanda. It doesn't have to be this way. It can't be. We both deserve to be happy. This is best for both of us. It's a hard choice, but really it has to be. I'm sorry that you're upset, but you have to be strong. Life will go on."

"No, it won't. It can't," she said raising her voice.

"Think about our beautiful children, Amanda. They need you. Go on, go home. They're waiting for you."

"You came before them. You can't leave me."

"I'm not leaving you but we can't be together anymore. We aren't good for each other. It'll be hard at first, but time will heal the wounds. Go on, go home, ah?"

"I'll go if you take me," she said, sobbing helplessly.

"I can't take you. I can follow you to make sure you make it all right."

She did not answer. She just stood there silently in the darkness and reached for him. He pulled slightly back, grabbing her wrists.

"No, come on. You must go. Come on, get in your car."

He gently eased her arms down. She began to cry. He took her by the shoulders and turned her toward her car. With his arm around her, and she leaning her head toward him, they walked to her car. He opened the T-bird's door and handed her in.

"I want you to promise me that you're coming home," she said.

He did not answer. He was going to shut the door but she stopped him.

"No. I won't go until you promise. You have to."

He still didn't answer but pushed on the door to close it. "I will follow you. Come on. Let's go."

He went back to his pickup, got in, and turned on the engine. He waited for her car to ease slowly onto the road and stayed close behind her. Aldo could see the house from a distance. He would have loved to stop and see the children but knew it would only antagonize Amanda at this moment. He truly did not want to hurt her. The wounds must heal on their own.

As she pulled into the garage, he stepped on the gas and went by her. She rolled down her window in time to see the truck, but she could not see him. She held onto the steering wheel and cried. She stayed in the car alone for several minutes, crying helplessly. She did not dare think that it was over. It could not be. Tomorrow she would call him for lunch. He would come over before the children were home, and they would be together again, just like old times, and she would be his figurine.

Dulce rocked in front of the television set. *This is a critical time*, she thought. She had witnessed the scene from the safety of the small kitchen window. She had expected scenes like these, and she watched anxiously as her nephew dealt with the situation. She looked only at him. She knew what Amanda was up to, but she was not sure how he would react. Would he fall for it again? She could not interfere, no matter how painful. She wanted very much to protect him, but only he could help himself. When she saw him embrace her and walk her to the car, her heart sunk. *She is doing it again. That devil's daughter,* she thought, then reproached herself for thinking this way of the late Guillermo. God forgive him for his sins. But yes, he had been a devil and Amanda was just like him.

Dulce saw her sobbing and laughed to herself. *They are crocodile tears*, she thought. Amanda did not love Aldo. She was in love with her position, something she thought only she and her family had. It was no way to live, thinking one was something special. And what about Aldo? Dulce could never understand it. Theirs had been a huge mismatch, yet they had managed to live together for all those years. At what price, she didn't know.

Dulce saw him get into his pickup and drive after Amanda's car and did not know what to make of it. Was he coming back? She let go of the curtain and went quietly back to her living room, turned the set on, and sat down on her rocking chair. It got pretty lonely at night. She missed her neighbors and her trips to the market. It was not the same here and she had been elated when Aldo had moved in. It brought all the good memories back, and she tried desperately to remind herself that he could not stay. So she suffered alone, waiting for that inevitable moment when her nephew would leave again.

She was so deep in thought that she was startled when she heard the door open.

"Did I scare you? I'm sorry. I guess you didn't expect me back after that, ah? Well, I'm back," Aldo said.

She was embarrassed by his comment, knowing that she had spied on him and that he knew it. Slowly, she smiled. She was so happy he had prevailed over Amanda.

"I'll get your dinner now. Go take a bath."

Joe and Aldo's decision to go to Tampa was an ambitious one. Tampa was far from Miami, yet they considered it only another big city, like Orlando and Jacksonville. The two men had never been afraid of taking on new business. They had now synchronized their operation. As soon as a deal was made, Pablo took over the mechanics of delivering the goods. He would hire the men they needed. Transportation was now handled by Red who had given up his shop in Hialeah to become their full-time, in-house supervising mechanic. Rebeca followed through with the customers by phone, with Aldo making the initial call. It had become a close-knit network made up of a few trusted people. Their success had been tremendous.

Aldo drove Joe's 1956 Chevy on the expressway out of Miami. He was the only one who had sat behind its wheel but even he could not escape Joe's suspicious eye. The lightest departure from the center of the road or an abrupt turn could set him off with warnings to be careful. As they left the outskirts of the city and got on the Florida Turnpike, Aldo set the speed at 60 miles per hour. They traveled smoothly and entered Tampa around 10:00 A.M. and Joe took over, telling Aldo where to turn and where to stop. They met their man at the office of a market chain. Ralph had arranged the meeting. Joe and Aldo sat across the manager's desk. He was definitely an office man. Despite the heat, he wore a jacket and high collar, and he talked softly to them as he reclined in his chair. Why should he buy their product? What did they have to offer his company that other local distributors did not? The biggest hurdle seemed to be that Joe and Aldo were from out of town. The fact that their business came from Miami made it suspicious in his eyes.

Aldo learned a great deal from the meeting. One had to know one's territory and competitors. One never came onto someone else's territory without knowing how competitors there operated. It was apparent that the area was highly dependent on the local distributors who offered the markets a long tradition of low prices and fast service. It would be a hard nut to break. How could they surpass such service from so many miles away? He had given the man a theoretical answer but not the right one, he knew. The obvious answer and only answer was that they could not compete with the others unless they started a new operation in this area. And he wasn't sure they were ready for it.

With these thoughts in mind, Aldo went back onto the Florida Turnpike. They had not made a deal, but they hadn't failed. Joe promised him they would be back and take the town by storm as they had done in Miami, but Aldo had other ideas. This time Joe was wrong. They would never get off the ground in Tampa or any other far away city unless they first scouted the area and set up shop there. He let Joe talk until it seemed that he would never shut up. By then they were back in Miami. They had not stopped for lunch, and it was now late afternoon, so Aldo made it a point to stop in Hialeah.

"Why Hialeah? What's there?" Joe asked.

"There's a nice little strip of Cuban stores in the area that I would like to see."

"I thought you were hungry, buddy."

"I am. Let's go for Cuban food."

"Oh, no. I can't stand the coffee."

"Then ask for American coffee."

They drove to Palm Avenue and stopped at a small restaurant. Palm Avenue was a one-way street, splitting east from west, widely traveled and beginning to show signs of commercial life. Aldo had heard about it. The small Cuban shops that had opened up in the area had their work cut out. They were away from the stiff competition of their compatriots' businesses in the Southwest, but they also did not have the patronage of the growing Cuban population in that area. In a way, it was a new culture shock to be dealt with.

Aldo and Joe walked in through the front glass door. To their left was a small counter, open to the sidewalk, where several people gathered smoking cigars and drinking coffee. Aldo and Joe got a table inside. A waiter brought two menus in Spanish, and Aldo asked him for one in English for Joe. As the waiter went into the back, Aldo looked behind Joe and saw a tall brunette with large penetrating green eyes and an innocent smile. She was dressed in the restaurant's black and white uniform. She came over to their table to bring them water and courteously asked them if they were ready to order.

"My friend here needs a menu," Aldo said. "In English. He doesn't speak Spanish"

"I'll see that he gets one," she said.

She turned away to go back inside. Joe winked at Aldo and smiled. It had been a long time since he had looked at another woman. With a few exceptions during his teens, Amanda had been his only love. He had loved her, had given her his youth and all the best he had to give. He had gotten used to married life and knew no other. Thinking about another woman, he felt clumsy.

"It's none of my business," Joe began, "but as a friend, I must ask you, are you and your wife having trouble?"

"Yes."

"Anything that I can do to help?"

"I don't think so," Aldo said.

"Why don't you give it a while, ah? These things have a tendency to flare up and then die down. I tell you from experience."

"Okay," Aldo said, taking the menu from the waitress. He spoke to her in Spanish. "Can you bring him some American coffee?" He's dying for a cup."

"He's American," she said looking at him for the first time.

"Yes. And I am Cuban, like you."

"I know," she said shyly.

Like many other families, Mercedes's life had been torn apart by the latest political events in Cuba. She had been forced to flee the country with her two small boys while her husband had been incarcerated for alleged treason to the revolution. The rest of her family stayed behind. Arriving in Miami without hardly any money, she had gone from job to job and had started as a waitress in this small restaurant. She was a beautiful woman who had never, worked before and was unaccustomed to the advances of the men around her. But she had learned how to deal with it and had found a sympathetic employer who understood her situation. She had been lucky. She worked to support her two sons and never, during the year she had been in the United States, had looked at another man. She waited to be reunited with her husband.

Aldo and Joe ate their late lunch while discussing their Tampa meeting. It was now close to 4:00 P.M., and they had been away from the warehouse all day. Aldo went to a public phone booth near the entrance and called his office.

"Aleida," he said, "We are now in Hialeah. We should be there in about a half hour. Any problems?"

"Some," she replied, "But Pablo is here. Some trailers didn't arrive today, and we are short. Rebeca has a list of things for you. I guess you'll see it when you get here."

"You want me to speak to her now?"

"Yes, but wait. Amanda has been calling. She wants you to call her back."

"Can I ask you a favor?" he said, ignoring the comment. "Can you ask her if she'll let the children visit with you tonight so I can see them."

"Sure. I'll do that."

"Now, connect me with Rebeca."

They talked about the events of the day. Outside of Pablo and Joe, she had become his most trusted employee. She could fill in for him with such efficacy that he seldom had to dwell with a problem after his return from a trip. She was more than just a secretary. She could handle any customer, no matter how difficult, and any emergency that came their way. She was as gifted as men like Entrante and Puntiel, ambitious, driven, dependable.

"Let's go," Aldo said to Joe as he came back to the table. "They want us at the warehouse."

"Problems?"

"Nothing serious."

Aldo placed a dollar bill under his glass for the waitress. She was at another table taking an order. She felt his gaze on her but did not acknowledge it. Although she found him attractive, it was taboo to even think about him. She would never deceive her imprisoned husband even in her thoughts.

The following Friday, Aldo and Joe entered Miami's town hall followed by Joe's wife, Maureen. Aldo and Joe both wore suits. Maureen wore a blue silk dress. The humid afternoon made their clothes sweaty. It had been a long time since Aldo had worn a tie, but the occasion called for one. He was the best man in Pablo's wedding. It seemed all like a dream but it was real. Pablo and Ana were getting married.

Joe led the way. He had been in this old building many times and knew his way around. He pushed the creaky mahogany door open. There were some benches lined in front of a reception window with a door on the side. There were several other people filling out forms. Joe went to the window and announced that some of the wedding party had arrived.

"Let me know when everyone is here," said a woman wearing glasses from behind the window. "Can't do anything until everyone has arrived, sir."

"Well, we're here. We might be getting married, too, if someone is available."

"All right," she said, acknowledging his humor, "but that is not on the calendar, sir. You have to call and schedule it first."

"I first have to divorce my wife."

"You might just have to, if you keep talking that way."

"I will sit down and be a good boy, okay?"

"Very well, sir."

Aleida, Ana, and Amanda, came in a few minutes later. Aleida and Amanda wore tight, knee-length dresses and high heels. They each wore bouffant hairdos and pearls around their necks. The children came behind them and all three ran excitedly toward their father when they saw him. Behind them came Pablo with Dulce who wore an elegant blue dress and flowers pinned to her chest. Since Pablo did not have a mother, it was appropriate that she present the groom as her son. She had, after all, acted as his mother all his life. Last came the bride, wearing a white satin dress with long sleeves, high-necked collar, and a white veil. Her beautiful black hair was loose around her shoulders. Streams of small yellow and white flowers had been pinned to it, and she looked dazzling. She carried a large bouquet of flowers.

They all rose when she entered. She had obviously waited for Pablo and Dulce to enter the room. This was her moment. Aldo and Joe stood up. Joe, always the gallant, rushed over to kiss the bride's hand.

"You are the most beautiful bride I have ever seen," he said.

Maureen, slowly got to her feet, embraced her, and kissed her cheek.

"God bless you Ana. You look beautiful."

The old wrinkled lady stepped back and nodded in approval as she stared at Ana's wedding dress. Then Aldo came forward and hugged Ana. She put her arms around him, holding her bouquet tightly in one hand.

Joe went to the window and announced to the attendant that the wedding party had arrived. The woman looked at the bride through the glass then disappeared inside. The side door opened, and she allowed them all to come in. They went through a large room filled with cubbyholes and desks. The woman led them into a room in the back where they were met by a uniformed police officer and the judge, dressed in his black robe, sitting behind a large desk.

"Good morning, and welcome," the judge said in a hoarse voice. "I guess I don't need to ask who the bride is but I do need to ask who the groom might be."

Joe broke out laughing and the others followed.

"Oh, we all want to be grooms with such a pretty bride."

"Yes, I'll say," agreed the judge. "Okay. Well, I'm delighted to see you all, and I hope that you will have a good ceremony and that you have good memories of these chambers where many people have been married before. Now, let's see."

He put on a pair of reading glasses and shuffled through some papers until he found what he wanted. He began reading the names.

"Ana Diaz, is that you?"

"Yes," Ana said.

"Okay, good," the judge said smiling at her. "Now, who's Pablo?"

"I am," Pablo said.

"Good, very good. Sergeant," he said to the uniformed police officer in the room, "you want to line them up?"

"Sure."

He walked towards the group and asked Ana to stand next to Pablo. He asked who the witnesses were and had Aldo stand next to Pablo and Aleida next to Ana. Amanda, the children, Maureen, and Dulce stood behind them while Joe positioned himself next to the judge, snapping his Kodak camera.

"Sir, do you have a ring?" the judge asked Pablo.

"Yes."

"Very well," he said. "Take it out and have it ready."

He stood up and began perusing a form. He then began the ceremony by warning the groom and bride about the nature of their commitment. He quickly read the form and then asked the groom to put the ring on the bride's finger. He told them they could kiss and wished them good luck. The officer took out a certificate and asked all four to sign. There was deep silence in the room as each of them signed the document. Then Pablo and Ana kissed again, and they all applauded. The judge stood up and shook hands, first with Ana, then Pablo, Aldo, and Aleida.

"Good luck to you all."

"Good luck," the officer said.

They walked outside together. Aldo held each of his daughters by the hand. Amanda did not talk to him but stayed close by, following him with her eyes. Outside, the group conversed for a short time. It was barely 11:00 A.M. and it already felt oppressively hot. Summer was coming. Aldo watched as Pablo held his bride. It had taken considerable effort on his part to appear normal during the ceremony but now that it was over he could let his feelings go. He would have never dreamed that they would end up this way. He smiled at them as he held Clara and Teresa. He met Ana's gaze briefly. She looked quietly happy.

One by one, they all hugged her and wished her well. Aldo waited his turn and kissed her cheek. She held him and patted his back. Then Aldo embraced Pablo and congratulated him. He brought Frank over and had him shake hands. They all headed for Aleida's apartment where they held a small reception. The groom and bride cut a cake and they all had champagne while Joe took pictures. It was not the type of wedding that Guillermo Diaz would have dreamed of for one of his daughters, but it was a memorable one.

In following weeks, Amanda's calls to Aldo tapered off. Aldo refused to speak to her and instructed Rebeca not to connect her calls unless she was calling about the children. Gradually, Amanda's pride asserted itself as Aldo knew it would. She was hurt, but time was beginning to heal her wounds, and she got her pride back. Her father had taught her and her sisters that purity one did not mix with those born below your social level. There was a reason for this, and to lower one's status was a regression that sooner or later, would be regretted. Aldo had been a peasant. Despite his success, he could never deny his origins. Why should she demean herself? She had borne him three children, and she had caused her father a lifetime of grief with her marriage, something for which she could never forgive herself. It was he who should be chasing her. So, she would wait and let him come to her.

The trouble with her reasoning was that it always came in spurts. Amanda was not consistently rational. Time had proven that. And during her most irrational moments, she might do the opposite of what she may have truly intended. Aldo knew her well. He had been patient. He had loved her, but now he had made his decision, and he never went back on his decisions. Their relationship had not worked. They were not happy. Amanda, especially, had been miserable most of the time. Perhaps she did not know it yet, but he was doing her a favor by leaving her.

The phone rang in and after a brief exchange, Rebeca paged her boss who was somewhere in the warehouse.

"There's a phone call for you," she said curtly.

Aldo picked up the receiver. Frank was standing next to him. The boy was beginning to spend his afternoons after school with his father. The twins came sporadically, but their visits were also increasing. Aldo recognized Hortencia's soft voice.

"I will be leaving in another half hour," she said in Spanish. "Can we meet half way between here and my house?"

"Important?"

"Isn't it always?"

"I can't leave until after 7:00 P.M. I have loads coming in tonight."

"Oh," she said regretfully. "Can't we have dinner together?"

"Yes, later."

"All right," she said, "I guess it'll have to be."

"I'll call you."

He put the receiver down and went back toward the forklift. He climbed in and continued moving crates of boxes from a trailer to the edge of the walk in freezer. A budding romance had developed between the two. Hortencia had not asked Aldo out outright. It would have been improper for a respectable woman of her era, but she made it possible for him to take an interest. How could he not?

He was, after all, separated from his wife, and he was a prize too valuable to waste. She found excuses to call him. Their conversations were business-like at first but gradually became more personal until, almost casually, she met him for dinner. She was deeply infatuated with him. Aldo, on the other hand, did not reciprocate. He lusted after her, but it ended there. He sensed something artificial about her as with her make up and dress. In his mind, she could have well fit the role of Guillermo Diaz's daughter.

Meanwhile Aldo's trips to Hialeah became more frequent. He patronized the restaurant on Palm Avenue every day and became acquainted with his favorite waitress. What attracted him about Mercedes was her unpretentious manner. She was a hard-working woman and very good looking, but she seemed detached and uninterested in any man. Then one day Aldo noticed her distress as she waited on tables. He could tell she had been crying, and he heard one of the waiters quietly tell another that her husband had died. One local radio station in Miami had read her husband's name among others who had recently been executed by the Castro regime. Such announcements were now common as the rebels moved to crush the slightest opposition. The waiters' comments reminded Aldo of his own brush with death while in prison. He had been saved only by Ana's and Pablo's devotion and tenacity.

As he was leaving, Aldo walked up to Mercedes and offered his condolences which she quietly accepted.

"Anything I can do, I'm at your service," he told her.

"Thank you. I appreciate that," she replied and smiled at him.

From that day on, Aldo looked at Mercedes in a different way. She was alone now and her quiet courage reminded him of Ana.

Aldo devoted himself to his work. His only goal was to make his business grow, so he and Joe continued their practice of visiting new markets, no matter how remote, to offer their product. They went back to Tampa three or four times until, in January of 1962, they received word that one food chain was willing to buy their product, insisting only that it be fresh.

Aldo thought about this new opportunity. For days, he and Joe argued the pros and cons. Aldo favored a piecemeal approach in entering the new market, keeping their overhead at a minimum, whereas Joe, always the aggressive salesman, wanted to attack the market as they had in Miami. Finally, they compromised and agreed to rent a warehouse in Tampa. They would start small to test the market.

Early in the spring, they began operating the new warehouse. Although small, it required a large investment of time. Already, Joe and Aldo were spending at least one day of a week in Tampa. But the venture soon paid off. The pair began visiting stores in the Tampa area. Gradually, they built a clientele of medium-sized markets that slowly began placing small orders. This time, they did not have the advantage of Joe's connections in Miami where he knew everyone so they had to rely on Aldo's personality and well-thought-out presentations. The strong young man with the courteous manners always made a good impression on his American hosts. Then he could always count on Joe to carry the conversation with a fast-pitched joke.

The April dawn was breaking in the horizon when Aldo pulled off the expressway on their way out of Miami.

"Where are you going?" Joe asked.

"Let's get a quick breakfast."

"Oh, not again," the old man complained.

"You don't want breakfast, ah?"

"I always want breakfast but that's not really why we're going, is it?"

"I'm hungry."

"You want to see that beautiful Cuban with the green eyes. That's the real reason."

Aldo did not respond. The old man knew of his infatuation. It was written all over Aldo's face. And he couldn't blame him. Mercedes was a beautiful woman and wished he was twenty years younger. She was a decent, hard worker. From the stories Joe had heard, she was also virtuous and never gave the men in the restaurant an inch. Joe wondered how Aldo would break her reserve. Could he? Joe had also heard that Mercedes's husband had been executed in Cuba and he was saddened by it. It was like an old-time war movie, the attractive woman left behind loses her husband in battle while the male predators circle around her. But Aldo was a nice man, and Joe could tell he had more than a passing interest in the green-eyed beauty.

"What do you like," Mercedes asked in broken English as the two men sat on one of the tables by the entrance.

"Me, I want a cup of coffee," Joe said merrily. "My friend here got other ideas, can't you tell?"

She smiled at him while looking down at her order book. Joe marveled at her being hard at work this early. He had learned enough about the Cuban culture to know that this was unusual in their macho society. A woman working? But knowing her circumstances, Joe felt sympathy for her.

"I'll have a coffee with milk and buttered bread," Aldo said in Spanish.

Joe caught them as they exchanged glances. No doubt about it, Joe thought. It was only a matter of time.

"Listen, buddy," Joe said as she walked away, "I'm really sorry about her husband and all but how long do you think she'll mourn? I think she is ready now."

"Oh, Joe," Aldo said shaking his head.

Joe was a nice old man and he could get away with a lot, Aldo thought and was glad Joe was his friend.

"When are going to ask her out? You know, a movie may be? A nice dinner in Miami Beach?"

Aldo said nothing. He merely glanced at Joe as a mischievous boy. Mercedes came back with a cup of black American coffee in a mug.

"Cream?" she asked.

"Yes," Joe replied, "thanks. Listen," he said, "I gotta bring you to our warehouse one of these days so you can teach us how to make some of this coffee. Would you come?"

"What's he saying?" Mercedes asked Aldo in Spanish.

"He wants to bring you over our warehouse so you can teach him how to make coffee."

"Yeah, yeah," Joe repeated shaking his head.

Mercedes grinned then glanced at Joe and back at Aldo.

"Tell him it will be a pleasure."

"We're going to bank on that," Aldo broke in. "It will be our pleasure to have you."

She did not reply, feeling a little embarrassed, so she went back to the kitchen for his coffee. She had a long day ahead. At 7:00 A.M. she would run home for a few minutes to get her kids ready for school. Then she would go back to the restaurant to wait on people until late in the afternoon. She thought about her future and felt fear. There was no hope in sight. No husband that she could count on. No relatives she could rely on. She would have to make it on her own. The tall man sitting at the table with the American was no different than the other men. Always trying to make out with her. They all wanted the same thing. He was no different and she felt disappointed.

The new venture in Tampa seemed to be going well. After the new warehouse was opened Aldo and Joe never looked back. They gained a store weekly, then they began planning their next move: Orlando, a middle city in Central Florida still known, as a country town but with a lot of potential. They hired an experienced salesman and a manager for the warehouse in Tampa and went on to seek new business in Orlando. It was October of 1962 and a world crisis had developed between the United States and the Soviet Union over Cuba. It would change the destiny of thousands of Cubans who were leaving their homeland in droves.

It was past 7:00 P.M., and Aldo sat at the counter at Puntiel's restaurant. He was quietly listening to the men's comments regarding the crisis. Joe was already home, and he was meeting Pablo here on his way back from Orlando. It had been over a year since Mercedes's husband's death and she had agreed to see Aldo socially. Some of the men's faces in the restaurant were somber, others were elated. Miami was in turmoil as troops descended on the area, prepared for a military invasion of the island. There was no doubt that the Americans meant business this time.

"An invasion will cost thousand of lives on both sides," a man pointed out. "Let's not kid ourselves."

"If the Russians don't move the missiles, there is no need for an invasion," another man said. "The whole island will be blown up."

"Don't even say that," one waiter said gloomily. "What about our families, our friends?"

"This is the price we all have to pay for being politically irresponsible," Puntiel said. "We allowed a monster to gain power, and now we must depend on a powerful nation to eject him. Do you think the Americans care about our families? Of course not. The United States has only one problem to resolve, and that is to get rid of the threat to their country, which right now is Castro and the missiles. They have to get at the root of the problem and they are going to do it as inexpensively as possible, even if it means destroying the whole island. That's what's happening, and that's why we are doomed."

Aldo thought that took guts. Puntiel was a businessman. He could not afford to upset his customers with pointed comments. His role was only to provide a neutral and amenable forum where his compatriots could meet and vent their frustrations. Statements like the ones he had just made could antagonize some of his customers. Yet it was the correct thing to say. Puntiel spoke from the heart, regardless of who disagreed. It was the truth. All the men in this room had, in some way, participated in forming of the new government, some by making a donation, some by supporting the rebels, some by merely saying nothing. They had permitted a new breed of men to gain control of the country. Unquestionably, the whole population had given the rebels their total support, thus causing irreversible conditions that had led to a utilitarian regime.

The Cubans arriving daily in Miami told horrors about the life they had left behind. If Batista had been a tyrant, the new system was pure slavery. Conditions were deteriorating throughout the country. One did not trust his neighbor and the populace was to think, how to behave. Allegiance to the revolution must be, above all, unquestioned. Planes were arriving daily in Miami, loaded with émigrés, and many of the embassies were swamped with asylum seekers. Anyone with wealth, education or skill, thought only of leaving. The most valuable resource the country had, its people, was being depleted.

The majority of Cubans in the opposition felt that the United States had an obligation to intervene. After all, since the end of the previous century, Cuba had been dependent on the Americans who had nurtured it and guarded it like their first born. What had gone wrong? Why had the Americans now left them?

"You say it's our fault, right?" one of the customers said, "but this whole affair could have been resolved last year if Kennedy had had some balls. You talk about being politically irresponsible," the man stressed, now getting up from his seat, "well, look around you. What could be more irresponsible than putting the whole world at the brink of nuclear war over a small island and a band of renegades, which is what the rebels are? It was only a year ago that they could have made Castro disappear with a couple of their planes and they passed up the opportunity. How does that make any sense? Now they are ready to go to war with Russia over Cuba. It's irrational. You know what, Puntiel? They owe us. The United States owes us after what they did at the Bay of Pigs."

The man sat down again. His face was red from anger. It was time, he thought, for the Americans to act the humanistic giant that they purported to be.

"I agree with you about the Bay of Pigs, but you are missing my point. The United States did not put Castro in power. We did. It's like Hitler in Germany. Who can the Germans blame for their troubles but themselves? Same with us. We can't pass the blame to others. It's our problem. My point is, if you rely on someone else to do your dirty work, then don't complain about their methods. They'll use whatever is necessary to get the job done. That's all."

There was a moment of silence among the men. Tears rolled down the face of the waiter. At that moment the telephone rang.

"It's Pablo for you Aldo," Puntiel called.

Aldo took the receiver from Puntiel and moved to the end of the counter. The restaurant had grown. Puntiel had expanded by taking over the space next door. There were now twelve tables. Despite fierce competition, he had maintained his resolve to retain the family atmosphere. Most of the other cafes that had opened nearby offered an open-street counter to their customers. There, men and women gathered to order espresso, pastry and drinks without having to come inside. But Puntiel didn't. He didn't care that they labeled him old fashioned. He was. Here if one wanted to eat, one would have to come in and sit at a table. Had he wanted a candy store, he would have bought one, he figured. His place was a restaurant.

"Hello," Aldo said. "Where are you?"

"One of our drivers got into an accident, not a bad one. But I had to come to the police station where he was questioned to pick him up. Guess who I saw here."

"Who?"

"Remember the man who ran the fights that night you fought?"

"Mr. Murphy?"

"Yes. He is being held there."

"Do you know why?"

"I've asked one of the officers. He said they arrested him for running illegal prize fighting. Imagine that."

"Yes. I can imagine."

"Can we meet at the warehouse? How long are you going to be at Puntiel's?"

"Not long. I was only waiting for your call. I will see you there later."

Aldo hung up. He got inside his old pickup and as he pulled into the expressway, he passed a convoy of army trucks and trailers. The crisis was real, Aldo thought. If the Americans invaded the island, Castro would clearly disappear. What would happen to this Cuban community? Would they go back to claim their possessions and leave the American dream behind? Aldo doubted it. As for him, there was no going back. He had cast his lot here, and here he would stay, but he would never forget where he came from.

As he got off the expressway, Aldo went uptown and pulled into the parking lot of the southwest police department, the same building where Ana and Pablo had been married a few months before. He walked up to the entrance and went to the receiving desk. A uniformed officer sat behind a high desk, looking down at him through dark glasses.

"Can I help you, sir?" The officer asked.

"I am looking for a Mr. Ronald Murphy. Is he being held here?"

"Hold on, sir. I'll get someone to help you."

The desk officer turned back toward another, saying something that Aldo could not hear. A few minutes later, a sergeant came into the room through a small side door. He walked up to Aldo.

"You are looking for Ronald Murphy?"

"Yes."

"We have him. He's downstairs. The judge just set bail for him at twenty five thousand dollars, ten percent."

Aldo looked pensively at the sergeant for a moment. Luckily, he had not had the opportunity to learn first hand about American justice. He was happy to be able to claim that his only experience with law enforcement had been in Cuba under Castro's guerrillas. But he understood immediately.

"Does it mean he can be released with two thousand five hundred dollars?"

"Hey, very good," the sergeant exclaimed pointing a finger at Aldo. "You didn't know that, ah?"

"I would like to pay his bail."

"You do?" the officer looked at him curiously. The scars on Aldo's face told a story. "Are you a boxer son?"

"I was at one time."

"Is that where you know Ronald Murphy from?"

"He's someone I used to know."

The officer didn't take his eyes off him. He had participated in the raid when Murphy was taken. Perhaps they had missed this one. But the man before him didn't look like one of Murphy's lackeys. No, this guy was real, and he had never seen him before. No doubt he must have fought for Murphy at some point. Not knowing why, he felt some admiration for him.

"How are you paying his bail?"

"By check."

"Okay, come inside with me, son."

Aldo followed him inside a small office where the officer sat behind a desk. He pulled a manila folder from a drawer and then sat behind a typewriter.

"Sit down," he said. "This will be ready in a minute. Might as well make out your check."

Aldo reached into his shirt pocket and took one of the business checks he carried. On his trips with Joe, he always carried two or three checks in case they had to front any expenses. He leaned on the desk and began writing.

"Make it payable to the City of Miami," the officer said.

Aldo scribbled the words and signed it. He waited until the officer turned towards him and then handed him the check.

"Let's see here," the officer said inspecting the check. "This is from P, J & A Distributors. Oh, that's the nice outfit off the Palmetto highway. Can I have some identification sir? Are you authorized to sign this check for the corporation?"

"I am," Aldo said, handing him his driver's license.

The officer took it and looked from the license to Aldo several times.

"How are you associated with this business, Mr. Ochoa?"

"I am the president."

"Very well."

The sergeant picked up the telephone. In a few moments, a door slammed shut and another officer brought Murphy up. He was wearing prison garb, a khaki shirt and khaki pants. It reminded Aldo of the Batista soldiers who had stopped him one night on Christmas Day. He glanced at Murphy. He hadn't changed much since he had last seen him. He was completely bald now, and his skin had sagged around the eyes. Murphy looked at him intently, as if not quite recognizing the face.

"Your friend here bailed you out," the sergeant said. "Hope he's not working for you, Murphy because we'll bust him too."

"I don't know this guy," Murphy said.

"Not that it means anything," the sergeant said. He turned to the other officer. "Give him his clothes. We have to keep the money as evidence."

"I need my money back," Murphy protested.

"You ain't getting your money, Murphy. That goes to the prosecution. And don't give me any crap now, ah? Leave while you can."

"You want a ride?" Aldo said to Murphy, getting up from his chair.

"Right now, I'll take anything."

"I'll wait for you outside," Aldo said.

As Aldo got inside the pick up with Murphy behind him. Murphy waited until he was inside, then he shook his hand, smiling broadly at him.

"Don't think for a minute I don't know who you are," Murphy blurted. "I didn't want those suckers to think I knew you. You don't need to be implicated. How the hell have you been, ah?"

"I've been fine. What happened to you?"

"Oh, just the old same crap. They busted my ring last night. Those mother fuckers. Hey, but listen kid, now that I found you, you've got to fight for me again. I can make us a lot of money. You can get yourself a new car."

"I don't need a new car, Murphy. I'm fine."

"Why'd you do it kid, ah?"

"I don't know. I wanted to help you out. Why don't you come work for me and leave prize fighting?"

"Are you kidding me, kid? That's my life. Listen, I have never forgotten that night when you were in my ring. It was the most beautiful thing I've seen. What a sin for you to waste that talent."

Aldo listened to him as he took the expressway to Miami Beach. Murphy had a room past One Hundredth Street. Aldo pulled into a dirt driveway and dropped him off at a small house near 151st. that looked deserted. There was no car parked nearby. Murphy probably didn't need any. He was quite a character.

That night, Aldo relaxed in front of the television set in his aunt's apartment. The news were filled with controversy. The reporters had somber faces and spoke only of the impending nuclear conflict with Russia that could explode at any minute now. It was ironic that such impending disaster could come from a small island in the Caribbean. Around ten o'clock, Mercedes rang Aldo. She had been home all evening and wanted to know why he had not called. He told her he had gone to bail an old friend out of jail. She pressed him for details, and he said he would tell her tomorrow over breakfast. He fell asleep on the sofa until Dulce woke him to go to his room.

The next morning, Aldo had breakfast with Mercedes at her restaurant in Hialeah. The two sat together drinking milk and coffee while dawn broke. These were treasured moments. Mercedes had brought Aldo happiness and love and he appreciated her quiet, loving nature and reciprocated. Best of all, she was a complete woman. It was clear she did not need a man to survive, which was what had initially attracted him to her. She was a woman who knew how to look after herself if need be. That was the spark that ignited the flame.

There were no out-of-town trips scheduled, so Joe was not with him. Maureen's health had deteriorated, and the old man tried to spend as much time with her as he could. He had hired a nurse to watch her during the day, a luxury he could have never afforded had he and Aldo not crossed paths.

Aldo met Joe at the warehouse later that morning. He hung around the office for a few minutes until Rebeca made the daily calls to their other warehouses in Tampa and Orlando. Aldo and Joe then headed for North Miami where they visited a local supermarket that they had begun to serve. The meeting was short. The manager was not in, and Joe could only manage to get his card and a promise to call. All business had been hampered by the current crisis. Many people thought it was the end. A confrontation was inevitable and Miami was at the doorsteps of all the trouble.

In the afternoon, Aleida brought the girls to see Aldo. Frank was out at a baseball game. She and Aldo had never discussed what had happened between him and Amanda. The divorce had been quickly settled, and Aleida remained as a go between, bringing the children to him and delivering messages. She worked as a second to Rebeca in the office.

After most of the help had left, Aldo took his daughters to the back of the building and began sorting the heavy new boxes that had come in. After 6:00 P.M., two men would be in to put them away. They would work until midnight and leave the platform empty for the next day. A watchman would work from midnight until morning to receive any night deliveries and look after the place. Aldo's early operation was now huge and the work never stopped.

The two girls sat behind the receiving desk, writing in their school notebooks. They had grown equally in size and shape. One could not tell them apart. They both had long, light-brown hair, small noses like their mother, and round little faces. With their gray school uniforms, they reminded Aldo of the privileged children he had once watched walking to the Catholic schools in his native city. He was happy for them. They had been lucky.

He was thinking about Murphy as he lifted a box to look at a label when a noise behind him got his attention. He turned quickly and looked straight into the bearded face of a man. The man was holding a pistol, and after Aldo noticed him, he brought the gun inches from Aldo's face.

"Don't move, motherfucker, or you're dead," the man said. "Where's the cash, come on."

"I have no cash."

"Oh, yes you do, motherfucker. Where is it?"

The man's hand shook as he spoke. Aldo could see that he was nervous. He knew he was seconds from being shot but that didn't worry him. His daughters were only a few steps away, and he would have to protect them at all cost. Then the man made a mistake. He suddenly moved his shaking hand away from Aldo and pointed it at the twins. They were Aldo's entire life, everything he lived for, and then he made a mistake. With the speed that had made his trainer proud in Cuba, he reached for the man's hand, gripped his wrist, and yanked it toward him, away from the girls. The move startled the man whose eyes opened wide as he pulled the trigger, whether reflectively or deliberately, Aldo would never know. It was an easy shot. The barrel was only an inch away from Aldo's chest, and the bullet shattered his heart. Aldo slumped back from the impact, falling against the wall of boxes, blood exploding from his chest, and lay still.

No sooner had the gun gone off than the man dropped it, turned quickly around and ran towards the main door and out of the building. Pablo had entered the front office at that moment and was going for the telephone as he heard the shot. He stopped and turned to make sure he had heard right and then heard the sound of rushing footsteps behind him. It took a few seconds for reality to sink in, but the children's cries left no doubt that something terrible had happened. He ran towards the back, not knowing exactly where, and followed their hysterical screams. He saw them from the corner of his eyes, standing at the edge of the desk, their faces wet with tears. They were okay but where was Aldo? He saw the puddle of blood traveling fast towards him on the floor and then Aldo's body, sitting down, his torso twisted sideways and his head slouching forward. Pablo began to shake as he touched him, seeing the lean tall boy running towards him through the dirt paths among the huts in Rios years ago.

"Pablo, Pablo, come with me. My father's missing. Help me look for him. Let's go, let's go!"

Pablo had followed him that day and always. Together they had found Aldo's father's body.

EPILOGUE

Two weeks after the funeral, Ana knelt on the red velvet cushion of a padded *prie-dieu*, directly across the small altar of Our Lady of Charity. The Cuban immigrants who had flocked to the Miami area had not only brought their food and music but also their saint. The small church located in the heart of southwest Miami shone bright on this Sunday morning, its stained-glass windows reflecting the sunlight on the polished floors of the chapel.

Ana crossed herself as she whispered her last Hail Mary. She also said the Lord's Prayer and begged salvation for the soul of Aldo Ochoa. Her mother Francisca had taught her how to pray. As a kindergarten girl, she had found it difficult to learn the rosary. The sisters from Saint Teresa had complained to her mother that she mumbled the words. So Francisca had taken charge, as she always did in time of crisis. She had sat with Ana at night, slowly making her repeat the words one by one. That was how she had learned.

It had been a sad scene at the funeral parlor. When Ana saw Aldo's body she lost all control. All those years of holding back had suddenly overcome her. She had rushed towards the coffin as she entered the room and laid her head on his cold chest, crying inconsolably. She was grateful to Aleida who had discreetly removed her to another room, away from Amanda's downcast eyes and from the rest of the crowd that had just witnessed the weakest moment in Ana's life. Ana had tried to tell Aldo in so many ways, for so many years, that she loved him more than life itself, but she could not say it or show it. Only Francisca, the smart lady with the penetrating olive eyes, had known long ago. And she had immediately figured out what to do. She had done what any other caring mother would have done to save her daughters from discord and hate. But had she? Hadn't her mother favored Amanda? Hadn't she really failed Ana? Her mother, the perfect strategist, had missed badly. In her last thought before the virgin, Ana asked to be forgiven for being selfish.

Aleida and a man had rushed toward her. The man enveloped Ana in his long arms and dragged her away from the coffin. She had never seen him before. From his physique, she guessed later that he was a boxer, probably one of Aldo's old friends. The man was an American, bald and red like a lobster. She took comfort knowing that someone who had been close to Aldo had touched her. Then she thought about her husband and wondered if he had witnessed the ugly scene. She did not think so. Pablo had been so impacted by his friend's death that he could not bear to look at him and he never made it to the funeral.

The man had revived her and given her water. His name was Murphy, Aleida said. He was a good man who had known Aldo and now worked for Pablo at the warehouse. Somehow, he seemed to relate to Aleida, her youngest sister, the one who had always served as the bridge in the family. But not even Aleida could bring Ana and Amanda together again. The two sisters had not spoken to each other since the day they last argued. Ana could never forget how Amanda had treated Aldo and Amanda saw Ana as the traitor who had secretly wooed her husband.

Ana made the sign of the cross as she stood. She walked to the center aisle, faced the main altar, and genuflected. She turned and walked toward the open entrance where Aleida and the children awaited her. She dipped her right hand in the basin of blessed water and again crossed herself, looked back at the altar one last time, and went outside. She slipped her black *mantilla* off her head, folded it and placed it inside her purse. At the bottom of the stairs, her nephew and nieces were talking to their friends. Amanda had not come.

"I'm listening to them," Aleida whispered. "They're so smart."

"…So how can you tell them apart?" A chubby boy of twelve was asking Frank in English.

"I can. I always could. My uncle Pablo could, too. He never had any trouble. Now, my aunts, that's another story."

"Are there other twins in your family?"

"No, not that I know of. My grandparents came from the Canary Islands, and we kind of lost track of the family history. Some day one of us will travel there and look into it. It would be nice to know your family tree."

"Yeah. For sure. Listen," the boy told him, "come around the gym after school tomorrow. I like how you hit the bag. You're fast."

"I don't know," Frank replied. "I don't really care for boxing that much. My father was a boxer."

Ana and Aleida descended the twelve marble steps onto the sidewalk. Ana reached for the girls' hands but Frank grabbed them before she did. He was tall for his age. His arms were long and his shoulders were starting to broaden. He held the twins by the hand and walked ahead of the group. A policeman stepped over the crosswalk and signaled for the traffic to stop. With his other arm, the patrol man waived the children across. Wearing their Sunday dresses and their prettiest hair bands, Teresa and Clara seemed to radiate hope as they looked back at their aunts, giggling and prodding them to follow. They were beautiful. It was too early yet to know whether they carried the same resilience so prominent in their parents' generation.

Only time would tell.

ABOUT THE BOOK

THE VERY CULTURAL STORY OF Aldo Ochoa and his family who migrated to the United States during the early years of the Castro regime from Cuba. A detailed presentation of the drastic changes brought about by the 1959 revolution and how they affected the population at large, causing a massive exodus never seen before in the history of the island. America is the dream land for the families that arrive and thrive in the area of South Florida. They find the American dream alive and well but in the end fate seems to play a fast one on the adventurous Aldo. A passionate tale of romance and adventure.